_1_
<u>OLIVE</u>

It was a Monday in early October and I was hungover for the third straight day. By noon, I vowed never to drink again. Of course, I'd said the same thing the previous two days and some good that had done. It's not that I was a big drinker, but with a petite frame like mine, I tended to feel it the next morning.

And this had been a particularly long weekend, as my best friend since grade school, Kayla Martin, had been visiting, and yours truly was in charge of showing her around Los Angeles. Once the sightseeing, hiking, and productive part of the day were over, Kayla wanted to see the nightlife that LA had to offer, so I obliged. Friday consisted of bar hopping in West Hollywood, Saturday landed us down by the beach in Santa Monica, and Sunday had ended in between the two at The Belly Flop, the bar where I worked.

I was back at The Belly Flop Monday morning, and at 11:46 a.m., two hours after dropping Kayla off at the airport and forty-six minutes into my shift, I made my vow that alcohol would never pass my lips.

"Or at least until Friday. And no more shots," I told my co-worker, Sheri.

"Well, no wonder you get drunk so easily, Olive, you weigh a hundred pounds soaking wet," Sheri said.

Olive Fairbanks, that's me.

"A hundred fourteen!" I said authoritatively.

It didn't help that at only twenty-six years old, I wasn't a seasoned drinking vet like some of my regulars. And I certainly had those. The Belly Flop consisted of a largely male, largely older crew. The owner of the bar, a ceaseless flirt named Barry Gant, thought I was attractive and would increase business when it came to this clientele. It appeared he was right. Since I had started, my shifts consistently made more money than the other day shifts.

I couldn't believe it had been three years since I had been hired, fresh out of UCLA. I'd majored in creative writing, always having known that I wanted to become a writer. A travel blogger, if I had the choice, but mainly I'd just gotten gigs like "The Top Ten Burgers in LA" and other cream-puff articles that any of a million people could have written.

My parents, and most of my friends, thought I should have gone out in the real world and gotten a 9–5, even if it was something low paying in the writing or publishing world.

"We didn't pay four years of tuition at UCLA to have you serving drinks to old men," my mother had told me more than once.

But as my father used to say, I could be a hard-headed young lady. I knew that a regular 9–5 job wasn't really over when it ended—there'd be the commute, work-related things lingering on your mind, preparing for the next day, overtime, etc. The Belly Flop was two minutes from my apartment and once my shift was over, the day's work didn't hover in the air. I wasn't splitting the atom, after all.

This allowed me, at least in theory, to do a lot more writing than a standard 9–5 would have.

Recently, however, while I should have been spending more time writing at my beloved Coffee Bean on San Vicente Boulevard, especially on the weekends, I found myself out at bars more often than usual.

"Okay, how about this for a concession?" I said to Sheri. "I won't have a drink until I've gotten to Chapter 10 of my novel."

"What chapter are you on now?"

"Three."

"So what's that, a few weeks?"

"The way I've been writing, it's probably more like a few years," I sighed.

I had started my first novel, in the young adult romance genre, back in August, and here it was October and I was only a few chapters in. I'd become a bartender to spend more time writing, but with the exception of the occasional creampuff article I mentioned earlier, I really hadn't done much.

Maybe my mother was right.

"Hey Olive, want to have a shot with me?" Mark Midfield, a retired construction worker, said from across the bar.

"I hate this place," I whispered to Sheri.

I walked over to Mark and politely declined his offer, but poured him his favorite shot, a Woo Woo, which consisted of vodka, cranberry, and peach schnapps. I always found it comical that a retired construction worker, blue collar to the core, would order a shot called a Woo Woo with no sense of irony.

I walked back over to Sheri.

"Your sobriety is off to a good start, Olive," she joked.

I often thought I had been misnamed, given I clearly didn't have what should be a requisite for anyone named Olive: the skin color to match it. My last name of Fairbanks dated back centuries in England, and no one would mistake Anglos for having skin of an olive tone.

"Let's see if I can resist the charms of the old men here," I whispered to Sheri.

The Belly Flop had been around since the late 1990s, when Barry Gant bought it from its previous owner, renaming it in the process. While I didn't love The Belly Flop as a name, it was certainly preferable to the connotations of a bar called Savages, its previous reincarnation.

The decor was cheap Los Angeles, and while it wasn't a dive per se, Architectural Digest wouldn't be knocking on our door anytime soon. Still, a well-designed circular bar in the middle gave people room to walk freely on either side. It was flanked to the right by a huge room where people would go

THE
BARTENDER

This novel is dedicated to the Bay Area baristas who think I'm a responsible, upstanding citizen and to the Los Angeles bartenders who know better.

to watch their favorite sporting events. The Belly Flop liked to pride itself on being a sports bar, though there were several other bars in the vicinity that truly catered to their sports fans. We just said we did. The third room was usually vacant during the day, but would get going at night, playing loud house music or hip-hop once the sun went down. The Belly Flop became more like a club at night, and I was happy to miss that.

So were my elderly day drinkers. They were always gone long before the music started.

For the day shifts, I was always given a server. Sheri and I worked well together, and I was always happy to see her on the schedule. A couple of the other girls—and yes, it was always women who served—could be what my mother used to call Debbie Downers and I hated to hear them gripe.

Of course, I realized that I was doing my fair share of griping on this day. I generally had a very sunny disposition, and decided to revert back to that.

"Let's talk about something more interesting than my hangover. How's it going with you and Zane?" I asked Sheri.

The first shift on Monday was one of the quietest ones of the week. Since I had taken care of Mark Midfield and the two other older men at the bar, I knew we had a few minutes.

"Hot and heavy." Sheri said laughed.

"Tell me more," I pleaded.

"A lady never tells."

"Is this where I say, If only a lady were present…"

Sheri gave me a playful push. "How about you?" she asked.

"Perpetually single."

"Not for lack of opportunities."

"Who, him?" I said, subtly motioning to the oldest guy in the bar, a man deep into his seventies.

"Don't be coy, Olive. You're one of the most beautiful girls in West LA. You're skinny, but have curves in all the right places. We all wish we had your body, and that dirty blonde hair never has a strand out of place."

"Keep going," I joked.

Sheri laughed again.

She was finishing up her schooling at Cal State Northridge while working a few shifts a week, and at only twenty-two. It made me feel old—yes, I know twenty-six is still very young, but feeling old is more a state of mind than an actual number.

"And by the way, my hair was a mess this morning. Why do you think I went with this?" I asked, grabbing my ponytail.

"Just stop. You know you're hot."

While I didn't always feel as pretty as she said, I decided to just go with it. "Thanks, Sheri."

"So, back to your dating life…"

If I were a lawyer, I would have argued it was a leading question.

"Well, maybe in my coming weeks of sobriety, I'll go on a few dates."

"Now you're talking," Sheri said.

"Olive," the septuagenarian yelled from the other side of the bar, "can I get another Old Fashioned?"

"He's old fashioned," I said to Sheri, smiling as I jokingly shot myself with my index finger.

The day went on like this for a few more hours, of which every second felt like a minute. At least my hangover finally dissipated. One thing to appreciate.

"Thank God for small favors," I told Sheri.

The bar was starting to pick up and we couldn't spend much time chit-chatting, but Sheri had come over to pick up an order, so we had a few seconds.

"Well, would you look at this?" she said.

My back was to the front door. "What is it?" I asked.

"Maybe the most handsome man I've ever seen."

"You say that every week," I said, not yet turning around.

"But this time I mean it. Just take a look. Better be subtle, he's walking this way."

I turned. Sheri wasn't lying. In front of me came one of the handsomest, sexiest men I had ever seen in my life. He stood probably 6'3", with tight-cropped, light blond hair. His blue eyes came as no surprise with his complexion. My first thought, one I later regretted, was that he would have been the perfect Aryan specimen.

He had wide shoulders and a skinny waist, exemplifying the V shape that I found so irresistible in a man, and walked in a way that told me he was used to getting what he wanted.

"I better serve that table." Sheri winked and walked away, leaving me alone with the approaching stranger.

"How can I help you?" I mustered, and thought I pulled it off without any slip-ups.

The man looked up, as if he hadn't realized I was right in front of him.

"I'm sorry, I didn't see you right there," he said, smiling at me the whole time.

It was only one sentence, but he seemed like a nice guy. I'd met enough handsome guys in LA who turned out to be assholes, but my first impression said this guy was more down to earth.

"Can I get you a drink?" I asked.

"Not yet, it's only 2:30. I don't start drinking on Mondays until 2:45."

I liked his sense of humor, but that lagged in second place behind his devastating smile.

"Not that there's anything wrong with that," he added, nodding in the direction of the older men in the bar.

I found myself laughing.

"Don't badmouth my regulars," I whispered.

"Think I saw them at an AARP meeting last week."

"Wow, you must be older than you look."

He smiled at me again and I felt one of my knees buckle. "Sadly, I'm only twenty-eight. And my name is Austin."

Austin extended his hand and I took it, holding on just long enough to give him something to think about.

"I'm Olive and twenty-six."

"That's a long-lasting olive. I usually finishing eating those things in seconds."

I would have found the comment creepy coming from most guys, but from this one, I found it downright alluring.

"I'll let you get away with that."

He smirked. "So now that we've got our names and ages out of the way, what's next?"

Though not exactly sure what was going on, I enjoyed the give and take. "I guess we'd ask each other where we're from."

"I'm from Norfolk, Virginia," Austin said.

"Really? I'm from Richmond."

"I've done that I-64 from Norfolk to Richmond more than you know."

"Tell me about it. We used to do it every summer weekend to get closer to the beach. Of course, it wasn't always Norfolk. We liked some other towns better."

Austin faked being hurt. "How dare you slight my hometown!"

"Let's be honest, Norfolk is an easy target."

He turned around and waved his hand in the air as if he was leaving. "It's been fun," he said.

I laughed, knowing he would turn around and come back toward me. He did just that.

"So what brought you here?" I asked.

"To The Belly Flop?" He looked around the bar. "Actually, I'm new to town. Moved a block away about a week ago. Really just checking out the businesses around me."

"Found any you like?" I asked playfully.

"Just one," he said.

Our eyes met and we held it for several seconds.

"What are you doing after work?" Austin asked.

"Hanging out with you," I answered.

_2_
<u>AUSTIN</u>

Killing Olive wasn't in the original plan, but it became a necessity as time went on. It wasn't something I wanted, you have to believe me. But Becca had her own plans. I had come to enjoy my time with Olive, I really had. Even if she was just a pawn in our little game.

Our terrible, perverse game.

I guess I should start at the beginning.

I came into this world on July 19th, 1990, at Northside Hospital in Atlanta, Georgia as Jared Austin Jenkins. I went by Jared my whole life, and I'd guess less than 10% of my friends knew Austin was my middle name. Which is why Becca had me adopt it when I agreed to go to Los Angeles.

But I'm getting ahead of myself again.

My childhood was normal, the middle kid surrounded by two sisters. My mother was a homemaker and my father was the foreman of a construction company. I'd probably be characterized as a precocious kid, but nothing out of the ordinary. Certainly not indicative of what I'd become.

My life changed, and not for the better, when I met Becca Poe in eighth grade. Or to be more accurate, when our lips met. She was a transfer student and we found ourselves at the same party one night early in the school year. Like plenty of parties at the time, we ended up playing Spin the Bottle at some point.

Sure enough, Becca spun the bottle and it landed on yours truly. It was already awkward having to kiss a girl at that age, but kissing a total stranger in front of others made it even more uncomfortable. The kiss was sloppy, with our lips at awkward angles, and I heard a few laughs from the other thirteen- and fourteen-year-olds in attendance.

It's not like Becca wasn't desirable. She was very pretty, with long, curly strawberry blonde hair. Of course, that would change many times over the years. She was nothing if not a chameleon.

Danny Dufner, the alpha male of the eighth grade, decided we should escalate from Spin the Bottle to Two Minutes in the Closet, another popular game of the time. Everyone was intimidated by Dufner, and no one had the balls to stand up to him, so the game commenced.

Almost as if by karmic intervention, Becca and I were again matched together. What followed laid out the type of person that Becca Poe was; I was just too young to realize it.

"We should give them a show," she whispered to me as we entered the darkened closet.

"Like what?" I said.

An impressionable adolescent at fourteen, I felt fine following her lead. Even though I had known Becca Poe for just over an hour, she was quite obviously a Type-A personality.

"Let's make it seem like we're having sex."

I didn't think it was a good idea and reluctantly told her so. And then I looked in her eyes, and knew she wasn't going to budge.

She pushed her back up against the door, preventing anyone from forcing it open.

"We'll make them wait," she said.

She grabbed a bottled water from her purse.

"Here, put this in your hair. Make it look all wet and messy."

I didn't know why, but I couldn't say no to the girl in front of me. I did as she instructed. She grabbed the water bottle and did the same to hers.

They knocked on the door two minutes later and that's when Becca started letting out some small moans. The people on the other side of the door initially laughed, and then we heard a few gasps. This only emboldened Becca, whose moans grew louder and louder.

She forcefully grabbed me at one point and motioned for me to pound on the inside of the closet as if we were having sex against the wall. Suddenly all sound ceased from the other side of the door, and I imagined no one wanted to miss a noise from our end. Finally, after three minutes, Becca let out a series of cries, which even at my young age and being a virgin, I knew were meant to emulate an orgasm.

A minute later, we emerged from the closet, wet hair and all. She had also undone a button on her blouse and made sure the top button of my jeans was undone as well. She had seemingly thought of it all.

The faces were priceless. Danny Dufner went right up to Becca.

"That was all fake," he said.

"Shows how little you know about sex," Becca said. "Just like I figured."

She stared at him and it was Danny Dufner who broke eye contact first.

The toughest kid in class had been emasculated by a fourteen-year-old girl. There were many smiles from the boys in the room who Danny Dufner had picked on over the years.

I should have known from that moment on that Becca Poe was going to be trouble. But it's not like I could tell anyone that it had all been a sham. I was now the guy who'd had sex with one of the hottest girls in the eighth grade. And I liked the attention.

Becca didn't mellow out in the intervening years. If she didn't like a girl, she would spread a nasty rumor on Myspace, which had started blowing up in our early high school years. If a guy turned down her advances, she'd get the word out that he had a small penis or was terrible in bed.

Despite all this, we remained friends. I can't tell you why. She had an allure for me that was tough to break. Rumors always thrived that we were dating, but we had never done more than kiss on that infamous first night. Everyone else still thought we had sex at the party in question, and it was never disproven. They also knew that Becca Poe had made Danny Dufner cower in fear, and people became afraid of her as high school wore on. So the story persisted.

Over the years, I grew into my body, and into a charismatic, good-looking young man. I was no longer the impressionable eighth grader. By senior year, I was no longer remembered as the guy who'd had sex with Becca Poe. I was the one girls wanted to spend two minutes in the closet with. I was a starting forward on the basketball team of Roswell High School, which was just outside of Atlanta. I also played wide receiver for the football team. I was popular and a decent student. I had it all. Unfortunately, I also had a bit of a temper.

In April of 2008, I was a few months away from graduating high school and everything seemed great. Set to attend Virginia Tech in the fall, I planned to try and walk onto the football team, even though I knew it was a long shot as they had a very good program. I had a rotating crop of two girlfriends, Laurel and Jackie, whom I had somehow prevented from knowing about each other. Life was good.

If you said I had a bit too much testosterone going through my veins, you wouldn't be wrong. And it's what got me in trouble.

At lunch one day, I was approached by Max Underwood, one of the biggest nerds we had at Roswell. Actually, Max was a nerd, dork, and a loser all rolled into one. Had I picked on him from time to time? In a word, yes.

He handed me a note. I read it as he walked away.

Meet me at the bleachers by the football field at 3:00. If not, I'm telling Laurel and Jackie.

Seething, I approached my locker after fifth period and leaned my shoulder into it, hard, causing a huge dent. Some people saw it, but they wouldn't dare call me out. They were scared of me. With my quick temper and withering put-downs, I had become the male equivalent of Becca Poe.

Sure enough, Max Underwood waited for me by the bleachers. Football wasn't in season and no one was using the field, so we were alone. I had remained livid throughout the day and was not in a good mindset as I approached him. I admit that.

He tried to extend his hand for me to shake, but I, already seeing red, pushed him down to the ground.

"It's none of your fucking business, Max, you fucking loser."

"I wouldn't want them both to know you're screwing the other."

I couldn't have been more pissed. I held him down by the neck and punched him twice, hitting him near his eye, followed by his cheekbone.

He started crying like the little bitch he was. It surprised me that he could even get a word out, but he did.

"And maybe I'll tell everyone that you and Becca didn't do anything either. It's so obvious."

That put me over the edge, although I'm still not sure why. I could have gotten any girl I wanted; it's not like I needed that old story any longer. But just the fact that he knew, and dared to let me know, elevated me to a new level of depravity.

I kept holding him down and hit him twice more, as hard as I could, exploding his nose on the second punch. I knew it was broken when I felt the bones crunching as my fist connected.

For a moment I worried I had killed him, but I heard him breathing. I didn't know what to do, so I just went home. The whole rest of the day I expected the police to show up at my door, but they never came. I couldn't explain it.

It would be a few years until I knew why.

_3_
<u>BECCA</u>

Unlike that pussy Austin, I wanted to kill the bartender from the very beginning. Olive! What kind of name is that anyway? If it was my choice we would have drowned her in a bathtub full of gin or vodka, adding some vermouth for good measure. Look, a dead Olive floating on top of the booze!

You'll have to excuse me for my sense of humor.

It's hard to remember exactly when and where I turned into the depraved bitch I've become. Which probably means I was like that all along. I've been called a whore, a leech, and an evil genius. They are probably all true in some respect, and the last one I take as a genuine compliment.

And there has never been a more evil, more genius plan than the one that brought Austin to Los Angeles. Well, really he was Jared to me, but I thought it was better if he didn't use his real name when I had him meet Olive.

Fucking Olive.

My childhood was littered with mistakes and brilliance, and they were not always mutually exclusive. Some overlapped, no question. Two events stand out above all others, and they both happened in the spring of my senior year at Roswell High.

The first one I undertook was the Great Bullshit fundraiser. Yes, I named it myself.

It was late March of 2008. I'd been working menial jobs like babysitting or delivering papers, and my parents (both good people, this apple did fall far from the tree) had agreed that if I saved up $2,000, they would match me and I could buy a used car.

I would do anything I could to make this happen. Riding the bus my first three years of high school was about the most humiliating thing in the world. It was just me, dirty poor whites, and minorities. An exaggeration? Sure. Not my first and wouldn't be my last.

Keep in mind, the bus to Roswell High was fine. It was a nice, prosperous area. However, it was boring as hell, and if you wanted to have any fun, you had to head into Atlanta for the weekend. And being carless, practically every weekend, I'd have to take buses with the minorities and poor whites I so despised.

It's not like my parents were rich—we were firmly in the middle class—but they certainly could have afforded to buy me a cheap used car. In their minds, making me work for it was going to give me some overarching view of the world. Make me sympathetic toward poor people's plight.

Guess what, it didn't work.

Grudgingly, I raised the $2,000, my parents matched it, and I was able to buy a shitty 2001 white Volkswagen Golf. It had taken me over a year to save up the money and I vowed never to work such inane jobs again. I was adamant about that. I was not going to be some poor schmuck for the rest of my life.

So I came up with a plan.

My motivation came from all the little fundraisers that people did as kids. Sponsor me for this, donate to that, etc. I remembered one specifically where all the boys in town raised money for Little League based on how far they could hit a baseball. Parents made pledges from a few pennies to a quarter per foot. For example, if you pledged a dime for each foot and the Little Leaguer hit it two hundred feet, you donated $20.

It was softball season around Atlanta, so I would steal a page from the Little Leaguers' playbook. Why should boys get all the advantages?

I knew what I was trying to accomplish had to be completed within a day. If it lasted any longer, people might catch on, and I'd surely get caught.

On Saturday, I printed out a flyer saying that Beecher Hills High School was having a softball fundraiser on that Monday, with all money going to improve women's sports at the school.

I didn't go to Beecher Hills, but I chose it because it was one of the poorest high schools in Atlanta, with a huge percentage of students living below the poverty line. I thought it might make donations just a little bit easier to come by if potential donors thought I went to a horrible school like Beecher.

That Sunday morning, I decided not to shower. I wanted to look as pathetic as possible. I wiped off all the residual makeup from the night before, reapplying a little dark blue around one eye. Whether it looked like a black eye or not would be in the eye of the beholder. Anything to make me look more pitiful.

I told my parents I was going to a friend's and set off in the direction of the richest suburbs of Atlanta. The plan was to walk from house to house. If they saw a car, even my pathetic Golf, they might not be as inclined to give. While the money supposedly would go to a school, it was really the person at the door (me) who they would base their donations on.

So I was going to be walking.

Buckhead and Virginia-Highland, two of the richest areas in suburban Atlanta, lay within minutes of each other, so I decided to knock those two areas out. The houses were extraordinary; my parents' home looked like a shoebox in comparison.

I parked the Golf just outside the beginning of Buckhead and set off on my way. I had a binder holding tons of flyers and forms that people would fill out to verify how much they donated. It all seemed very official.

The first house I approached was an old Victorian that had either two or three stories. It was hard to tell. When I was ten years old and knew that more than anything else I wanted to become rich, I used to study the architecture of rich homes. It was my way of planning for a more prosperous future. Victorians were almost always equated with wealth, so this home was easy for me to identify.

I knocked on the front door and immediately heard someone on the other side. As soon as the woman opened it, I dropped my binder to the ground, all of my forms spreading out on the expensive brick. This wasn't a coincidence, mind you; I had thought of it on my drive over that morning. Just another detail to make me look miserable and encourage these rich assholes to pony up their money to little old me.

I would look like a responsible young lady for the majority of the time, but throwing in a few pathetic moments might lower their guard.

The woman—in her fifties, with an old-school haircut that didn't make her look any younger—was on my side immediately.

"Oh, you poor child."

Just as I started grabbing the forms and putting them back in the binder, I "accidentally" dropped them again. This was an Oscar-caliber performance. Finally, I had rustled all the papers back into the binder and I looked up at the rich older woman with my most feeble face.

"I'm here for a fundraiser that our high school is having tomorrow. Beecher Hills, maybe you've heard of it?"

The woman's eyebrows turned up. She had most assuredly heard of Beecher Hills and either felt bad for me or looked down on the people who went there. Probably both.

"What type of fundraiser is it?" she asked.

"I'm on the softball team, and we barely have enough money for bats, mitts, bases, uniforms, and all that stuff. So we are asking people to either make a donation to our team, or pledge money per foot I hit the softball at the fundraiser."

"Of course I'll help you out, sweetie!" she said.

Gullible bitch!

"Oh, that's great. You're a generous soul," I said instead.

"Do you take credit card?"

I knew this was a possibility, and I'd had an answer prepared.

"You can, but they didn't give me that responsibility. If you want to pay by credit card, you have to go down to Beecher Hills and pay at the office."

I knew there was no way this rich snob was going to the hood of Atlanta.

"How about a check?"

"If you want to donate with a check, me and one of my coaches will be coming by tomorrow to collect them after we hit the softballs. They don't give me that responsibility either." I sheepishly grinned.

"What are my other options?"

"You can give a one-time cash donation today. And then obviously me and my coach wouldn't be by tomorrow."

I was counting on the fact that these people wouldn't want me returning the next day. Of course, I wouldn't be returning anyway, but they didn't know that.

I certainly wasn't going to have the ability to cash their checks. So I had to convince them to give me cash, and I guessed that ensuring I wouldn't be back the next day might just do the trick.

"I'm not sure I'm going to be here tomorrow, so maybe it's better if I just give you a donation right now," the lady said.

"Oh, bless your heart," I said.

I can safely say that I had never used that phrase before, but it seemed perfect in the moment. I thought she'd eat it up.

"Give me just a moment," she said.

She came back a few minutes later with three crisp $20 dollar bills. I had made $60 in the span of a few minutes and knew I could never go back to babysitting, where you wouldn't make that in a night.

I thanked the woman profusely and as I walked down her driveway, I looked out at all the other extraordinary homes. I was going to make a lot of money.

The next three hours were spent in Buckhead and the following three hours in Virginia-Highland. I had brought a little fanny pack where I put the money, but I didn't dare count it as I went from house to house. That could wait until I got home.

Finally, after a long day, I picked up my crummy Volkswagen Golf at the base of Virginia-Highland and drove back to where my parents and I lived. I said a quick hello to them and headed off to my room, locking it behind me.

Sitting down with the fanny pack, I really had no idea how much it held. Anything over a thousand dollars and I would be ecstatic. I took the money out. There were several hundreds, loads of twenties, and some tens and fives littered in as well.

Rich people didn't deal in one-dollar bills.

I counted it, recounted it, and finally added it up a third time. I couldn't believe how much it was. I had raised $2,145. Okay, I know I hadn't "raised" it, but "scammed" is such an ugly word.

I made a little fan out of all the money and pretended to air myself with it. $2,145! More money than I had saved in a year performing jobs that I couldn't stand. This was the type of job I could get used to. I felt smart, like I had outwitted the elite of Atlanta. I fanned myself a few more times and then put the money back in the fanny pack and hid it in my closet.

There was still a problem I had to deal with. There were probably twenty or thirty people who thought I would return the following night to pick up a check from them. If no one came by for a few days, I feared they'd call Beecher Hills, who'd likely notify the police.

I made a plan for this inevitability as well. For every house that promised to give me a check the following day, I had written down their address. That night, I designed and printed up a new leaflet.

It read: *Beecher Hills would like to thank you for your support. Yesterday, we got a huge donation for the softball team and will not be coming by to pick up your checks. We've raised enough. We appreciate your generosity.*

I printed out a few dozen copies and the following night I put them in the mailbox of each house who expected a return visit from me. I was certainly on my way to being a career criminal. I can't lie, I enjoyed it. I slept well that night.

A few weeks later, I saw a segment on the local news in which people from Buckhead were interviewed. Apparently, some young lady had canvassed around their area and they had given money to a made-up cause.

They had no suspects in the case.

My first foray into illegality had been a successful one.

My second major undertaking in the spring of my senior year was a lot more villainous. In the fake fundraiser, I'd just fleeced some rich people who weren't going to miss their money. I hadn't given it a second thought. But my next enterprise did involve someone getting hurt.

The aforementioned Austin was at the forefront of it. Yes, he was still Jared at the time, but I'll refer to him as Austin. After all, it was once he came to LA as Austin that all the fun started.

Austin had reaped all the benefits of my pretending to have slept with him in the eighth grade. He was considered a Romeo and it certainly helped his sex life heading into high school. Was I considered a Juliet? Absolutely not. I was labeled a slut, skank, and other things worse.

What a double standard!

But I didn't tell anyone the truth. The fact was, I enjoyed being the notorious one.

Austin became exceedingly popular and although we remained friends, sometimes I wished I could trade my beloved notoriety for his popularity. After all, it was I who had helped propel him to his newfound status. I also recognized the charisma he had in abundance, thinking it could come in handy in my future endeavors. Having a handsome face like that on your side couldn't hurt.

I'd heard through the grapevine that Austin was sleeping with both Laurel Cruise and Jackie Agnew. Apparently, this hadn't gotten back to either of the two girls. Sounds impossible, but Laurel was a volleyball player who hung out with the athletes while Jackie was one of the richest girls at our school, preferring to talk about expensive clothes and jewelry. They were in different social circles, so I understood how Austin was able to do it.

I employed the help of Max Underwood, a pathetic excuse for a human. There's nothing wrong with being a loser, but when you beg and plead for people to move you up in social circles, you are something worse than a loser.

Max would always try to hang out with more popular groups once the lunch bell rang. He would be rejected from each group, and you'd see him move around the quad of Roswell High looking for people who would let him join them.

If you were the empathetic type (newsflash, I'm not), I see how you might find it sad. Not me. I saw an opportunity.

I approached Max one morning and told him to follow me. There aren't many places in a high school where you can get peace and quiet, but I knew a little area beyond my locker where no one would be able to see us.

He followed me like a little puppy dog, and when I looked around and didn't spot anyone, I made him a proposition.

"And if I go through with this, you'll make sure I become more popular?"

"You have my word, Max."

I said it like my word meant something. It doesn't.

Max agreed to do it. I reiterated to him that under no circumstances was he to say my name. Even if Austin punched him, which I considered a distinct possibility. I banked on it, in fact.

My plan couldn't have gone any better. I arrived ten minutes early and hid behind the bleachers in a place where I knew Austin wouldn't be able to see me. When he arrived, I started filming. No, my 2008 cell phone didn't take videos like the ones of today, but it did the trick.

I recorded as Austin attacked Max right off the bat. He had become a hothead. If a little nerd like Max Underwood told him he was going to tell Laurel Cruise and Jackie Agnew about each other, I knew Austin would react confrontationally. I couldn't have guessed he'd be quite as vicious as he was, but I found myself smiling the whole time.

Austin was now mine for life. This video would be a life-ruiner.

After Austin left the field, I went over to Max and feigned shock.

"I thought he was just going to push you, I didn't know he was going to attack you!"

"I think I need to go to the hospital," he said.

"I'm going to go now, Max," I said, since I couldn't be around when the ambulance, or the cops, arrived. "Just remember, girls love scars. And that includes black eyes and broken noses."

The little weakling actually smiled through all the blood on his face.

As I turned to go, I whispered to him, "You can't tell anyone how this happened. If you do, I'll deny it and you will never become the popular person you so want to be. Just say you were playing on the bleachers and fell on your face. Or that you got jumped by people you didn't know. But don't mention me or Austin."

If they found out that Austin had done this, then my little video was worthless. But I knew how Max ticked, and by dangling popularity in front of him, I ensured that he'd keep his mouth shut.

Max returned to school two days later, a big gauze pad covering his nose. He looked even more pathetic than usual. I found myself laughing. Like this guy ever had a chance of becoming popular.

A few weeks later, he started pestering me about introducing him to some prominent kids. I had to stretch it out, slowly introducing him to a few friends at a time. If his bid to get accepted by others went down in a heap of flames immediately, he might have started reconsidering our little deal.

Over the next several weeks, I introduced Max to about five of my friends, but none of the relationships even got off the ground. Max was a lost cause.

In early June of our senior year, Max Underwood committed suicide. Maybe I was supposed to feel guilty, or at least a bit sad, but I didn't feel either.

Actually, I was happy. Now nobody else knew I'd set up Austin.

Plus, this only made his actions worse. He had beaten up a little weakling who committed suicide a few months later.

Austin was going to do whatever I wanted.

_4_
<u>OLIVE</u>

It was the best first date of my life. Even though for most of it, I felt more like a tour guide.

Austin had come back when my shift ended and we decided to just walk around Santa Monica together. That's when I started channeling my inner docent.

"Eat there."

"Don't go there."

"You have to try this."

While it was unconventional, Austin told me it was just what he was looking for.

"I've learned more in the last hour than in the week I've been in LA. I'd much rather hear the opinion of someone who lives here than read another Yelp review."

He held my hand a couple of times as we walked the streets. Maybe it was a bit presumptuous for a first date, but I liked it. He had a firm grip and I felt safe.

After walking around for more than ninety minutes, we decided to get some dinner. There was a new bar called Gramercy on 24th and Wilshire and I'd heard great things about their food. As we approached, we saw a huge, gorgeous mural of Anthony Bourdain outside of the bar. He had been one of my heroes, and I asked Austin to take a picture of me in front of his portrait. He obliged.

The bar itself had a nice ambience to it. It wasn't that big, but it somehow felt spacious, with a long bar to the right and seating to the left, where we grabbed a booth. A friendly bartender walked over and took our order. I realized he didn't have a server on yet, and I felt privileged to have Sheri helping me out at The Belly Flop.

"I'll take a light beer," Austin said.

I realized I was being put to my no-drinking test earlier than I thought.

"I'll take an iced tea. Not the Long Island version."

The bartender smiled, gave us some menus, and went back to the bar.

"I'm a bit surprised," Austin said. "I take a bartender out and then she orders something non-alcoholic."

"Was a long weekend. Hope that's not a problem."

"Not at all. Watch this."

Austin walked over to the bar, and I could hear him change his order from a Coors Light to an iced tea.

As he came back, I couldn't help but check out his body. My mouth watered.

"No drink for me. In solidarity with you."

"You can't be this perfect," I said.

"I'm not," and he met my gaze with a serious look in his eye. "I add a teaspoon of sugar to my cereal every morning."

"My God, you should go straight to hell."

The bartender came back over and set our iced teas down. We'd barely had time to scan the menu, but I had seen a sandwich that looked great.

"Have you decided what you'd like to eat?"

"I'll take the chicken sandwich," I said.

"Do you have any Frosted Flakes with some sugar?" Austin said.

The bartender looked on, not knowing what to say.

"I'm only kidding. I'll try the burger. Medium rare."

"You're a troublemaker," I said as the bartender walked away.

"Olive, you have no idea," Austin said.

"Enough small talk. What brought you to LA?"

"I want to be an actor," he said, but started smiling right away and I knew he was kidding.

"Yeah, you and half this town."

"Would you hold it against me if I was?"

"Of course not. I'm a writer, and we're almost as ubiquitous as actors."

"Using a word like ubiquitous shows you're probably a good writer."

"Thanks," I said.

"The truth is, I was just tired of the East Coast. After Norfolk, I went to college at Virginia Tech, which is right around the corner. And then I went and worked in New York for the last several years. I needed a change."

"What type of work do you do, if you don't mind me asking?"

"In New York, I was doing financial stuff on Wall Street. I won't bore you with the details. Same thing every day."

"You must have made good money?"

"I did. That's why I'm not in a rush to find a job out here. I'll probably just take up surfing for a month or two and then start looking at jobs again."

"I'd say October probably isn't the best month, but this is LA after all."

"Seriously. It was like eighty-five today. I love it."

I love you, I thought to myself. He was handsome, funny, self-effacing, and everything I could want. Things seemed to be going great.

"What do you write about?" he asked me.

"I had a travel blog, but I discontinued it earlier this year. Hard to be a travel blogger when you're in LA most of the year. I write those Top-Ten lists from time to time. 'Top Ten places Austin should see while in LA!' Those. And I've got a novel in the works. A young adult romance novel. Probably not up your alley."

"What, because I'm a guy, I can't be romantic?"

"I think this place is romantic," I said, and stared at Austin.

I was being much more upfront than my usual self, but he brought it out of me.

"It is," he agreed.

"Truth be told, even though I'm writing a romance novel, my first true love was mysteries."

"I love a good mystery," Austin said. "Tell me more."

"Not much more to tell. I was just infatuated with Nancy Drew as a young woman."

"You're still a young woman."

I blushed.

"Thanks. I'm talking as an early teenager. I read every Nancy Drew novel. Knew them like the back of my hand."

"Remind me not to commit a crime around you."

"I'll catch ya!" I said and winked at him.

The food arrived a few minutes later. The rumors had been true. Gramercy had some great food. The chicken sandwich was served on a skinny block of wood, adding to the aesthetics. Austin seemed to be enjoying his burger as well.

"Now this was a good choice, Olive."

"Thanks."

"This might be in my rotation."

"Didn't know you had a rotation."

"Yeah, it goes The Belly Flop on days you work and then to Gramercy."

"That's some rotation." I smiled.

"Hopefully, we'll get to add some as time goes on."

If he had asked me then and there to go back to his place, I likely would have. That wasn't my style, but there was something about him, and it would have been hard for me to say no.

But the offer didn't come and that was probably for the best.

"What days do you work?" he asked, after he had paid our bill. I had offered, but he insisted.

"Usually Monday through Thursday. Occasional Friday. Get off roughly around six, but that changes day-to-day."

"Then you go work on the novel?"

"I guess you could say that. I'm two months in, but have only finished three chapters."

"What's the opposite of a bullet train?"

"Exactly. Although I've vowed to get more done in the coming months."

"Maybe we can fill your weekends with some other fun as well," he said seductively.

I leaned up and kissed him. It was impulsive, coming out of nowhere, but I didn't regret it. He responded in kind and we shared a five-second kiss.

"As much as I'd like this to continue, I think this is a good point to stop," he said.

My legs were weak and I didn't want it to end, but I knew for the long-term health of our relationship, it was advisable.

Once we left, we exchanged information and planned to meet when my last shift ended on Thursday.

Sheri worked with me again on Tuesday morning, and we stood in our little corner of The Belly Flop where we'd talk, far enough away from the patrons to not be heard. Bill, the seventy-something-year-old man, and Mark Midfield were back for the second straight day. Not that this was a surprise. They were there every day of the week, while others, like the supposedly retired private detective Richard, only came in a few days.

I bet he's no Nancy Drew, I thought to myself, remembering my conversation with Austin about my favorite fictional detective.

I knew I'd only thought of Richard because of my conversation about my favorite fictional detective.

"Slow down," Sheri told me for the third time.

"I'm sorry, it's just, you know…"

"Been awhile?"

"Yeah. But I don't just mean sex, I mean the potential of falling in love."

"Damn, girl, all this from one date?"

"You saw him. But more than his looks, he was charismatic and funny and romantic and—"

"And and and! I get it!" Sheri yelled, but I knew she wasn't mad.

"I almost feel like you introduced us," I said.

"No, I just got out of the way and let nature take its course. I do expect an invite to the wedding, though."

"It's in the mail," I joked.

Sheri looked at me somewhat seriously. "Maybe you should slow down just a little bit, Olive. He sounds awesome and he probably is all you say, but guys are never perfect. You're making him out to be a god."

He seemed like one to me, but I said, "You're right."

"I mean, you've been out on one date and haven't even had sex yet. Maybe he's terrible in bed."

"I doubt it."

"So do I," Sheri said and we shared a laugh.

"Olive, do you want to have a shot?" Mark Midfield said from across the bar. It was like clockwork.

I walked to his side. "I appreciate the offer, Mark, but I'm taking a little time off." He looked sad. "But I promise my first drink back will be a Woo Woo with you."

That made him smile. "Get my old friend Bill a shot as well."

"You want a Woo Woo, Bill?" I asked.

"I'm not one to turn down a free drink. Thanks, Mark."

"You got it, Bill."

I poured two Woo Woo shots and set them in front of the two men.

"To our health," Mark cheered.

"Or lack thereof," Bill replied.

I returned to Sheri. It was still early and we didn't have much work to do.

"So when's the next date?" she asked.

"Thursday after work."

"Is that going to be the day?"

I showed her my crossed fingers.

"It's funny," she said. "Just yesterday we were talking about your lack of a love life and now you're dancing in the clouds."

"I know, it's great."

"You better call me on Friday with all the details. I'm not going to see you until Monday."

"I hope there's a lot to tell," I said, and then let out a little squeal.

I wasn't sure what was wrong with me. Sure, it had been a few years since I'd been this excited about a blossoming romance, but I was acting like a high-schooler.

"What if he orders wine at dinner?"

"We went down to Gramercy yesterday. He ordered a beer and I ordered an iced tea. When I told him I didn't want a drink, he switched his order to an iced tea as well."

"Maybe he is a keeper," Sheri said.

"Let's hope."

A party of seven walked into the bar.

"To be continued," Sheri said, and walked in their direction.

The next few days took forever. I was playing phone tag with Austin, but I wanted more than that. The shifts on Wednesday and Thursday were torture, but as I got off work on Thursday I had a big, goofy grin on my face. I went home, showered, and threw on a small black cocktail dress.

I eagerly waited for Austin to come and pick me up.

_5_
AUSTIN

If it was any other time, place, or situation, I would have taken Olive home and banged the shit out of her after we ate at Gramercy. God, was she sexy. Her eyes pleaded with me to take her home as I ate my cheeseburger and drank my stupid iced tea that I'd only ordered to appease her. But Becca and I had a bigger prize looming, so I pretended to be the good boy that I most assuredly was not.

When she leaned up and kissed me, I almost said fuck it (literally), but once again I managed to resist. I'm not sure how. Olive was as beautiful a girl as I had taken out in a long time. Too bad this wasn't going to have a fairy tale ending for us.

Fucking Becca.

I graduated high school never having heard from the police over the Max Underwood incident. I was worried every day for several weeks, just expecting a knock on the door at any time. I even tried to avoid Max when I saw him in the corridors of high school. Me, walking away from an unimposing wimp like Max Underwood. It didn't make sense, but I really didn't want to look into the guy's eyes. I knew what I had done was wrong, terribly wrong, and I wasn't quite sure why he hadn't reported me.

A month and a half after the incident, Max Underwood committed suicide. I felt sad, but not guilty. He'd obviously had a whole lot of issues and I didn't think my assault had pushed him over the edge. Still, I'm not a monster, and I did say a little prayer for his soul. I felt bad, I really did.

As time went on, I thought less and less about it. I went off to college at Virginia Tech (not everything I told Olive was a lie) and tried out for the football team, to no avail. I decided it was time to concentrate on my studies, and I was your average student for the next year and change.

Early in December of my sophomore year, I found out the real reason Max hadn't gone to the police. At that time, I lived off campus with three friends I had made in the dorms.

At two p.m. on a Saturday, we sat home watching Virginia Tech play Florida State in the ACC championship football game. If it was a home game, we would have tailgated all morning and yelled our asses off at Lane Stadium, but for the conference championship game in Charlotte, North Carolina, we had a group of friends over to watch instead. We were up 35-24 to start the fourth quarter when we heard a knock at the door. My roommate, Aaron Hield, sat closest to the front door and went to answer it.

"Jared, it's for you," he said.

Keep in mind, I was still Jared at this point. I walked to the front door and, for a second, didn't recognize the girl standing there.

She had long, curly black hair, which threw me off for a moment. But then it hit me.

"Becca?"

"Took you long enough."

"What have you done with your hair?"

"I've become a dark brunette. For a few months, anyway."

"It's great to see you," I said.

"Thanks."

We went in for an awkward hug, and I kissed her on the cheek. Truth be told, it wasn't great to see her. Becca had become more and more about Becca as we grew older, and she had already been selfish to begin with. Her showing up now didn't seem random. It was something sure to benefit her in some way.

"What are you doing here?" I asked.

"Do you have a place we could talk?"

"Sure. Let me just watch the end of this game."

I brought Becca to the family room and quickly introduced her to everyone. Our group consisted of ten guys and Becca became the third woman.

Rooting for your college football team is probably number two on a college man's wish list, but number one is beautiful women, so many of the guys gave a double take when I introduced Becca.

I wasn't a fan of her new hair, but she was still striking. She had long, tanned legs and a push up bra that made her breasts look bigger than I remembered. And her face was flawless. Badmouthing her hair would just be nitpicking. She was still gorgeous, I had to admit it.

We held on to beat the hated Seminoles 44-33, putting everyone at the party in a good mood, myself included. It wouldn't last.

After the celebrating ended, Becca turned to me.

"Can we talk somewhere private now?"

"Of course."

I high-fived a few more of the guys and took Becca to my room on the second floor. We had tried to clean up the place before the game, but it was a half-hearted attempt and I could feel her judging.

"Hey, it's better than a frat house," I said.

"I guess."

We got to my room and I opened the door for her. Time to find out what she was doing in Blacksburg, Virginia knocking on my door. She hadn't gone to college after graduation, but besides that I didn't know much about what she had been up to. As far as I could tell, she didn't have any social media.

"I think you should sit down," she said.

"Is something wrong, Becca?"

"I've got something to show you. And I know you are going to get pissed off when you first see it. But please, control your emotions. As much as it's going to sting, I'm going to give you a great opportunity once you've settled down."

I had no idea what she was about to show me, but coming from her, it was going to be a bombshell. She wouldn't have traveled to my college campus for something minor.

She sat next to me and raised her cell phone to eye level. She pressed play on a video and a split second later, I knew what it was.

"You fucking bitch!"

"I said to control your emotions. Just watch."

"I can't believe you recorded this."

"Watch!" she yelled.

I obeyed, watching as I pushed Max Underwood to the ground and punched him twice. Then he said he'd tell people that Becca and I didn't do anything. I went nuts, punching him twice more. His nose exploded under my second blow and you could see blood gushing from it.

I wanted to turn away, but Becca made sure I kept looking at it.

Mercifully, the video ended.

"And you're the one who recorded it?" I asked, trying to calm down.

"Yes."

"Did you know it was going to happen?"

"Yes."

"You told Max Underwood to say those things?"

"Yes."

"And you told him not to go to the police?"

"Yes."

"Jesus, Becca, you're a psychopath."

"Yes. Oh wait, that wasn't a question."

She smiled as she said this, and I couldn't help but feel I was in the presence of evil. I was far from a saint, but this was beyond the pale.

"You know he killed himself, right?"

"Is that rhetorical? You know that I know."

"And you don't feel guilty?" I asked.

"I'm not aware of such a word."

"You're immoral to the thousandth degree."

"Are you done ranting? I haven't told you the opportunity this video will present for you."

"The opportunity to go to jail."

"Well, yes, there is that. But that's why I'm so confident you're going to choose option number two."

I bowed my head, sure I wouldn't like what was to come.

"What is the other option?"

"How about we get rich together?"

I raised my head.

"I've brought you some homework," Becca said.

She laid down multiple pamphlets, all relating to Amyotrophic Lateral Sclerosis (ALS), also known as Lou Gehrig's disease.

"What exactly am I going to be doing?" I asked.

"Staying out of jail."

_6_
<u>BECCA</u>

I had never planned on going to college. I know it was expected of intelligent people, and while I fit that description, it wasn't for me. Spending four or five years in a classroom and coming out with a whole bunch of debt? No, thanks.

Life is short and I planned on being in the black when I was in my early twenties. College would have left me in the red.

So I did the most illogical thing a newly nineteen-year-old girl could do. I moved to a city where I didn't know a soul. San Francisco. Silicon Valley was spawning new young multi-millionaires every day and I wanted to be where the money was. I took a flight into San Francisco International Airport in October of 2008, a few months after graduating high school, ready to start my new life.

My parents always knew I was a bit of a wild child, to say the least, and this only confirmed their beliefs.

I had a little over $9,000 in my checking account. I'd saved the money from my fake softball fundraiser and made a few thousand more in various scams to close out my senior year. I'd received a few grand more as graduation presents and I sold my 2001 Golf for $2,800. Finally, when my parents realized they couldn't talk me out of moving to California, they gave me a thousand dollars more.

Nine grand was hardly a windfall for a city as expensive as San Francisco, but it was enough to get me by in the early months. After all, it wasn't like I planned on paying rent for long. I'd find a sugar daddy for that. Or better yet, one of those young Silicon Valley multimillionaires.

I located a room for rent in a five-bedroom house in the Haight Ashbury section of the city. It wasn't ideal, but when the median rent for a one bedroom reached $2,500 a month, concessions had to be made. I paid $900 a month, and although it was a good deal, nine grand wouldn't last long at that rate.

I didn't like my hippie roommates, so I spent most of my time outside of the house, which turned out to be a good thing. My dreams weren't going to come true surrounded by incest, lava lamps, and strobe lights. I had to inform my roommates more than once that it was no longer the Summer of Love in San Francisco.

As you can guess, they weren't the biggest fans of mine. Not that I gave a shit.

I made sure to wear a sexy outfit any time I went out looking for guys. I'd hang out in cafes near dot-com businesses, hoping to catch the eye of one of those young millionaires. I went on a few dates and I made the mistake of admitting my age. No one wanted to date a nineteen-year-old. I couldn't even get a drink with them.

I went to Alana, the one girl in the house I could deal with, and asked her how I could get a fake I.D. Alana was newly twenty-one and went out to the bars a lot, so I figured she might know someone.

"I'll get back to you in a few days," she said.

It didn't take that long. The next day she brought some shady looking guy with two sleeve tattoos back to the house.

"Becca, this is Devin."

Alana left us alone.

"I heard you're looking for a fake I.D.," Devin said as he not-very-subtly looked me over.

I caught him.

"Hey, eighteen is legal for what I'm looking at," he said.

I wanted to grab the chair next to me and slam it across his face, and then stab him with one of the shards, but I needed him for the moment. And maybe in the future. For a woman who planned to live a less than legal lifestyle, a man who supplied fake I.D.s would be a good person to know.

So I held my tongue, but I'd never forget what he'd said.

"I just want to get an I.D."

"And what do you want to use this I.D. for?"

"Why does it matter?" I asked.

"Well, Becca," he said, scanning me over once again, "if you're just looking for an I.D. to get into bars, that's easy. But if you're looking for an I.D. to set up a fake bank account or something more sinister, then that's going to cost you."

"What's the difference?"

I had suddenly become very attentive.

"For an I.D. to get into bars, I can just give you a stolen driver's license. For more mischievous endeavors, you'd need multiple forms of identification."

While I wasn't ready for anything like that, Devin had certainly piqued my interest.

"For now, I just want an I.D. to get into bars. But I may be in touch down the road."

He handed me a business card. It said he was a tattoo artist and worked at a place called Tit-for-Tat.

Gross.

"Can't exactly highlight my side job on these cards," he said.

I found myself grinning at the despicable man across from me. I'd love to tattoo him. With a big knife.

"So, we need someone who has long, dark hair in her early twenties."

I changed my hair quite often and had gone with the long, black hair before setting off to San Francisco.

Devin opened up a fanny pack, and I was reminded of the one I used to collect my fake donations in Atlanta. He looked through it a few times and took out two I.D.s he thought might work.

Lillith Jacobs was twenty-three, from Colorado, and had hair similar to mine. At 5'8", she stood two inches taller than I, but I didn't think that would be a big problem. We both had green eyes and I thought it might work.

The other I.D. belonged to someone named Rachel Mounds. She was twenty-six and also had long, brown hair.

"I don't think I can pass for twenty-six," I said.

"You're probably right," Devin said. "Lillith it is."

"What twenty-three-year-old goes by Lillith?" I asked.

"Go as Lily."

"I think I will."

The price tag was steep, a hundred bucks, but it seemed like money well spent. Lillith had one of the hologram I.D.s, and as long as I didn't fuck up, I could use it until I actually turned twenty-one myself.

"We have a deal," I said.

"Keep that business card. You can call me for anything you want. And I do mean anything."

I had my I.D. now and there was no reason to continue being nice to Devin.

"If you were the last man on earth, and it was just you and me, I'd jump off the Golden Gate Bridge."

I leaned in closer.

"You're fucking disgusting."

Devin didn't know what to say. I had scared him and it made me happy. Served the sexist asshole right.

"You can go now," I said.

Devin timidly walked toward the door.

Lily Jacobs paid immediate dividends. Protocol in Silicon Valley stated the guy would ask you out to coffee for a first date, and assuming you got along, the second date would be at a bar for a drink. I could now say yes to the second date.

For all intents and purposes, I was twenty-three years old.

Or so I thought.

One of the very first guys I dated was a thirty-year-old man named Gary who'd have stood 5'9" if he borrowed my heels. He was immediately smitten with me and I had him eating out of my palm after a few dates. He wanted to keep me close and told me he could get me a job at Facebook, where he was already a Vice President of something.

He said I'd have to start at the bottom, but could rise up quickly if I worked hard. There were two problems with this. One, I wasn't a twenty-three-year-old named Lillith Jacobs and filling out a W-2 with a fake name was just asking for trouble. Two, and more importantly, I didn't want to work. It wasn't in my makeup. I wanted to be handed wealth, not have to move up the ladder for it.

After I turned down the chance to work with him, Gary and I went downhill pretty fast. We were done less than a month later. It wasn't a total loss however, as I had been bought several expensive dresses, and hadn't paid for a meal out in three months. If I'd held out longer, I might have started getting some spending money, but it was time to move on.

I didn't want to be hanging out with some short-ass guy anyway.

The next guy I dated was a lot taller than Gary, but he wasn't as big a baller. He worked for some small start-up and barely made $100k a year. We didn't last long either. The guy after him worked for a company called Twitter that I hadn't heard of yet. I broke up with him less than a month in. A few years later, I heard he ended up becoming one of Twitter's high-ranking officers.

C'est la vie. He was shitty in bed anyway.

I dated guys all over the Bay Area until I finally met the one that changed everything.

Jeb Costner was twenty-six when I met him. When he first introduced himself, at a coffee shop less than a mile from Google headquarters, or "The Campus" as they called it, he used both his first and last name. Luckily, he looked a lot more like a young Kevin Costner than he did Jeb Bush.

Jeb was handsome, witty, and all other things that a woman might like in a man. If I was the type who could settle down and get married, he might have been the one. But I'm not.

He looked at me from across the cafe. It was October of 2010. I had just turned twenty and resorted to using the name Lily at all times. I figured if I ever got involved with something that needed me to be twenty-one years old, it was better to be known as Lily.

We made eye contact a few times and Jeb walked over to me.

"I'd like to get your next coffee."

"Oh, that's very nice of you," I said, trying to sound down to earth and modest. It was hard.

"You're welcome. What are you having?"

"An Americano would be great. I'm Lily."

"Jeb Costner," he said.

Jeb picked up his laptop bag and went to the nearest barista. He returned a few minutes later with an Americano and what looked like a latte.

"Thanks," I said.

"I come to this cafe a lot. I think I would have known if I'd seen you here before."

The insinuation that I was beautiful didn't come as a surprise, but I took note. It would make this easy.

"I live in the city, but have a friend who lives down here. I'm supposed to go see her later today, so decided to get a coffee first."

"She work down here?"

"Yeah, at Yahoo," I said, making something up on the fly.

"What's her name? I work at Google and know a great many people down here."

I spouted out the first name that came into my mind. "Maddy Smith."

"Can't say I know her," Jeb said.

"She's new there. I'm not surprised."

"I'm pretty good with accents. Yours is somewhere from the South. But not the rural South, it's a city accent. I'm going with Atlanta."

I was fucking impressed. "You nailed it. Now that's a rare talent."

"Thank you. I don't always pick the precise city, but I'm usually in the ballpark."

My I.D. still said Colorado, and in case it came up later I decided to nip it in the bud.

"I grew up there, but lived in Colorado the last few years before moving to S.F."

"Do you work for one of the dot-commies?"

"No, I don't think I'm as smart as y'all." I emphasized the Southern expression and smiled seductively at Jeb.

"Everyone has their own talents. I'm sure you're very smart, Lily."

I kept the smile as I said, "Yeah, I've got some talents."

We agreed to our first official date a few minutes later. He would come pick me up and take me to Morton's, a renowned steakhouse in San Francisco. Jeb was breaking protocol and taking me to an expensive dinner right away.

It was guys like Jeb that had me move to the Bay Area. He was rich, willing to spend it, and found me downright beautiful.

I vowed not to fuck this one up, at least not until I got what I wanted.

The first date turned into a second, and we were officially dating a few weeks later. I'd moved to a new place in the Mission district and Jeb couldn't stand it, so I'd spend large chunks of my days at his beautiful condo in Sunnyvale, right in the heart of Silicon Valley. It turned out he was Head of Marketing for Google and making money hand over fist.

He was good in the sack as well, and we had some great times those first few months. Jeb spoiled me rotten, and while I'd protest when he bought me an expensive dinner, I'd always "let" him win out and pick up the check.

The one thing he didn't like was that I wasn't working. He often used the phrase "The devil makes work for idle hands" and told me he'd find me something. I despised work, but I liked spending time with Jeb, and was getting accustomed to day trips to Monterey, expensive restaurants, and rooftop bars.

Jeb came into the condo one day, obviously exhausted.

"You look tired," I said.

"Long day at work," Jeb said. "Was doing stuff for me and for you."

My eyebrows rose. "For me?"

"I told you that I was going to find a job for you. And I did!"

I feigned happiness. "Thanks so much, baby. What is it?"

"Looking after a rich old lady."

My mind started running like a hamster on a wheel. Rich old lady sparked many images, and in most of them I fleeced the old bag for some of her money.

"That sounds interesting. How'd you find it?"

"It was pretty random, actually. I was talking to Ted at work, the guy you met at the Tonga Room Tiki Bar last week."

"Yeah, I remember Ted."

"Anyway, I told him that you were looking for a job and he said his mother could use someone to look after her."

"Look after her?" I asked as I visualized changing diapers and giving her pills.

"Nothing too bad. You're not going to be her nurse, if that's what you thought."

"It crossed my mind."

"I guess the job title would be more like 'chauffeur.' Joan, that's her name, is in her early eighties and doesn't drive anymore. But she's hardly the type who likes to stay at home. You're going to have to keep up with her."

"So I'd be driving her around town?"

"That would be a lot of it, yeah. And if she gets tired, you'll probably do errands for her."

"How often?"

"Ted said we could just start off with three days a week."

I thought it was three days too many, but I kept it to myself.

"That doesn't sound so bad," I said instead.

"I think it would be good for you, Lily. And trust me, they would pay you well. Joan Gandy is San Francisco royalty. You'd probably be meeting some pretty famous people."

The job suddenly sounded quite enticing.

"I'd love to do it. Thanks, Jeb, you really went out of your way for me."

"It's my pleasure doing things for you."

I figured it was my time to do something for him. This couldn't be a one-way street if I planned on keeping Jeb. And with this new opportunity with Joan Gandy, I had no plans on screwing things up.

I grabbed his hand and led him to the bedroom.

Joan Gandy was eighty-two, going on forty-two. My God, could this woman get around. Jeb had two cars, and loaned me his one-year-old convertible BMW. Must be nice to have that as your backup car. Joan would have me take the top down as we drove around San Francisco, stopping at her usual haunts.

Which turned out to usually be bars and restaurants. This eighty-two-year-old could outdrink a nineteen-year-old frat boy. She liked a Maker's Mark and Coke, but it's not like she'd have to tell the bartender. They all knew what Joan Gandy drank.

I received immediate respect since I came with San Francisco royalty. I wouldn't have had to pay for a drink, I was sure of that. But given I was the one driving her around town, having a drink was off-limits.

At times Joan would shoo me away if she needed to have a private conversation. Other times, she'd ask me to sit by her and I'd feel part of the team.

Truth be told, I really liked Joan. She was tough and could be a bit rude. She was no wilting flower. She'd speak her mind, and that intimidated many men.

I was reminded of when I eviscerated Danny Dufner back in the day. It's something that Joan Gandy would have done.

About ten days in to my new job, we were having lunch at the Cliff House in San Francisco, a restaurant that dated back decades and sat along the Pacific Ocean. It was known for the whales and dolphins swimming along outside its huge bay windows. We didn't see any on this afternoon, but I wouldn't have seen them anyway. I was trying something out on Joan Gandy.

"How long ago did your husband pass, Joan?"

It was the first time I had broached the subject.

"It's been about fifteen years now, Lily."

"Do you miss him?"

"No!"

That wasn't the answer I expected and I said so.

"He was an asshole," Joan said. "I'm glad he's gone."

We were more alike than I could have thought.

"In what way?"

"An asshole in all ways. An alcoholic and not the nice kind like me. He could be abusive. And he was fucking half of the rich women in San Francisco. He especially seemed to like widows."

"I'm sorry to hear that," I said.

"It's okay, dear, that was a long time ago. As you can tell, I've been getting along just fine without him."

"That's for sure."

"Tell me about you, Lily. I feel like I'm always the one talking."

I had been rehearsing a story for the last few days and decided to try it out. "Nothing special, I guess. Grew up in Atlanta with two brothers. Started high school there, but our family moved to Denver my junior year."

"Why is that?"

"My older brother has a terrible disease and the hospital in Denver was better suited to deal with it."

"I'm so sorry. What is it?"

"He has Lou Gehrig's disease."

"I know it all too well. Had a friend who battled it. So your parents just shipped you and your brothers to a new city? Leaving all your friends back in Atlanta?"

I tried to look sad. "Yeah, it was tough. Listen, I love my brother more than anything and I completely understand why my parents did it, but it wasn't easy for the sixteen-year-old me."

"How is he now?"

She was biting, just like I had hoped. Time to set the hook.

"Not too well, actually. My parents just can't afford to keep him in this hospital anymore."

"He's still in the same hospital?"

"He's in and out. He had several good years, but the disease has taken a turn for the worse as of late."

"And he must still be pretty young."

"He's only five years older than me. He got the disease a lot younger than most. One of the earlier cases the doctor had every heard of. Everyone thinks it's an old man's disease, but people do get it in their twenties and thirties," I said.

"Oh, my dear Lily, that's heartbreaking."

"Yeah, it's been really difficult for our family."

"Is there anything I can do?"

"I really like your company, Joan, but I've only known you a few weeks. I can't ask you to help." I put on my puppy dog face. The hook had been set.

"I've got more money than I know what to do with. I'd like to assist your family," she said.

"It would be such a huge help, Joan. I'll tell you more about it in the coming days," I said. "And can you not tell your son? He might have it get back to Jeb and I haven't spoken to him about this yet."

"Why not?"

"It's just too personal. I'm not even sure why I opened up to you. I guess I just trust you, Joan."

I was way too good at this. Joan's eyes looked like they were tearing up.

"I think we'll be able to do something, Lily."

"You're a wonderful woman, Joan."

"Remember, I'll be gone this weekend, but I'll see you early next week."

"That's right."

Joan got up from the table and we looked out on the Pacific Ocean. I had to agree it was beautiful, but not as beautiful as the evil plan brewing in my brain.

I knew what I was going to do that weekend without Joan. It involved a trip to Virginia Tech, an old video, and an older friend.

_7_
<u>OLIVE</u>

Austin and I made love after our third date. Do they still call it making love? Whatever, we had sex, we banged. You get the idea. It was glorious. We were in perfect sync and I couldn't have asked for anything more.

We started to become inseparable over the next few weeks. We ate at a new restaurant every night, or if we weren't going out, we'd catch up on the latest Netflix series. The night always ended in bed and we seemed very compatible in that department. The euphemism "Netflix and chill" could have been coined with us in mind.

The only thing was, he didn't seem to want to meet my friends. A few times I suggested hanging out with my crew so he could meet everyone, but Austin always refused. I didn't like it, but I was sure he had his reasons. Maybe it was too early on and he wanted to make sure we were going to last. Maybe he was just a shy guy, although that didn't appear to be the case. Maybe he was jealous and didn't want to meet my guy friends, though that didn't seem likely either.

I was fine with it. The only thing better than hanging out with my friends was hanging out with Austin. He'd surely meet everyone at some point, so I paid it very little mind.

We had many exciting dates to start, but one stood out from all the others. Austin called me on a Saturday morning and asked if I had the day free. Happily, I did. He said he'd pick me up in an hour.

I got ready, dressing casually and bringing a warm jacket as he had requested. He picked me up and we headed down to the ocean. Marina Del Rey, to be exact. We parked the car and started walking toward the marina itself, looking out at the extravagant yachts.

"You didn't buy a boat?" I asked, secretly hoping he had.

"Only for the day."

I turned toward him. "You're kidding!"

"Do I look like I'm kidding?"

"Wow, you've outdone yourself. Which one is ours?"

"We're down a little bit."

We approached the water and the boats all lined up in a row. Austin guided me to the left and we walked down a row of vessels I couldn't afford if I worked at The Belly Flop for 150 years.

"Don't tell me we've got one like this?" I asked.

"I'd have got you a yacht twice as big as these, but considering it's just us, it might have been a bit excessive."

"A small boat is just fine," I said.

"Well, I would hardly call it small." Austin grabbed my shoulders, turning me toward the boat I was about to pass.

It was gorgeous. An oversized speedboat, it probably would have fit fifteen people. Maybe more. It had to have been thirty feet long and was painted in white and light blue. The name on the side of the hull read *To Olive*.

"You didn't monogram this for me, did you?"

Austin laughed. "No, I didn't do anything that drastic. But I was walking down here yesterday and saw this boat. I knew I had to take you out on it. I waited around for an hour, but no one came. Finally, someone walked up from a neighboring boat, and I told him I wanted to rent this one for the day. I asked him for the owner's phone number, but he said he wouldn't do that. He asked for my info and said he'd contact the owner, who would get back to me if he was looking to rent it."

"And he was willing to?"

"It took a little convincing, but he came around to my side. Telling him it was for an Olive pushed him over the edge."

"I'm speechless, Austin."

"We're going to have ourselves one hell of a day."

"Did you find out who Olive was?"

"Yeah, it was the man's wife who passed away recently."

"Oh, no," I said.

"It's not a sad story. She was pretty old and the man said she got fifteen good years with this boat."

"The thing looks like it's brand new."

"I know, it's crazy."

"I don't know how to thank you for this," I said.

"I'll think of something," Austin said and smiled devilishly.

I asked him to get into a selfie with the two of us and *To Olive* in the background, but he said it would be better if it was just me and the inscription instead. It dawned on me that we didn't have any pictures together yet, but I didn't mention it. Hardly seemed the time.

After the picture, Austin helped me get on the boat and we set out from the harbor. I had been on a few boat rides in my life and one of my favorite parts was looking back at the land as we headed out to sea. It was like a beautiful separation.

Austin put on some cheesy captain's hat that made me smile.

"You're a natural," I said.

"I had a wealthy friend in Savannah who used to let me play captain on his boats."

"Savannah, Georgia?".

"Yeah," Austin said, pausing for a second before he continued. "I'd go there most summers for a week or two. Mostly to get to drive boats like these."

I realized how little I knew about Austin. He had grown up in Norfolk and went to Virginia Tech before working in New York City—that was about the extent of it.

"Tell me more about your childhood?" I said, snuggling up close to him as he drove the boat.

I had stopped looking at the shore and now we both stared at the blue, unforgiving ocean ahead.

"It was boring, that's why I don't talk about it all that much. High school was ordinary and Virginia Tech was your typical college experience. I moved to LA to experience new things, not dwell on the past."

He kissed me and I could tell he didn't want to talk about it, so I let it be.

"You're right," I said. "Plus, why talk about the past on a day like this? It's gorgeous out here."

"You know how you just switched from looking at the shore to looking at the water in front of us? That's me, forgetting about the past and looking toward the future."

It was a wonderful analogy, I had to say.

We got out of the harbor and Austin pressed the pedal to the medal. I had never moved faster on a boat. I almost wanted to tell him to slow down, but I found it so exciting that I didn't want it to stop.

At one point, he took his goofy captain's hat off and put it on me. He grabbed me and put me in between himself and the ship's wheel.

"This is called the helm." He had to yell as the wind sprinted by our ears.

It was exhilarating as all hell, going way too fast on the open water. He stepped away and let me man (woman) the helm for a few minutes. I'd take a peek over at him to make sure I was doing it right, and he'd say I was born to be a captain.

After a few minutes he came over and brought down the speed abruptly. We must have been five miles out from shore and there wasn't another boat to be seen. He brought the To Olive to an idle and gazed at me.

"Looks like we're all alone out here," he said.

I knew what was going to happen next, and you're damn right I was looking forward to it.

"Do we need to anchor the boat?" I naively asked.

"Baby, we're several miles from shore. There's no anchor in the world that's hitting the ocean floor from here. We'll just coast for the next few minutes."

"It's never just a few minutes."

"Then we'll coast longer," he said.

He led me down to the bottom of the boat, where, grinning, he said, "Would you like to see the bedroom?" His shirt was off by the time we got there. Soon mine was too. The sex was as great as always, and it seemed somehow more exotic knowing the boat was just drifting around the Pacific Ocean.

Just when I thought it might be over, Austin grabbed me and carried me back to the main level. I half expected a boat to be coasting by, seeing us in our birthday suits, my legs wrapped around his. Luckily, it wasn't to be.

Austin set me down to gather some blankets and towels, which he lay on the deck of the boat. I could tell this wasn't going to be the most comfortable position, but the environment was so intoxicating that I couldn't resist. He was as gentle as I could hope for and it turned out having sex on the floor of a boat wasn't all that bad.

I finished, then he finished, and all was good with the world.

We stayed out on the boat for five hours in total. Austin must have reminded me four times to put on more sunscreen. It was October, but in LA that meant a temperature of eighty degrees for most of the day. Remember, I was Olive in name only, and my skin could burn if I wasn't careful. We made love one more time, but this time we remained belowdecks.

As we headed back to shore, there was no denying I'd become smitten with Austin. It had only been a few weeks but I felt it quickly heading toward love. It felt like being aboard a runaway train, unable to find the brakes.

Austin finally made his second appearance at The Belly Flop a few days later. We were having a birthday for Barry Gant, the owner of the bar, and when I told Austin, he actually seemed interested in attending. A lot of my friends were going to be there, so this was a big day for me, introducing a new boyfriend to what must be a bunch of people waiting to judge.

I would also have to deal with Barry himself. He was a generous boss, always throwing parties, giving us gift certificates to local businesses, granting time off when we wanted. But he had taken a liking to me early on in my employment and it had never waned.

Over the years, numerous fellow employees had told me Barry asked them whether I was still single. He could be up front about my looks and I understood the way he always looked at me. Not that I would date a sixty-year-old man anyway.

Barry was still handsome, but his wavy hair always appeared unkempt and he had a gut that made it look as if the buttons from his signature Tommy Bahama shirts were going to explode. I thought the majority of women who hung out with him did so for his money. And while that might be enough for some women, it wasn't for me.

That being said, his flirting was generally in good fun, and I thought Barry had a good heart.

But now I had to see how he reacted when he learned I had a boyfriend.

It turned out I had nothing to worry about. Austin arrived fashionably late since I had to get there early and help set up. Barry owned a bunch of bars around Los Angeles, but we held the party at The Belly Flop because it had the highest capacity, and that turned out to be a good plan. The place was popping.

I pointed out Barry to Austin, having alerted him earlier that day to the possibility that he might be in for a little ribbing from him. Austin went right over and they appeared inseparable. Every time I looked over, they seemed to be laughing their asses off. I had to give it to Austin, he could be charismatic as hell.

About twenty minutes later, Barry approached me. This time his requisite Tommy Bahama shirt was red with white martini glasses splattered all over. It was pretty hideous.

"Olive, your boyfriend has quite the personality," he said.

"Thanks. We're still pretty early on," I said.

"No, I think he's a keeper, I really do."

"Thanks, Barry. I wasn't sure what you'd think of him."

Barry looked at me. "I deserve that," he said. "I admit it, I've thought you were the most beautiful employee I've ever hired. I'd wanted to do some naughty things with you. But I'm over it and I'm happy you're happy."

I could have been offended by his statement and would have been in my rights. But he had said it with a certain sweetness, if that's possible.

"I appreciate you saying that, Barry. Well, maybe not the naughty part, but the rest of it."

"I'm sorry, Olive. I'm still a chauvinist pig. What can I say?"

"It's never too late to become a better person."

"You're right. Alright, I'm starting over at sixty-two years old."

"I sense a little sarcasm there."

"I can't promise miracles. I'm still going to be attracted to pretty women."

"Well, this one is off the market," I said.

"So you're calling yourself pretty?" He laughed.

"I just meant that I'm no longer single."

"You sell yourself short, Olive. Do you know how many girls I've hired in the last several years between twelve restaurants? And if I think you're the most attractive of them all, then of course you are pretty. To say the least."

I didn't know what to say, so I just said, "Thank you."

"Now where is that boyfriend of yours? I want to hear some more of his stories."

We looked up and saw Austin headed in our direction.

I couldn't be happier.

_8_
AUSTIN

I was hoping to be done with Becca after helping her out in San Francisco. I had pretended to be her sick brother in front of an old woman named Joan Gandy. After learning everything there was to know about ALS, I even tried to show some of the early symptoms I'd read about. I slurred my speech and let a few things drop right out of my hand, including a cup of coffee on her expensive rug. I gave what I thought was a thoroughly convincing performance.

We drove away from the woman's mansion in a convertible BMW. I didn't even want to know how that had fallen into Becca's lap.

She wanted to have lunch after we had finished with Ms. Gandy, but I told her I needed to shower after what we'd done.

"You don't want me sending my video to the authorities, do you?" she asked.

"Of course I don't. Just like I don't want to tell them that you're fleecing some old lady."

"Ms. Gandy giving me $50,000 would be like you or I giving a stranger a dollar."

"$50,000? Jesus, Becca, that's a lot of money."

"Would you like to get a taste?"

I was a poor college student at the time, but I knew right and wrong, and this wasn't right. I had grown up a bit from the obnoxious, testosterone-fueled menace who had beaten up Max Underwood. I was by no means perfect, and I could still be a bully when it was unnecessary, but I knew going down the rabbit hole with Becca wouldn't end well.

"No, I don't want a taste. I want to get back to Atlanta and have Christmas with my parents."

"Say hi to all of our old friends. Go say hi to Mr. and Mrs. Underwood, they probably still live there."

"I'm no longer that guy who beat him up."

"You keep telling yourself that. Just know that your life would be over if I ever released this video to the public. I could send it out to any of your prospective employers after you graduate from college. I'm sure they'd love to hire you after seeing that."

"What is it you want, Becca? I helped you out here like you wanted. I'm done with this."

"That is yet to be determined," she said.

I no longer had the temper I did in high school, but in that moment I wanted to strangle the life out of her.

"Go spend your $50,000 and have a great life. I'm sure you've got all these Silicon Valley millionaires buying you clothes and paying your rent anyway. Fifty grand should last you ten years."

"You know me so well. It's a wonder we never got together."

"We did. Don't you remember Two Minutes in the Closet?"

"How can I forget? Made you the Romeo you became."

"It may have helped in the beginning, but women were always going to like this," I said, pointing at myself.

"Yeah, you sure have changed."

"Screw you!" I said.

"I'll be in touch."

"I may not answer."

"Then I guess I'll just have to post my little video on social media."

I knew I was screwed. That video really could ruin my life.

"Please don't do that. I helped you out here."

"You did and I appreciate that. Just make sure you answer next time I call."

That call wouldn't come for several years.

I graduated from Virginia Tech, so I guess I should take pride in that. Unfortunately, after that my life was a series of bad luck and worse choices.

No, I wasn't working on Wall Street like I had told Olive. More like I was on "I've hit a Wall" Street.

I stayed in Blacksburg, Virginia after I graduated, and that was my first mistake. While it was a great college town, the opportunities weren't bursting at the seams for recent college graduates. It didn't help that I'd majored in Sociology, which rarely led to an obvious post-college career.

People had suggested becoming a teacher, but I didn't enjoy the time I had spent in the classroom. Why would I want to spend my next thirty years stuck in one?

My parents threw out some other ideas. A psychologist. A job in PR. Law school. Business school.

In the end, I decided to go into the one thing I knew I was good at: sales. I could be charismatic, charming, and convincing, the three Cs that helped make a great salesman. And yes, I know charismatic and charming are quite similar. But our boss thought it sounded good.

I took a job at a place called Shelor Toyota, located in Christianburg, just eight miles from Blacksburg. My parents were disappointed and my friends didn't understand why, so I told everyone it was just a way to make some money before I decided on a career.

Truth be told, I didn't know what I wanted to do. A lot of things interested me, but nothing I wanted to do full-time. I loved cars, however, and anyone who ever met me could tell you I could talk your ear off, so selling cars didn't seem like such a bad gig.

And I was pretty good at what I did. I won Salesman of the Month twice in my first year. Well, whoop dee fucking doo, I hear you saying. But while everyone else was laughing at me, I pulled down close to a hundred grand a year. My friends who had taken more "reputable" jobs brought in barely half of that.

I also had a cute girlfriend, so yeah, I guess the first year after college wasn't so bad. But it went downhill from there.

A college town created a lot of distractions, and I started to cheat on my girlfriend with younger girls. I mean, I was still young myself, but I was dating and screwing freshman in college, often barely over eighteen years old. No, it wasn't illegal, but pretty slimy. I didn't care. I felt lost, not knowing what I wanted to do with my life, so fucking young girls seemed to pass the time.

My nose got me in trouble as well. I'd never tried cocaine while in college, even though it had presented itself several times. I still considered myself an upstanding citizen at that point. Selling cars was humbling, and since I no longer fooled myself that I was on some upward track to stardom, I started dabbling in the white powder.

At first, it was just once or twice a month at parties. Like most drugs, it wears you down, and six months in, I was doing it every Friday and Saturday. And then some Thursdays. And the occasional Tuesday.

This went on for a long time.

I was fired from Shelor Toyota after three years at the job. I was twenty-five. To be honest, it was amazing I lasted as long as I had. There had been rumors around the shop about me dating young girls and dabbling in nose candy. They could overlook the first, but the second turned out to be a problem.

My boss, a nice gentlemen who had been more than fair with me, warned me numerous times when I'd come to work with bloodshot eyes. I didn't listen. I was a car salesman, I didn't really give a shit if I got fired.

And when a co-worker caught me doing lines in the bathroom one day at work, the time had come. My boss called me and told me it was over. I didn't even put up a fight, knowing he had no choice.

I tried to say goodbye to most of the girls I was dating around town and called my parents. I was moving back to Georgia.

My enjoyment of—I wouldn't call it an addiction—cocaine proved surprisingly easy to give up. When I moved back to Roswell, just outside of Atlanta, I lived in my parents' house, and neither the allure nor the connections were there for me. I think I enjoyed the social aspects of it more than I enjoyed the actual experience. I'm sure many addicts hate people like me, but I can honestly say once I returned home, I never had the urge to use it again.

That didn't mean my life was all hunky dory.

I was twenty-five years old and living at home. I never told my parents I had been fired, much less the reason why, and they just thought I had grown tired of Blacksburg. Which wasn't entirely untrue.

My father got me a job in construction. He was the foreman of a company, and even though I had a college degree, he thought I should start at the bottom. My father was a pretty intuitive man, and I think he realized there'd been more to my leaving Blacksburg than I let on.

Because of this, he thought starting me off doing some really tough construction work would be good for me. He wasn't wrong.

The next couple of years weren't bad. I lived at home for the first year, partly because I was low on money (the money I made at Shelor Toyota had largely gone up my nose) and partly because it kept me out of trouble. Not cocaine—I figured I was done with that— but from getting in trouble with women.

After a year, I decided the time had come to move out. While I wasn't going to attempt to have girls all around town like I did in Blacksburg, I didn't want to live in a monastery either. And that's what my parents' house had felt like.

I continued working for my father's construction company. Several times he offered to try and get me a job in corporate, but every time I turned him down. I enjoyed doing the hard manual work and had become friends with a lot of my co-workers. I started to realize that maybe I was a blue-collar guy at heart. And despite having a college degree, there was nothing wrong with that.

My two sisters had gone away for college and never moved back, so I think my parents actually liked having one of their children close to home. I'd go to my parents' every Sunday and have dinner, sometimes doing the cooking myself. No, it wasn't five-star material, but it wasn't half-bad either.

This went on for a few more years. I went through several more girlfriends and I was faithful to most of them. Getting a girlfriend was not a problem. I had the looks and I could be alluring to the opposite sex. Girls fell for me in a matter of days.

The problem was keeping them. They'd hit the seven-year itch several months in, when they realized that although I was handsome, charismatic, and good in bed, I wasn't really going anywhere. I had no aspirations for the future and remained content working in construction. And I certainly wasn't ready to have a child. That had been a deal breaker for a few of the women.

One day I woke up and I was twenty-eight years old. It didn't seem possible. Where had the time gone?

I knew it happened to everyone, but time sure seemed to fast-track me. The last few years had been more of the same. I wasn't exactly happy, but I wasn't unhappy either. I'd been sure there was something better out there, I just wasn't willing to look for it.

On a Tuesday night in early October, I was alone in my apartment. I was single and enjoying the downtime, knowing that with my history it wouldn't last. I blew through a Netflix title every few days. This time, it was some cheesy end-of-the-world movie called Bird Box.

I was midway through it when I heard a knock at the door. I got up and opened it.

A girl with short, bleached blonde hair in a pixie style stood at the door. She was tanner than usual and more beautiful than ever.

"Hello, Austin," she said.

"Hi, Becca. Why did you call me by my middle name?"

She let herself inside and shut the door, not waiting for me. It didn't appear she had changed much.

"We'll get to that," she said. "How have you been?"

I found myself grabbing some dirty clothes from the floor and throwing them in the closet. I didn't usually go out of my way to impress anyone, but Becca still held that power over me.

"I've been good," I said.

"Working construction for your father, I hear?"

"It's not so bad."

"You were always good with your hands," she said, and even though we never dated, I knew what she was referring to.

"Subtlety is not your specialty, Becca."

"No, I guess not."

"So how did it end with that old lady in San Francisco? I haven't seen you since then."

Nor had I wanted to.

"She gladly gave me the money, but I had to get out of Dodge soon thereafter. They were starting to get used to my tricks in the Bay Area."

"Where have you been since?"

"Here and there. Two countries, three states."

"And I'm guessing not a real job during that time," I said.

"Unlike you, I'm not good with my hands."

I laughed in spite of myself. "So why are you here, Becca?"

"We are going back into business together," she said and smiled at me.

"I've got a job. I'm happy here."

She looked around, observing the mess I had made of my apartment. She didn't have to say a word to make her feelings heard.

But of course, she did say something. "Should I show you a certain video from years ago?"

"I looked up the statute of limitations. For assault it's only like five years."

"Oh, I'm not going to the police. I was going to post it on social media, send it to your parents, your father's boss at the construction company. Maybe send it to Max Underwood's parents. Send it to Roswell High. Maybe they can rename those bleachers in your honor."

I had the same urge I'd had several years previously to strangle Becca Poe right then and there. In all likelihood, she hadn't told anyone she was visiting me. I could kill her and then find a way to dispose of the body. But I knew I wouldn't.

"You're a fucking bitch," I said instead.

"I've been called worse."

"If I agree to help you, this has to be the last time. You give me the original video and we destroy it together."

"Gladly. The money we could make from this score will make that old lady's money look like a drop in the ocean."

While I had turned down the money in San Francisco, it wouldn't be as easy this time around. I sometimes struggled to pay my bills and some extra spending money—possibly a lot extra—would certainly be welcomed.

"How much are we talking?"

"I'll tell you that on the way."

"They way to were?"

"The City of Angels, Austin. Los Angeles, California."

"Why do you keep calling me Austin?"

"You'll find that out on the way as well."

"I need to call my father and tell him I need some time off. How much time?"

"Ask for a month," Becca said.

"That long?"

"Yeah, it could be. And don't you dare mention me."

"I won't. When do we leave?"

"Tomorrow."

"You booked a flight?"

"Nope, we're taking a road trip."

"Are you crazy?"

"Crazy like a fox. I don't want evidence that we took the same flight."

I shook my head. Becca was crazy, but she was the smartest kind of crazy.

"How'd you know I'd say yes?"

"You didn't have a choice," she said.

She held her cell phone toward me and I could see the video of me pummeling Max Underwood.

_9_
BECCA

Like I did Olive, I had planned on killing Austin from the very beginning. It's why I told him not to mention coming out to California with me to his father. He was going to take part in a second highly illegal venture with me and would be too big a risk going forward. So my plan was to have him floating dead in the metaphorical martini with Olive. Except their actual death would probably be much more violent.

Joan Gandy had been a piece of cake. Austin, posing as my brother, played his role to perfection at Jane's house. The makeup I had applied made him look ash-white and much older than me. He walked gingerly, looking very frail. Not easy for a buff man like himself. He had really researched Lou Gehrig's disease and went into detail with Jane about how his body would change in the coming months.

"If I make it that long," he added, seconds before he dropped his coffee.

It took a few more weeks of manipulation, but Joan Gandy gave me a blank cashier's check for $50,000 to put toward my brother's health care. I told her it had to be blank because I wasn't sure what hospital my brother would be going to just yet. She seemed to buy it. While she was still with it at 82 years old, there is a certain gullibility that comes with being that age. I used that to my advantage.

I made the check out to Becca Poe and cashed it one day. There were some questions from the bank, but they couldn't refuse me the money. The check was good and it was addressed to me.

I asked her not to tell her son or Jeb Costner about my "brother," and she seemingly never did. I was already making my plans to be rid of Jeb, but I couldn't put them into practice right away without raising suspicions. So I stayed in the relationship for five more months, trying to get as many free dresses out of him as I could, knowing the finish line approached.

I continued to work for Joan Gandy, since I couldn't just leave that job either. Truthfully, I did enjoy her company. She wasn't the psychopath I was, but she was every bit as tough.

One day, a week before the breakup with Jeb, I told her how much I appreciated everything. I told her my brother had checked into a new hospital in Denver that specialized in ALS, that he was doing better, and that he made sure I thanked her a million times.

Joan Gandy was so delighted, she looked like she had cured cancer. In that moment, I thought I could probably go for more money, but it wasn't worth the risk.

I lied to Joan, telling her Jeb was becoming too constricting for me and that I had to break up with him. She told me she hated men like that, always wanting to keep their woman in check. Reason #318 that I liked Joan Gandy.

I told her I'd still come by and visit her from time to time. She seemed to buy it. I kissed her on the forehead.

"Thanks for everything, Joan."

"You're welcome. Take care of yourself. And your brother."

"I will."

I never saw Joan Gandy again and moved out of the Bay Area a short time later. Jeb Costner told me how much he loved me and wanted me to stay. I told him to get over it.

I could be a cold bitch.

The next several years passed. I lived in Canada and Scotland for a few months each, as well as Boston, Dallas, and Phoenix. At different times, I went by Carly, Mimi, Jessica, and Holly.

I almost always had a sugar daddy, and tried to avoid dipping into the fifty grand. But life is not cheap and over the years my checking account slowly dwindled. I was living in a crappy apartment in Phoenix, which was a decent city, but didn't move fast enough for me, so I decided to move where the action was.

Los Angeles.

If I couldn't make a big score in LA, than I had lost my touch.

I first heard the name Barry Gant about three weeks after moving to LA, on a date at a way too expensive restaurant in Beverly Hills. My date, six years my junior, was so obviously trying to impress me that it was almost comical. Now an "old lady" of 28, I still had my looks. And my legs. And my sexuality. Let's be honest, I still had it all.

People always say how beautiful the women are in Los Angeles, and they're right, but there are some damn fine marks in LA as well. I'm sorry, did I say marks? I meant men. Not that there's any difference to me.

Anyway, we sat in this outdoor garden-type restaurant, eating foie gras or abalone or some other food I hoped to be able to afford for myself someday, when I heard two women talking at the table next to us.

"And this guy, this Barry Gant, went into his safe and showed me like $500,000 in cash," the younger, more attractive one said.

She was trying to whisper, but not doing a very good job.

"You've got to be kidding me!" the other one said.

The one who mentioned Barry Gant was probably thirty, with dark, curly hair. If Barry Gant had a type, then I was screwed with my newly blonde pixie-style haircut. The other woman was probably only in her mid-thirties but gave off a matronly feel.

"He even let me grab one of the bricks. That's what he called them. I'm guessing they were like twenty grand each or something."

My date said something about the weather and I nodded, pretending to agree with him while I concentrated intently on the conversation next to us.

"Too bad he didn't let you take a brick home."

"Yeah, tell me about it."

"Have you seen him since?"

"No, it was a one-time thing. The guy is probably sixty years old."

"What does he do?"

"He owns a bunch of bars around town."

"Where does he live?"

"Pacific Palisades. It was an ordeal just to get there. We had an Uber, but we had to stop at his front gate and then he must have pushed thirty buttons to get into the house. More like a mansion, really."

"Well if you had half a mill in your house, wouldn't you do the same?"

"Are you enjoying your meal?"

I realized that question was not coming from the table next to us. Actually, it had been addressed to me.

"It's to die for," I said, using some cheesy-ass line I thought the guy might like.

He kept talking so it became hard to hear what the table next to me was saying, but I had heard enough.

It was time to learn more about Barry Gant.

Home at my apartment in Santa Monica that night, I went on Google. I sat on my balcony overlooking the Pacific Ocean. No, I didn't have as much money as I'd once had, but I wasn't about to slum it either. I'd tried that in Phoenix, but I told myself never again.

If a big score was in my future, I might as well live it up before then. And my one-bedroom condo two blocks from the beach certainly fit the bill.

It had been rented by a woman named Nikki Mills, my go-to I.D. at the time. I had lied about an ex-husband stalking me and asked if I could just pay cash for several months in advance. They were willing to overlook the background check after that.

I hadn't wanted to leave a trace of Becca Poe in LA in case I found my big score. And now I believed I had.

I kicked my feet up on the low hanging balcony and looked down at my laptop. Barry Gant didn't have a Wikipedia page, but plenty of articles about him provided no shortage of information. I read several of these and put together a picture of the man.

Barry Gant was born in Odessa, Texas in 1956 and had come west to attend the University of Southern California, never to return to his home state. He worked a wide array of jobs in the hospitably business, starting as a dishwasher as an eighteen-year-old freshman. He graduated to serving and then bartending, all while still attending USC.

He got his degree in Hospitality Management, and it appeared Barry Gant knew what he wanted to do at a young age. He took a job as a manager of a bar/restaurant and worked that for five years. When the original owner wanted to sell the place, Gant put the money together to buy it, borrowing some from his wealthy parents back in Texas.

He was only twenty-seven years old, but everyone knew he'd be a successful owner.

Gant was quoted in one of the articles saying it was the only time he borrowed money from a human. After his first restaurant was successful and he paid off his parents, he was easily able to get bank loans. Gant owned five bars by the end of the 1980s and bought another five bars in the 1990s.

During the recession of the mid-2000s, Gant, ever the smart businessman, sold three of the restaurants he thought were most at risk. When the economy picked up a few years later, he went all in, buying five more bars in the span of three years. He currently owned twelve bars across Los Angeles.

It appeared that Gant had been a lifelong bachelor, but that didn't mean he wasn't in the company of beautiful women. If you went to Google Images, you couldn't help but see Gant at a Lakers game with a woman barely old enough to buy a lottery ticket. There were also numerous pictures of Gant drinking with young women at his bars across LA. The guy obviously liked to party and I could use that to my benefit.

I closed my laptop and started to brainstorm how to get into Barry Gant's mansion in the Pacific Palisades.

I decided a few days later that getting invited into his house would be the easiest approach. No need to include anyone else. Less chance of something going wrong. And men had a way of falling for me pretty easily. I didn't see why Barry Gant would be any different.

While reading the articles about Gant, I had written down all of the bars they'd mentioned. The one closest to me was named Angel's, I assumed after the City of Angels.

I walked in there three days after first hearing of Gant. A young woman with pink hair worked behind the bar.

"Can I help you?" she asked.

"I'm a writer for a local paper and wanted to do a piece on Barry Gant. Do you know where I could find him today?"

"What's today?" she said rhetorically. "Wednesday. I'm not sure where he is today, but I know he gets a drink at The Belly Flop around noon every Thursday."

"The Belly Flop?"

"Yeah, it's about twenty blocks east of us. Just get on Wilshire and head away from the ocean. It's on 27th and Wilshire."

"Please don't tell Mr. Gant I'm coming, I'd rather try to sell him myself."

"My lips are sealed."

I woke up the next morning, spent some time looking through my closet, eventually put on a revealing light orange dress, and made my way east on Wilshire Boulevard. I was sure that the woman at Angel's hadn't said anything, so I adjusted my plan. Instead of being a reporter, which could easily be disproved, I decided to just use my sexuality to have him make a pass at me. I'd play hard to get, but eventually it would lead back to his mansion.

I parked a block up the street and headed toward The Belly Flop. I didn't like the name, but when I walked in, it pleasantly surprised me. I had expected the walls to be adorned with pictures of girls in bikinis doing belly flops into a pool. It wasn't like that at all, but actually somewhat classy. It begged the question of how it got its name, but that's something I could find out later.

A pretty woman with dirty blonde hair stood behind the bar. If forced to guess, I'd assume she was a few years younger than I. My watch read 11:54 and I hoped I had beat Barry Gant there.

I sat halfway down the circular bar on the left side. The bartender approached me.

"Welcome to The Belly Flop. Can I get you something?"

"I'll take a greyhound. Tito's if you have it," I said.

"Great choice," she said. "I drink the same."

I couldn't have cared less, but I smiled at her.

I wasn't one to drink at noon on a Thursday, but I figured it might give off a slutty, desperate vibe that Barry Gant might seize on. Plus, a little vodka and grapefruit sounded refreshing.

I didn't have to wait long for Gant to make his appearance.

The bartender made my drink, and as she set it in front of me, I heard a loud voice coming from the entrance.

"Olive, my dear, how are you?"

"Hi, Barry."

"You never call me Mr. Gant anymore. Well done. We're going to make a bartender out of you yet."

The bartender, Olive, smiled, but it seemed more perfunctory than anything.

"I'm no dummy, I remember."

"How's business been the last few days?"

"The day shifts have been getting busy around 2 p.m. or so."

Barry Gant sat down and I was able to get a good view of him. He was easy on the eyes for a man in his early sixties. His full head of wavy brown hair had gone silver on the sides. Having no grays on top at his age seemed suspicious, and my guess was that he dyed his hair. He definitely had a beer gut, and there was a bit of sloppiness about the way he dressed, but he was still handsome. Maybe because of the first name, I imagined him as a fatter version of Barry Gibb, whom my mom had loved dearly.

He did have a horrendous Tommy Bahama shirt on, one that looked like a bunch of four-year-olds had thrown random colors together.

Not that any of that mattered. For 500k, or any percentage of that, I'd sleep with him. You could be sure of that.

"That's all you, Olive, you bring the crowd in."

"I try my best."

"A week from Friday we're having a big party at one of my Hollywood clubs. Would you like to join me?"

Was this guy blatantly hitting on his employee? It sure seemed that way.

"My oldest friend comes into town next weekend. Can I bring her?"

"The more the merrier. Bring her along. Listen, Olive, I have to hit the little boy's room. Can I have a Jack and Ginger when I get back?"

"It will be here waiting."

Barry Gant walked toward what must be the restrooms and I saw a chance.

"I think he likes you," I whispered to the bartender, Olive.

She looked at me, clearly unsure whether she should trust me. Her boss was returning in a few seconds and I'd put her in a tough spot.

"Oh, he's fine," she said, but she rolled her eyes and I knew what she meant.

"Nice to meet you. I'm Holly," I said, choosing the name I had used in Phoenix.

Just another degree of separation. Not Becca. Not even Nikki.

"I'm Olive, pleased to meet you as well."

And that's the first time I met Olive Fairbanks.

She seemed like a very pleasant woman, but I saw her merely as a means to an end. To get me closer to Barry Gant.

He returned a minute later and finished half of his Jack Daniels and ginger ale in one swig. He looked in my direction and Olive sensed it.

"Barry, I'd like you to meet Holly," Olive said.

I extended my hand. He looked me up and down, giving me a limp handshake.

"Nice to meet you," he said. "Now back to next Friday night, Olive. How about we meet for some dinner first?"

I had never seen a guy so disinterested in me. Maybe it was the pixie haircut—but I knew better. It wasn't me. It was Olive. Barry Gant was infatuated with his bartender.

I sat there finishing my greyhound while starting to formulate my plan. Olive was going to be my in to Barry Gant's mansion. And my old friend from high school was going to be my in to Olive.

_10_
<u>OLIVE</u>

"Jesus, Olive, I'm just asking a few freaking questions. Don't make it such a big deal."

It was my first indication that Austin wasn't all he was cracked up to be. It came the morning after Barry Gant's birthday party, when we'd had such a great time and Austin had been so charismatic. All of my girlfriends who had been there said what a catch he was. I'd agreed.

But the next day, he sprawled out in bed as I prepared for work, showing no intention of getting up, even though it was my apartment. I wondered if he would ever look for work himself.

We'd had a great time together, no question, and I really was falling for him, but I didn't just want him sleeping in till noon every day. He didn't seem like he had any motivation, an inconsistency with the successful man who had worked finance on Wall Street.

He finally woke up and asked five straight questions about Barry Gant. I figured he'd deduced that Barry had a crush on me and he didn't like it. That made sense, but the questions became tiresome.

"Enough about Barry Gant!" I yelled.

And that's when he told me not to make such a big deal out of it.

"I've never even kissed the guy," I said. "If that's why you keep asking. He's so not my type."

"So you've never been to his house?"

"I shouldn't even dignify that with an answer, but I will, and this is going to be the last time I mention Barry Gant. No, I have never been to his house!"

Austin finally realized he was driving me nuts. He got out of bed and walked over to me.

"I'm sorry, Olive. Just a little jealous is all. He's your boss and quite obviously has a crush on you."

It made perfect sense.

"Don't worry about it," I said. "I understand."

"It's the first time I meet your friends and all I see is that old, fat guy staring at you the whole time."

"I thought you were having a good time with him."

"I pretended to. But you know what they say: keep your friends close, but your enemies closer."

"Barry Gant is not your enemy. You have nothing to worry about."

"Alright, Olive. I'm sorry."

He kissed me on the back of the neck and I told him I accepted his apology.

"I think I might go out today and look into some possible employment," he said.

We had seemingly squashed the whole Barry Gant thing and then he talked about getting a job. I decided to forgive him for my earlier annoyance.

An hour after I opened, The Belly Flop was slammed. One of the bigger companies in Santa Monica had decided to have their lunch break with us. I wished they'd called ahead. I was stuck with Tiffany, not the co-worker you wanted when it got busy. She was abrupt with customers and when you had a group of thirty or more people, which meant a corporate card was likely being used, you didn't want to piss off the people who could make your day tip-wise. I wished Sheri had been there.

It turned out that along with eating, they were drinking as well, and The Belly Flop became the place to be for lunch. Mark Midfield, Bill the seventy-something, the private detective Richard Levert, and some of the older clientele didn't like the noise coming from the tables, but people passing by on Wilshire seemed to, and we had many walk-ins.

You need a crowd to create a crowd. Sounded illogical, but there was some truth to it.

Somebody was indeed using a corporate card, because when Tiffany came back with the tip they had left, her usually dour personality did a 180 and she a had a smile from ear to ear. They had tipped $400 on an $800 tab. A 50% tip!

As they started walking out, Tiffany and I thanked them profusely. They had not only tipped us well, but helped create a crowd that lasted until I got off at six that evening.

Austin was still out looking at potential job opportunities, so I decided to go to the Coffee Bean on San Vicente Boulevard and get some writing done. It was my favorite place to write and I often took an outside table to enjoy the great Los Angeles weather. That day was no different.

My time with Austin had prevented me from getting much writing done. It was time to change that.

Some days you're just in the zone, and this happened to be one of them. I put on my indie music playlist, which consisted of songs by Future Islands, Fleet Foxes, Local Natives, Parquet Courts, and other bands that didn't have two-word names. Almost immediately, my fingers were typing the ideas my brain sent them. I had finished three chapters in the previous several months, but on this day I busted out two chapters in a few hours.

I didn't know if it was the good day at work, the lucky playlist, or my new relationship with Austin, but no matter the reason, it was the most productive writing day I'd had in months. Finally, after a fruitful three hours, the ideas started to slow down, and I packed my laptop into my backpack and bid Coffee Bean adieu.

I was very happy with myself as I went home that night.

Austin called me an hour after I got home, asking if I wanted to go to dinner the next day. He said he had some big news and sounded genuinely excited.

_11_
__AUSTIN__

I never really had a choice but to come out to Los Angeles. I knew Becca's video could ruin my life, not to mention what it would do to my family. My father would inevitably have to fire me, and my mother would never look at me the same. I could live with getting fired, but it would kill my mother and I couldn't have that happen.

So I came out to Los Angeles. And I wandered into The Belly Flop, using my good looks and charisma to make a pass at Olive Fairbanks. It had worked better than I ever could have imagined. Her eyes, those beautiful blue-green eyes, told me all I needed to know within minutes. She was mine.

I probably pushed our relationship a little quicker than I generally would have, but Becca wasn't in this for the long con. This was something she wanted to get done fast.

Less than two weeks into my "courtship" with Olive, I met up with Becca at a tucked-away coffee shop in Koreatown. Her hair was still short and blond, but some of her dark roots had started to come in. Knowing Becca, a change of hairstyle was only a few weeks away. She went through hairstyles like most people went through pairs of socks.

"Thanks for meeting me," she said.

"You said it was an emergency in the note."

Becca had made it abundantly clear on our drive to Los Angeles that we would not be communicating by cell phone. She'd leave notes under my apartment door if she needed to talk, and one led me to the coffee shop on this day. She had sublet an apartment for me for a month. It stood a few blocks from The Belly Flop, which I knew was no coincidence. It was nice and probably expensive, but she wanted me to say I'd worked on Wall Street, so that was necessary.

"Yeah, I may have exaggerated about that."

I was pissed. "What is it that you want, Becca?"

She stared at me with indignation.

"Never call me Becca again," she said. "Use Nikki if you have to, but better yet, don't use any names."

Becca had requested a table in the corner, but her head was still on a swivel.

"It's time to start escalating things with Olive. I was walking around Marina Del Rey and saw a boat named *To Olive*. If that doesn't get her eating out of your hand, then nothing will. I talked to the owner, using all of my sexuality. He never had a chance. It's yours tomorrow for a six-hour block."

"Jesus, how much did that cost?"

"I said I used my sexuality. Don't you ever listen, Austin?"

I was beginning to really despise Becca. She had been nothing but trouble since the day I met her, and she was just becoming a bigger bitch as each day passed.

"I listen," I said. "And you know what I haven't heard? Exactly how you plan on getting the money from Barry Gant. All you've told me is to romance this girl, but I still don't know the whole endgame."

"This is my gig, Austin." She had taken to calling me Austin at all times. "You are merely on a need-to-know basis."

"What if I want out?"

"Then you know what happens. I mail copies to several Atlanta TV stations. They'd love that local angle. I address one specifically to your mother, one to each sister, and one to your father. You can all watch it together at Christmas."

She was intolerable!

No one knew that I was out in LA with Becca, and I started to wonder if I could get all the money and do away with her once and for all.

It wasn't the first time it had crossed my mind.

"Austin?"

I hadn't answered and she saw the proverbial hamster running on the wheel that was my brain.

"Don't get any crazy thoughts, Austin. You're going to do what I say. And if you do, you're going to get a lot of money yourself."

"Okay," and I almost said *Becca*, but caught myself.

"So I want you to be at your most charismatic and most romantic on this yacht. Given how smooth you were driving boats when we were younger, so that shouldn't be a problem. Fuck her brains out and make her want to do anything you're going to ask going forward. Because we are only a week or so away from asking her to help us get into Barry Gant's house."

"I'll do my best."

"Leave me a note tomorrow once it's over. I want to know how it went."

I left a note at Becca's apartment the next day, telling her the boat ride couldn't have gone any better. Olive was eating out of my hand. I even shared some of the more salacious details from our time drifting on the ocean, hoping it would make Becca jealous.

She had looked at me as a project early on. However, I had a feeling she started to find me attractive as our teenage years went along. But she wasn't like regular girls. I knew that if we had sex, even if I performed like an Olympic champion, she still wouldn't fall for me. I didn't think Becca knew what love was. She just saw men as a means to have physical enjoyment and then spit out.

I couldn't tell Becca, but I was starting to feel a little something for Olive. Unlike Becca, I still had a heart. I wasn't falling in love with Olive, but I enjoyed our time together and there's something to be said for that.

I needed to find out exactly what Becca had planned with Barry Gant. Maybe I'd be able to put my own little wrinkle in it.

12

BECCA

As far as I could tell, my plan was working to perfection. It appeared from afar that Olive had really fallen for Austin. I'm the first one to have seen his potential, back when I knew him as Jared. He had this easygoing confidence that worked on most women. Did I know that he would be Olive's type? No, but there was a pretty darn good chance. And it looked like I was right.

That had been the easy part of the plan. Figuring out how I was going to get out of Barry Gant's mansion with the money and without getting caught by the police? That was more problematic.

Austin had been perfect for recruiting Olive, but I needed someone a little more prone to violence when it came to dealing with Barry Gant. And not the Max Underwood type of violence. I meant the kind that necessitated a gun.

I had another perfect man in mind.

Chet Watkins couldn't have been more aptly named. A tough S.O.B. whose name just sounded like someone who had a screw loose, Chet Watkins actually had a lot more than a few screws loose.

I met him when I was living in Phoenix, my last city before Los Angeles. I was Holly Cutler at this point in time, and we had met at, of all places, a laundromat. The apartment I rented didn't have a washer and dryer. It was a dump in a shady part of town, and I knew I wasn't going to stay in Phoenix much longer. I was meant for greater things than a shitty little apartment where I had to venture out to do my laundry.

I ended up at Premium Laundromat one day. It was far from premium and the clientele were either poor Hispanic families, drug addicts, or white trash. Sometimes the last two were one and the same. It reminded me of the bus rides I had so despised in high school. I didn't like a single thing about the laundromat or its customers.

Chet saw me from across the room, and probably wondered what an attractive girl like me was doing at Premium Laundromat. He walked in my direction and I looked him up and down. He had a sleeve tattoo, but that's not what made him so menacing. He had a look like he wanted to kick the ass of anyone he saw.

His intensity was disarming, even for someone like me, who had dealt with some bad dudes over the years.

"You're way too pretty for this laundromat," he said, trying to be charming, but his intensity trumped any charm he might have had.

"I'm not as innocent as I look," I said.

"I didn't say anything about innocence."

"It's what you meant when you said I was too pretty for this place."

Chet was impressed, I could tell. He certainly didn't expect the girl in front of him to give it back.

"You're a tough little cookie, aren't you?"

"I can be."

"How about we go get a drink sometime?"

"As long as you know this ain't going to last long. I'm not staying in this godforsaken place much longer."

"I don't blame you."

"Alright, what the hell, I'm up for a drink."

I knew I had read Chet right the first time we went out. He took me to some dive bar with one jukebox, two pool tables, and three customers with all of their teeth. The night was going fine and I actually enjoyed my time with Chet, even though he was a loose cannon just ready to go off.

And it didn't take long for him to do just that.

He'd gone to order a drink at the bar when one of the many people lacking in teeth came over and tried to hit on me. The man was probably approaching fifty, his red and black flannel shirt smeared with white paint. Chet saw him talking to me.

"Hey, motherfucker, get your own girl."

"She's your girl? This looked more like a first date," the man said.

"She came with me. That makes her mine."

Just about every girl I knew would be petrified in this situation, but I was fascinated.

"I don't see a name tag saying she's yours."

This made Chet go from mad to livid. He walked from the bar, and though the other guy got in a defensive stance, he never had a chance.

Chet punched right through his hands, connecting flush with his cheek and knocking him down. I thought it might be over then, but it wasn't, as Chet proceeded to stomp on his head several times until he was obviously done for. The guy bled profusely from a head wound.

Some of the other people in the bar looked over at Chet, but obviously didn't want a piece of him.

"Let's get out of here," he said.

We ran to his pickup truck and got the hell out of there as quick as we could.

"Will they call the cops?" I asked.

"No, they aren't going to do shit. A little dive like that probably has fights every night. I saw some drug deals going down too. The last thing that bartender wants is the police to show up."

I believed Chet. He apologized for all that had happened, not knowing that I didn't give a shit. I enjoyed violence and it actually turned me on as well.

I slept with Chet that night.

We remained friends and occasional fuck buddies during my time in Phoenix. I found out that Chet was a two-time felon, just biding his time until he got his third strike. With his temper, it was inevitable.

He confessed to me that he had sold drugs for several years in Texas, but got tired of being on the bottom rung of the business, so one time he stole a bunch of meth from his boss, moved out of the city, and started selling large amounts on his own. It didn't last long and he was picked up and thrown in jail for eighteen months.

His second arrest was for beating up a drug dealer beyond recognition, nearly killing him. That didn't surprise me at all. He got fifteen months in prison for that.

While our modes of operation varied, mine usually involving the wealthy and his based on drugs, we weren't all that different. We both wanted one huge score.

Unfortunately, I knew that wasn't going to happen in Phoenix. I told Chet one day that I was moving.

"But I may be in touch," I said.

"I'll be game for whatever it is you want."

"Anything?"

"Any fucking thing!" he said.

I got ahold of Chet Watkins one day. Austin and Olive had progressed along, and I knew we were getting close, so it was time to get him out to LA.

I prided myself on having thought of every possible nuance. For that reason, I decided not to call Chet's cell phone. If I ever became a suspect, phone calls and texts would be an easy way to tie me to the crime.

It's the reason I had driven all the way to Roswell to talk to Austin: so we wouldn't be taking flights from Atlanta to Los Angeles at or around the same time. Investigators looked for things like that. And I was smarter than your average criminal.

These were the reasons I didn't call Chet directly.

We had often frequented a bar named Chalky's. He went there almost every Saturday night, so I called on a Saturday and asked for Chet. Less than a minute later, a man came to the phone.

"Hello?"

"Hello yourself, Chet."

"Holly, how are you?"

I made a note that I'd have to keep my names straight.

"I may have something for you in Los Angeles. Are you interested?"

"Is it big?"

"Makes your drug deals look like the work of children."

"When do you need me?"

"Soon. This is all going to go down pretty quick."

"I've got nothing to do here. I could get on the road tonight."

"You're drinking at Chalky's. And I don't need you tonight."

"Alright," he slurred. Yeah, no need for him to be on the road tonight; he'd never make it to me if he drove while this drunk.

"And I don't want you to call my cell phone under any circumstances." I still had the cell phone when I lived in Phoenix, so it occurred to me that it could become a problem. I decided I'd get rid of it, just in case he tried to call it. I had enough burner phones to get by on. "Do you hear me?"

"Yes."

"I mean it. No phone calls. There's a Shell station on Wilshire and 17th Avenue in Santa Monica. You can GPS it. I will meet you there at 8 p.m. tomorrow night. Can you remember that?"

"I'll write it down."

"We're going to do this thing right and leave no ties to each other. So no cell phones."

"I've got it. I'll see you tomorrow night at the Shell station."

"Good. And Chet?"

"Yeah?"

"Bring a gun."

_13_
<u>OLIVE</u>

As we sat down for dinner the next night, the questions about Barry Gant kept coming. They had met at Barry's birthday and seemed to have a good time, but nothing that would explain Austin's utter fascination with him.

And he knew I didn't like it. Yet, he continued.

The waiter came over and took our orders. Still, the questions went on non-stop.

I decided to confront him.

"Why do you keep asking about Barry Gant? We already went through this at my apartment!"

"Well, that's why I invited you to dinner tonight," he said.

"To talk about Barry?" I sarcastically asked.

"I'm thinking about opening up a bar!"

"Huh?"

It was news to me.

"Yeah, I'm really considering it. That's why I've asked so many questions about Barry."

It suddenly made more sense. I had assumed he'd been asking out of jealousy, but Austin hadn't seemed the jealous type.

"I was trying to keep it on the down low," he continued. "As you know, I made a lot of money on Wall Street and don't know what to do with it all. What if, and now just hear me out, I bought a bar and I paid you a big salary to run the place? You'd make much better money than you do from the old men at The Belly Flop."

It didn't sound like such a bad idea.

"What do you know about running a bar-restaurant?" I asked.

"Nothing, but I do know how to hire the best people. And I'm sure you know many, many people who know how to run a bar or a kitchen."

"I do," I said.

"So, you're interested?"

"You're throwing it at me pretty quick, but obviously I'd be interested if it turned into something feasible. Running a bar is not easy work."

"I know. That's why I have you! You've been doing this for three years, you know how a bar works."

"I'm intrigued."

"So that's why I've been asking so much about Barry Gant. I wanted to get your feel for him and see if he's somebody who might help us."

"He's a tremendous flirt, especially toward me, but he's also a great businessman. You'd be learning from one of the best." I said.

"Well, let's make it happen!" Austin said.

We cheered, clinking our glasses as we waited for our food to arrive. The restaurant turned out to be sub-standard, but Austin was so happy we still had a nice dinner.

_14_
AUSTIN

I noticed that Olive was getting tired of my questions about Barry Gant, so I came up with an ingenious idea to explain it all away.

I wanted to open a bar.

In my discussions with Becca, I could tell she didn't know exactly how to get into Barry Gant's house. From what she had overheard, his front gate had a computerized keypad to get in, so you couldn't just do it by brute force. We were going to use Olive in some way. After all, that's why she had me come to Los Angeles. But Becca hadn't decided how.

And I had solved that all by making something up on the fly. It was perfect.

Olive would talk to Barry, who would remember me from his birthday party, and he'd gladly invite us into his home. I bet he'd secretly like to show Olive around, hoping to impress her in case she ever dumped me.

I'd let Becca deal with what would happen once we entered Gant's home, but I had the notion of a hundred thousand dollars dancing around in my head.

That's the amount Becca had promised me.

I reminded myself to stop by Becca's apartment and tell her what I'd thought of. I'd be sure to let her know that it was me, and not her, who had solved our dilemma.

I arrived at Becca's place the next day, looking forward to her telling me my idea was ingenious. I hated to admit it, but I was still a little scared of Becca, and proving to her that I had done well was like bringing straight As home to my parents.

I knocked on her door and she opened it, then shut it immediately upon my entry. She remained very paranoid about anyone seeing us together. And phones were off-limits. She'd made that clear several times.

"Everything okay?" I asked. Even in her apartment, I decided not to use her name.

"Everything is fine. I just think we should start being vigilant."

I heard a noise from one of her rooms. "Gentleman caller?" I asked.

She ignored me. "What do you want?"

"I found our way into Barry Gant's house."

"Let's hear it."

I told her my idea, and like a child, waited for the praise that I was sure to come.

_15_
BECCA

I was proud of Austin, but also a little jealous. His idea of feigning interest in opening a bar and using that to get into Barry Gant's house could be genius. It was believable, and I'd always thought that having Olive as a willing participant would be easier to pull off. I had considered kidnapping Olive and using her phone to text Barry Gant, but too many problems went along with that.

Of course, Austin's plan wasn't without its problems. First and foremost, what if Barry Gant said he'd rather have the meeting at one of his bars? Or an office? But this is where we had our wild card: Olive. When I first met Barry Gant, I could tell how infatuated he was with her, and my guess is he'd do anything to get Olive to see his house.

If Austin could just sweet-talk Olive into suggesting that they meet at his place, Barry Gant would cave. I was sure of it.

Chet Watkins had gotten into town the previous night. I told him that a friend was coming over and he had to be quiet. Sure enough, a loud noise sounded thirty seconds after Austin walked in the house.
Chet was a fucking idiot.

I pawned it off as some one-night stand and didn't think Austin's suspicions were raised. I couldn't have them meeting each other.

That wouldn't be advisable, considering I planned to have Chet kill Austin after we got the moncy at Barry Gant's house.

Yes, I was going to have my childhood friend killed by some thug I'd known for a few months in Phoenix. Austin and I had too much history together and if he ever grew some morality, he could send me to jail for a long time.

It was going to be easier going forward without him in the picture.

As my plan came to fruition, I had the utmost confidence it was going to work. I'd have no ties to Olive Fairbanks or Barry Gant. Only a few dipshits in Phoenix even knew that I was friends with Chet Watkins. And they knew me as Holly, anyway. No one from Atlanta or Roswell had a clue that I was in Los Angeles, nor that I had kept in touch with Jared Austin Jenkins over the years. And I had told him not to tell a soul.

More than that, there would be no texts or phone calls connecting me to either one. Those would have probably been the easiest way to have been caught. But I was way too smart for the police.

Finally, I'd be sure to wear gloves at the crime scene. Sorry, officers, no DNA.

My big score was coming soon and nothing, and no one, was going to stand in my way!

_16_
<u>OLIVE</u>

Austin had been acting like a kid at Christmas since our dinner. The idea of opening a bar had taken over his every thought. We must have spent an hour a day talking about potential names. Our top three in order were Happiest Hour, Just Another Irish Bar, and 26 Olives, in honor of my name and age. We decided to ask Barry for some help, knowing ours were all pretty weak.

Austin thought we'd have a better chance of getting an official sit-down if it came up organically, so the Thursday after our dinner, he planted himself at The Belly Flop, waiting for Barry Gant's weekly visit.

Like clockwork, he arrived a few minutes before noon. Sheri was working with me and she, Austin, and I were sitting at the end of the bar when Barry walked in. Mark Midfield sat opposite of us, waiting to finish the Woo Woo he had just ordered. Richard Levert, the private detective, was quietly sipping on his beer. Bob, the septuagenarian, was missing, likely one of his unending string of doctor's appointments.

"Olive!! How's my favorite bartender doing?" Barry was never subtle.

"Happy Thursday, Barry!" I said.

"And Sheri is on too! We definitely have the A-team on today."

"Ah, thanks, Barry," Sheri said.

"Shit, even Mr. Handsome, a.k.a. Austin is here."

"You remember me?" Austin said.

"Of course. How could I forget the charismatic man who landed the cutest girl in LA?"

"Hardly," I said.

"You don't know your own beauty, Olive. Now set me up with a Jack and Ginger and let me pick your boyfriend's brain. Maybe I'll get some pointers."

I poured Barry his go-to drink and set it down in front of the seat next to Austin, who gave me a wink. Barry took the seat. He and Austin started talking immediately.

This looked like it was going to be a two-way conversation for a few minutes, so Sheri and I walked over to the other side of the bar. Two young men who had just turned twenty-one within the last month came in and ordered Long Islands.

It made me feel old, remembering that was my go-to drink when I was in college, since it gave you the biggest bang for your buck. Two of those things and I was fine for the night. I could never understand how my guy friends could throw back six or seven. I'd have been dead.

"It looks like Austin and Barry are fast friends," Sheri said.

"I can't tell if Barry truly likes his company or just wants to get close to him because of me."

We both looked over as they laughed loudly.

"No, I think he genuinely likes him," Sheri said.

It was hard to argue with her.

"Happiest Hour? That's the dumbest name I've ever heard of," we heard Barry say.

Since Austin was having the conversation he wanted, I kept my distance.

"What are they talking about?" Sheri asked.

"Austin is considering opening up a bar-restaurant in LA and wanted to run some ideas by Barry."

"You could do a lot worse."

"That's for sure. There's probably no one in LA who knows more about opening bars then him."

We heard his voice again.

"Just Another Irish Bar? Oh my God, your ideas are getting worse!"

"How about 26 Olives?" Austin asked.

Sheri and I had headed back in their general direction.

"Now you're talking," Barry Gant said. "That sounds like a bar."

"It would be a combination of Olive's name and her age," Austin said.

"I thought it was her name and the amount of days you guys have been dating," Barry said.

Sheri cackled.

Austin looked at me and laughed nervously. We realized it was somewhere right around there.

"Oh, I'm just being a jerk," Barry said. "I'm sure a lot of guys have named bars after a girl they've dated for a month."

He'd tried to make things better, but really just made everything more awkward.

And it did get me thinking. Did I really know Austin that well? He had taken me out on a boat named To Olive, and now he was talking about opening a bar with me. Possibly with my name in it!

Maybe it was time for me to take a step back.

"How about you suggest the name of a bar, Barry?" Austin said, trying to change the subject.

Barry clearly enjoyed the needling he was giving Austin, who looked like he'd rather be anywhere else.

"How about Young Love?"

I heard Sheri trying to withhold another laugh.

"C'mon, Barry," I said. "He's trying to get some advice from someone who obviously knows a lot about the business. You should feel honored."

His mood softened. Austin turned toward him.

"Actually, what I really wanted, Barry, was to sit down and pick your brain on how to open one up. Not here at the bar, though."

Austin looked down at Barry's near-finished drink. "Olive, can I get Barry another Jack and Ginger?"

"Yes, you may," Barry said before I could respond. "We could meet at my office early next week."

"Your office sounds too stuffy for an old friend like Olive and a new friend like me," Austin said.

He had just been offered a chance to do a sit-down. I couldn't understand why Austin didn't just say yes.

"You didn't say Olive was coming," Barry said. "In that case, I'd like to invite you guys to my house in the Palisades. Let's do it right."

"How can we say no to that?" Austin said and smiled up at me.

"Next Tuesday works best for me. I'll text Olive the address. I've got to be at another one of my bars until seven, but we can meet at eight o'clock. I'll bring back some food."

"Nine works fine. Thanks so much for this opportunity, Barry."

"Jeez, Olive, your boyfriend is already calling me by my first name."

"I know, I think he has a bigger crush on you than he does on me."

"He'll probably end out naming his first bar Barry's."

We all laughed.

"I can live with being the punching bag," Austin joked.

"Hmm," Barry said. "The Punching Bag. I'm imagining a bar surrounded by a room full of punching bags where you can go take out your anger."

"You guys are crazy!" Sheri yelled.

Everyone was having a good time, myself included. But something, a very small something, reverberated in the back of my brain. It was saying that this whole Austin/Barry meeting seemed a little contrived.

_17_
<u>AUSTIN</u>

The meeting at The Belly Flop with Barry Gant had gone better than I could have imagined. In our talk beforehand, Becca and I decided that we couldn't be the ones who suggested meeting at his house. He'd be too suspicious if I just brought it up, especially considering how much money he kept there.

Becca had been right as usual. She said to drop Olive's name and maybe that would get him to bring up his house. When Barry mentioned his office, I thought we were fucked, but that's when I remembered Becca's advice and decided to name-drop Olive. He folded like a cheap suit, volunteering his house for the meeting.

I went by Becca's apartment later that day and told her that everything was set for next Tuesday at eight p.m. She had us leave the apartment and go down to the garage to talk in her car. I assumed the gentleman caller from the other night was staying with her again.

For some reason, she took great interest in the fact that Barry said he'd be at another bar until seven p.m. on Tuesday night.

She started going over the plan with me. It was brilliant, I really had to give it to her. I was taking a huge risk, but it seemed worth it for the possibility of a hundred grand.

Plus, I'd be out from under Becca's control. I would make sure she deleted the video of me beating up Max Underwood. That part would just be ceremonial, because I was sure she had copies, but that didn't matter anymore. If we pulled off the heist at Barry Gant's house, she could never threaten me again. I'd have my own dirt on her, dirt that would land us both in jail for a long, long time. The video would no longer mean anything.

We went over the plan one more time. It would begin with me picking up Olive on Tuesday night. Becca said to act as normal as possible, not giving Olive any reason to suspect a thing. We needed her to ensure that Barry opened his front door. After that, Olive became inconsequential.

Unbeknownst to Olive, when I picked her up, Becca would be in the trunk of the rental car I'd been driving around in LA. This would get her on to Barry's premises without having to go through security.

When Olive and I pulled up to his residence, I would park the car, and when I took the keys out of the ignition, I'd immediately press the "open trunk" button on the fob. I had tried this many times and it was one of those trunks that only opened upward a few inches. Some open all the way up, which might have been seen by Olive's peripheral vision, but we didn't have to worry about that.

As Olive and I arrived at the front door, we would knock and Barry would open it. Becca had said the next part was very important. I was not supposed to enter the house right away. Instead, I should stand directly in Barry Gant's line of sight, making small talk if necessary. I was much taller than Barry and he wouldn't be able to see over me. This would give Becca time to approach the front door. In case Barry saw her and tried to shut the door, I was supposed to subtly put my foot in the door jamb. That would give Becca enough time.

Becca would be wearing a mask of some sort and carrying a gun. When she arrived at the door, she'd order us inside. Once there, she'd have the three of us get on our knees with our arms behind our heads. The next part was going to be a little tricky, but I thought it would work. She was to take the butt of the gun up and slam it on the back of Olive's head.

As petite as Olive was, I had no doubt this would knock her out. I worried that it could cause irreparable damage, but didn't voice this to Becca. The alternative was killing her and I didn't want that. As I'd said, I really had enjoyed my time with Olive. Was she just means to an end? Yes, but I still cared about her. At least a little bit.

After Becca knocked Olive out, she would do the same to me. Whether it worked or not, I would fall to the ground as if I'd been struck unconscious. I told Becca to really give me a proper slam. Would make our story all the more airtight if I had a huge gash and hopefully some blood.

Once Olive and I had been dealt with, it would just be Becca and Barry Gant, and I had no doubt that with a gun, Becca would get the money from Barry. We hadn't talked much about what would happen after that. She said her goal was to let him live. Why risk alerting the neighbors with a gunshot? It made sense.

If I was not knocked unconscious by her blow to the back of the head, I was to wait 30 minutes until I called 9-1-1. If I remained unconscious for longer than that, Becca told me to just call the cops once I came to. This would give her plenty of time to get out of Dodge.

The cops would arrive and ask a million questions, but Becca assured me there would be nothing tying me to her. I had told no one that she was the reason I had come to LA, so it made sense. We'd never texted each other, which had been very astute on her part. Not that any of that would matter. The cops would never suspect Becca Poe. She'd be wearing gloves and a mask. Nothing would ever get tied back to her. So even if they suspected I was in on it, there would be no proof that I had colluded with someone.

As for my lies to Olive, they could easily be explained away. I'd just say I had been trying to impress her. I didn't want to tell her I was some poor schmuck, so I'd made up an identity as some Wall Street bigwig who wanted to open a bar. It wouldn't be the first time that a guy lied to a girl. And with nothing to tie me to the robbery, it didn't really matter.

There was one thing I hadn't understood, so I finally asked Becca.

"Why were you so happy when I told you Barry Gant will be at another bar until 7 p.m. on Tuesday?"

"It will give me time to disable the cameras I'm sure he has."

I felt like I was missing something.

"If you're going to wear a mask, why do you care about the cameras?"

"Oh, Austin. It wouldn't look very good if the cameras caught me getting out of the trunk of your car, would it? They might even suspect that we acted together."

She was right. As usual.

"I'm sorry, it's just so much to take in," I said.

"Leave the planning to the grownups," she said.

Fucking bitch.

_18_
BECCA

I had never been much into music, but I was playing everyone like a fiddle. I felt like some maestro at a concerto. It was that beautiful.

Chet had been staying at my apartment since he arrived. I'd told him we'd be ordering in for the entirety of his visit. I assumed my plan was foolproof and there was no need to take any undue risks. If, by some chance, they came to suspect me or Chet, I didn't need people testifying that they had seen us walking around Santa Monica together.

So we remained indoors.

I had always enjoyed sex, but purely for the feeling of it. No attachment or staring into the eyes of my partner after the fact. That was for the birds. With Chet and I being basically landlocked in my apartment for several days, I figured, why not get a little satisfaction out of it? So we did have sex a few times each day.

He'd want to talk about it afterward, but I'd just roll out of bed and go do something else. This two-time felon had assaulted God knows how many people in his life. And I was the one with more emotional distance. Explains a lot.

Part of the reason for the sex was the enjoyment, but I also wanted Chet to think we were a team. He may not have realized it, but he was taking the biggest risk of all. I had to make sure he thought there was no way I was going to fuck him over. I would have fucked over anyone in the world for $500,000, but he didn't have to know that.

I didn't worry about Chet Watkins. He was practically under my thumb.

Sunday and Monday took forever. I had never been more excited, or nervous, in my entire life. This was the score of a lifetime. Everything would be different from here on out. No conning old ladies, no living in a shitty one-bedroom in Phoenix.

Sure, I had planned it meticulously, but there's never a perfect crime. Movies like *Dial M for Murder* taught me that. Even my favorite literary character, Bud Corliss from *A Kiss before Dying*, managed to get caught and killed. Sometimes, the smallest little detail can derail an otherwise flawless crime.

So I went over the plan again. And again. And again.

The next thing I knew it was late Monday night, and I decided to get some sleep. The next day was going to change everything.

_19_
__OLIVE__

Something hadn't been right for almost a week. It was hard to put my finger on it, but Austin was acting different. He hadn't been the doting guy that he'd been for the first several weeks. Something was obviously on his mind, but when I brought it up, he'd say he was fine.

Other things were bothering me as well. He never introduced me to a single friend of his. He said he'd moved to Los Angeles for a clean break and that he didn't know a soul in town, but it rang hollow to me. Everyone knows at least one person in Los Angeles.

His former job aroused some suspicion as well. When he started bringing up the idea of opening a bar, I told him that he must have made a lot of money at his Wall Street job.

"Yeah, they paid well."

"Who?" I asked.

"My employer."

And no, he didn't volunteer the name of his employer. I didn't even find out his last name until a few weeks after we started dating. Jones, he told me in a rush, as if it was the rudest question he'd ever heard.

I wasn't ready to concede he was lying, but if you were going to lie, Jones would be a pretty easy name to go with.

I googled Austin Jones; Austin Jones Norfolk, VA; Austin Jones Wall Street; Austin Jones LinkedIn; and a few others, and while the searches produced pictures of many Austin Joneses, none were of my Austin.

He told me more than once that he had wiped his social media clean. It didn't stop me from looking for Austin Jones on Facebook and Instagram, but I didn't find him.

Maybe nothing was out of the ordinary, but I found that less likely each and every day. I started thinking that maybe something had happened back east, and he didn't want anyone to find out about it. And that's why he made a fresh start in California.

It seemed possible, and I hoped it was the case. Maybe I probed a bit too much. We'd only been dating a month and maybe he'd slowly open up to me as time went on. I knew how guarded some guys could be, and perhaps Austin was just a little more guarded than most.

So I decided to give him the benefit of the doubt. Second thoughts arose about potentially opening a bar with him, however. I had a good gig at The Belly Flop. I wasn't sure I was ready to leave.

That decision could wait until after our meeting with Barry Gant.

Austin was a nervous ball of energy Tuesday morning. He reminded me of a cat, bouncing off of walls and chasing his own tail. I knew he'd be eager, but this was definitely more nerves.

I got ready for work. Usually Austin would leave at the same time as me, but he asked if he could stay at my place for another hour before he went home.

"Is everything alright, Austin? You seem a little jumpy."

"I'm fine," he said, but I could tell he wasn't. "Just excited about this opportunity."

"I know what excited is, this is the opposite of that."

"Anxious and excited, I guess. Having a chance for my lifelong dream to come true."

"I thought you just started thinking about opening a bar when you moved out here."

"I meant my life in LA."

He was being weirder than usual, which was saying a lot considering how he'd behaved the last several days.

"Get some more sleep," I said. "You'll feel better when you wake up."

"Thanks. What time are you on till?"

"Six."

"Okay, I'll pick you up at 7:30 and then we'll head to the Palisades and Gant's house."

Austin was already calling Pacific Palisades "the Palisades" like a seasoned LA vet.

"Sounds good. Remember, this is an exciting day for you. Treat it as such," I said, suddenly feeling like the only adult in the room.

"I will. Sorry I'm not myself today, Olive."

"It's fine. Get your charming side back before we meet with Barry."

I ended on that and walked out the door.

I had criticized Austin for being nervous, but to be honest, I felt the same way at the Belly Flop. You know when you have the feeling that something isn't right, but you can't place it? That's how I felt all day.

It didn't help that Sheri and I got slammed with several different big parties that afternoon. Unlike myself, Sheri was happy-go-lucky all day long. She seemed more excited about what would happen that night than I did.

"Have you thought anymore about what you're going to name the bar?" she asked during one of the rare downtimes of the day.

"I was thinking Sheri's," I said.

"Very funny."

"Haven't thought much more about it, honestly. It's just come out of left field so quickly. This guy wants to buy a bar so soon after moving to LA?"

"This guy? What the hell, Olive. I thought you were falling for Austin."

"I was. I am. I don't know, he's changed since this whole 'opening a bar' thing started."

"How so?"

"It's hard to describe. Like he's looking past me toward the future. Like this meeting with Gant is the be-all and end-all. He's given me so much less attention over the last week or so. I feel like I've been used and he just wants to have Barry help him with his business venture."

"I think you're reading way too much into this, Olive."

"You might be right. But my woman's intuition is telling me that something is up."

"Well, it's hard for me to argue with that. I guess we'll know in a few weeks if he's still with you."

"Maybe I'll be dumping him," I said.

It had certainly crossed my mind. The first two to three weeks of dating had been heavenly, but this felt more like purgatory.

"He's handsome as hell, but you're still the catch in this relationship, Olive."

"Thanks, Sheri. For everything. You know what, if Austin refuses another double date with you and Zane, I'm getting rid of him."

"Don't be so drastic."

"I'm not. He knows how much you mean to me and still refuses to go. What kind of man does that?"

"Someone who's thinking about opening a bar with the beautiful girl he's falling for."

I laughed in spite of myself.

"I'm not so sure," I said.

"You guys were in early dating bliss just last week," Sheri said.

"You're right, maybe I'm being too tough on him. Call me tomorrow and I'll give you all the details."

"I will. And by the way, Mark Midfield is trying to get your attention."

"Woo Woo," I said, trying to sound as much like a train as I could.

The crowds slowed as the day moved on and Sheri and I were able to spend the last hour gabbing away. We had moved on from my relationship with Austin to talk about girly stuff. It was a nice, much-needed break.

My replacement arrived a few minutes late, but I was able to get out of work at 6:15, which gave me plenty of time to get home, shower, and get ready for the night. It wasn't going to be formal, but I wanted to look nice.

I half-expected Austin to still be there when I got home, but mercifully, he was gone. The fact that I felt happy he wasn't there didn't bode well for our future.

Showering for the second time of the day, I wiped off all the grime you get by working as a bartender. I picked out a cute, light blue dress that was pretty casual and threw on a short, subtle necklace that didn't approach my cleavage.

I thought it best, considering this would be a meeting with someone who had a crush on me and the guy I was dating. Maybe one reason Austin hadn't been himself was because he'd be asking for help from someone who obviously lusted after me. That had to put him in a tough spot.

I decided to give him the benefit of the doubt. For the night, at least. If this really was all he said it was, then it truly would be a big night for him. I should at the very least be the supportive girlfriend.

Were we boyfriend and girlfriend yet? We didn't go around saying that, but it sure felt like it.

I was starting to get a little crazy. I took a deep breath and decided to settle down. A few minutes later, I heard Austin honk from downstairs.

Wouldn't a real man come to the door and knock?

I walked downstairs, got into the car, and we took Wilshire down to Lincoln Boulevard, where we started heading northwest toward Pacific Palisades. Austin had given me a kiss on the cheek when I got into the car, but the feeling that something was off still permeated the air around me.

"You ready?" I said.

"I think so. It's not like it's a job interview, I should just try and enjoy it."

I decided to be blunt.

"I'm looking forward to this being over. I feel like it's caused some friction in our relationship that wasn't there before."

"Baby, I think we are fine."

He didn't even look over at me when he said it.

We drove a mile on Lincoln and then took a left, two rights, and a left before arriving on Latimer Rd., which would take us right into the Palisades. I'd attended a few parties there over the years, though I'd hardly call myself a regular.

It was one of the richer areas of Los Angeles, and that was saying something. The homes, inevitably huge, mostly had an open feeling to them, with views of the Pacific Ocean. J.J. Abrams, Ben Affleck, Judd Apatow, Kobe Bryant, and other famous people called it home.

I wouldn't be living there on a bartender's tips, and I knew the only reason I had been invited in the past was because people thought I was hot. Specifically, men. Barry Gant being at the forefront. He had invited me to his house many times, but I'd always been able to make excuses. Now I was finally making my maiden visit to his house.

Austin had his cell phone in a stand above the dash and the voice from Google Maps told us where to go. We took a few rights after entering the Palisades and then I heard the voice saying, "You have arrived at your destination."

Austin drove up to the huge gate outside of Barry's residence. He pressed the button on an intercom to the left.

"Hello?" a voice said.

"Is this Barry?"

"Barry who?" the voice said, but we recognized him.

"Very funny," Austin said. "Do you have to let us in?"

"I will be doing so momentarily."

A buzzer went off and the massive gate started opening inward. We proceeded up a newly paved driveway to approach the house.

"Amazing," Austin said.

"I'm sure it gets better," I said.

As we arrived at the top of the drive with the sun setting, we got a panoramic view of the Pacific Ocean. Phenomenal. We were a week before day light savings ending, and it would be pitch dark at this time in a week, but on this night, we were there at the perfect time. The floodlights illuminating the ocean didn't hurt, either.

The house itself stood two stories tall and spurted off in different directions, with very little uniformity. Out front, there was a circular driveway to park your car, a lawn, and an infinity pool in which you could look out at the ocean.

Spectacular wasn't a strong enough adjective.

Austin parked the car near the front and I saw Barry open the front door and head our way. We got out of the car.

"So, what do you think?" he asked.

Austin answered first. "It's the most beautiful home I've ever seen."

"And you haven't even seen the inside," Barry deadpanned.

"I don't know if I'd have to. I could just sit in that pool and look out on the ocean all day."

Barry ignored Austin and turned toward me. "Olive, dear, what do you think?"

I hated how he had called me dear, but now wasn't the time. "It's more than I expected. And I had huge expectations coming in."

Barry smiled at that, and I knew it made him happy to see me impressed. "Let's go inside. I think you are going to like what you see."

We started walking the forty or so feet between our car and the front door. Barry looked over at me, no doubt gauging my reaction. Which was impossible to hide. The house was as nice as any I'd ever seen.

Austin had a weird expression on his face. He held the fob to the car and appeared to be locking it. Like someone was going to rob his car here!

He looked ashen white.

"Remember, this is an exciting time," I whispered to him. "Don't be nervous."

What had happened to the confident guy who first walked into the bar and swept me off my feet?

On the threshold, Barry Gant input numbers and slid his finger on some sort of security system. All three of us faced the massive front door as, like the gate to his house, it opened inward.

Peeking in, the first thing I saw was a marble staircase heading to the second story. As the door continued to open and I got a fuller view of the inside, the most opulent place I'd ever seen, I heard some footsteps behind us.

We all turned around at the same time.

A large man headed our way, wearing a mask. A white, baby doll mask with cuts or perforations around the forehead. Down around the nostrils and chin, it turned a grimier color, at odds with the porcelain-like white of the rest.

I'd never seen anything creepier.

"Get inside," the man said.

His menacing voice and the gun at his side only added to the looming fear.

My body started to shake, but I did as he instructed. We were being robbed, and in the moment, I just hoped he wasn't going to try and kill us.

I looked at Barry, whose expression told me to keep doing as the man said. When I turned to Austin, I detected real fear.

I had never been more scared in my life.

I took a few steps inside.

"Get on your knees," the man said, and I started to weep, frightened with every fiber of my being. There really wasn't any choice, so I got on my knees. I gave one last thought to my family and friends, fully expecting to be shot in the back of the head.

The man was behind me, but in my peripheral vision, I saw him raising the gun up. I said a final, quick prayer. A split second later, everything went black.

_20_
<u>AUSTIN</u>

As I was getting ready to leave my apartment and go pick up Olive, I found a piece of paper on the doorstep.

It read: *I couldn't take a chance of people seeing you help me into the trunk. I'm going to do it myself. When you come down here, just get into the front seat like nothing is out of the ordinary.*

I was using the rental car that I'd had since getting to Los Angeles. Becca had a spare set of keys illegally made, so she'd be able to lock herself in the trunk without my help. I wasn't quite sure why she didn't do it with me present, but she was doing all she could to not have us seen together, so I guess it made sense.

Walking down to the car a minutes later, I paused just behind the trunk.

"You still in there?" I asked.

It was a dumb question, but I had to make sure.

"Yes," she said.

I got in the front seat and headed off to pick up Olive.

When I approached the gate to Barry Gant's house, I knew we were in for a treat. It didn't disappoint as we headed up the driveway and looked out on to the bright, blue Pacific Ocean. The next several minutes were going to be life changing, but you'd have to be a robot not to take in the beauty of it all.

Barry Gant came out to meet us. Becca and I had assumed he'd just open the front door, but I thought his leaving the house might actually work to our advantage. Now, when Becca emerged from the trunk and came after us, all our backs would be turned.

We started toward the front door and I pressed the car fob to release the trunk. I had to make sure not to turn around and draw Olive and Barry's attention. Barry reached for the door and for a split second, I thought maybe Becca hadn't been able to get out.

But then I heard the footsteps.

We all turned around to see someone quickly approaching us, a terrifying baby doll mask covering their face.

I knew immediately that something was seriously wrong. It wasn't Becca moving toward us.

A male voice yelled "Get inside."

Without being sure what was going on, I grew very scared. Change was never good in a situation like this.

What was Becca doing?

The man with the gun made forced us into the house. I stood to his left as he ordered Olive to get on her knees.

I saw him raise the gun and bring it crashing down on the back of Olive's head. I was sure he had killed her. The man was big, and he brought it down with such force that it let out a cracking sound.

Barry Gant shuddered. "Oh, Olive," he said.

A few seconds later, a second person with an identical grotesque mask appeared. It had to be Becca.

"Where is the safe?" the man asked Barry Gant.

"I don't have a safe. What are you talking about?"

A sinister laugh came from behind the baby doll face. "I'm only going to say this once." He cocked his gun as he said it. "We know you have a safe. If you play dumb, then I'll just shoot and kill you. Would you prefer that?"

"No. Don't shoot!" Barry yelled.

"That's better. Now take us to it."

"Are you going to let me go if you get what you want?"

"Of course. We don't want to kill anyone. If we don't have to."

"How do I know you're telling the truth?"

"If you keep this up, I'll kill you and find the damn safe myself."

Barry Gant didn't respond immediately. The man's voice was raspy and menacing. I had a feeling this wasn't the first crime he'd committed.

"Okay, follow me," Barry finally said.

I looked at the person I presumed to be Becca. Her baby doll mask with protruding cheekbones looked in my direction, but she said nothing. Nor should she. We were not supposed to know each other. But I wondered why she or the man hadn't hit me with the gun yet. I was supposed to be knocked out by this point.

And who was this guy she had brought? I had to assume she was afraid she couldn't do all this herself. If that was the case, I could forgive her, but she should have told me.

I looked down at Olive. A huge gash in the back of her head released blood that had begun to cake on her hair. I assumed she was still alive, but the blow easily could have delivered a subdural hematoma. I hoped this would end soon; I didn't want Olive to die.

If she died, it was on me. Sure, this was Becca's plan, but I had gone along with it and courted Olive the whole time. I would be just as guilty of Olive's death.

Barry started leading us in the direction of the marble staircase. Following him came the man with the gun, then me, and then Becca.

We made our way up the staircase, taking each step very deliberately. When Barry arrived at the top, the man told him to stop, allowing us to catch up.

"Now where?"

Barry led us past a bedroom, grandiose as any I'd ever seen. The four-poster bed had been covered in gold, along with the crown molding throughout the room.

We arrived at a huge walk-in closet. The thing was bigger than some studio apartments.

He had probably seven suits on one side. The other side had at least fifty Tommy Bahama-like dress shirts, obviously something he preferred to wear. On the floor, dress shoes waited near the suits and upscale tennis shoes near the island shirts.

At the far end of the walk-in closet, which had to be forty feet long and twenty feet wide, there was a huge perforation in the shape of a square.

"Is that the safe?" the man asked.

Becca still hadn't said a word.

"Yes," Barry said.

"Well, get at it, then."

Barry looked around the room, staring at both Becca and I for a long moment. He walked to the safe and stood at the center, making it impossible for us to see around his big torso.

Twenty seconds passed and nothing happened.

"What's taking so long?" the man yelled.

"You have to move the safe dial five different times back and forth. It's not easy."

"Just fucking hurry up."

Less than fifteen seconds later, the safe clicked and the door creaked open. Barry Gant tossed something over his shoulder and it landed on the floor between the three of us. A brick of money, probably a foot long. It was actually four separate, smaller bricks taped together, two bills long and two bills wide.

If it held anything less than $25,000, I would have been shocked. We all looked at it in awe.

I realized something was amiss before the others did, seeing a small movement from Barry Gant out of the corner of my eye. As we stared at the money on the floor, he swiveled from the safe, and before I knew it, he had pulled out a little pistol, firing it at the other man. The noise in the walk-in closet was deafening.

The man fell backward, hitting one of the walls. Barry must not have struck a vital organ, as the man remained very much alive and still held his own gun. He fired twice and I saw part of Barry's head blown off. I heard myself scream, but oddly, no sound came from Becca.

Barry Gant's blood caked all over the pristine white walls of the walk-in closet. He'd fallen back and his arms were spread out on the floor below. The top of his forehead was missing.

We looked at the other man, who was seriously hurt.

"Take my mask off, it's hard to breathe," he said.

I did so, not recognizing the man under the baby doll mask.

"You're going to be okay." I didn't know what else to say.

"I should have known he might have a gun in the safe," he mumbled as blood starting coming out of his mouth.

"I'd suggest you don't talk anymore," I said.

I sat there with him for a few more seconds, wondering why Becca wasn't by his side. I turned around to look at her, and as I did, I heard the man scream.

"No! Don't do it! You fucking bitch!"

Becca had picked up Barry Gant's gun and pointed it at the man. She did not heed his cries, raising the gun and firing twice, right in his chest. The man and I looked at each other and then his eyes went blank. Dead.

I stood up and glared at the woman in the baby mask.

"Becca, what the fuck are you doing?"

"Tying up some loose ends," she said, and I knew once and for all it was her. "Come to think of it…"

That's when I knew Becca wanted to kill me.

I could run for the door or try to attack her. The walk-in closet stretched so long that I'd never make it to the door, so I decided leaping toward her was my only chance.

I took one step in her direction and was about to jump in the air and tackle her. But I never got there. The light from the gun went off twice. Becca had put two bullets in my chest.

As I crumbled to the ground, I looked up at the woman above me. Becca stared down at me with disdain, a little smirk on her face, the baby doll mask now hanging on the top of her head.

"Poor little Austin," she said, and her smirk got a little bigger.

How had it all ended like this? I knew Becca was evil, but I never guessed she was this depraved.

I tried to hang on a little longer, but I felt the life leaving my body. The pain started to diminish, and that's when I knew it was all but over. I raised my eyes to Becca one last time. She still looked down at me, appearing to enjoy every second.

I couldn't stand the sight of her, and closed my eyes for what I knew would be the final time.

My heart stopped pumping a few seconds later.

I was dead.

21

BECCA

To say that everything fell into my lap would be the understatement of a lifetime. Through meticulous planning, I had prepared for almost any eventuality, but never could have expected the good fortune that was thrown at me.

And I do mean fortune in more ways than one.

My plan had changed a few times in the weeks leading up to the robbery. Initially, it was just going to be Austin and I, and we would let Barry and Olive live. I scrapped that right away. Not because I needed to have bloodshed, but there's no way we could have gotten away with it.

If we let Olive and Barry live, the investigators would have had a field day with Austin.

Why were you so eager to meet with Barry Gant? Had you ever told anyone else of your interest in owning a bar/restaurant? How were you going to get the money? Why did you tell Olive that you had worked on Wall Street? Why did you really come to Los Angeles? We can give you a plea deal, if you just tell us who planned this.

There's no way Austin would have stood up under questioning. He'd send the police my way and I'd spend the rest of my life in jail. That wasn't going to happen.

But I did tell Austin most of my plan, and he seemed to buy it. Dumb motherfucker.

My second plan, and the one I went with, involved my old friend Chet Watkins. I knew he'd be up for anything, and when I told him he would get a hundred thousand dollars, he would have killed his own family.

On the night in question, I had Chet go to the Palisades and look for cameras out front of Gant's house. I couldn't have the police see us getting out of the back of Austin's rental car. That would change it from a home invasion to an obvious inside job, with Austin being involved.

Chet left my place at 5:00 and I told him he had to be back by 7:00 so we had time to get into the trunk of the car. Chet returned a little after 6:30 and told me there had two cameras looking out on the driveway. He had spray-painted them and then attached a dark Glad bag over each one before hopping the closest fence. He was sure he hadn't been seen, but had worn a hoodie just in case.

We went over to Austin's apartment, less than a half mile away. I slid a note under his door. I couldn't have him see Chet get in the trunk, so I made the logical excuse that I didn't want to be seen with him on the street. We walked down to where his car was parked and both jumped into the trunk, waiting until no one was wandering around.

A few minutes later, I heard Austin's voice asking if I was in the trunk. I responded in the affirmative and we set off to Barry Gant's. Once we parked, Austin did as I instructed, unlocking the trunk as he walked toward the house.

Chet followed them inside and he knocked out Olive, as I had outlined. It didn't make sense to shoot her right away. That might make Barry Gant less willing to cooperate, which was of the upmost importance. And despite Chet's gun having a silencer, I thought holding off on gunshots until after we had the money was advisable. I didn't want some neighbor hearing and calling the police. Although neighbors in the Palisades were pretty spread out and I didn't think we had too much to worry about, I still didn't want to take any chances.

I'd decided to have Austin come with us to the safe. I didn't want Chet to shoot him for the same reason, fear of the police being called early. I also didn't like the idea of Chet trying to knock him out. Austin was a big man and I was afraid Chet couldn't lay him out with just the butt of a gun.

I wasn't going to let Austin live, however. I'd told Chet that after we got the money from Barry Gant, we'd kill Austin and Gant. We'd head back to where Olive was, finish her off with a shot to the back of the head, then be on our way.

Chet Watkins would be the only one with a gun, so my plan was to let him live. Not that I needed him alive for any reason, I just really didn't have much of a choice. We'd go our separate ways. I told him to wear gloves and hoped that neither one of us would leave any DNA, so that this would remain a cold case forever.

If Chet happened to get caught and ratted to the police, he knew me as Holly Cutler. I'd done away with the phone I had in Phoenix and one day, when Chet wasn't looking, I deleted Holly Cutler from his phone.

Good luck with that, investigators.

And then I was given the present of a lifetime!

When Barry Gant shot Chet Watkins and then Chet blew the top of Barry's head off, I realized I had an opportunity.

Dumb-ass Austin crouched on the ground, trying to comfort someone he had never met before. What a weak person. He deserved what he got.

Or more precisely, what I gave him.

It all happened very quickly, but I realized that if I killed Chet and Austin with Barry Gant's gun, it would look like everyone involved in the robbery had been killed. Whether the police thought the robbery was planned by Chet and Austin or just Chet didn't really matter to me.

I only had a few seconds, but it was a chance to leave no ties, and I had to take advantage of it. I grabbed Barry Gant's gun and shot Chet twice in the chest. Austin and I both saw him die instantaneously. Austin looked up at me with pleading eyes, asking me what the hell I had done. I don't think he realized in the moment that he was the last thing tying me to this crime, but he my evil intentions definitely registered. He made a move toward me, but I was far enough away to react. I raised the gun and also shot him twice through the chest. He fell backward, landing next to Chet.

I made an unnecessary comment, showing him what a cruel bitch I could be, and then watched his eyes roll back in his head.

I set the gun down next to the corpse of Barry Gant.

It was his, after all.

I took the few steps toward the safe.

Please don't say I did all this for nothing, I thought. Please be more than just that one brick.

Turned out it hadn't been for nothing. Not by a long shot. The safe was massive and it held probably twenty-five or thirty bricks, just as big as the one Barry Gant had thrown on the ground. The woman I had overheard at the restaurant was mistaken. There was more than $500,000 in the safe.

Then my heart sunk. Inside the safe, on the left, a little panic button flashed red. Barry Gant must have pressed it as he grabbed the gun. I assumed it went directly to the police.

I had to get the fuck out of there. I couldn't risk going back to the front door and finishing off Olive. I'd leave by the back.

I grabbed the pillowcase I had brought and started filling it with all the money there was, leaving the one brick on the ground that Barry had thrown our way. It had blood all over it and I wouldn't be using that.

Then a brilliant and agonizing idea came to me. If I was going to make this look like a robbery where everyone got killed, I couldn't just take all the money. I had to leave some behind.

It pained me to no end, but I grabbed two bricks from the pillowcase. I put one back in the safe and let the other fall on the ground.

Now at least $60,000 remained in the room. Maybe it was $75,000. I'd imagine even the best detective would assume no one had escaped.

Who the fuck would leave three bricks of cash behind?

It was time to get the hell out of there. I put the baby mask in the pillowcase and briskly made my way from the room and down the staircase. When we walked in, I'd seen a back door and decided to take that. The police, when they arrived, would undoubtedly use the front.

I opened the back door and locked it behind me. I then took off the gloves I had been wearing the entire time and put them in the pillowcase. My body had been covered in sweats from neck to toe, I had a mask on, and I had been wearing gloves. I was positive I had left no DNA at the scene.

People said there was no such thing as the perfect murder, but they were wrong. I had just committed it. Well, murders, but who's counting?

A hundred feet from the back of Gant's house was a fence. I took the pillowcase and tossed it over and then lifted myself over after it.

It wasn't easy, but there was no chance a fence would keep me from that kind of money.

I started walking away from the Palisades, taking off my sweatshirt and wrapping it around the pillowcase so it didn't look so obvious.

It was heavy as hell, but what choice did I have?

A few minutes later, I got to a main street, where a few police cars passed me. I smiled, about to get away with it all. And with several hundred thousand dollars to boot.

There still was one connection. Olive. I probably could have grabbed Chet's gun, gone downstairs, headed toward the front door, and shot her in the back of her head. But once I saw that Barry Gant had pressed a panic button, I couldn't risk it.

I didn't worry about Olive. I had lagged back as Chet approached the house, so she never saw me. And she'd been knocked unconscious by the time I walked in.

The way my luck was going, Olive had probably already succumbed to her injuries.

__22__
<u>OLIVE</u>

The faint sound of police car sirens pierced in my ears. I thought I heard a door being broken down. The sounds seemed real, but I couldn't be sure. It's like I was dreaming, even though I was, at least partially, awake.

All at once, I came to and immediately reached for a pain in the back of my head. Coagulated blood appeared on my fingers. I tried to remember what had happened.

Several police officers—there must have been five or six of them—stood over me.

"Where is everyone else?" one of them asked.

"Who?" I said, still in a daze and trying to get my bearings. I looked around at a house I had never seen before, and then it hit me. I was in Barry Gant's house. Austin and I had come here to meet with him.

The officers spotted the wound on the back of my head. One stayed with me and the others moved through the house.

"Send an ambulance to 4126 Alta Mura Road in the Palisades. Young woman, mid-twenties, with a pretty bad head wound."

I knew they were talking about me, but it still didn't register for a few seconds.

"Am I going to be okay?" I asked.

"It's a big gash, but I think you'll get through it," the officer said. "But you're lucky we found you when we did."

"What's going on?"

"That's what we're here to find out. You don't remember anything?"

"I came here with my boyfriend," I said and tried to recollect what happened then.

I started to sit up, but the officer laid me back down.

"You know what, why don't you just rest?" he said. "We can find this out later."

My awareness fading and returning, I heard the officers rummaging through the house, and a few minutes later, coming down what sounded like some stairs.

"Three deceased at 4126 Alta Mura," one of them said.

I had been going in and out of consciousness, but that I heard well. Three deceased! What the fuck had happened? Two of them had to be Austin and Barry Gant. I started crying. Austin killed? I couldn't believe it.

Everything had seemed so surreal, but hearing that people had been killed made it way too real.

Austin? Barry? I started sobbing louder.

The officer tried to comfort me, but then the doors opened and two EMTs rushed to my side. I was still crying as they loaded me onto a gurney.

I cried for Austin, for the man I had dated for the last month. For a man who, until very recently, I thought I was falling in love with. And I cried for Barry, who may have been a flirt, but was a good man at heart.

They started wheeling me out of the house. They had said three were dead. And that's when I remembered the man walking toward us with that creepy baby mask. I tried to remember all I could before I fell back out of consciousness.

I awoke in a hospital bed. A nurse told me I'd been brought to Saint John's Health Center in Santa Monica. My hands immediately went back to my head injury, but felt only a huge gauze pad protecting it. Less than a minute after I woke up, two LAPD officers walked in, accompanied by a doctor. The first officer was a white guy in his early forties with a tight blond crew cut. The second was African-American, several years younger, but with the same close-cropped hair.

The doctor, a woman also in her forties, spoke first.

"Olive, you've suffered a pretty serious head wound, but you are going to be okay. These two detectives want to ask you a few questions and I said it's alright if you are up for it."

"Sure," I said.

The doctor left the room.

"I'm Phil Liston and this is my partner, Nate Washington," the white guy said. "We're homicide detectives with the LAPD."

They both extended their hands to shake. Nate then took the lead.

"We're really sorry to question you this soon after suffering a head wound, but any immediate information we could get would be extra helpful."

"I work at a bar called The Belly Flop on Wilshire Boulevard. The owner is a guy named Barry Gant, whose house we were at tonight."

My room had a window. I looked outside and saw nothing but pitch black. It somehow made it more eerie, being interviewed by the LAPD this late at night. My thoughts turned to Austin for a second. I still couldn't believe he was dead.

I was having a tough time concentrating.

"Is Austin Jones one of the people who died?" I asked.

"Austin Jones?"

"Yeah, he was my boyfriend. He's the reason we were at Barry Gant's house. Austin was considering opening up a bar and Barry owned twelve of them across LA."

"Maybe he should have been named BAR-ry," Phil Liston said.

Nate Washington glared at his partner.

"I'm sorry," Liston said. "That was completely uncalled for."

I looked in Nate Washington's direction, thinking Phil Liston didn't deserve my respect.

"Tell us everything that happened today, Olive," Detective Washington said.

"I woke up. Austin was staying at my place. You didn't tell me whether Austin died."

I just assumed he had, but now I held out hope.

"We'll get back to that, Olive."

Now, I was confused. Austin had to be one of the deceased. Didn't he?

"No, I want to know now."

Officer Washington grabbed a photograph from a manila envelope he had brought in.

"Is this your boyfriend?"

It was several years old, but it was undeniably Austin.

"Yes. Is he dead?"

"He is, Olive. I'm sorry."

"And Barry Gant is dead too?"

"Yes."

I started crying again, but managed to get myself under control. I could cry later. But I needed to finish the interview.

"Why didn't you just tell me that right away?" I asked.

The officers looked at each other and I knew something was up.

"What the hell is it?"

"You said your boyfriend's name was Austin Jones?"

"Yeah, as far as I know."

Detective Liston finally felt confident enough to get back into the conversation. "Olive, this person's name was Jared Jenkins."

My world began to spin. Had this whole relationship been a charade? Was I being used to get to Barry? Why had he lied to me about his name?

"His middle name was Austin, however," Detective Washington said.

That calmed me down a bit. Maybe he went by Austin and the officers didn't know it yet. And maybe he was trying to get a new start and that's why he said his last name was Jones. There were a lot of maybe's, but conceivably this had all been a misunderstanding.

"Was he from Roanoke, Virginia?" I asked, fearing the worst.

"He was born in Atlanta, but we're not sure yet if he grew up there. Listen, Olive, we'll get back to this, but for now we really need to know about the rest of your day."

My head still spun. I wasn't sure if it was from the revelation about Austin or my head wound acting up. I needed to concentrate and talk with the officers.

"Like I said, when I woke up, Austin was staying at my place. I went to work at The Belly Flop and returned a little after 6:00 p.m. Austin was gone.

He came and picked me up around 7:30 and we headed over to Barry's house in the Pacific Palisades."

My mouth was parched. "Can I get a sip of water?"

Officer Liston grabbed a water bottle from a tray and gave it to me. I could tell he was trying to get back in my good graces after his tasteless joke. I took a huge swig.

"We got to his place and there's a gate at the front. Barry opened the gate from his end and we drove up toward his house. The views of the Pacific were amazing. That's all Austin and I were talking about. We parked the car probably forty feet from the front door and Barry came out and met us. We walked to the door. Somewhere right around then, I can't remember if it was before or after, we saw someone coming toward us with a gun. He had on a mask of, like, a baby porcelain doll. It was really disturbing."

I grabbed the bottled water and had another big sip. "He ordered us inside and had me get on my knees. And then I don't remember anything."

"We think the man hit you with the butt of his gun," Officer Washington said.

"That sounds logical," I said.

"And that's all you remember?"

"Yeah, I think so. It's all a little hazy."

"Actually, you're doing great. How did you and Austin meet?"

"At The Belly Flop."

"Did he show an interest in Barry Gant early on?"

"Not right away. But he met him one day, and then every day it was questions about Barry. I thought it was weird."

"What type of questions?"

"How many bars he owned. The names of the bars. Where he lived."

"Where he lived?"

"Yeah, he asked me if I'd ever been to his house. He actually had a good reason to be suspicious. Barry Gant used to flirt with me a lot. I mean, he did it with several of the girls, but everyone knew he really had a crush on me."

I looked around the barren hospital room. This was all so bizarre.

"Had you ever been to his house?" Detective Liston asked.

I had seen enough police procedurals to know this was a question to see if I would incriminate myself.

"Of course not!" I yelled. "I really hope you guys don't think I had anything to do with this."

"We don't," Washington said.

"If I ever wanted to go to Barry Gant's house, I had plenty of opportunities."

"Okay, Olive."

"You haven't even told me what exactly went down. I'm not answering any more questions until you tell me that."

They looked at each other.

"Well, obviously we can't give you specifics, but we think this was a pre-planned robbery."

My head started spinning once again.

"And you think Austin was involved in it?"

"That's what we are trying to figure out."

Officer Washington took out another picture from his manila envelope. "Do you know this man?"

He showed me a mug shot of a guy somewhere around thirty. The man had a menacing look on his face, and a tattoo on the right side of his throat looked like it headed down toward his arm.

"No, I have no idea who this is."

"Have you ever heard the name Chet Watkins?"

"No," I said. "Was he the third guy who was killed?"

They looked at each other again.

"Yes."

"How was he involved?"

"Listen, Olive, we appreciate your position, but we can't give away any more information. We're going to let you go back to sleep now. But I'm sure we'll have more questions in the morning."

The officers said their goodbyes and left me alone in the quiet, soulless hospital room. I was back asleep within a few minutes.

The next morning was more of the same. The officers came in and interviewed me, asking many of the same questions as the night before.

They were still tight-lipped, but when I was alone in my room, I turned on the T.V. and watched local news stations reporting on the robbery. Three people had been killed and they mentioned a young woman who survived at the scene.

It was more than bizarre to hear myself mentioned on the news. Luckily, they hadn't disclosed my name.

The report said they didn't believe the public was still at risk, and that the perpetrator or perpetrators had been killed in the course of the robbery. This led me to believe Chet Watkins was a confirmed perpetrator, the one with the baby mask, while they were trying to figure out if Austin was a co-conspirator. Although they referred to him as Jared Jenkins.

I had so many feelings and thoughts, I didn't know where to start. Foremost in my mind was whether Austin's and my relationship was a real one. Had I been duped all along? Had he targeted me? If he was part of this robbery from the beginning, then I almost assuredly had been.

The reports also said that $75,000 dollars had been left at the scene, confirming that no one got out alive. Except me, of course.

Three people dead for $75,000?

What a fucking waste!

Later that day, the doctor I'd met the previous night came in and checked on my head. She didn't seem too worried.

"You suffered a concussion and there is a big gash, but nothing permanent. It's a nasty, bloody flesh wound, but still just that. I'm recommending that you get released in a few hours."

For the first time, I thought of my parents. I loved them very much, but wasn't particularly close to them the last few years, a lot of it being because I had chosen to work at a bar. Plus they still lived in Virginia and it's not like that was right around the corner from Los Angeles. But obviously they deserved to know what had happened.

"Do you have a phone I can borrow? I need to call my parents and tell them what happened."

"Why don't you tell them yourself?" the doctor said, and I knew what was coming next.

A minute later, in walked Terri and George Fairbanks. My father had recently turned sixty-five and still had a good deal of dark hair for a man his age. My mother was sixty with a beautiful complexion and long, light brown hair. They looked ten years younger than their ages, and most people still considered my mother beautiful.

She didn't look it on this day, tears having made her eyes bloodshot and puffy. I felt bad that they had to go through this with me.

They both came to my bedside and alternated giving me big hugs and a kiss.

"Oh honey, I was so worried when we got the call last night. There were no flights out, so we set up one for first thing this morning. Just landed and took an Uber to the hospital," my mother said.

"I'm just glad to see you're alright, Olive," my father said. He was a man of few words.

The doctor excused herself and left us alone.

"Tell me everything," my mother said, too theatrical for my liking.

I summarized everything that had happened.

"So the police aren't sure if your boyfriend was involved?"

"No, I don't think they know. They're certain this other guy Chet was, but they're unsure of Austin."

"But you said he lied about his name to you?" my mother asked.

That certainly didn't look good.

"Yeah, he did. Although his middle name was Austin, so I just don't know."

"Why didn't you tell us about this guy?"

"We'd only been dating for a month, Mom."

"Terri, why don't we deal with that stuff later? I'm just glad to see you're alright, Olive."

It was the second time my father had used the same exact phrasing.

"Thanks. You guys didn't have to fly all the way out to see me. The doctor told me it's just a superficial head wound."

My mother looked at me intently. "If you ever have a daughter and you get a call in the middle of the night that three people are dead and she is going to the hospital, I hope you go fly to see her."

Well, when she put it that way.

"I understand, Mom. I'm just telling you guys that I'm going to be fine."

"George, how many times did I tell you that the bar business can be shady?"

"Mom, please not now!" I yelled. "This has nothing to do with my job."

I said and believed that, but it did have something to do with the owner of The Belly Flop, so my mother wasn't completely off base.

"I'm sorry, Olive. You're right, I should just be worried about you right now."

This wasn't the time to argue.

"Thanks, Mom. I'm glad you guys came."

"Olive, the doctor said you are going to be released later today. We've got a room at some hotel in Santa Monica and we'd like you to stay with us. We fly back on Sunday, so all we ask is that you stay with us on Friday and Saturday night."

I wanted to get back to my apartment, but my parents had flown all the way out here to be with me, so I agreed to it. "Of course."

"Great. I'm going to go check your mother in at the hotel, since we came directly here. Call me when you're released and I'll come get you," my father said.

"You don't have a car, Dad."

"I'm getting good at this Ubering thing."

My mother and I got a nice laugh out of that. It helped ease the tension that had built up.

"Okay, Dad, we'll go Ubering together."

They smiled and I told them I'd see them again in a few hours. My smiles wouldn't last as I was once again left to my thoughts of whether I was just a pawn to Austin.

The next few days went by in a blur. I had two more interviews with the LAPD and then spent both nights at the Wyndham Santa Monica, a stone's throw from the Pacific Ocean. I wondered why I had ever wanted to go back to my pedestrian apartment. It was a bit odd staying in a hotel with a shared door to your parents' room, but the hotel itself was gorgeous and my mother and I bonded as we walked around the city, hitting up the world-famous Santa Monica Pier.

We even got a drink at the hotel bar downstairs, after my mother made sure I called the doctor and got confirmation I could imbibe. I realized it was going to be my first drink since the day I had sworn off alcohol. That was also the day I had met Austin.

I planned on sticking to my plan of drinking less, but after almost being killed, it didn't seem all that important in the moment.

So I sat down with my mother and ordered a cocktail. The bartender brought it over and smiled at both of us.

"The bartender seems like a really nice guy," my mother said.

"Yeah, we're not all bad people," I said.

"I deserve that," she said. "It's only because I want what's best for you."

"I get it, Mom. And who knows if I'll ever bartend again? With Barry dying, I don't know what's going to happen. I mean, I was at his house when he died. I'd be a sideshow bartender and everyone would want to know details."

"Do you have enough money saved up to get by?"

"I'm fine, Mom. I've made pretty good money and I don't really have any expensive spending habits."

"If I lived in LA, I'd be at those shops on Rodeo Drive every week."

I laughed. My mother and I were having a nice time bonding—ironically, over a drink.

"Well, keep us posted. If you get laid off and need to borrow some money, just let us know."

"Like I said, Mom, I'm fine."

"I'm glad to hear it, Olive. I love you."

I hugged my mother and a tear came to both of our eyes.

"I love you too."

"When we first got the call, it was almost midnight our time. You should have seen your father. He was a mess."

"I'm sure he was."

"I wasn't much better."

"Thanks for coming, Mom."

And she hugged me like she'd never hugged me before.

They flew back to Virginia on Sunday and I went back to my unremarkable apartment.

Monday was going to be a big day. I had to meet with the general manager of The Belly Flop, and before that, with Detectives Liston and Washington for hopefully the last time. My time at the Wyndham Santa Monica had been great, but I hadn't slept well with all that had happened. I made up for it when I got back to my own bed and slept eleven hours on Sunday night.

_23_
BECCA

When I escaped after the robbery, and got back to my apartment, the first thing I did was change my hair color.

As I walked on the streets below the Pacific Palisades, several cars had driven past me. It was after 8:00 at night but a bleached blonde pixie haircut would stand out. If the officers started interviewing people who lived in Gant's neighborhood, maybe one of them would mention me.

I had kept Chet indoors for the entirety of his trip, but Austin and I had met in public a few times. If someone recognized him from the news, maybe they'd tell the police they'd seen him with some bleached blonde as well. And if an officer heard twice about a bleached blonde with a pixie cut, I was sure they'd get suspicious.

I hadn't come this far to be caught now, so I dyed my hair pitch black that very night. I vowed to pick up some extensions the next morning.

After the dye took effect, I sat down and set the pillowcase in front of me. I couldn't control my enthusiasm as I started counting the money. First off, I counted a single brick. It held four stacks of bills that had been taped together. Three of the stacks were $6,000 each and the final one was $7,000. The brick did, in fact, hold $25,000.

Then I counted the bricks. Twenty-seven!

I did the math and it came to $675,000! I couldn't believe it myself. I was fucking rich! People were dead, but I didn't give a shit about them. I had wanted to be rich as far back as I could remember, and now I was!

It was exhilarating just touching all the money.

I went to sleep that night, and while a normal person might have tossed and turned after having killed people, I slept like a baby.

An extremely rich baby.

Just as I had departed the Bay Area a few months after fleecing Joan Gandy, I knew I should get out of Los Angeles soon. Everything had gone my way, but there was just no reason to chance it. I gave my landlord my one-month notice.

I followed the investigation as closely as I could. In the first few days, that meant watching the local news. I had a huge smile on my face when I first heard a newscaster say, "There is no more risk to the public." From what the local reporters could gather, the people who committed the crime were dead. They were unsure if Chet Watkins had carried it out on his own or whether he had Jared "Austin" Jenkins as a partner, but either way, there were no other suspects out there.

I also took great pride when they mentioned that $75,000 had been recovered at the crime scene. One blonde newscaster, who couldn't have been older than twenty-five, said, "I think it's pretty obvious that there's no robber still on the loose. I mean, who would leave that much money?"

"Give that dumb blonde a raise!" I said aloud.

I could get away with that, since my formerly blonde hair now resembled an oil slick.

I didn't agonize about being caught, but I did have one worry. I had $675,000 in my apartment. I became a hermit of epic proportions, hardly ever leaving the house.

When I did get out of LA, I couldn't just take it with me to South America or Europe or anywhere where a flight was needed. I had to figure out how to launder $675k.

First world problems, I know.

One other thing gnawed at me. What if the girl I had overheard at the restaurant in Beverly Hills went to the police? She could say that she'd seen way more than $75,000 in the safe when she was there.

But what did that really prove? Nothing. Just because Barry Gant had hundreds of thousands at one time, doesn't mean he'd have that months, or possibly years, later. The girl never specified how long ago it had been.

And maybe she had moved out of LA. Or hadn't heard about his death, although that seemed unlikely. Maybe she was married and didn't want to go to the police and tell them about committing adultery.

I started to worry less and less about it. And even if the police believed the safe had held more money than the $75,000 grand, they still had nothing linking me to the rest of it. Nor any person. Luckily for me, Chet Watkins and Jared (no need to call him Austin anymore) were both deceased.

There was the time I had met Olive Fairbanks for all of two minutes at The Belly Flop. I doubt it even registered with her and I paid it no mind. I'd heard on the news that she was out of the hospital and going to live. So I guess my run of luck hadn't been quite as perfect as I thought.

This Olive would be allowed to live.

For now.

24

OLIVE

"Hi, Olive," Officer Nate Washington said as I entered the West Los Angeles Police Station early on Monday morning. It was going to be my sixth interview in less than a week and no, I wasn't looking forward to it.

His partner, Detective Liston, was nowhere to be seen. I'd had a better rapport with Washington, so I'm sure that was why he met me alone.

"Good to see you again," I said.

He walked me to one of the several gray doors that all had matching silver door handles. The place showed the personality of a vacant parking lot.

We entered the office and he shut the door behind him. I had expected a big conference room, but it turned out to be just him and me in a crammed little space.

"I'd like to start off with some good news, Olive."

I could use some.

"We are, for all intents and purposes, closing the part of the investigation that involves you."

"What exactly does that mean?"

"It means that we don't think you are involved. We may have questions that run ancillary to our investigation which we may need you to answer, but they will not question your involvement."

"A bit longwinded, but it sounds good."

"It is good, Olive. Listen, we never thought you had any part in it and we're sorry we had to drag you into so many interviews, but we just had to know."

"Thanks. Do you think that Austin was involved?"

"Do you mean Jared?"

"Yes. I guess."

"I can't tell you everything, obviously, but I think you deserve a few answers."

"Thanks."

"*We don't know* is the honest answer. My gut tells me yes, but we still haven't found a connection between Jared Jenkins and Chet Watkins. In fact, we can't even find a time they were in the same city until the robbery itself. But he set up the meeting and repeatedly lied to you, so while I can't prove it, I'm guessing he was involved."

"This whole thing is so weird."

"You can say that again. I've been doing this for ten years and I can't think of a case more mind-boggling."

"Did they all kill each other at once?"

I knew I needed to tread lightly, but I thought Nate Washington had taken pity on me for what I'd been through. We seemed to trust each other.

"We know that Barry Gant had a gun in the safe. We believe he took it out, turned, and first shot Chet Watkins, who was also armed, three times, and then Jared Jenkins twice. Chet Watkins did not die immediately, so he shot Barry Gant right through the forehead. Watkins then succumbed to his injuries in the time it took the police to get there."

"Seems so convoluted and yet wrapped in a bow all at once. Is that possible?"

"That's well said, Olive. It's both ridiculous that all of these things happened at once and also not only possible, but probable. We found no other DNA in the room and no evidence that anyone else was involved."

"Maybe Chet Watkins was just a lone wolf," I said.

"It's possible. But there are some other factors that don't look good for your ex-boyfriend."

"Like what?"

"I'm wondering why they didn't just knock him out like they did to you. If he wasn't part of it, why take him up to the safe?"

I had no answer to that.

"What else?" I said, dreading what more I'd hear.

"All the lies he told you. That he was a stockbroker or some bigwig on Wall Street. Or that he was from Norfolk, when there is zero evidence he's ever been there, much less lived there."

I bowed my head. "I was used from the very beginning, wasn't I?"

"That would be my guess."

"But why?"

"My suspicion is that the guy you knew as Austin thought you were his in to Barry Gant. How many people knew your boss had a crush on you?"

"Pretty much everyone who had spent any time at The Belly Flop. All my regulars certainly knew that Barry had a thing for me."

"And how would they know Barry had $75,000 in his safe?"

"I have no idea."

"I believe you, Olive."

I exhaled. It was nice to know, even after all that happened, that the police believed me. Or at least, Detective Washington did.

"Why did you tell me all this information? It doesn't seem like something cops would usually do."

"I do have some ulterior motives. I and my partner, who couldn't be here today, thought that if you knew this information, you might be able to help us down the road."

"How, exactly?"

"If you hear that Jared Austin Jenkins was hanging out with someone else in the neighborhood."

"He wasn't. I would have known."

"I don't mean recently. This could have been months ago."

"Impossible. He only got here a month ago or so."

"Are you sure about that?"

"No," I admitted.

"We're trying to find someone who knew both Jared and Chet Watkins. Who maybe put them in touch with each other."

"Sorry I can't help. I don't even know who Chet Watkins is," I said.

"It's okay, Olive. But, listen, if you hear anyone say that they've been to Barry Gant's house before, I want you to tell me. I don't care if it's your oldest regular or your favorite co-worker. We think this was some sort of inside job. We don't necessarily mean by The Belly Flop, but someone must have alerted Mr. Watkins or Mr. Jenkins that there was money there."

"I'll let you know if I hear anything. None of my co-workers have been there, though. They used to joke that I'd be the first."

"Jeez, he really did have a crush on you, didn't he?"

"Yeah."

"Okay, I think that about wraps it up for now, Olive. Thank you for answering all the questions."

"You're welcome."

"How is your injury doing?"

"I don't even think about it. Unless people mention it."

Detective Washington smiled and raised his hands in surrender. "I'm sorry."

"It's fine," I said. "Is there any way I can get updates on the investigation?"

"You got a lot more information today than most witnesses would."

"I know."

"We'll likely be having one more meeting next week. Maybe we'll see if we can throw you a bone."

"Why are you so nice to me?" I asked.

"First and foremost, we're trying to get to the bottom of this. But I also realize how used you must feel."

"Yeah, men can be jerks."

"Well, your boyfriend paid for it with his life."

"Yeah," I said, not knowing what else to say, and suddenly feeling bad for Austin.

Detective Washington recognized the awkward silence.

"I'll show you to the front. Thanks for coming in today, Olive. And please, if you hear or see anything suspicious regarding Barry Gant or Jared Austin Jenkins, get in touch with us. Even the smallest thing."

"I will. Thanks for sharing some info with me."

"You're welcome. Don't share it with anyone else, please."

"Who am I going to tell?" I said rhetorically.

And all of a sudden I felt very lonely. My parents had just left and my boyfriend, whether fake or not, was dead. I didn't have many people I could talk to who weren't wearing a uniform.

Detective Washington led me to the front door. He told me to keep my head up. I said I would and we said goodbye to each other.

Next on my Monday morning tour was Tiffany Van Dyke, the general manager of The Belly Flop and a few of the other Barry Gant-owned bars. I had met Tiffany many times over the years and she always seemed pleased with the work I was doing. She was in her mid-thirties with bright red hair, always accompanied with bright red lipstick. A bit overweight, she wasn't lacking in curves.

She'd given me a couple of dirty looks early on when she saw Barry flirting with me, but I think she gradually figured out that I wasn't instigating it. If anything, I tried to resist his wooing.

It was weird walking into The Belly Flop for the first time since Barry had died. I spotted Mark Midfield and a few other regulars. He usually loved to talk, but he just nodded his head in my direction. I'm sure they assumed I had nothing to do with Barry's death, but it would be awkward to work here again.

Tiffany was in the corner of the bar where Sheri and I would usually have our little talks. I missed Sheri. She had sent a few heartfelt texts, but with my interviews with the police and my parents in town, we hadn't been able to meet up. I didn't see her on this day, either. Some new girl was with Tiffany going over things.

"Hi, Olive," Tiffany said, seeing me approach.

There were only about eight people in the bar, but it seemed like all of their heads turned toward me at once. I guess I couldn't blame them. After all, I was present when Barry Gant was killed. I'd have probably looked too.

But I didn't like the feeling one bit. I felt like an animal at a zoo.

"Hi, Tiffany. Sorry I'm a few minutes late, I had to meet with the police for a last time."

"It's no problem, Olive. This is Jen, she's one of our new trainees."

"Nice to meet you," I said, feeling her eyes all over me.

One of the night bartenders, Bryce Cannon, came over and gave me a nice hug.

"I'm sorry for all you've been through, Olive."

"Thanks, Bryce, that means a lot."

"Let me know if you need anything."

I had always liked Bryce. He was honest and a stand-up guy. He had a longtime girlfriend, so we had never done anything together, but I knew he was one of the good ones.

"Thanks so much. You covering my shift?"

"Technically Tiffany is, but I'm going to cover for her while you guys talk."

"Which we should do now," Tiffany interrupted.

Bryce gave me one more hug and made it last. I was grateful.

Tiffany walked me back to the The Belly Flop's two offices. The one for Barry was rarely occupied, but the other was often used by managers on duty, or in Tiffany's case, the general manager.

I sat on a cold tin chair that, even though I had jeans on, made the backs of my legs fill with goose bumps. Tiffany sat in the chair behind the lone desk in the room. It was very cramped, much like the police station.

Tiffany spoke first. "First off, I'd just like to extend my sympathy, Olive. No one should have to go through what you went through."

"Thanks."

"I know that Barry had a crush on you, and I always appreciated how you were able to resist him without causing any friction. You deftly handled it."

"I appreciate that," I said, deciding not to mention the dirty looks I got early on from her.

"It's been very morose around here without Barry. Yeah, he was a ceaseless flirt, but he had a good heart and these bars were more fun with him around."

"I agree. His flirting almost became like a badge of honor for me. He never crossed the line and we actually enjoyed each other's company."

"You were definitely one of his favorite employees," Tiffany said, stating the obvious.

"He was part of the charm of working here."

"Which makes this all the tougher," she said, and that's when I knew I was going to get fired.

"Are you letting me go?" I asked.

"We're not firing you, Olive. But we don't think it's advisable to have you working here right now."

I understood, but that doesn't mean I had to like it.

"So, it's like a suspension?"

"Don't make this tough, Olive."

"I'm not."

"I can't have someone on call here who is part of a police investigation into the owner's death."

"They've cleared me. Everyone knows I had nothing to do with it."

"I know that. Do you think every drunk guy who sees you working is going to be as nice?"

She had a point. I could already imagine it. *Have you tried Olive's Bloody Mary? It's extra bloody!*

"How much time are you giving me off? I do have bills to pay."

I didn't tell her that I had over $10,000 saved up and could last on my own for a while.

"We were thinking about revisiting this in a month. By then, the investigation will likely be over and the whole incident will be in people's rearview mirrors."

A month didn't sound so bad. I could concentrate on my writing. If I could put the horrors of what happened out of my mind. Concentrating might be difficult.

"I'm assuming it would be unpaid?"

"Olive, this isn't the NBA. You don't get a paycheck if you're sitting on the bench."

"Even if the player wants to play?"

I didn't know much about sports, but I thought it was as good an analogy as any.

"My hands are tied. And this decision is final. I'm sorry, Olive."

I was done fighting, and not even sure why I had tried. The month off sounded better and better.

"What's going to happen with the bars?"

"Barry had an estate. It looks like a sister who lives in Texas may inherit them. I talked to her and I don't think there are going to be huge changes. For now, she wants the multiple GMs, myself included, to keep running them as before."

"Is there going to be a funeral?" I asked.

"Barry's will said no funeral. He wanted to be cremated, which may have already happened. I know he wanted his ashes spread in the Pacific and up by the Hollywood sign."

"Fitting," I said. "He really was a big deal in this town."

"Opening twelve bars is not an easy thing to do."

It made me think of Austin, who claimed he wanted to open one. It would get me thinking about whether I had been used our entire relationship, and I didn't want to go down that rabbit hole for the twentieth time.

"So should I just get back in touch with you in a month?"

"Yeah, let's do that, Olive. You've been a great employee for the last several years. Hopefully, this isn't goodbye."

It sure felt like it.

After my meeting with Tiffany Van Dyke, I went home and broke down. I had been pretty strong considering all that had happened, but now that my interviews with the police were over and my job was too, at least temporarily, it just all hit me at once. I cried for Austin, I cried for Barry, and even cried for Chet Watkins, whoever that was.

But mostly, I cried for myself. I had never been a gullible fool, and generally had pretty good taste in men. It looked like both of those patterns had been broken with Austin, or whatever his name was. Even in the unlikely event that he was just an innocent bystander, he had lied to me about multiple things in our relationship. Why?

It got me thinking. I had money saved up and was unemployed for the next month. What if I went back to Austin's hometown and did some investigating? I needed some closure. I had to know if I had been a pawn in his game from the very beginning. I'd modeled myself a little Nancy Drew when I was a young girl. Maybe it was time to see if I had it in me.

I started looking at flights to Atlanta.

_25_
BECCA

I decided to make a trip to Atlanta to see my parents once my lease in LA ended. They still lived in Roswell, just minutes from Atlanta, in my childhood home.

My ultimate destination was going to be nowhere near where I grew up, but I figured it would be nice to spend a few days with the parents before I left for a long time.

At least, that's what I told myself.

To be honest, I never cared much for my parents. They were decent people and they loved me, but I had always looked down on them. They could never rise out of the middle class and that pissed me off to no end. They had never made their mark on the world and I held it against them.

I can't remember the last time they called me. Even with my variety of cell phones over the years, I still had my "main" one they could have reached me on. From their perspective, I was a money-grubbing witch who could never hold down a job and just had sugar daddies taking care of everything for me.

Not anymore, Mommy and Daddy. Somebody's rich!

I wasn't the most introspective person, but obviously I occasionally wondered why I ended up the way I had. And I came up with a pretty simplistic answer. Whatever benefitted me most was the right answer, regardless of the repercussions for others.

While little Max Underwood was getting his ass pummeled, I didn't worry about how it might affect him. I was just happy that this gave me dirt on Jared/Austin and would pay off for me down the road.

When Chet Watkins was shot, I didn't think "Oh my gosh, some guy I was friends with (and fucked a few times) is going to die." I was too wrapped in my own good fortune. An opportunity for me to get out of the robbery scot free.

This could be considered monstrous, but from my perspective I was just looking out for my own self-interest. Did I cross the line? Of course, but life was a full contact sport. I was prepared. These weak men I always encountered never seemed to be. Shit, even the worthless bartender Olive survived the robbery.

Three men died and two women lived. It's like with the praying mantis, where the females eat the males alive. Those were my spirit animal.

Of course, that's not totally fair.

I'd also kill any woman who ever got in my way.

_26_
<u>OLIVE</u>

My love of Nancy Drew started at a young age. I used to read Edward Stratemeyer's novels religiously, and tried to find similarities between myself and the heroine of the books. I read Stratemeyer's Hardy Boy books as well, but they never spoke to me like Nancy Drew did.

At eight years old, I told people I wanted to be a sleuth when I grew up.

"A sleuth?" they would say, laughing at me.

"Sleuth! S-L-E-U-T-H." I'd adamantly spell the letters out.

At eleven years old, I'd graduated to saying I was going to be a private detective when I grew up.

I'd still get quizzical looks, but not the laughs that the word sleuth enticed.

For two main reasons, my dream of being a private detective slowly went away. First, boys. I started to notice them more and more as I entered my early teenage years, and going home and reading a Nancy Drew novel seemed boring in comparison.

I knew they found me attractive and I found many of them attractive as well. I started to become girlier as I grew up, caring more about makeup and looking good to catch good guys than I did about catching bad guys.

The other thing that started to discourage me was that I realized, unlike in Nancy Drew books, there was likely to be a lot more violence and grime for a real-life private detective. You couldn't just outthink someone and solve the case.

Nancy Drew had made her way into my psyche a lot lately, no doubt through a combination of the horrific crime I had been a part of along with my upcoming trip to Atlanta. I was reverting to the eight-year-old me, styling myself a now twenty-six-year-old Nancy Drew.

I was going to finally be a sleuth.

I laughed at the absurdity of it all, knowing I wasn't cut out for this type of work. That being said, I really wanted to find out what had gone down at Barry Gant's house. I wanted to know if Austin was involved. I wanted to know if I had been used the whole time.

No, that's not true. I didn't want to know. I needed to.

I considered going down to see the officers once again, but put it off. I would wait until just before I departed for Atlanta so I'd have the most up-to-date information before I went off on my wild goose chase.

And let's be honest, that's exactly what it would be. I was no Nancy Drew. I was a cute, twenty-six-year-old woman who screamed in pain if I smashed a nail.

I had about as much business going on this little adventure as my eight-year-old self did. Namely…none.

Still, I knew it was going to happen. I could be really stubborn when I wanted to be.

I went ahead and booked my flight to Atlanta.

BECCA

The three weeks after the murders had been very quiet. And that was a good thing. No news was good news. I felt tempted to call the police station and ask if there had been any progress on the investigation. I'd have used a pay phone (turns out they still had those in some corners of LA), but decided against it. No reason to involve myself.

One question I wanted answered did get the better of me, however. I called The Belly Flop one day and asked if Olive was working. The woman sternly said that Olive was taking a break from The Belly Flop for now.

I had assumed as much. How could they keep employing her if she had been present while her boss, the owner of the bar, had been killed? Even if she had nothing to do with the crime, it would still just be too uncomfortable.

"Poor little Olive," I said, even though I didn't believe that at all.

I was about to ask the bartender if she knew Olive's phone number, but I reconsidered.

I'll be honest, I wanted to needle Olive a little bit. Leave notes on her apartment door.

So it was Jared, not Austin, huh?

Guess you're lucky it was just a blow to the back of the head.

Should have been four dead instead of three.

I could have scoped out her place and seen her reaction when she read the letters. It would have been great.

Of course, I would never follow through on it, but just the thought put a smile on my face.

Why couldn't I just leave well enough alone?

I had more money than I knew what to do with. If I was able to invest it right, it would last a long time.

But still, a part of me wanted people to know. I wanted to be heralded as the evil genius that I was. What was the point of committing a crime if you couldn't rub it in people's faces?

That could wait, I decided. *Concentrate on where you're headed after Atlanta*, I told myself.

My lease was up in four days when I finally made my way down to the office. I signed the papers in the bullshit name I had used and thanked them for my time there.

No credit cards. No debit cards. All cash, all the time. No evidence that Becca Poe had ever stepped foot in LA. I truly had committed the perfect crime.

OLIVE

"Take a seat wherever you'd like," the flight attendant said as I boarded the plane.

I had chosen Southwest Airlines to fly to Atlanta. The airline got a lot of crap online, but they had always been easy for me. No need for a seat assignment, just sit where you want.

I checked a bag and brought a backpack with a few cosmetics and my laptop in the cabin. I was hoping to do some research on my flight over. Nancy Drew never had the internet, but I planned on using it to my benefit.

The morning before, I had met with Detectives Washington and Liston for what I guessed would be the last time. The case was still open, but they weren't out looking for more suspects. They didn't believe that anyone besides Chet Watkins, and possibly Jared Austin Jenkins, were involved in the robbery. And since the perpetrator or perpetrators had been killed, it was no longer a murder investigation.

They believed Austin was involved, but still didn't have any evidence. They knew he had lied to me every chance he got, but that wasn't enough to prove he took any part in planning the robbery. They couldn't find a connection between Austin and Chet Watkins, making it very problematic to conclude they worked together. Austin didn't have a weapon on him or any incriminating texts.

So despite their assumptions, with no evidence, he had to be listed as an unwilling bystander.

I knew differently. Or, at least, I thought I did. Something had been off with him in the days leading to the murder. I told myself that maybe he just had a lot on his mind. New city, new girlfriend.

But I didn't really think that.

I know what I saw and felt. Austin had changed. Of course, maybe he hadn't changed and that had been him all along. But he was different from when I first met him. Of that, there was no doubt.

What neither I nor the police could answer was how Chet Watkins had known Barry Gant. Or known of him. And how had he found out that Barry would have so much money in his safe?

Chet Watkins had been in Phoenix ten days before the murder. He wasn't employed at the time, so it was hard for the officers to pin down exactly when he had driven to LA, but officers guessed it was around that ten-day mark.

There was no evidence that Watkins had ever spent any real time in Los Angeles, which made it unlikely the robbery had been thoroughly planned for any protracted period.

Officer Washington speculated that the following happened.

"Chet Watkins, who was known as a big drinker in Phoenix, stumbled into one of Barry Gant's bars in LA. Gant, who had a big mouth, must have said he was the owner of several bars, or that he owned a big house in the Palisades. Watkins overheard this and decided to rob Gant."

I had to admit, it made some sense. Barry was always a bit of a loudmouth and I'd heard him brag about his house dozens of times. When a longtime criminal like Watkins heard something like that, he may have taken the chance.

"How would he have known he had a safe?" I asked.

"He probably didn't. But he knew he was rich and would have things at the house that were valuable. If he found a safe, all the better."

"It seems possible," I admitted.

"More like probable," Officer Liston said.

"If that's true, Austin was just a horribly unlucky bystander."

"I know," Detective Washington said. "That's what throws me for a loop, because I've been assuming that he was involved. I just don't know anymore."

I had left the police station a few minutes later.

As I sat on the plane, waiting to take off for Atlanta, I thought back on our conversation. Chet Watkins, lifetime criminal, overheard the braggadocio Barry Gant and decided to rob him. It sounded more and more believable.

Originally, I had planned the trip because I thought Austin was part of the robbery and I wanted to find out why. Now, I wasn't so sure that Austin wasn't a victim as well.

Maybe my trip had become one to acquit, not convict, Austin. Although in the back of my mind, I still feared the worst.

Either way, there was no turning back now. The wheels came up and the plane set off toward Atlanta.

We landed four hours later at Hartsfield-Jackson airport. I'd read that it had been the busiest airport in the world, measured by passenger traffic, since 1998, but I was able to get to baggage claim within ten minutes, arriving just as my bag made its way around the luggage carousel.

I stood in the cab stand for another ten minutes, and when asked where I was headed, I named the Holiday Inn Express on Cone Street. I had been able to book it for only $75 a night. It's a big reason why I'd decided to stay on a Wednesday and a Thursday. Weekends jumped to $200 nightly.

The cabdriver was nice enough, although he looked back in his rear-view mirror a few too many times for me. Just once, I'd like to spend a day as a guy, not getting creepy looks all day long. It must be nice.

We arrived at the hotel at 2:48 in the afternoon, and although the woman at the front desk said check in didn't start till 3:00, they were able to fit me in.

Wonders never cease.

I walked up to the room myself, having turned down a bellhop.

The room was basic, and not spacious by any means, but for under a hundred bucks a night, it was just fine. I took out my laptop and started wasting time on the internet. My plan was to head over to Austin's parents' sometime around 6:00. I wasn't sure if they worked, so I didn't want to head over too early and be stuck sitting around for a few hours.

I'd read a few obituaries of Austin and some mentioned his parents. After that, it wasn't too hard to find out their location in Atlanta. I had not called their house, and wasn't sure how my visit was going to go over.

I fell asleep on the hotel bed and awoke a few hours later. I looked over at the bedside clock as I got up. It was time to go meet Austin's parents.

They lived in in a suburban town called Roswell, twenty miles north of downtown Atlanta. As my Uber approached, a great many of the houses impressed me. The neighborhood was much more spacious than Los Angeles. People had lawns, big driveways, and room to do what they wanted.

It made me a bit jealous. Almost everyone I knew in LA rented apartments, and having your own space was a luxury beyond most of us.

The area looked upscale, but as the driver slowed down and dropped me off in front of the Jenkins home, it didn't stand out like so many of the others. A perfectly reasonable house, but not extravagant like so many I had seen in the neighboring areas.

I paid the cabdriver and paused as I looked out on the pale green house in front of me. It felt weird, almost like going behind Austin's back, but I reminded myself of all the times he had lied to me. After all, he'd said he'd grown up in Norfolk.

Was that all for my benefit? Had he found out that I grew up in Richmond and picked a city in Virginia? One that wasn't too close in case I started name-dropping?

I decided I could think about that later. For now, I was just here to share my condolences with his parents. Or at least, that's what I told myself I was doing.

My inner Nancy Drew had other ideas.

I knocked on the door once but received no answer. I was about to knock a second time when I heard some footsteps approaching. The door opened for a woman of about sixty, her hair a mixture of red and gray. She had big, blue eyes, but nothing else reminded me of Austin.

"How can I help you?" she asked.

"Nice to meet you. Are you Mrs. Jenkins?"

"I am," she said trepidatiously.

"I was a friend of Austin's from LA," I said.

"Austin?" she said, and I quickly realized my mistake. "No one ever called him that."

"He introduced himself to me as Austin," I said.

"Hmm, that doesn't sound like him."

"I was dating your son, Mrs. Jenkins. I promise you that I knew him."

"Wait, are you the girl who was with him when he died?"

"I am," I said and showed her the back of my head, which was starting to heal, but you could still see the wound.

"Oh, I'm so sorry. Please, come in. I'm Linda."

"I'm Olive."

She escorted me in the house. Like its outside, it was nice, but nothing to write home about. The living room, to the right as we walked in, held three fading couches. To the left, a hallway led, I assumed, to the bedrooms.

I looked around for some family photos, but didn't spot many. I had hoped to see what Austin looked like as a younger man.

"You can sit here," Mrs. Jenkins said.

It was a pale green couch that matched the color of the home. She pulled up a chair and sat next to me.

She seemed old and fragile, much older than what I guessed her actual age to be.

"I'm sorry about that blow to the head," she said. "We were out in LA for a few days, identifying Jared's body. They sure haven't given us many answers."

"Me, either," I said. "As of now, they don't have any evidence your son was involved."

I expected her to say *"As of now?"*, but instead she surprised me.

"It's probably only a matter of time."

"Wait, you think he was involved?" I asked.

"I hope I'm wrong, but it sure seems like it."

"Why do you say that?"

"He leaves Atlanta in a rush, never telling us he is going to LA, and then a month later he's killed in a robbery? Terrible coincidence if he wasn't involved."

"I wasn't involved. It was a terrible coincidence for me."

She looked me over, seemingly trying to figure out if I could have been involved despite my denial.

"Then why would he tell you his name was Austin?" she asked.

I had become the defender of Austin. It certainly wasn't what I expected.

"Maybe he was trying to get a new start in a new town. With a new name."

"Yeah? What was he doing for work?"

"He didn't have a job yet. He was considering opening a bar."

Mrs. Jenkins let out a huge laugh. "I'll have to tell Harold that one."

"Harold?"

"My husband. Jared's father. He's out of town right now."

"Why couldn't your son open a bar?"

I couldn't get used to saying Jared, so I had to resort to "your son."

"Well, unless LA is a whole lot different, you still need money to open up a bar."

The cops had told me he didn't have much money in his checking account, but it hit home even harder coming from his mother.

"He seemed to have a little money. He paid for a lot of our meals. He even chartered a boat for us."

"I'm sure he had enough money to get by for a month or two. But we were talking about opening a bar. I'd be shocked if Jared had more than $5,000 in his checking account."

All of my worst fears were being confirmed.

"Did you guys ever spend time in Norfolk?"

"Virginia?"

"Yeah."

"Never been to Norfolk. Although Jared did go to Virginia Tech, so it's possible he did."

"But never lived there as a child?"

"No, he grew up in this very house. And we never took a trip to Norfolk, Virginia."

When we had talked, he had seemed pretty well acquainted with Norfolk. I don't know if he'd conducted research online or if he visited there while in college, but he obviously hadn't spent his childhood there like he'd said. Just another lie.

"Do you have any idea why he would have lied to me?"

"No."

"What was he like?"

"He was a good boy. He could always be very charismatic. And the girls always loved him. Especially the cute ones."

She meant to compliment her son, and me, but instead, I felt like I'd been exploited.

"And manipulative," she added, maybe seeing my emotions on my face. "He could be that too."

"How so?"

"I'm sure you don't like hearing this stuff, Olive."

"You're right, but I need to hear it," I said.

"I think he used girls. I mean, I know he found them attractive, but I think he dated ones that could help him in some way. He'd date a popular one. Then a rich one. Then one whose father could help him out. You get the idea."

I was starting to feel more used by the moment. But what could I give him? The answer was obvious: Barry Gant.

I suddenly wanted to get out of the Jenkins house. I wasn't a big fan of Linda Jenkins.

She seemed to read my mind. "I'm sorry about this all, Olive. I thought you said you wanted to hear it."

She was right.

"I do, it's just not easy to hear."

"My advice to you would be to forget about my son. Be lucky you got out of that robbery alive. I don't believe in coincidences. He moves to LA on the fly, starts dating a girl who has a rich boss, and then that boss gets robbed and he's hit in the crossfire? I ain't buying it."

She made a convincing case.

"Did he have any friends in Los Angeles?" I asked.

"Not that Harold or I knew of. We talked about it after we I.D.'d his body out there. It didn't make sense. Why are you going all the way to Los Angeles without a job or at least some friends to hang with?"

"That's what I'm trying to figure out," I said.

"Don't. Like I told you, just let it be. Jared is just going to let you down in the end. Even in death."

"Are any of his old friends in Roswell or Atlanta?"

"Did you not listen to me, Olive? Let this be."

"Why so adamant, Mrs. Jenkins?"

"He was my only son. Right now, he died in a robbery gone bad. But the police have not said he was involved. I can live with that. If you keep snooping around, I'm sure you are going to find something that ties him to the crime. And then this whole neighborhood will know we raised a criminal. Do you think I want that?"

I understood her point.

"But you've basically told me you thought he was involved."

"Because I was hoping that would be enough closure for you. Plus, you aren't the police. You're just a little n…"

For a moment, I thought she was going to say Nancy Drew.

"Nag," she said.

I wasn't even close. I realized it was time to go.

"What high school did your son go to?" I asked.

"Roswell High. I hope you aren't going there."

I decided it was better to lie.

"No, just curious. I should be leaving. I'm sorry about your loss," I said.

"I'm sorry if I came off as a bitch. I just don't want to spend time thinking about how Jared died anymore. I want to remember him as the cutest little kid you could ever imagine. That's what I try to hold on to. But then you come here and bring it all back to the front."

"You won't hear from me again," I said, ready to get the hell out of there.

"Tell the police to leave me and Harold out of it too."

She walked me to the door and let me go. I shivered when I got outside, even though it wasn't all that cold. That's the effect that Linda Jenkins had had on me.

It was too late to stop by Roswell High School, so I decided to leave that for the next morning. I took an Uber back to the Holiday Inn Express and started to wonder why I ever came to Atlanta.

I was in a no-win situation. Either the guy I was dating had been involved in the robbery and had put me in harm's way, or he wasn't involved and didn't deserve to die. Although, as I looked back on my conversation with Mrs. Jenkins, the odds that he wasn't involved seemed less and less likely.

Austin had lied to me about everything. His hometown, his finances, his job. Even his name.

I woke up the next morning after having read in bed for most of the evening. I showered and threw on a long, denim skirt with a t-shirt of The xx, one of my favorite bands. I don't know if I'd made a subconscious choice because I was going to Roswell High School, but I'd definitely dressed younger than my age. It was weird to think that these high schoolers would look at me as old. Where'd all the time gone?

I took another Uber ride north of the city and passed a lot of the same roads as I had on the previous day. Austin's high school stood only a mile away from his childhood home. I began wondering if he walked to school each day, trying to recreate Austin's high school years.

Had he been an asshole back then? Was his mom right about him using people at a young age? Or did he just wait until he met me in LA?

I knew thinking about being used wasn't going to help me, but I couldn't stop.

Mercifully, we arrived.

The Uber driver dropped me off in front of a black and white sign that said Roswell High School, having a big green R on top. The school itself was surrounded by extraordinary fall reds and oranges, with trees and bushes surrounding the campus. A lot more beautiful than my high school back in Richmond.

I walked to the front entrance, still not sure exactly what I was going to do. Austin had been twenty-eight years old. One thing he hadn't lied about, as the obituaries I'd read had confirmed it. None of the existing students would know him unless they had a much older brother or sister. If I was going to get any information, it would have to be from a teacher or a counselor.

Kids milled around as I entered the campus, and I hoped with my denim skirt and rock band shirt that I might just blend in. Maybe it was wishful thinking.

A few security guards stood near the front, but I wasn't asked to show an ID. I just mingled with a group of students and entered when they did.

As I walked up the hallway, looking for a central office, I got some looks from a few of the high school boys. I'm sure they wondered who the new girl was. That, or they thought I was a young mother. Ugh!

"Nice shirt! The xx rock," one of them said.

I couldn't help but laugh.

I kept walking and finally saw what appeared to be the main office. Inside, I was greeted by a teenage boy with one of the worst cases of acne I'd ever seen. I felt bad for the kid.

"Hi, how can I help you?" he asked.

"Hello. This is going to be a weird question, but I was wondering which one of the counselors has been around the longest."

The young man looked at me, not grasping what I had asked. "Excuse me?"

Just then, a woman in her mid-fifties approached the front desk. She was tall, had long, white hair, and was going on three hundred pounds.

"It's certainly a weird request, Jonathan," she said. "Hi, I'm principal Evelyn Gillingham."

"Nice to meet you, I'm Olive Fairbanks."

"What can I help you with, Olive?"

"How long have you been the principal?"

"Almost fifteen years now."

Evelyn Gillingham would have been his principal.

"Did you know Jared Austin Jenkins?"

Her face dropped, and I noticed Jonathan look up when I mentioned the name.

"Why don't you come into my office?" she said.

We walked back until we arrived at Evelyn's personal office. She motioned for me to sit in a fading leather chair facing her desk, which she sat behind.

"I was the principal when Jared was here. How did you know him?" she asked.

There was no reason to lie.

"I was with him when he died. I was the woman who was hit in the back of the head."

"Oh, I'm so sorry. Obviously, that was a big story back here. It gave our high school a lot of publicity for all the wrong reasons. More like notoriety, I guess. Local boy killed in a robbery of a rich guy from LA. And then it came out that he might have been involved. It's been tough."

"For me too," I said. "I'm just trying to find out anything you remember about…Jared."

Despite the visit to his mother and now his school, I was still not used to calling him Jared.

"Sure, I remember him. He was a good athlete and a decent student. I know he went to Virginia Tech after he graduated, which meant we did our job. We're always happy if they go to a four-year university after finishing here at Roswell."

"What was he like, though?"

"Well, Olive, we've got about 2,000 students here, which means about 500 graduate each year. So, it's not like I know them all closely."

"I understand."

"That being said, there were rumors that Jared wasn't the best guy. That he bullied several of the students. He played basketball, football, and had a big ego. I wish everyone in high school was nice to their fellow students, but we know that's not always the case."

It was weird to hear Austin being characterized as a jerk and a bully. He had been nothing but nice with me for the vast majority of our time together. Of course, it was looking more and more like his courtship was all an act, so I'm sure he only wanted to present his good side.

"Did he have a lot of friends?"

"He was good looking and a great athlete. What do you think?"

"Yeah," I said, my mind thinking about many things at once.

She picked up on it.

"So why are you really here, Olive?" Evelyn asked.

"He and I were involved romantically. And I'm trying to find out if that was all just a ruse, or whether he really cared about me."

"I completely understand. But do you think you're going to find that information out at his old high school?"

"Probably not," I confessed.

"I'm guessing his friends or parents would know more."

"I met his mother yesterday. She didn't want to have a whole lot to do with me."

"I'm sorry," Evelyn said.

It was getting time to go. Evelyn had been nice and polite, but she was right, this wasn't going anywhere. I had one last question.

"Who was his best friend? Maybe I could get some info from him?"

"It's weird. I know I told you earlier he had a lot of friends, but I'm at a loss to remember his really close ones. Maybe people were friendly with him more out of fear than some undying love for him. Do you know what I mean?"

"I do. We had assholes at our high school also."

"I'm sorry you have to hear all this, Olive."

"It's alright. I need to hear it. I was dating a jerk."

"Maybe he changed, but yes, the high school-aged Jared Jenkins would classify."

"I think it's time I get going. Thanks for your help, Evelyn."

"You're welcome. Sorry I couldn't be of more help."

I rose up from my chair and headed toward the door.

"You know what," Evelyn said. "Thinking back, he was pretty close to Becca Poe. They were always hanging out together even though I don't think they ever dated. You may want to look her up."

"Okay, thanks."

"But tread lightly. That girl was trouble."

29

BECCA

My ego soared to an all-time high after committing the perfect crime, but even I was prone to making bone-headed decisions from time to time. Looking at flights to Atlanta was one of them. How did I think I was going to get $675,000 through airport security? I wasn't sure if they could see cash when you put bags through the metal detector, but no way I was going to chance it.

Turned out I would be driving to Atlanta.

Like in the rest of my life, I hadn't made any long-lasting connections in LA, so there was no one to say goodbye to. Which was kind of the point. I left no trace of ever having lived in Los Angeles.

The closest I had ever gotten to a long-lasting friendship was with Jared/Austin, and we know how that ended.

On an early Monday morning, I made my way up Wilshire Boulevard, got on Interstate 405, and said farewell to Los Angeles. It hadn't lasted long, but it sure had been profitable. I patted the suitcase loaded with cash as I made my way out of town.

My route to Atlanta consisted of driving through California, Arizona, New Mexico, Texas, Oklahoma, Arkansas, Tennessee, and finally, Georgia. I stayed at nice hotels, knowing stops in dives always increased the chances of getting mugged.

And with as much money as I had, getting mugged was something that I couldn't allow. As I drove across the United States, I started to think that maybe it was time to get a weapon. It wouldn't be difficult, especially the further south I got. Gun laws were so lax, I could probably just have used one of my fake I.D.s to secure one. But I decided that could wait.

I ended out finishing the trip from LA to Atlanta in just over three days, arriving on Thursday. I had enjoyed the time alone, but that was now going to end.

Time to deal with my parents and the millions of questions that I was going to be bombarded with.

I slowly made my way toward my home, passing so many pillars of my childhood as I drove. The local high school, my favorite movie theater, even the house where I had kissed and then pretended to have sex with Jared Jenkins.

Roswell usually brought back lousy memories, but I tried to concentrate on the good ones as I drove through the town. It had been several years since I'd been home and I knew my parents were going to be curious as to what I had been up to. I would have to lie, but I wasn't going to go out of my way and create some alternative universe. They knew I used men. But they'd be a bit surprised if I told them I'd killed a few this time.

I couldn't mention I had been in LA. When I called my mother and told her I was coming home, she asked if I had heard that Jared had been killed in a home invasion. I played dumb. No reason to get them wondering about Jared and I being in LA at the same time.

Truth be told, they'd just be happy to be rid of me after a few days. People generally don't like to hang around a woman they perceive as evil. Imagine knowing that you had been the ones who'd raised her.

I arrived home. There were two parts of Roswell: the very nice and the average. Roswell was a prosperous town with a median income of probably around $100,000, so the majority of people lived in great homes. I'd say 80%. The other 20% or so, and Jared's parents qualified there, lived in decent homes. Nothing to write home about, but they weren't god-awful.

As I looked out on my childhood home, I still couldn't believe my parents made me take the bus with all the riff-raff in and around Atlanta. They were well off enough where they didn't have to treat their daughter like some girl living off of food stamps. Damn them!

I had to say, the house looked nice. It had aged well, unlike my parents themselves, who looked old as I saw them waiting at the door.

Roswell was a safe neighborhood, so I put the suitcase in the trunk. Still, it wasn't ideal and I realized I needed to find a way to launder the money. And soon.

But I didn't have much choice at that moment. The last thing I needed was my father taking a peek into one of the bags as he helped me unpack. There would be a lot of explaining to do if he saw the bricks of $25k.

My parents, Mason and Sue Poe, started walking in my direction, fake smiles attached to their faces. I couldn't blame them. I really hadn't accomplished shit in my decade since graduating high school. Unless you counted getting men to pay for your every need. I don't think they did.

They had raised me as well as they knew how. They disciplined me when necessary, but also showed their love.

But I was trouble from the beginning. In fact, I would be the poster child for Nature in the Nature vs. Nurture debate, because my parents tried as hard as they could, and I still ended up being a manipulative soul. A murderous one as well.

"Hi, Becca." My mother spoke first.

She was only fifty-four, but looked more like seventy. Her formerly brown hair had gone gray. I don't know why she didn't just dye it, but maybe she liked the grandmotherly look. My father was fifty-eight, and while he didn't seem quite as old as my mother, he appeared to be in his mid-sixties or so.

I wondered if all the problems they'd had with me had contributed to their premature aging. Probably. Not that I cared.

"Hi, Mom! It's great to see you," I said with unnecessary aplomb. "And you too, Dad. You guys look great."

Obviously they didn't. I don't know why I was unnecessarily mean. It just came naturally.

"What brings you back after all these years?" my father asked.

His always-present glasses looked more like goggles now. It added to his aged appearance.

"I might be moving out of the country and just wanted to say goodbye to you," I said.

To be honest, I didn't know where I was going next, but it was fine with me if my parents thought I was out of the country. If, against all odds, the cops somehow made it to my parents, telling them I was out of the country could only help. I wasn't going overseas, however. There were 675,000 reasons to stay.

We walked toward the front door, which my father held open for both of us. It reminded me of Austin and Olive about to enter Barry Gant's home when Chet started approaching. Who knew that Olive would be the only one who would get out alive? Plus me, of course.

I sat down on a fading leather couch that had been around since I was a child. My parents sat across from me on a much newer model.

"So what country is it? And why?" my mom asked.

I knew it was going to be awkward, but it had gotten off to an even rockier start than I anticipated.

"Germany," I said, making it up on the fly. "I've met a new guy."

"Shocker," my father said.

"I think he might be the one," I said, lying out of my teeth. There was no man, and there was certainly no "one." Never had been, never would be.

"That's nice to hear, Becca," my mother said, but I could tell she wasn't buying it either.

We had about ten more minutes of painful small talk when my father said the following:

"Becca, you are free to stay here a few days or a week if you want, but once you leave, we don't want you coming back."

"Excuse me?" I said.

"You heard me. Your mother and I are tired of all the lying, Becca. You've been trouble since you were born. Maybe some of it is our fault, but we also think you've had every chance to turn your life around and never have. When was the last time you had a job? I really don't even know. Have you ever?"

I wished Chet Watkins was still around. I'd have hired him to do something to my parents. I really would have. Maybe I'd find someone in the future to make a return visit to Roswell for me. I certainly had the money to pay for it.

But despite my feelings, I decided to play nice. Or as nice as I could be.

"If that's what you want, then fine. I'll never set foot back in Roswell again. Is this what you want also, Mom?" My focus had been on my father, but when I looked over at her, I could see she was on the verge of crying.

"Maybe it's for the best, Becca. But I'll always try to remember the good times."

My father jumped in. "What, when she was three years old? She's cared about no one but herself since around that age."

"Mason, that's not fair. Becca was good for longer than that."

My mother was trying to be complimentary in her own weird way.

"Yeah, I was probably like five before I turned into Satan."

Sarcastically, I tried to exaggerate their assertions, but let's be honest: I had just put something in motion that ended with three people dead. I was actually much worse than they realized.

"I'm sorry, Becca. It's our final decision."

"Well, it's a pleasure being home."

"You can still stay as long as you want," my mother pleaded.

"I'll stay here tonight, but then I'm out of here tomorrow morning."

"Becca…"

"Just stop, Mom."

I really should have left right then and there, but I was exhausted after more than three days of driving. I excused myself and went to my childhood room. It brought back memories, but as you may have guessed, I wasn't the sentimental type. A couple of old yearbooks on a shelf caught my attention. I flipped to a photo of Jared.

"Thanks for making this all possible," I softly said.

I took out a pen and wrote *R.I.P.* next to Jared, adding a smiley face. I don't know why. Probably because I was a heartless bitch.

My ruminating about the past over, I lay down on the comfortable bed, one of the few things they had changed about the room. The new mattress was much more relaxing than the one I'd slept on as a kid. There had always been a loose spring that would find its way to my back when I least expected it.

Usually while having sex with one of the high school eunuchs I always ended up with.

I fell asleep at some point, but was woken up by a knock at the door.

"Becca, there's someone here to see you."

I thought I was still dreaming. No one knew I was back in Roswell. And then a shiver went up my spine. It had to be the police. That was the only explanation.

"Who is it?" I asked.

"Some girl. Younger than you, I think. Said her name is Olive."

A second shiver went up my spine. What in the flying fuck was she doing here? I literally had no idea.

"Mom, please tell her I'm not feeling well," I said.

Then I realized I had to go to the door. If my mother asked Olive what she'd come about and she mentioned Jared/Austin, things could get ugly. The last thing I needed was my parents, who were now officially against me, thinking I had anything to do with the robbery in Los Angeles.

Okay, fine, murder.

Olive had only met me for about two minutes in Los Angeles. And I looked completely different now. I'd had my blonde pixie hair when I stepped into The Belly Flop that day. My hair was now long and pitch black. If I could make the conversation a short one, I didn't think she'd recognize me.

"Actually, Mom, I'll go say hi."

"Who is Olive?"

"An old friend. I told her I was coming back for a few days."

"I don't remember anyone named Olive that you grew up with."

"Her real name is Jenny," I said; anything to get my mother off my back.

I left my room and approached the front door. I decided to speak with a distinct Southern accent. I'd certainly heard enough in my day. Anything I could to prevent her from recognizing me.

The door was ajar and I saw Olive waiting there. I wanted to find out how the hell she had found my parents' house, and by extension me, but I also wanted this to be as short a visit as possible.

My mother followed me, and if she listened to our conversation she'd soon know that Olive and I weren't old friends. So as I said "Hello," I shut the door behind me, leaving Olive and me alone outside.

"Hi, are you Becca?"

"I sure am," I said, with an exaggerated twang.

"This may sound weird, but did you know Jared Jenkins?"

"Sure, I remember him. Haven't seen him since high school, though."

I saw Olive's face fall flat. This must have been a huge letdown.

"Why?" I asked.

"I'm sorry, I'm probably wasting your time. He died recently and I was wondering if you might have any information."

"Jared died?" I asked, and started quietly crying.

It was a skill I had perfected over the years.

"I thought you would have known."

She looked deflated. I had nipped this potential problem in the bud less than a minute in.

"I don't really talk to old friends much. People in high school were mean to me," I said, looking as pathetic as possible.

I could tell this wasn't what Olive had hoped. She wanted to get the hell away, but I had to know one thing.

"Jared knew a lot of people. Why did you come here?"

"I went by your high school and your principal said you two were close."

"That was a long time ago. Olive, was it?"

There's no way she could have remembered me as the girl in LA. At that time, I had been dressed up with four-inch heels and bleached blonde hair. Now I was in grubby sweatpants with long black hair and an over-the-top accent.

"Yeah, Olive. Sorry I wasted your time," she said.

"No problem. Good luck," I said.

"Thanks." Olive started to walk away.

She was only here because our old principal, Evelyn Gillingham, had told her. And now she was gone. I had nothing to worry about from Olive Fairbanks.

_30_
<u>OLIVE</u>

I left Becca Poe's parents' house with more questions than answers. My first surprise had been to find Becca there at all. After I met with the Roswell High principal, I had googled *"Becca Poe Roswell"* and learned nothing of substance. It made sense. She and Austin had graduated from high school just over a decade ago. It was very unlikely she still lived there.

I managed to find a Mason and Sue Poe who lived in Roswell, the only Poes in the city. When an older woman answered the door and I mentioned Becca Poe, I was shocked to hear her tell me she'd go get her. Poe was an uncommon last name, so I had assumed it was her parents' house, but I hadn't expected Becca to be there.

As I stood outside and talked to her, I wasn't sure how to feel. She acted polite enough, doing nothing egregious. But I had a lingering feeling that something was off. The accent seemed too over the top. I had spent the last few days in Atlanta and hadn't heard a single accent like hers.

There was also a part of me that felt like I knew her. Or had met her. I couldn't place it, even when I tried to focus. I was a bartender who dealt with several hundred people on a weekly basis. Very possibly I was mixing up Becca Poe with somebody else.

The principal's warning about her had stuck in my mind, but Becca herself had done nothing to substantiate that. Yet I also found it weird that she hadn't heard of Austin's death. If she was close to him back in the day, how had that news not gotten back to her? Especially in their hometown.

In the end, none of that mattered. Becca Poe was living in Roswell, Georgia, with her parents. She couldn't know anything about a robbery that had happened several weeks ago in Los Angeles.

It looked like my Nancy Drew experiment wasn't going to be a bestseller.

Young woman goes to the town of the man she was dating and finds out absolutely nothing of importance.

Not exactly a tagline that would grab your attention.

I got back to my hotel with plans of keeping my return flight to LA the next morning. I checked the internet to see if there had been any updates on the robbery at Barry Gant's house, but nothing came up.

I flipped off my laptop and started reading a novel I had brought. I was all alone in a big city and looking forward to getting back to LA.

The brain is a weird, magical thing. Sometimes, an idea will be hovering in the dark recesses, and suddenly make an appearance when we least expect it.

I took an Uber the next morning back to Atlanta's Hartsfield-Jackson airport and checked in for my flight. Ten minutes before we were about to board, it hit me.

I did know Becca Poe! It had finally pushed its way to the front of my mind.

She had been in The Belly Flop a few months back. Probably a week before I met Austin. It was a bit hazy, but I remember she had asked a few questions about Barry Gant. That stuck out.

Her hair had gone from blonde to black and she'd looked more attractive on her previous visit to the bar, but that's only natural. She'd worn sweats when she talked to me outside of her parents' house.

But no doubt remained in my mind. It was the same woman.

I didn't have much time with my plane about to board, but I once again googled "Poe" and "Roswell," trying to find her parents' phone number just like I'd found their address. I couldn't find it, but since Becca's parents were older, I thought maybe they'd have a landline.

When I was young, my parents used 4-1-1 to find out people's home numbers. To my surprise, it still worked and I got the number for Mason and Sue Poe.

It was only 8:00 a.m., but I didn't really care about being polite anymore. Becca Poe was on my radar now.

"Hello?" came the voice of her mother.

"Is Becca there?"

"Whoever this is, you've got some great timing. She's about to step out the door. Becca, it's for you," I could hear her say.

A few seconds later, someone approached the phone.

"Mom, can I get some privacy?" the voice said. And then, "Hello?"

"Hi, Becca. This is Olive. We met yesterday."

"What do you want, Olive?"

"I just wanted to ask one question."

"And what would that be?"

"Have you been in Atlanta for the last several months?"

"I have."

"No trips to Los Angeles?"

"I've never been to Los Angeles in my life."

"Then how come I remember seeing you in my bar a few months ago?"

"Different woman. I've been in Atlanta the whole time. Sorry."

"Your accent sounds a little different today."

"Must be the reception. You know how these old landlines are," Becca said.

"You've got an answer for everything, don't you?"

"I guess I do."

"So, I'm going to ask you one last time. You haven't been in LA in the last several months?"

"Precious little Olive, how many times do I have to tell you that? I've been in Atlanta, hitting up our local community pool. I just love doing belly flops off the high dive."

My whole body froze. I couldn't respond for a few seconds.

"Belly flops, huh?"

"They are my favorite. Next time I'm going to float an olive on top of the pool. And just squash it as I land."

"Is that a threat?"

"You seem nice, Olive. This game isn't meant for you."

"You sure seem to be admitting a lot."

"I'm not admitting a single thing. Not that it matters. I'm too smart for you."

"It almost sounds like you're enjoying this," I said.

"No almost about it. I love it. I'm going to give you a warning now, Olive. If you go to the police, I'm going to pay you a visit in Los Angeles. I'm going to guess you live in a blue and gray building off of Wilshire Boulevard."

I felt like I had been hit in the stomach. She knew where I lived.

"So I was set up from the very beginning? You and Austin and whoever Chet Watkins was."

"I've never heard of those people."

"But you've heard of The Belly Flop?"

"The Belly Flop? No, I was merely talking about *doing* belly flops."

She seemed to be backtracking. I wondered if she feared she was being recorded.

"Why me?" I asked.

"Listen, Olive, I think I'm going to hang up now. I hope you don't go to the police with your silly and false accusations. I'd hate to have to pay you a visit."

"You killed them all, didn't you? It seemed too perfect that everyone shot each other, Mexican-standoff style."

"You've got an imaginative mind, Olive. A regular old Nancy Drew."

That was another gut punch. Austin and I had discussed my love of Nancy Drew, and he must have told her. She knew much more about me than I did about her. Had Austin told her about our sexual life? I felt violated.

I'd held up well considering the circumstances, but the voice on the other end was starting to scare me.

"Stay away from me," I said.

"That's contingent on you, Olive."

I was not sure why the next words came out of my mouth.

"Bring it on, you fucking murderer."

There was a long pause.

"I'll be seeing you again soon, Olive. You can count on it."

I hung up the phone and my whole body started shaking.

I didn't have time to calm down. A minute later my flight was called. It was time to head back to Los Angeles.

_31_
<u>BECCA</u>

"I'll be seeing you again soon, Olive. You can count on it," I said.

But I didn't mean it. At least not yet.

The last place I wanted to be was in Los Angeles. I wanted to deal with Olive down the road, but for now, it was time for me to disappear. I was sure she'd alert the police, so I'd be going as one of my many aliases for the near future.

I had to give it to Olive. She turned out tougher than I had assumed. She was still involved in a game she shouldn't be playing, but she didn't wilt at some of my comments. I'll give her that.

My mother walked back out to the kitchen. She smiled at me, which meant she hadn't listened in on the conversation.

"Are you really leaving, Becca? You just got here last night."

"Mom, you can't have Dad tell me that he never wants to see me again and then expect me to stay here and pretend everything is hunky dory."

"We hadn't heard from you in years. Can you blame your father, Becca?"

"Who is Becca?" I said.

My mother gave me a puzzled look. "Huh?"

"When I walk out of the door in a few minutes, there is no more Becca. I'll be dead to you guys just as you will be to me. I'd say it's been fun, Mom, but you know what? It hasn't."

My mother started to cry. I didn't care. I walked by her as I went to my room. It was time to get out of Roswell. For fucking ever.

For a woman who had so meticulously planned the perfect robbery, it seemed a little weird to be unsure of where to go next. Maybe that was for the best. With the police after me, which seemed likely after my conversation with Olive, it was probably better I didn't know where I was headed. If I didn't know, how the hell could they?

And yes, I probably should have kept denying and denying over the phone to Olive, but that's just not how I'm built. Plus, this made it more fun. My own little cat and mouse game. Me versus the police. And down the road, me versus Olive. But that was going to be easy. She wouldn't even see me coming. That was in the distant future, however. For now, it was time to get out of Dodge. And by Dodge, I meant Roswell, Atlanta, and the South in general.

It was time to head north.

32

OLIVE

My mind was racing as I took my seat in 34C to fly from Atlanta to Los Angeles.

Do I go to the police? Do I move apartments? Is Becca going to come after me?

I needed to go to the police. I was not going to move. And the third was to be determined, but I found it unlikely.

If she took part in the crime, which she basically admitted to me, why would she want to come back to Los Angeles, in the middle of an ongoing investigation?

I made a mental note to buy a dead bolt for my apartment, however, and maybe install a camera. I'd seen ads for cameras, relatively cheap. This was my life we were talking about, after all.

A baby two rows ahead of me sporadically cried throughout the flight. A handsome man sat right next to me.

And yet, all I could think about was Becca Poe.

I recreated our conversation. Had she admitted guilt? Not exactly, but by alluding to The Belly Flop and mentioning Nancy Drew, she made it obvious that she knew who I was. And the fact that I met Austin a week or so after Becca came into my bar was just too big of a coincidence.

Did they know that Barry Gant carried $75,000 dollars in his house? Had they used Austin to get to me, knowing I would lead them there? It seemed like that wasn't even a question anymore. All signs pointed to yes.

I'd alluded to Becca that I thought she could have been present at the robbery. Was it possible? Why would she leave $75k behind? Surely she would have taken it.

Unless there was a whole lot more than $75k. And she left it behind to make it look like everyone involved had been killed.

It was next-level criminality, which didn't mean it wasn't true.

My theory had some problems, however. After all, I didn't remember seeing a woman before I got knocked out. My last memory of someone walking toward us who was undeniably a man.

Also, Austin and Chet Watkins had been killed by Barry Gant's firearm. How could Becca know that Barry Gant was going to shoot them both? And why wouldn't he then shoot her?

Despite my interesting theory, it seemed unlikely that Becca Poe had been present at the robbery. But that didn't mean that she hadn't been the mastermind. Of that, I was almost certain.

Austin seemed nervous leading up to the night at Barry's. Becca seemed cool as a cucumber when we talked.

Austin wasn't mastermind material. Becca was.

Against all odds, I slept well the night I arrived back in Los Angeles. I must have been so exhausted from my trip to Atlanta that it superseded my nervousness. I didn't wake up till almost noon, when I put in a call to the LAPD.

"Officer Washington speaking."

"This is Olive Fairbanks. I was wondering if I could come in today."

"Olive, do you know we've had over twenty-five murders in Los Angeles since the ones you were involved in?"

"Then I guess you don't want to catch the killer."

"The killer? They killed each other."

"Okay, fine, the brains behind the operation. The ringleader. The mastermind."

"When can you get here?"

"Twenty minutes."

"I'll see you then."

I drove down to the precinct and Detectives Washington and Liston welcomed me. As had become custom, Liston deferred to Washington.

"So, what have you got?" Washington asked.

"Her name is Becca Poe," I said.

I spent the next five minutes detailing my trip to Atlanta, my meeting with the principal, going to Becca's parents' house, talking with her, remembering she had come to The Belly Flop, and finally my call where she all but admitted she was part of the conspiracy.

The officers didn't interrupt, letting me say my piece.

Surprisingly, Detective Liston spoke first.

"We don't encourage members of the general public to investigate crimes on their own, but I understand why this case is so personal to you. You've done some good detective work."

"So you think I might be right?"

"It's hard to say. You are fighting an uphill battle. There was no other DNA found in the house, on the gun, or on the $75,000. No suspicious phone calls or texts from either Jared Austin Jenkins or Chet Watkins to a woman who might have been involved. Doesn't that seem highly unlikely if this Becca Poe was in on it?"

I had to admit that it did.

"But we will check it out," Liston continued. "I can promise you that."

I had walked into the precinct with so much confidence, but it was slowly diminishing. The officers were saying all the right things, but I could tell they weren't fully on board with my story.

I knew I was right about Becca Poe, but I understood their side too. No DNA. No texts. No phone calls. Unless you counted my phone call. And that wasn't nearly enough.

The detectives promised to follow up on it and we vowed to meet the following week.

_33_
OLIVE

TWO MONTHS LATER

I hadn't met up with the detectives a week later. Or two weeks later. Or even two months later.

I'd called several times and they had told me that Becca Poe was not considered a suspect.

They told me there was no evidence that she had ever been in Los Angeles. No house owned, apartment rented, or hotel room checked out around the time of the robbery by someone named Becca Poe who was between twenty and forty years old.

They had contacted Becca's parents, but they had no idea where their daughter had taken off to. As far as they knew, their daughter had never spent any time in Los Angeles.

More and more murders had taken place across LA in the intervening months. While the Pacific Palisades murders garnered a lot of attention early on, I hadn't seen anything in the news in weeks. It had drifted from the public consciousness.

On the rare occasions I talked to the detectives, they'd tell me the case was still theoretically open, but they had more pressing needs. The last time I had called, Detective Washington asked nicely if I could give the calls a break.

It was over. At least in the eyes of the LAPD.

I had to go a different route.

Of all my old regulars at The Belly Flop, Richard Levert was the quietest. And the most aptly named. In our infrequent talks, he'd told me that he was a retired private detective. I was sure he had heard thousands of time in his life that "Dick" was the perfect name for a private eye, and I didn't feel the need to be Captain Obvious, but it stuck in my mind.

Richard told me he was retired, but he was only around fifty years old. I'd also seen a few shady-looking figures come talk to him at The Belly Flop over the years, so I wasn't sure just how retired he really was.

I decided to find out. My journey to being the next Nancy Drew had turned out to be a non-starter, so I wanted to give a real private eye a chance.

The LAPD had forgotten about Becca Poe. I hadn't.

I walked into The Belly Flop on a Thursday morning in early January. It was like the new year was giving me a new start. And hopefully some new eyes when it came to Becca Poe.

My money had started to dwindle and I'd realized it was time to get a job again. I had never received an offer to return to work at The Belly Flop and I started to realize that ship had sailed. I understood why.

I'd spent that morning giving my resume to a few bars and restaurants across Santa Monica. I had to include that I had bartended at the Belly Flop, obviously, but I just hoped they didn't ask too many questions about why I left.

The two months without working had been great for my writing. I was all the way up to Chapter Twelve, probably a third of the way through my novel. I was proud of myself.

But Becca Poe still dominated my thoughts when I wasn't writing. Early on, I thought every noise outside of my apartment could be her. That passed with time, but she still entered my consciousness daily.

And it's what brought me to The Belly Flop on a cold (for LA) winter morning.

What's nice about having regulars at your bar is that they really do keep to a specific schedule. Richard Levert had always been a Thursday and Friday regular. That was it. I'd never seen him any other day. In fact, I had most Fridays off, so Thursday was the day I would see him the most.

I smiled as I walked in and saw Richard sitting in his regular spot. I hadn't been in The Belly Flop since our GM, Tiffany Van Dyke, had effectively fired me back in early November, but not much had changed.

While serving old men drinks for a living might not seem like a dream job, I'd had a lot of good times here. I had laughed a lot, occasionally drank a lot, and met some interesting people from all over the world. Being a bartender wasn't all that bad.

I didn't recognize the new girl behind the bar, but as I approached it, several regulars recognized me.

"Olive!"

"Look who's back!"

"So good to see you!"

To the surprise of no one, Mark Midfield offered to buy me a Woo Woo. I said if I could take a rain check and have it in a half hour, I was in.

After I'd said all of my hellos, I approached Richard Levert, who had been his usual quiet self, although he'd smiled and waved in my direction.

Richard always had facial hair, just in varying degrees. Three days of scruff counted as clean-shaven for him. On this day, he had a full beard, which I actually thought made him look quite handsome. Well, maybe not handsome, but distinguished.

There was the scar that took up about three inches of the lower left of his face, however. It was tough to ignore, but I had never mentioned it to him. The full beard could only hide so much of it.

When I had met him, his beard was about half brown/half gray, but gray had definitely got the upper hand over the last three years. He wasn't all that tall, but he had tremendously strong arms, especially his forearms. The muscles and veins would contract when he went to sip a Guinness, his beer of choice.

"Hi, Olive. It's nice to see you."

I leaned in closer so people couldn't hear us.

"You too. Listen, Richard, do you think you could give me two minutes outside? There's a few things I'd like to ask you."

"Sure thing. I'll meet you out there. You can go first."

It was expertly done. He allowed me to walk out first so it wasn't obvious we were going to talk together. It certainly wasn't conclusive, but my first impression of Richard Levert as a private eye was a good one.

True to his word, he arrived outside a minute later.

"What is it, Olive? I'll be honest, this clandestine meeting is unlike you."

"If I tell you something, you know how to keep a secret, right?"

"Of course. It's a very important attribute in my line of work."

"So you aren't retired, are you?"

"I only take cases I'm really interested in. Semi-retired, I'd say."

I knew it. I leaned in closer to him and whispered, "Would it interest you if I said that the real mastermind of Barry Gant's murder is still on the loose?"

"I'd love to hear all you know, Olive."

"I want to hire you to do some investigating, but there's a minor problem."

"What's that?"

"I don't have much money left. I haven't worked since The Belly Flop effectively let me go. I've got about $5,000, although I did just apply for jobs this morning."

"Don't worry about that for now."

"Thanks so much, Richard. It's not like I'm totally broke. If your inquiries require you to fly somewhere, then I'll pay for it. And I can pay you a small hourly wage."

"This means a lot to you, doesn't it?"

"Of course. I was almost killed. Two people I knew were killed. Three total. And I think someone may have profited from it."

Richard took a long pause.

"Profited? I thought all the money was recovered at Barry Gant's house."

"No one knows how much he had in that safe," I said. I still wasn't sure if Becca had been at the scene of the crime, but I thought it was a possibility.

He paused again.

The back lot of The Belly Flop was almost always quiet, but a couple walked past us at that moment.

"Let's not talk here," Richard said. "Here, take my number down. I can meet up tomorrow if you'd like."

I entered his number into my phone.

"Thanks so much for your help, Richard."

"Don't thank me yet. Let's just see where this goes."

I met with Richard the next day at a quiet little diner on Pico Boulevard in Santa Monica. They knew Richard and gave him a booth in the corner. I imagined he had done a lot of business there over the years. He ordered a Reuben sandwich, and despite not being very hungry, I ordered a BLT for myself.

"So, lay it out for me, Olive. What do you know?"

I told him everything, leaving nothing out. He said "interesting" at least five times, but never interrupted.

"So what do you think?" I asked upon completing my account.

"If that phone call happened like you said, it sure sounds like an admission of something. The cops didn't follow up?"

"They did. But there was no woman's DNA on the scene, no incriminating texts from Austin or Chet Watkins to a third party, and no trace of Becca Poe ever having lived in LA."

"The cops' hands were tied."

"I know. That's why I came to you," I said.

"I'll take your case, Olive. We can deal with the money later. It's not common in my profession, but let's assume for now I'm taking this case pro bono."

"Thanks so much, Richard."

"Let's meet here next Friday at the same time and I'll tell you what I've found out."

_34_
<u>BECCA</u>

I did indeed go north. For two terrible months. I forgot how cold Boston and New York could be in the late fall and early winter. I booked a room in one hotel in each city for the entirety of my stay. Considering how much money I carried with me, it was way too dangerous to be continually ambulatory.

It's not like I could just deposit the money in my checking account, however. The IRS would come calling. More importantly, I feared the LAPD were monitoring my checking accounts, and if I deposited something as small as even ten grand, I wouldn't have an answer as to how I had come across that much cash.

So while I had good reasons for not doing anything with the money, I needed to get a house or a permanent apartment and install a safe. Moving around was just too risky.

A safe to keep my money safe. What a perfectly named word.

And I needed to get out of the cold weather.

I had been thinking a lot about Los Angeles. I had even called the LAPD saying I was a relative of Barry Gant's and asked if there were any updates on his murder. Not that I could put much stock in it, but I'd been told there was no new news. Better than the alternative.

It was still too early to move back to LA, but I knew I wanted to move close.

So I considered cities in the West.

There would be advantages to living in a city where cash was king. Where having hundreds of thousands of dollars wasn't unheard of.

I had a new destination in mind.

Las Vegas.

35

RICHARD

As a private investigator, I often got questions about the worst situation I'd ever been put in. Whenever I was asked that, I'd tilt my head so they could see the three-inch scar on the left side of my face.

And I'd tell the story of Jasper Miller.

He'd been the ultimate loser. Not someone born in the hood or raised as poor white trash. Someone like that at least had an excuse. No, Jasper Miller was the son of a Hollywood executive father and an actress mother.

Born with a silver spoon in his mouth, he grew up in Malibu and the Hollywood Hills. By the time I got his case, he was thirty years old and had fucked half of the actresses in Tinsel Town. I'm not sure he'd ever held a job, living off of his trust fund. He was constantly on the local news—slapping a woman, leaving no tip on a three-grand bar tab, getting a DUI. Always in trouble.

He came into my life in 2004. I was only thirty-eight and my private detective business was doing well. I made good money, had a lovely wife at home and two teenage boys. I would often get jobs from Hollywood types who I'd built up a nice rapport with.

Patsy Williams was an up-and-coming actress who had been the third lead in a few blockbusters and was going to be the next big thing. But she was in love with Jasper Miller, somehow managing to overlook everything she had heard about the guy. They had a six-month courtship and were married. Patsy was only twenty-two years old.

Jasper Miller got back in the news, but this time for all the right things. They'd say how he'd matured, leaving the partying Hollywood lifestyle behind. There was talk about Jasper and Patsy having a child.

But as time went on, Patsy realized she had made a huge mistake. While the media fawned over the new Jasper Miller, Patsy was stuck at home with a maniac. And one day, Jasper Miller crossed the line.

Patsy Williams entered my office late in 2004, and the first thing I noticed was her huge black eye. It didn't look like a fall. It looked like a punch. I didn't say anything, but knowing she was married to Jasper Miller, I had my assumptions.

I'd done work in the bars of Hollywood from time to time and heard about what a privileged jerk the guy could be. Rumors said that he had beaten up a few of his previous girlfriends and now I saw the evidence firsthand.

I suggested going to the police, but Patsy Williams didn't want the attention. I couldn't blame her. She was becoming famous, and even though it wasn't her fault in the slightest, a story like that could slow her ascent.

"So what exactly is it you want me to do?" I asked.

"I'm planning on divorcing Jasper, but I wanted to get some dirt on him before I file. I know he's cheating on me," she said.

It was one of the most common kinds of cases I got. A spurned lover hired me to see if their husband or wife was cheating. In this case, though, Jasper Miller was not only cheating on Patsy (I had no doubt), but he'd also hit her.

She offered a lot of money, and I knew I was going to take it, but this is the type of case I might have taken for free.

Keep in mind, this was a long time ago, when I still had my scruples. I took the Olive Fairbanks case pro bono out of greed. I know that sounds incongruous, but it's true. Only once I heard there might be money out there did I take it.

Anyway, within a week, I had evidence of Jasper Miller cheating. In a seedy motel off of Vine Street, I took pictures of Miller walking into the room with a 6-foot blonde on his arm. My camera was of the highest quality and left no doubt what the two would be doing. A few of the shots captured them kissing as they entered the room.

I told Patsy what I had. She asked me to come up to her house in the Hollywood Hills with the pictures.

"You sure you don't want to come to my office?" I asked.

"I'd rather you come here. Don't worry, Jasper went up to Santa Barbara for the day."

I agreed to meet her in an hour, being sure to bring the photos. I drove up into the Hills and parked in front of a house I'd never be able to afford. I knocked on the door three times, but didn't hear an answer. That worried me. I shook the handle and noticed it wasn't locked.

It probably wasn't the smartest thing to do, but I pushed the door open.

"Patsy, are you here?

"Patsy, it's me, Richard."

I didn't hear anything. I took a right into what looked like the living room.

That's when I saw her. She sat on a couch, her face cut up and blood everywhere on the white upholstery.

"My God," I said and ran to her side.

Before I got there, I was blind-sided by Jasper Miller. He tackled me to the ground and quickly jumped on top of me. He carried a huge knife that he brought down toward me. I leaned up and grabbed his wrist, slowing its momentum.

But he had the angle on me, and I couldn't slow his hand completely. He took the knife and dragged it across the left side of my face, going as deep as he could. I screamed out in pain.

He lifted the knife again, preparing to slice another part of my face off. I went for his wrist and got a better grip this time.

It was then that I saw Patsy Williams walking in our direction. Her face was a complete mess and I worried she'd never look the same. But in the moment, my concentration was on the huge porcelain vase that she carried above her head.

She took a few more steps and brought the vase down on the back of Jasper Miller's skull. He was knocked out immediately, and I pulled the knife from his hand.

"Call 9-1-1," I yelled to Patsy.

She left to find a phone, coming back thirty seconds later.

"Here, give me the phone," I said. "And can you get me some duct tape?"

I called 9-1-1 and Patsy returned a minute later with some duct tape. I didn't know how long Jasper Miller would be out and I wasn't going to take any chances. I grabbed his limp hands and put them behind his back, wrapping duct tape over and over.

Even if he came to, there's nothing he could do now. I stood up and felt my own face. I was bleeding pretty badly, but was more concerned for Patsy. She had gotten it much worse than me. I went and gave her a hug.

"Everything is going to be alright," I told her.

But it wouldn't be. Not for either one of us.

The police and an ambulance arrived several minutes later. I told the police what happened and they arrested Jasper Miller on the spot. Patsy and I were taken by ambulance to the hospital.

I got out two days later. I was going to be left with a nasty scar by my left jawbone, but other than that, I was alright.

Patsy wasn't so lucky. She had been cut over twenty times on her face, and even with many surgeries, she would never look the same. Her Hollywood star never rose again. Even with the best makeup specialists in the world, Patsy Williams' injuries would always be visible, which meant she wasn't viable as a leading woman any longer.

She got some smaller roles for a few years, but slowly faded into obscurity. Last I heard, she had returned home to Missouri.

Jasper Miller got twenty years for attempted murder and kidnapping, having kept Patsy against her will as he spent fifteen minutes cutting her up.

I could live with my scar and almost took it as a badge of honor, but the incident had a longer-lasting effect on me. Everyone now knew me as the guy who'd fought with Jasper Miller. And, completely unfairly, I was labeled as the guy who couldn't keep Patsy Williams safe.

That couldn't have been further from the truth, but it's the impression that lingered. Because of it, the rich Hollywood types didn't want to do business with me anymore. My jobs lessened in the months after the incident, and they came to a grinding halt some time later.

Without my high-paying contracts from the rich of Los Angeles, I had to resort to taking less than desirable gigs. I still had two teenagers at home and needed to make money. But without the bigger paydays that Hollywood gave me, I struggled. The lack of money had been a big factor in my wife and I eventually getting a divorce.

The incident in the Hollywood Hills had ended poorly for all of us.

It would be fifteen years until I got a case that might turn around my rotten luck. And it was brought to me by Olive Fairbanks.

I always knew that Olive was a sharp cookie. She didn't seem to buy my "retired" bit, and she was right. I wasn't retired. I was too broke to retire. In fact, I was too broke to drink more than a few days a week at The Belly Flop. I'd have preferred to be sitting on that barstool six days a week and looking at the beautiful girls go by. Olive included.

So while I didn't have any plans to take Olive's case, I played nice and heard her out as we talked behind The Belly Flop. And then she mentioned that there might be some stolen money still out there, so I pretended to be Mr. Sympathetic and agreed to look into things.

It wasn't out of the goodness of my heart, nor out of any empathy toward Olive or Barry Gant. I was a greedy son-of-a-you-know-what and I hoped to get my share of the money. If there was any. I had my doubts about Olive's assumptions, but now I would investigate. And hope she was right.

Being a private eye, private detective, private dick, or whatever else you wanted to call me had led me to gather some rather unsavory connections over the years. They were great with credit card receipts, plane tickets, rental agreements, and the like. That was the place I figured I would start.

If Olive was indeed correct and this Becca Poe had somehow come away with money from the robbery, then I looked forward to making her acquaintance.

After all these years of living poor, it was time to get my own nest egg.

36

OLIVE

Handing the case off to Richard Levert had been a relief. For the first time in a long time, I wasn't constantly worrying about what happened at Barry Gant's house. It didn't hijack my every thought. I was more relaxed than I had been at any time since, well, since I was dating Austin.

Which made me mad, since we really hadn't been dating at all. I was now completely convinced that Becca Poe had brought Austin to LA to court me, hoping I would lead them to Barry Gant.

It also pissed me off because the last time I remembered being happy was in the arms of a man who didn't give a shit about me. Even worse, he had put me in harm's way, and likely knew I might die.

I told myself the next man I fell for was going to be a dorky, nice guy who only had the best intentions. At least, that was the plan.

I got some good news: I had been hired by a Santa Monica bar called Rick's Tavern on Main, a reference to Main Street, where it was located.

A neighborhood bar, it had a great clientele. I'd only been there once, but when you worked as a bartender, word got around about the good and bad spots to work at, and Rick's always had a great reputation.

So things were looking up for me, at least on the employment front.

My first shift started a few days later and it went by in a split second. Time always flies when you're busy and I spent the day learning where all the bottles and taps were. Rick's definitely had a different vibe than The Belly Flop, with a much younger crowd. I'm sure it wasn't always the case, but on that day, Richard Levert or Mark Midfield would have been the oldest men in the bar.

I saw two cute guys that I would have liked to talk too, but things just moved too fast that day. The woman training me, a pretty brunette named Zara, made sure to tell everyone that I was on my first shift. She meant it as a preemptive strike in case I was slow or didn't get a drink just right. But I liked it, because if either of the two guys heard her, I felt sure they'd come and visit Rick's again.

And hopefully I'd have more time to talk.

I went home after that first night. The ivy had started to grow over the entrance of my apartment complex, overtaking the white awning. I often wondered why I had stayed at the complex after being threatened by Becca Poe. It was extremely melodramatic, but I thought of people going back to work after a terrorist attack. The whole "you can't let the terrorists win." I felt I'd have let Becca win if I just moved apartments right away.

That being said, every time I entered my complex, my head was on a swivel. And I had certainly proved my toughness, not moving out right away. I no longer needed to stay. Now, with my job down near the beach of Santa Monica, maybe it was time to get a new apartment.

As I approached my door, I heard a quick noise coming from my left. It was just a cat scurrying through, but as always, it gave me pause.

37

BECCA

Within a few days of moving to Las Vegas, I wondered why I hadn't spent my whole life there. Wow, what a city! I loved the hustle and bustle of the Las Vegas strip. You could easily get lost in the sea of tourists, rich gamblers, and even the ones looking for a $5 steak deal at one of the seedier casinos.

I loved it.

I had only been to Vegas once in my life, when I was living in Phoenix. I'd been trying to play a guy named Roger, and when he invited me to Vegas a few weeks in, I took it as a good sign. When we arrived at our room at Circus Circus, I knew we weren't going to last. Roger thought he was crazy when he upped his blackjack bet from five to ten dollars and I couldn't wait to be done with him.

But this time was different. I had found my home. The only drawback was that it was January and I'd have to wait a few months to enjoy a Vegas summer.

I had changed my hair again, now shoulder-length and red. I figured the whole investigation had come to a grinding halt, but there was no reason not to be safe. And maybe, just maybe, Olive was out there looking for me. Sure, if she saw me up close, she'd know me, but from afar, she wouldn't recognize the auburn shade I'd chosen.

She'd seen me as a blonde and a dark brunette, but not as a redhead.

And I thought the color was perfect for Vegas. It drew attention, and while I didn't want attention from Olive or the police, I did want it from the wealthy men visiting the casinos. Sure, I had enough money to last years, if not decades, but I could be a greedy bitch. Okay, not could be. I was.

I really only had one worry in the world, the same one I'd had since I left Barry Gant's house with $675,000.

How was I to launder it? I couldn't just carry the money around forever, but I also couldn't put a large sum in the bank. I'd have no way to explain how little old unemployed me had come across so much cash. I had several fake I.D.s which were fine for fooling a guy or a gullible landlord, but none of them would work for opening a checking account. I wasn't that sophisticated.

I still had a checking account in my own name that had $1,600 in it, but I hadn't used it since I first moved to Los Angeles. I had taken out a huge amount of cash when I left Phoenix, not wanting to leave a paper trail when I was in LA. And after the robbery at Barry Gant's, I had been afraid to make a deposit, fearful the LAPD was monitoring me. Sure, I had designed the perfect crime, but there was no harm in remaining vigilant. So I hadn't used my checking account in over three months.

But it was time to do something. I remained constantly afraid of being mugged, even though I watched the money like the most observant hawk in the world. The suitcase that held it all—shockingly reasonably sized—rarely left my sight, and when out in public, never left my hand.

So after calling the LAPD one last time, from a pay phone of all things, this time pretending to be a reporter, I rested easy that the investigation into the murders was all but over. Finally, the time had come to stop carrying around a suitcase full of cash.

I went down to two local Las Vegas banks and opened two separate safety-deposit boxes under my own name. I figured if by some chance, even if it was one in a million, something happened to one, I'd still have $300k in the other.

It was a load off of my mind to get the money put away.

A safety-deposit box was a lot more subtle than depositing $600k into my checking account.

I kept $50k just for spending money, still not wanting to leave a paper trail. I'd continue to use cash. The other $25k had been spent over the last several months in Boston and New York. I realized that even though I had a shitload of money, it could go quickly.

Maybe it was time for another sugar daddy. No shortage of them in Las Vegas.

After getting the safety-deposit boxes, the next thing I needed was a place to live, having spent my first few days at the MGM Grand. I decided to rent a suite at Veer Towers, two residential high-rises located within the Vegas CityCenter located on the Strip. The Aria was the closest casino.

How easy. I found someone renting it out for six months on Craigslist. I gave him one of my fake I.D.s, but he barely looked it over. I was paying him in cash, after all.

A rich Asian, he was going back to work in Hong Kong or Singapore or one of those damn places. He wouldn't be coming back to check up on me for a long time. I gave him three months' rent ahead of time and told him I'd wire the rest of the money at the start of the fourth month. He was fine with that.

Once I got settled at Veer Towers, I spent the next week getting acquainted with my new city.

_38_
<u>RICHARD</u>

I didn't get much information on Becca Poe in the first few weeks of my investigation. Scratch that, I got zero information on her. And I was happy about it.

The fact that we saw absolutely no spending from any credit card, debit card, or gas card piqued my interest. I started to consider the possibility that Olive was right about this whole thing. Maybe Becca really had gotten away with lots of money.

If you never paid with a credit card, one possibility was you had a nest egg of cash built up. I hoped that was the case.

So, for a rare time in our business, I thought no news was good news. But then I got news, and it was a bombshell.

Sometimes in banking you get your news a little late. Things can fall through the cracks, especially if you're getting your information secondhand, which I most definitely was. So I wasn't surprised to hear about a transaction that had taken place several days earlier.

Hector Reyes worked in the information business, with ears all across the nation. He had been a loyal friend for years, not easy to find in this business, and he'd always gotten me the goods. This time was no exception. I'd given him instructions after meeting with Olive, but hadn't heard back from him since then.

"I've found Becca Poe for you," he called to tell me one day.

I was driving in bumper-to-bumper traffic on Interstate 405. I'd have welcomed any distraction, and this was the best kind.

"Great work, Hector."

"Well, I haven't found her per se, but I know what city she's in."

"And where would that be?"

"Sin City."

I smiled. It was a great city to launder or hide money.

"What do you mean, you haven't found her per se?"

"Well, it wasn't a hotel room or a gas station receipt or anything like that."

This dance had gone on too long. "Spill it, Hector. You'll get your money from me."

"She opened up two separate safety-deposit boxes in Vegas."

Jackpot!! My mind started seeing dollar signs. And the fact that she'd opened two separate boxes made me think it might be a huge amount.

"You've done great work, Hector."

"I know."

"Nothing else? No hotel bill or rental agreement?"

"That's it. She's like a ghost in the town except for the two boxes."

Better that I left it as it was. Hector was a great friend, possibly my best, but I didn't need to tell him all the money that might be in those safety-deposit boxes. I had learned to trust no one in this business, and that included your friends.

"Great work. And I'll send you the second half of your money tonight."

"Thanks, Richard. Pleasure doing business. Let's get some lunch soon."

"I'd like that," I said. "I'll call you next week."

I hung up the phone and started shadowboxing with my steering wheel. This was it! My big payday. Or at least, I hoped so. My confidence that Olive had been right grew and grew. Why else open up two safety-deposit boxes, but then leave no traces of having been in that same town?

I had a brief sinking feeling. What if she wasn't in Vegas, but just made the deposits there? She could have easily kept enough cash to live. In that case, she could be anywhere. And I'd be fucked.

But I didn't believe that. If you had two boxes with, potentially, hundreds of thousands of dollars in them, wouldn't you want to be in the vicinity? I know I would. No, I thought Becca Poe was definitely in Vegas.

And I knew, like everyone else, that $75,000 had been left at the crime scene. How much money would you have to make out with to leave $75,000 behind? The answer: a lot!

I did have another problem on my hands. Olive. I couldn't tell her the truth. She might go back to the cops with the information on Becca. They would investigate and I'd have no chance of getting my big payday.

I wouldn't be telling Olive. Which got my mind wandering. If I ended up making a deal with Becca Poe for some of her money, Olive would be the only one tying me to it.

But I was getting way ahead of myself.

I booked my flight as soon as I got home. Vegas was a big city, but it was also a pretty consolidated city if you wanted to be where the action was. I didn't think I'd have a problem finding Becca Poe rolling around the Strip on a regular basis.

I searched for pictures of Becca Poe of Roswell, Georgia online, but wasn't able to find anything besides a senior high school portrait. I called Olive and asked her to describe Becca for me. She asked if I had any leads and I lied, telling her I just needed a description for some of my connections. She seemed to buy it.

I finished the conversation with a very vague description of Becca. The one thing that stood out was that her appearances had been completely different the two times Olive had met her. Once her hair was short and bleached blonde, the other time long and pitch black. I could use that information. In my experience, women who drastically changed their appearance did it with panache, choosing something that stood out.

After all, why shapeshift all the time if you weren't going to stand out?

Lastly, I might have been assuming a lot, but I didn't think she'd be a blonde or a dark brunette. After she'd given Olive a reason to suspect her, she'd try to look different if there was ever a third meeting.

I didn't rule out any other hair color, but in my mind I imagined her with light brown hair. Or as a redhead.

__39__
<u>BECCA</u>

Vegas had been growing on me every day. Definitely a city for a grifter. In most places on earth, you'd have to roll around for days looking to find a mark. In Vegas, potential scores surrounded you every single time you set foot on the casino floor.

I had already successfully robbed two men of several thousand each. It's not like I needed it, but a little extra spending cash came in handy for an expensive city like Vegas.

Both went down in a similar fashion. I looked for a man at the craps table who had a lot of money in front of him. I'd start batting my eyes and looking at him with my bedroom eyes.

I also made sure he had no wife with him, but that he did have a wedding ring on.

There was a method to my madness. A married man would be far less likely to report a theft to the hotel. He'd have to say that a woman he invited up to his room had stolen the money. The last thing these guys wanted was a call to their wife a week later saying they had caught the woman who had been with their husband.

So I chose married men.

After they finished up on the craps table, I'd convince them to go to a hotel bar before we went upstairs. I'd order a few quick drinks and let nature take its course. Usually, and it was the case with both men, they had already been drinking excessively, so a few quick shots put them right over the edge.

I then escorted them up to their rooms, and yes, I realize the connotation "escort" has. I have no shame.

The first man was extremely drunk by time we left the bar. He never even made it to the cage to cash out. We started kissing on the elevator up, and I took his pants off as soon as we arrived in his room. As the foreplay progressed, I could tell he wasn't feeling well. He rushed to the bathroom and as he puked his guts out, I went to his pants. There I found three $5,000 chips and two $500 chips.

I grabbed one of the $5,000 chips. He was drunk and he was married, but if I stole it all, I felt sure he'd report it.

Once he came out of the bathroom, puke still on his face, no excuse seemed necessary and I just left. Five thousand dollars richer.

The second man wasn't as inebriated and had cashed out before we went to the room. We ended up having sex, and as he took a post-coital shower, I went in his pants and took about a quarter of the huge wad of hundreds he had.

I stayed until he got out of the bathroom, so as not to be too obvious. When I counted my haul later, it amounted to $3300.

So I'd made $8300 in the span of a week.

Did I need to do this? Obviously not, but I enjoyed it. I'd told myself many times that the robbery at Barry Gant's house had been all about the money. And that was true. For the most part. But part of me just enjoyed the risk. The action. The fear of getting caught.

I had orchestrated a triple homicide with no ties back to me.

I was an evil genius. And only getting better.

I was going to go down in history.

I felt bulletproof.

40

RICHARD

I had no immediate sighting of Becca upon getting to Vegas. It's not like I walked into Caesar's Palace, a woman walked by, and I knew it was her. This wasn't going to be that type of work. And I knew that.

I needed to do hard detective work, the likes of which I hadn't done in years. When I first started getting into my career, after failing to pass the bar exam for the fourth time, I thought I was the most brilliant private detective in the game. I might not make it as a lawyer, but I was plenty smart to work in my new industry.

Many brutes chose this line of work, and while I could play that card when necessary, I liked to view myself on a higher plateau. In my early years, I found people in Los Angeles who had ten different P.I.s looking for them. It wasn't my brute strength that led me to them. It was my ingenuity. My detective work.

And that's what it was going to take to catch Becca Poe.

I came up with a crazy plan in which I'd page Becca Poe at every Vegas Casino, pretending to be Olive.

First off, I needed a woman's voice. I called Cora Mendelsohn, my off-and-on girlfriend, and asked her for a favor. We were currently off, but she still loved me and I knew she'd do anything I asked.

"I want you to say, 'Meet me at the lobby bar in ten minutes. It's Olive,'" I told her.

She did it, but it didn't exactly sound right.

"Try to sound younger," I said.

"You sure know how to impress a woman, Richard."

"I'm sorry, honey." She always ate it up when I called her honey. "Just try to sound like you're in your mid-twenties."

Cora tried it a second time as I recorded from my end. It wasn't perfect, but it would have to do. I'd recorded it on one of my two cell phones— multiple phones being a necessity for any private eye.

I gambled that Becca Poe wouldn't exactly be the best judge of voices in that moment. She'd be so befuddled and in shock I probably could have used my voice.

"That will work, Cora, thanks!"

"What's going on, Richard?"

"I can't tell you now, but how about taking a vacation with me sometime soon?"

"That sounds nice," she said.

"Gotta run. I'll call you in a few days."

I was staying at The LINQ Hotel, which offered a pretty inexpensive room. I expected to be there several days, and I couldn't afford the $300 or more a night at a place like Wynn.

I could always hit up Olive if the bills became too much, but I didn't want her knowing I was in Vegas. For obvious reasons.

I'd arrived on Wednesday and devised my ingenious plan on Thursday, so Friday was the night to try it out. I couldn't just call up haphazard hotels along the Strip. On a Friday night, it could take quite a while to get from one side of the Strip to the other. Even if Becca Poe did go to the lobby bar after she heard my message, she wouldn't hang around forever. I needed to be in the vicinity of the casino I was calling to make it there on time.

If I missed the chance, and Becca learned that Olive was looking for her, I'd probably never see her again.

So I needed to do it section by section.

Deciding to start at the south end of the Strip, I took a cab to the Luxor. In my first attempt, I could knock out Mandalay Bay and the Delano, the Luxor, Tropicana, Excalibur, the MGM Grand, and New York, New York.

I was close enough to all of them that if she picked up the phone, I could easily get there in ten minutes. If she didn't answer any of them, I'd take a cab to a more centrally location for the next batch of casinos.

The Luxor, like most casinos in Vegas, was loud on a Friday night, and I started looking around for a quiet place. Midway through, I reconsidered. Having the background noise would be beneficial when I played the tape of Cora Mendolsohn's voice. It would make it more difficult for Becca to tell it wasn't Olive.

I tried Mandalay Bay and the Delano with no luck. They both seemed more than willing to page someone, although with cell phones, I'm sure that practice had dwindled sharply over the years. I waited on the line four or five minutes each time, but no luck. Next, I tried the Luxor itself, which would have worked out perfectly, but it wasn't to be.

The next four casinos brought nothing either. I was starting to wonder if my plan was as good as I had originally thought. I decided that it was, the problem being that even if Becca was at one of these casinos, there was no guarantee that she would pick up the page. I assumed that curiosity would get the better of her, but I couldn't be sure.

There was the chance she had settled in some apartment in the suburbs of Summerlin or Henderson. But from the little I knew about Becca, that seemed unlikely. She seemed like a woman who would want to be near the action.

I took a cab to the Aria to begin on my next block of hotels. I found a slot machine near the front entrance where I could get to the cabstand in a matter of seconds, and started my calls.

No luck with Aria or The Cosmopolitan. A false alarm at Bally's when they thought someone was on the line, but it had just been a mistake.

This was growing tiresome and I had completed less than half my route, not even considering the smaller casinos that were off the Strip.

Next up, Paris, which had a recreation of the Eiffel Tower out front. Though an average casino by Vegas standards, I'd stayed there in the past and never had a problem with it.

I called.

"Hi, you've reached Paris Las Vegas."

"I'd like to page someone."

"Just a second."

They transferred me to someone else.

"I'd like to page someone."

"The name?"

"Becca Poe, from Olive."

"Olive?"

"She's my niece and with me right now. She can't find her mom, Becca, who has no cell phone."

"Oh, I'm sorry to hear that. I'm sure we'll find her. Let me page her now. Please hold."

"Thanks."

I had almost given up at this point. There was no reason to get my hopes up when I was likely to just be disappointed each time. This was my tenth casino, after all.

A few minutes later, the same voice came back on the line.

"Told you we'd find her," she said excitedly. "Transferring you right now."

I readied my second cell phone with the recorded message of Cora Mendolsohn. I turned the volume up, ensuring Becca would hear it.

"Hello," the other end of the line said.

I positioned my two cell phones next to each other and pressed play.

"Meet me at the lobby bar in ten minutes. It's Olive," blasted from the phone. There was no way she hadn't heard it.

I hung up and headed directly to the cab stand. Three people stood in line, not bad for a Friday night. I just hoped I could get to the Paris lobby bar in time.

About eight minutes later, my cab pulled up to the front of the Paris. I threw the guy a twenty and told him to keep the change. Every second counted and I couldn't sit there and wait.

Luckily, I knew the layout of Paris and headed directly toward Le Central Bar. My plan was far from foolproof, but it wasn't feasible to have Cora name a different bar for each casino. I just hoped Becca would go to Le Central, the biggest and best-known of the Paris lobby bars.

Becca had no idea what I looked like or who I was, but I still felt I should be as discreet as possible. When she realized that Olive wasn't showing, she'd surely be suspicious and looking around. Better to not be recognized.

As I approached Le Central, I slowed and started looking around. I figured Becca would be easy to spot. While I only had a brief description of her and an old yearbook photo, she'd likely be looking around as if she was waiting for someone.

I scanned the front of the bar and didn't see anyone who fit her description: attractive, late twenties, likely but not limited to light-haired brunette or redheaded, looking over her shoulder.

I headed to the other side of the bar. And then I saw her—now a stunning redhead. I could see how the guys who partook in the robbery fell under her spell. Becca was beautiful and had a sexiness about her that you couldn't fake.

She stood about five feet from the bar, and as I had figured, her head was on a swivel. She tried to act composed, but there was no mistaking what I saw. I felt positive I'd spotted her.

I didn't dare get closer for fear of being remembered. I kept my eye on the bar, but I hoped she'd be heading for the cab stand when Olive didn't show.

After a few more minutes passed, Becca still stood there. She had to be considering that Olive wasn't going to show. Still, she lingered longer.

Finally, I saw her leave the bar and head in my direction. I assumed she was getting the hell out of Paris so I headed toward the cab stand.

I got in the line and less than a minute later, Becca Poe snuck in, a few people behind me. This wasn't my first rodeo and I knew exactly what I was going to do.

The line at the Paris was longer than at the Aria, and we waited nearly ten minutes to get to the front.

"Where to?" the man in charge of the cabstand asked.

"The Mirage," I said, making it up on the fly.

"One to the Mirage."

I got in the yellow cab.

"Can you pull over up here to the right? I'm actually following my friend who's a few cabs behind me. Not sure if we're still going to the Mirage."

I imagined this happened a lot in Vegas and I was hoping the cabdriver wouldn't ask any questions. He didn't, pulling over just as I had asked. I turned around and looked behind me, seeing Becca Poe get into the third cab after mine.

"That's the one," I said.

The cab pulled out and started following behind Becca Poe's cab. She approached Las Vegas Boulevard and took a right, heading north. My driver did the same.

"Please don't lose her. I lost my cell phone earlier."

We followed a little too closely for my preference, but it was better than the alternative of losing her. When we arrived at her destination, I wasn't going to get out and follow Becca. If she saw me at the bar, at the cab stand, and then a third time, surely she'd get suspicious.

We continued going north on Las Vegas Boulevard and I took in the lights of one of the most iconic cities in the world. Becca's cab eventually took another right and I could tell that she was headed to Wynn.

"Expensive taste," I said under my breath.

We followed Becca's cab to the front and I saw her get out. Maybe she planned on doing some gambling or drinking, but I severely doubted it. After the scare of a page from Olive, I was 99% sure Becca had headed back to wherever she was staying.

"You know what," I told the cabdriver. "I'm pretty exhausted. I think I'm just going to go back to my room at The LINQ if you don't mind."

"Whatever," the guy said. He couldn't care less about what was going on.

He drove out of the parking lot and started heading toward The LINQ. I turned around and looked at the majestic Wynn Casino as we drove away from it.

I'd be back there soon. Now that I knew where Becca was staying, I had the upper hand. Big time.

_41_
<u>BECCA</u>

I don't often get nervous, but my heart sank for a brief moment when I heard the page come over the loudspeaker at the Paris casino. Becca Poe, from Olive.

How did she know I was in Vegas? Was she with the police? Was I going to be arrested?

My anxiety evaporated when I picked up the phone.

"Meet me at the lobby bar in ten minutes. It's Olive," a voice said.

I had only met Olive two times, but the voice on the other end was most assuredly not her. I was still interested, of course, but no longer worried.

Lobby bars were easy to find in Sin City. Every casino had one, making it a good meeting point for people congregating on the casino floor. I had walked by the Le Central Bar at the Paris a few times since moving to Vegas and knew where to find it.

I headed there immediately, hoping to arrive before whoever had paged me. I got there within two minutes of receiving the page and took up a spot several feet behind the bar. I was able to see my side of the bar as well as anyone approaching from the other side.

About five minutes later, I saw a man approaching. He looked around, which shouldn't be a surprise, since a lobby bar was a place where people waited for friends, but the way he held himself made me think this was something different.

Somewhere around fifty, he had a big scar on the left side of his cheek. He was stocky and he could snap me like a pretzel if he wanted too.

He moved slowly, looking at both sides of the bar before making his way toward me. I had been expecting a woman, but this changed things.

I thought back to the voice on the phone. It had sounded a little distant. Had a woman even been on the other end of the line? Could it have been a recording? I wasn't sure, but what I was certain of was that this guy had my full attention.

He got within about twenty feet of me and I could feel his eyes take a quick look in my direction. Trying to be inconspicuous, he walked toward the other side of the bar. I didn't buy it. I could see him through the bar and it didn't look like he was waiting for anyone. Well that's not exactly true. It looked like he was waiting for me.

Several minutes later, I left the lobby bar and headed toward the front entrance of the Paris. When I got outside, he stood in the cabstand in front of me. I watched as he got in a cab. It pulled over about fifty feet ahead.

That's when I knew I was right.

"Where to?" the man asked as my cab got there.

"Wynn," I said.

No reason to let him know that I lived at Veer Towers. I got in and watched as we drove past the other cab, who immediately started following behind us.

I came up with an idea on the spot.

"What's your name?" I asked.

"Ron."

"Ron, I have a favor to ask."

"Sure," he said.

I had used my sexiest voice and Ron seemed pretty into it.

"There's a car behind us. This guy has been following me most of the night from casino to casino. It's getting creepy."

"That's terrible. What do you need?"

I figured the man at the bar wouldn't get out at Wynn. Not the smart choice. He had just seen me at the bar and the cab stand, and it would be pretty obvious he was following me if I spotted him a third time.

"I'm going to write down my phone number for you. If the man doesn't get out at Wynn, I'd like you to follow his cab, then call me and tell me where he was dropped off."

I took out a hundred-dollar bill and dropped it on the front seat.

"Could you do that for me?" I asked.

"Sure. What's your name?" he asked. "For when I call back."

That's not why he wanted to know, but I didn't care.

"Kelsey," I said, making up just another name in my long lexicon of fake ones.

We arrived at Wynn and I started to get out of the cab.

"Looking forward to your phone call," I said.

"You can count on me, Kelsey."

I walked to the entrance of Wynn. When I turned around, the man wasn't walking toward me, so it seemed he had stayed in his cab, just as I had assumed.

Thirty minutes later, I got a phone call.

"Is this Kelsey?"

"It sure is. Is this that sexy cabdriver?"

"Stop," Ron said, and it's almost like I could see him blushing through the phone.

"So what happened?"

"You were right, the guy stayed in the cab. I followed them and he was dropped off at The LINQ Casino. Do you know it?"

"I do. Thanks so much for your help."

"Kelsey, I was wondering if you wanted to…"

I hung up the phone. Like I would ever in a million years go out on a date with a cabdriver.

But he had delivered the information I wanted. I now knew where the mystery man was staying. I had the upper hand. Big time.

42

RICHARD

After following Becca Poe to Wynn Casino, I had the cabdriver take me back to my place at The LINQ Casino. It was only 9:30, but I hoped to be able to fall asleep early.

I knew who she was, what she looked like, and where she stayed. On top of that, I was bigger, stronger, and had the element of surprise working for me. I didn't see how I couldn't win.

That didn't mean I was getting cocky. This business could throw you a curveball sometimes, and I made sure I had planned for every contingency. Plus, it's not like Becca Poe had many good options. She could either go with me to the bank and give me half of her money, or I'd threaten to turn her in to the cops. I think she'd come to the right decision. And if there was as much money as I hoped, she'd still have plenty left for herself.

I googled the two banks' information and found out that they were only open until noon on Saturday. I didn't have enough time to finalize my plan and realized I'd have to wait until Monday to implement it.

I went to sleep with dollar signs spinning in my head.

I woke up Saturday morning feeling as good as I had in years. Yes, the looming payday had a lot to do with it, but I was also just in a good state of mind overall. At the top of my game. Paging Becca Poe and finding her that way, when no one else would have thought of it, had given a boost to my ego. And deservedly so.

I called Olive and told her no progress had been made. It was quite the whopper, but she didn't suspect a thing. How could she?

I decided to walk along the Strip and enjoy the fresh air. I left The LINQ and strolled through their outdoor area, past their version of the Millennium Wheel in England. Some nice bars had outdoor seating, but this early in the morning I didn't want the minimal haze that even one beer would bring.

Plus, once I got half of Becca Poe's money, I could drink every day for the rest of my life if I wanted. No more having two pints at The Belly Flop and worrying about how it would affect my bottom line. No more being late for rent every other month. No more having to take seedy jobs to make ends meet.

I doubled back toward The LINQ and walked into O'Shea's Casino, losing $5 on a slot machine. I exited through The LINQ and made my way back out on the Strip. It was a crisp January morning, hardly what you think of when you think of Vegas. The polar opposite of the hot, oppressive summers.

At least for me. Young people seemed to love the beach clubs and all that, but it was too much.

I walked through the Hilton and continued to head down the Strip, occasionally putting a few dollars in slot machines along the way. By the time I made it all the way to the MGM Grand, I had lost $25. Considering I had never been a big gambler, that was a lot of money to me. Of course, with my impending payday, I paid it no mind.

While I gambled as I went, the primary reason for the walk was to nail down my plan regarding Becca Poe. I always thought better when I was moving, and once I had finished my walk, I felt pretty sure I had finalized my plan. I walked farther than I realized, so I grabbed a cab back to the LINQ Casino.

I sat down at a breakfast spot called Hash House A Go Go and ordered a coffee and some pancakes. They arrived, literally the biggest pancakes I'd ever seen. I only ate half of them, but I did have three cups of coffee which made my mind laser-focused.

The bill came, which I paid, and I made my way back up to my room. I went over my plan one more time, incorporating a few minor changes. It was now perfect.

_43_
BECCA

Having the upper hand was one thing, but using that to my advantage was something else altogether. Obviously, I could have just gone to my banks and picked up the money and gone on the run again. But that would just be postponing the inevitable. The man had found me once and surely he could find me again.

Olive must have hired him. No one else knew who I was.

I guessed that the two safety-deposit boxes had led him to me. My place at Veer Towers remained under the original guy's name, and I couldn't think of another way in which he could have found me. If he did it through the banks, this guy had connections, and I'd never be able to set up another safety-deposit box without fear of being found.

And I couldn't live with the possibility that he'd go to the cops. They'd likely seize the money and assuredly put out a warrant for me.

My other option was to go back to carrying around six hundred thousand dollars in cash. I wasn't ready to do that again. It was too stressful to think every guy walking by you could grab your suitcase. It also made flying impossible, unless I wanted to risk going through airport security. And go to jail for life if I got caught? No, thanks.

There weren't many good options on the table, but getting rid of this guy once and for all seemed the most reasonable to me. I didn't want to spend my life running. I had done enough of that.

I considered two possibilities. One, the man had already called Olive, who in turn would probably call the police. This seemed unlikely. Why chase me around if you were just going to call the police once you found me? Second, and more likely, the man had been hired by Olive and either the two of them wanted some of my money, or the guy had gone rogue and wanted the money for himself.

And if that was the case, I had a second huge advantage. He wasn't going to kill me, at least not initially. He needed me to go to the bank first.

But I wasn't going to let it get that far.

I finalized my plan, knowing I needed to make a stop at a Rite Aid.

_44_
__RICHARD__

The rest of Saturday was unremarkable. I lost a little more money and ordered room service, falling asleep to some cheesy '90s action movie.

I woke up Sunday morning knowing I was one day away from my big payday. Early Monday, I planned to rent a car. I'd be ostensibly kidnapping Becca Poe and I couldn't drive around in a cab. I would park the car in Wynn's public parking garage.

Since I couldn't bring my gun on the plane, I would go buy a real-looking fake firearm. It's all I would need.

My plan was adaptable, but my goal was to spot Becca on the lobby floor as she waited to take the elevator to her room. I'd get on with her. There would likely be other people on the elevator, so I'd lie low until we reached her floor. I'd get off with her and as soon as no one was around, I'd pull the gun and tell her she was taking me to her room.

She was a criminal who likely had hundreds of thousands of dollars hidden in two Vegas banks. I knew she wasn't going to scream when I pulled the gun. The last thing she'd want to do was bring attention to herself. Another huge advantage for me.

Assuming she played along, we'd go to her room and I'd lay out her options. I could kill her or we could go to one of her banks, where she could give me half of the money she stole. She wouldn't make a scene at the bank for the same reason: Getting the police involved was the last thing that Becca Poe wanted. And assuming I did get half the money, I would let her go on living her life. At that point, we'd be basically co-conspirators, neither one able to turn on the other without incriminating themselves.

It was brilliant.

I spent most of Sunday in my room, finalizing the plan. I went down and walked around The LINQ Casino for a bit, but didn't feel like gambling. The next day would be the biggest gamble of my life, and nothing I could put down on the table would have the same luster. Not even close.

I returned to my room and ordered room service for the second time in two nights, getting a French dip and some French fries. Which was funny, because I didn't really consider either dish very French. The sandwich hit the spot; the bread turned out a little stale, but that didn't matter once it was smothered in the au jus.

Afterward, I took the rolling table and set it out in the hallway. I flipped through the channels, but nothing could hold my attention. It was 8:30 and I was too wired to fall asleep yet, so I decided to take another walk.

I took the elevator down and strode along the other side of the Strip, having seen the LINQ side the day before. I passed the Venetian and then crossed Las Vegas Boulevard, ending up in front of Treasure Island and The Mirage. I started to feel old as I remembered when Treasure Island and The Mirage were the new and trendy casinos in Vegas. Now, they were the dated ones, having been surpassed by Wynn, The Cosmopolitan, Aria, and so many more.

Walking through the Mirage brought back great memories of gambling there with my friends in the early '90s. One stood out.

My buddy Robbie Beltran was a real nut, let's just put it that way. His favorite movie back then was *Austin Powers: International Man of Mystery*. There's a line in the movie where Mike Myers' character Austin Powers, playing blackjack, stays while only holding a hand of five, saying: "I also like to live dangerously."

That was Robbie's go-to line back then. On the night in question, Robbie probably had six gin and tonics in him when he, I, and another friend, Sean, sat down to play some blackjack. Every time Robbie had less than an eleven (meaning he couldn't bust and should absolutely hit) he'd stay and say his go-to line: "I also like to live dangerously."

The first few times it was hilarious, there being just us three on the table. Even the dealer couldn't help but laugh before giving him a chance to change his mind. Robbie didn't, and miraculously, he won each time when the dealer busted.

It would have been great if it had ended there, but Robbie couldn't get enough of it. Soon after, a few other people joined our table, and while we were betting the table minimum of $10, they were betting $100 per hand.

About five hands in, Robbie got a four and a two. The new dealer, who hadn't seen our antics, went to peel off a card when Robbie interrupted him.

"Stay," he said.

"You have a six, sir."

He looked down across all the people on the table.

"I also like to live dangerously," he said.

Sean, Robbie, and I couldn't stop laughing. The other men were less than amused, but they waited to see what happened before passing judgement. Sure enough, by Robbie staying, the dealer hit two straight perfect cards and got twenty-one. The two guys got in Robbie's face and it almost came to blows before hotel security came over.

I looked at the Mirage blackjack tables and felt a confluence of emotions. On the one hand, I remembered the day incredibly fondly. Three twenty-something guys without a care in the world, causing trouble and just enjoying life.

But it also got me thinking about my present situation. Tomorrow I was going to basically kidnap a woman and have her hand money over to me. No, she hadn't come upon the money legally, but neither was it mine to steal from her.

I started to wonder what had happened to the younger me, the carefree one who would never have considered such a devious plan.

Life happened, I said to myself. *It hardened me up.* And as much as I channeled my younger, moralistic self, I still knew I was going to go through with my plan.

I needed the money.

I left the Mirage, trying to focus on the great memory of Robbie Beltran "living dangerously," and not on the day ahead. I continued walking toward Caesar's Palace, which had undergone some nice renovations in recent years. It had dropped from its height in the '80s as the premier destination in Vegas, but in the midst of its comeback, a lot of people thought Caesar's was desirable again.

The Forum Shops in Caesar's had long been my favorite spot to shop in Vegas. My ex-wife, Daisy, had loved it as well, and we could get lost there for hours if we wanted. She would do the shopping while I'd just follow her around, enjoying her company.

This was early in our relationship, before the whole Jasper Miller event and our economic problems that followed. Our children were young, and when we'd bring them to Vegas they'd be in awe of all the lights and massive hotels. It could truly be a wondrous city at times.

As I walked around the Forum Shops, I wondered why I had suddenly become so sentimental. It certainly hadn't been a characteristic that most people would ascribe to me. I knew why.

While I had morphed into a shady guy since becoming a private investigator twenty years previously, tomorrow would mark a new low. And my inner angel was trying to fight my inner demon to make me reconsider. That poor angel fought an uphill battle, however.

I reached the end of the Forum Shops, where they were in the middle of "The Fall of Atlantis" show I had seen numerous times over the years. The statues were much bigger and the show much better since I had last seen it. Around me, children gaped on their parents' shoulders, in awe of the talking statues.

I decided I needed to get out of there. I had to concentrate on what was going to happen tomorrow and stop being a sentimental fool.

Walking out of The Forum Shops and then Caesar's, I made my way back to Las Vegas Boulevard. considered heading back to the LINQ, but I decided to stop at The Bellagio before I did.

After crossing East Flamingo Road, I continued toward The Bellagio. They had a great water show and if it was coming up soon, I planned to stay and watch.

I approached the lake where the show took place and saw a young couple sitting there waiting.

"Do you know when the water show starts?" I asked.

"Someone just said three minutes."

"Great, thanks."

It would get crowded once it started, so I made my way up to the fence where I'd have the perfect view. I started to remember a couple of times Daisy and I had watched the water show together, but tried to push them out of my mind.

The young couple was right and a few minutes later, the show started. The song this time was "Fly me to the Moon" by Frank Sinatra. A great song no doubt, but I had always equated Andrea Bocelli with the Bellagio fountains. His "Time to Say Goodbye" had long been the song that they'd play during the show. It was almost depressing to hear any voice but his as the water shot up hundreds of feet in the air, even the great Sinatra's.

Still, I enjoyed the show. I was happy to have made it close to the fence. The crowd pushed at least fifteen people deep behind me.

I told myself it was time to rekindle my romance with Cora. She had always been fun in the short stints we had dated and now I'd have money to spend on her.

Finances, or lack thereof, had been the biggest reason Daisy and I had split up, and money had remained a concern of mine since 2004. I smiled. Despite all the sentimental feelings I'd had at the Mirage and Caesar's, I knew getting half of Becca Poe's money was going to make me an even happier man.

I listened to Frank Sinatra's voice and took in my surroundings as the show got close to wrapping up. I was absolutely going to bring Cora to the Bellagio fountains. They were about as romantic as you could get.

I was about to beat myself up about being over fifty and single when I simultaneously felt a pinch in my right hamstring and my right flank. I figured someone had just nudged into me, but then the pain got worse. It felt like a little knife was penetrating me. I looked to my right, thinking the person next to me must have knocked into me with something sharp.

"Did you bump into me?" I said.

"No," the man said.

I turned around, planning to confront the person behind me. Except, as I turned, I started to feel a little groggy.

A tall, skinny man looked down at me. "Are you alright?" he asked.

I didn't feel alright. My legs wobbled.

I saw a woman moving quickly, suspiciously, past the tall, skinny man. Something told me to keep my eyes focused on her. She walked out of the crowd and I kept watching.

Once she got past the mob watching the water show, she looked back. The woman wore a long coat and a hat that covered most of her face, but there was no mistaking who it was. Becca Poe stared right at me.

She raised her right hand and moved her fingers up and down as if saying goodbye.

It turned out she was.

My legs started to buckle and I found it difficult to breathe. I felt my body give out below me.

I collapsed to the ground. My breathing became more and more labored. I heard some voices, but I couldn't seem to get my mouth to say anything. I wanted to scream "Becca Poe did this," but nothing would come out. Getting more and more dizzy, I felt myself about to pass out.

At least, that's what I hoped.

I was wrong, however. There would be no waking up from this.

As I took my final breath, the last thing I ever saw were the bodies crowding around me and the Bellagio Fountains shooting off behind them.

45

BECCA

Early on Sunday, I went to a Rite Aid and picked up several packets of over-the-counter sleeping pills, some plastic syringes and needles you had to set up yourself, and a bottle of Clorox. I also bought several other items, just so they didn't get suspicious.

I went back to my room at Veer Towers and emptied what had to have been 50 sleeping pills into about a cup of Clorox and then loaded the concoction into two syringes. I imagined either the sleeping pills or the Clorox might have killed the man, but just to be safe, I combined the two. And then, to be even safer, I decided to plunge him with two needles full.

I prepped while wearing gloves, covering my bases as usual.

I grabbed the longest jacket that I had, knowing this would be the last time I'd ever wear it. I put the caps on the needles and set the two syringes in my jacket pocket. I also put a pair of flip flops and a denim skirt in with them.

I threw on a blonde wig, followed by a black baseball cap with some logo I didn't recognize. I fastened the hat tight to my head and pulled the brim down as far as I could to hide my face.

I first spotted the man in question at about 4:00 p.m., after having been at the LINQ for three hours with nary a sighting. He was walking out from the elevators. I had intentionally taken a seat at a slot machine where I could see people's profiles as they walked out of those elevators, while they were unlikely to see me.

I watched him, but not too closely, afraid he'd sense someone's eyes following him. As long as he stayed on the casino floor, there was nothing I could do, so I kept my distance. I looked completely, and I mean completely, different from Friday night, but I still couldn't let him see me, just in case.

After about twenty minutes, he made his way back to the elevators. I waited some more.

I hoped the next time he came down, he'd leave the confines of the casino and I could try the lethal syringes I had brought.

I had to wait four more hours, but finally, at 8:30 p.m., I saw him get off the hotel elevators once again. He was walking a little more briskly this time, which suggested he wasn't just going to loiter around the LINQ.

My suspicions proved correct as he headed out onto Las Vegas Boulevard, and I followed a safe distance behind. We passed the Venetian and crossed to the other side of the street. I continued behind him as he made his way to the Mirage, where he sat and looked at their blackjack tables.

I thought he might join and play, but he never did.

Next, he went into Caesar's Palace and the Forum Shops, a place I had come to know since moving to Vegas. I still followed at a safe distance, and whenever I saw him doubling back, I'd step into a women's store, knowing he wouldn't set foot in there.

He finished with the Forum Shops and headed back out of Caesar's. There was a point where I considered just walking behind him on the street and injecting him, but it would be too easy for some hero to tackle or restrain me until the police arrived.

But then I got lucky. I saw him going to the fence outside of the Bellagio lake, and few minutes later, the water show commenced. I waited until a big crowd gathered, which would make me more inconspicuous when I approached. But I couldn't wait too long, because I knew I had to inject him while the water show was going and a crowd was still gathered. It would be much easier to escape.

About five minutes in, several solid rows of people stood watching the show. I slowly, quietly made my way up toward the fence. When I got close, I grabbed both syringes from my pockets, taking the little tops off. Luckily, the sun was down and there were tons of people around, so no one could see what I was doing.

I started approaching.

When I reached him, I simultaneously pierced him in his right hamstring and right flank, plunging the needles as soon as they entered his skin.

After plunging them, I immediately pulled them out of his skin. It only took a split second.

At once, he turned on the person on his right as I blended back into the crowd.

He then must have accused the guy behind him, because as I turned around, I saw him looking past a tall man in my direction.

I subtly put the syringes into my purse, and as I did, his eyes focused in on mine. He undoubtedly knew it was me.

It was time to show him that he'd made a big mistake in fucking with Becca Poe.

I should have kept walking, but I had to let him know who had killed him. It was half the fun. Like seeing Austin's face when he realized I was about to end his life.

I curled my fingers, waving goodbye to the man, and his terrified expression made it all worthwhile.

Pure gold!

When the man didn't come after me, I knew my concoction was taking effect. I saw him go down to the ground.

It was time get the hell out of there. I started walking briskly, but not so fast as to draw attention.

And then it was time for the final implementation of my plan. As I got to the far side of the Bellagio Lake, the show was ending, and loads of people started matriculating into the Bellagio. I tried to blend into the crowd, and just as I was walking into the casino, I subtly dropped my hat so that I entered the Bellagio with my blonde wig visible for all to see.

I wasn't done. I went to the bathroom and stayed in there for almost an hour. There were so many lined up that no one knew I occupied the same stall for so long. When I was about to leave, I took off my pants and my tennis shoes, replacing them with flip flops and the denim skirt. I also took the wig off.

I exited the bathroom, but not before dropping my clothes, which I used to cover the syringes, into the garbage. Everyone was doing their own thing, and no one noticed me dumping a perfectly good jacket, pants, and pair of shoes away. I walked out of the Bellagio via a different exit than the one I had walked in.

In no time, they would come in and change out the garbage in the bathroom, and the murder weapons would be lost forever.

In all likelihood I had done enough, but I continued strolling along the Strip, blending in with crowds, and entering casinos before leaving through different doors than the ones I had come in through.

After three hours of roaming, I made my way back to Veer Towers. It had been so busy when I injected the man with the syringes that I didn't think there was any way a camera could have singled me out. Add to that, I changed clothes and wandered around the Strip for hours, and I just knew I couldn't get I.D.'d as the murderer. Assuming, of course, that he had died.

I eagerly waited to find out.

I woke up Monday morning and went to the *Las Vegas Review Journal* online. I didn't see anything on the front page, so I clicked on the section titled LOCAL. There, about halfway down the page, was the headline: *Tourist Dies at Bellagio Water Show.*

Richard Levert, a private detective from Los Angeles, died at approximately 9:10 last night during the water show in front of the Bellagio Casino. People next to him stated that as the show was ending, he went down to the ground and lost consciousness, never to regain it. An autopsy could take weeks, but for now, authorities believe it was likely a heart attack.

I couldn't help but laugh. A heart attack. Well, if that's what they wanted to think, I was just fine with that. Very possibly the attending medics hadn't seen the needle marks where I pierced him. And maybe they wouldn't do an autopsy at all if they truly thought it was a heart attack.

I liked the way everything seemed to be headed.

"A private detective from LA," I said aloud, now sure that Olive had hired him. The police wouldn't hire outside private investigators.

Was it time to get out of Vegas?

Even if the autopsy uncovered what had really happened, how exactly were they going to tie me to it? I had a long, dark jacket on and was wearing a dark hat pulled down tight on a dark night in Vegas. I was surrounded by people when I plunged the needles in to Mr. Levert (sorry we were never formally introduced, haha) and even if there security cameras covered the street, I doubted there was any way they could have seen the needles with all the people around us.

Furthermore, I then disappeared into the Bellagio for over an hour and walked out in flip flops, several inches shorter, and looking quite different.

For good measure, I walked in and out of several more casinos after that.

And guess what? They didn't know my name or where I lived, and would have no fingerprints.

I felt like I had committed another perfect murder.

I decided I'd stay in Las Vegas after all.

Just like the saying goes, "What Happens in Vegas, Stays in Vegas."

I kill myself.

Well actually, I kill others, but you know what I mean.

"Hey Olive, it's Sheri!"

I was surprised to see an incoming call from Sheri that Monday afternoon. It had been awhile since we'd talked.

"What's up, Sheri?"

"Sorry I haven't called lately, but I've got some bad news. One of our old regulars at The Belly Flop died."

My heart sank. "Who was it?" I asked.

"I'm sure you remember Richard Levert."

I started to choke up, but I couldn't let Sheri hear me.

"Are you alright, Olive?"

"I'm fine. Just sad is all."

"Yeah, it's too bad. He always seemed like a nice guy. Quiet and intense, but nice."

"How did you find out?"

"Mark Midfield told me."

"Where did he die?"

"In Vegas of all places."

"How?"

"Mark said they think it was a heart attack. Apparently it happened last night right out front of the Bellagio."

I hoped more than anything that it really had been a heart attack.

"That's terrible," I said, trying to sound calm. "Will you let me know if people are going to get together to remember him at The Belly Flop?"

"Of course. How have you been? I never see you anymore."

"Just busy working at Rick's on Main. I'm a little busy right now, but stop in sometime. I'd like to see you."

"Okay, I will."

"See you, Sheri."

"Bye, Olive."

I hung up the phone and dropped onto my couch. The tears started flowing before I even hit it. I had so many questions.

Did Richard really die from a heart attack? Could Becca have killed him? If she was in Vegas, would she stay there, or could she be coming for me next?

I got up, approached the door, and made sure the dead bolt was secured.

"This is driving me crazy," I said, making my way back to the couch.

I had last talked to Richard two days ago and he'd said there had been no progress. Was he lying? He'd seemed sincere, but that was easy to fake.

Maybe he'd traveled to Vegas for something that had nothing to do with Becca Poe. And Mark Midfield had heard he'd died from a heart attack. I told myself I had nothing to worry about.

But I didn't believe that. If I had to go with my gut, I'd say he was in Vegas trying to find Becca Poe.

Then why hadn't Richard told me? There was certainly one potential answer. I had been right about the money and he wanted some for himself.

I'd thought Richard was an honest man, but how well did I really know him? He'd occasionally complain about being low on money while at The Belly Flop. Maybe he saw his opportunity to get rich and took it. It seemed the most logical conclusion at this point.

If I was right, I had something more important to worry about. Becca Poe had outthought and outfoxed a private investigator. Someone bigger and stronger than her. Someone who knew who she was, while she would have had no idea who he was. And yet, she had won.

How the hell did I stand a chance?

I had Mondays off at Rick's on Main, so I took a late afternoon nap. I had become tired after thinking about all the possible implications of Richard's death.

My first inclination had been to call the police again, but I knew that wouldn't go well.

I'd have to explain that I didn't trust their police work, so I'd hired a private detective of my own. I didn't think it was illegal, but probably the police wouldn't look on it very fondly. More importantly, his death had been ruled a heart attack. There was no chance in hell of them sending members of the LAPD to investigate a heart attack.

So, I was back on my own. Austin was dead. Barry was dead. Chet Watkins, whoever he'd been, was dead. And now Richard was dead.

I knew I'd be next if I wasn't careful.

The next morning, I went to one of the dwindling number of pay phones in LA and called the Las Vegas Police Department.

"LVPD. How can I help you?"

"You should do an autopsy on Richard Levert, the guy who died outside of the Bellagio. It wasn't a heart attack, he was killed. And you should investigate someone named Becca Poe."

I hung up.

I deposited a few more quarters and placed another call.

"Clark County Coroner."

"You should expedite the autopsy on Richard Levert. He was murdered."

I hung up and wiped down the phone with my sleeve. Maybe I was being paranoid, but there was an outside chance they'd check it for the latest fingerprints.

I walked back to my apartment, looking to my right and left as I came to the complex. Becca Poe remained on my mind at all times, and I didn't see that changing any time soon.

As I entered my apartment, Sheri was calling back.

"What's up, Sheri?"

"Talked to Mark today. Apparently, Richard Levert asked to be cremated in his will and didn't want a funeral."

They couldn't cremate him without performing an autopsy first, could they? My mind raced.

"Okay," I said, sensing Sheri had more to tell.

"But we decided to do a little memorial at The Belly Flop on Thursday. It won't be huge, but I'm sure some of the day regulars and employees will be there. Be nice if you could stop in."

"I work from 11 a.m. to 4 p.m. What time is it at?"

"We're doing it from 3-6. Just stop by after work."

"I'll be there. Thanks, Sheri."

The next two days moved along at a snail's pace. I hoped I'd find out more information on Richard's death at the memorial, but until then, there wasn't much I could do. I couldn't exactly call the LVPD and ask if they had followed up on my phone call. And I was still writing off the LAPD. If I found out that the coroner in Vegas had ruled it a homicide, then I'd be willing to go back to Detectives Washington and Liston. But not until then.

On Thursday, after my shift at Rick's finally, mercifully ended, I drove directly to Richard's memorial at The Belly Flop.

Guilt started to blossom as I drove up. Had I caused his death? Would his family or friends see right through me? Should I just tell everyone what I had asked him to do?

I decided to wait until I knew what Richard had been up to in Vegas. If he was there gambling with some friends, then I saw no reason to tell everyone about hiring him. If it turned out that his trip had been related to Becca Poe, than I'd have a tougher decision.

I parked behind The Belly Flop and walked in the back door. I realized it was where I had my first talk with Richard about Becca Poe. It made me sad.

Around twenty people had gathered there. Ten or so were regulars that I knew. Five were employees, and I assumed the remaining five or six were family or friends. I had hoped for a much bigger turnout, but it wasn't going to be the case.

I hugged Sheri and said hello to some former co-workers who I hadn't seen in a while.

"Hey, Olive."

"We've missed you."

"Where have you been?"

They were all tempered by the occasion, however.

I had mixed emotions. It was good to see them all, but hard to be my effervescent self considering the circumstances.

Sheri took me by the shoulder. "Let me introduce you to his family."

I walked with Sheri around the bar. We passed Mark Midfield and a few other regulars on the way.

"I'll be back in a few minutes, guys. Let me meet his family first. And yes, Mark, I'll have a Woo Woo with you."

Mark Midfield lit up like a Christmas tree.

We arrived at the other side of the bar, where Sheri took the lead.

"This is Richard's ex-wife, Daisy. His children, Don and Ron. Cora, who is an old friend. And his sister, Charlene."

I shook everyone's hands.

"And what was your name, dear?" Daisy, his ex-wife, asked me.

"I'm Olive. I used to work here," I said.

Cora, the "old friend," did a double take as she looked at me. I looked back, but she reflexively dropped her gaze toward the ground. Something was up and I made a note to get time alone with her at some point.

"And what was Richard like as a customer?" one of his two sons asked.

I didn't remember who was Ron and who was Don.

"Richard was great. He was always respectful. He was quiet, but sometimes he'd open up to me."

"Wish he had opened up more to me," Daisy said.

"C'mon, Mom, not now," the other son said.

Cora remained noticeably quiet, although I did catch her looking up at me every few seconds.

"Get over here, Olive. Time for a Woo Woo!"

I could tell that Mark was drunker than usual. He had been the closest to Richard of all the regulars, so I guess he had good reason. It couldn't have been easy for him.

I said goodbye to Richard's family and Cora, walking back to the other side of the bar. A new bartender who I didn't recognize made a huge batch of Woo Woos and Mark Midfield told her to hand them out to everyone present.

Once everyone got one, Mark stood up and raised his glass.

"To Richard Levert! He was a good guy and I enjoyed all of our conversations at The Belly Flop over the years. I'll miss you, my friend. Rest in peace!"

Everyone raised their Woo Woos and clinked the glass of the person nearest them. I looked over at Cora and saw that she was staring right at me.

After I finished my Woo Woo, I nodded in Cora's direction, then bobbed my head toward the room that wasn't in use. Hopefully that would give us some privacy.

I told Mark and the other regulars that I'd be back in a few minutes. I hadn't been drunk since my friend Kayla's visit several months earlier, but I had a feeling tonight might be different. I excused myself and headed toward the room with all the big screen T.V.s.

Cora sat in the corner, shielded from anyone seeing her. I walked over to her.

"I could tell you did a double take when you heard my name," I said.

"Was it that obvious?" She smiled.

"Yeah," I said and smiled back.

"Richard called me a few days ago and wanted me to pretend to be you."

"What?"

"He called me on Friday. Wait, no, it was Thursday. I don't remember. Anyway, he asked me to record something for him."

I was even more lost.

"Record something for him?"

"Yeah, and it was meant to be coming from you. Unless there's another Olive I don't know about."

That seemed unlikely.

"What did he have you say?" I asked.

"*Meet me at the lobby bar in ten minutes. It's Olive.*"

I felt like I'd been punched in the gut. Richard had been in Vegas working on the Becca Poe case. I was to blame, at least in part, for his death.

"Do you know why he would do that?" she asked.

I played dumb. "I have no idea. Did he say anything else?"

"He asked me if I wanted to take a vacation with him. He was always broke, so that surprised me."

My guilt for the death of Richard Levert immediately began to fade. It sounded like he thought he was coming into some money. Like I'd guessed, he'd been after Becca's money himself. His own selfishness had got him killed.

"Did he mention where he was on the Strip? Or anyone else's name?"

"No. Honestly, it was a minute-long conversation. He was trying to butter me up. We've been dating on and off since he and Daisy got divorced."

"I won't say anything."

"It doesn't matter. Daisy and her kids know it. They think I'm a saint for dealing with him."

"Was he an unscrupulous guy?" I asked.

"We've known each other for twenty years, since long before we started dating. I would not have labeled him unscrupulous when I first met him, but I do think he was heading in that direction in recent years. He was half-broke all the time and he'd take any job to make a little money. Some of them were pretty seedy."

Cora's words left no doubt in my mind. Richard was going behind my back and trying to get Becca's money. Or to be more precise, Barry Gant's money.

It saddened me all over again. Here we were, sitting in one of the bars that Barry Gant owned and talking about a sleazy private eye who was trying to steal the money that Barry had been killed over. It was sordid stuff.

"And he didn't mention how he had ended up in Vegas?" I asked. I wanted to know how he had tracked Becca there.

"No. Like I said, the conversation was very brief. You still haven't told me why he was using your name."

Sheri peeked in the T.V. room. Her eyes went to me and Cora talking. It would be hard to explain why I was in the corner of a separate room talking to someone I had only just met.

"Cora, I think we should talk in the coming days. We're drawing a little attention to ourselves."

"Take down my number," she said.

I did, and we walked back to the main bar.

I had one more shot with Mark Midfield and the older regulars, but then stopped drinking. I decided I couldn't afford to be hungover. The situation with Richard Levert's death was fluid and I couldn't risk wasting a day feeling like shit.

The rest of the time had been filled with stories about Richard by his friends and his sons, and it made me realize just how little I knew about him.

No question, I was sad, but I couldn't help but think he brought it on himself. He'd been driven by greed, just like Becca Poe, but greed had gotten the better of him. While she was out there enjoying her money, Richard Levert was dead, lying on a cold slab somewhere in a Vegas coroner's office.

If he hadn't been cremated yet.

I left the party at 7:00 p.m. as it started to dwindle. When I arrived back at my apartment complex, as had become protocol, my eyes were on a swivel as I made my way up the steps. Not seeing anything, I walked briskly to my apartment, where I quickly put the key in and locked the dead bolt behind me.

It was no way to live.

47

BECCA

I was getting good at this killing thing. I'd always had a voracious appetite for crime: stealing, swindling, blackmailing, and all those other great -ing words.

But now I had grown a taste for murder, and I have to admit, I kind of liked it. I wasn't a Jeffrey Dahmer or a Ted Bundy who killed just to kill, but if you got in the way of my freedom, you were fair game.

And while I had caught a couple of breaks in the robbery/murder in the Pacific Palisades, the murder of Richard Levert had been a work of art. There was Da Vinci. Van Gough. Picasso. And Becca Poe.

A week had passed since his death and I hadn't read anything else in the papers.

I started reading up on autopsies and saw that in general, coroners had to have permission to perform one. They made exceptions when someone died under mysterious circumstances, and that's where I wasn't sure if Richard Levert fit the bill.

Would they perform an autopsy on someone who crumbled to the ground and died in Vegas? It had to happen all the time in Sin City. Most people would just assume a heart attack. I hoped the coroner thought the same.

I knew that nobody saw me inject him with the syringes. They were hidden under my jacket and people were jam-packed up near the fence to watch the water show. They were looking out on the lake, concentrating on the lake.

No one was looking for me. I had committed the perfect murder. Once again.

While I had become an accomplished killer, I had not stolen Barry Gant's money to then be caught and thrown in jail for life. I began to ask myself what the point was of stealing it if I just kept running from people all the time. I wanted to settle down and find a home base. To spend my money freely. To live like the social climber I'd always hoped to become.

Sure, I had skipped about ten steps on the ladder, but people didn't need to know that. I'd tell them stories of stock investments, summers in Martha's Vineyard, and famous people I knew. It's what I was meant for. As much as I enjoyed Vegas, the majority of the rich people there were just visiting.

When I was that little girl riding a bus surrounded by poor, scroungy white kids and poorer, scroungier minorities, I knew that I wanted to be rich. I wanted to get the adulation that comes with being rich. And I still wanted it.

I started going over all of the places I had lived. Los Angeles had been my favorite, without question. I loved hanging out in expensive Beverly Hills restaurants and just waiting to see a wealthy celebrity walk in.

When you were in LA, you were always close to the action. And I loved that shit.

It was time to move back to Los Angeles.

One of my character flaws—it must be admitted that I had a couple—is that I could never leave well enough alone. I had to let people know I'd gotten the best of them. It's why I turned around and waved goodbye to Richard Levert when he was seconds from dying. I should have just walked through the crowd and never turned around. But no, I had to take a risk and let him know I had won our little game.

And now, I needed Olive to know that I'd killed the private eye. Of course, knowing I'd murdered Richard Levert might dissuade her from hiring someone else, but my primary motive in telling her was selfish. I wanted Olive to feel guilty, to squirm at having caused the death of another.

She had tried to fuck up my life and now I wanted to fuck up hers. Smiling, I came up with another idea.

I started typing out an email to the LAPD.

I've got some information on the murder of Barry Gant, it started.

48

OLIVE

"Olive, this is Detective Washington from the LAPD."

It was three days after the memorial for Richard Levert when I got the call I had been hoping for. I hadn't told anyone about my own suspicions because as far as I knew Richard's death was still being ruled a heart attack. But obviously, the LAPD had some new intelligence. Hopefully, it included evidence linking the murder to Becca.

"I'm glad to hear from you, Detective Washington," I said. "Did you find some information on Becca Poe?"

"We'd like you to come down to the station when you get a chance."

"Sure, I've got today off. What time?"

"As soon as you can."

I figured it must be something really important.

"I'll be down there in twenty minutes."

I got ready, throwing on a pair of jeans and a sweater. On my days off, I'd usually be fine just roaming around in some leggings, but I figured the Los Angeles Police Department deserved better than that. I drove down to the precinct, finding a spot right out front.

The detectives were waiting for me as I entered.

"Follow us," Detective Liston said and I walked down the hall with them.

They had always been cordial with me, but something seemed different during the phone call and now at the police station. I wasn't sure what was going on, but I had an uneasy feeling.

We arrived at a conference room, where they asked me to sit down.

"You guys aren't very friendly today," I said.

They proceeded to sit across from me.

"We just wanted to go over what happened at Barry Gant's house one more time," Detective Liston said.

"How many times have we done this?" I asked.

"Just do what Detective Liston asks," Washington said.

He had always been kind to me, even more so than his partner, but suddenly it didn't seem that way. What was going on?

"I drove out there with Austin. I thought we were meeting Barry so Austin could talk to him about opening up a bar. Austin had expressed interest and Barry said he was willing to meet us."

"Did you always call Barry by his first name?" Liston asked.

"Yeah. I'd worked for him for three years. We knew each other pretty well."

"How well?"

I couldn't stand the man and his questions.

"He was my boss and I'd see him probably twice a week at The Belly Flop. As I've told you, he hit on me repeatedly over the years, but it was usually good-natured."

"If a guy was always hitting on you, I'd think you'd call him Mr. Gant just to make it more impersonal."

"What the hell are you guys trying to say? Why don't you go ask any regular who ever stepped foot in The Belly Flop? They all saw Barry hit on me many times. Just because I called him by his first name, doesn't mean I was asking for it. If that's what you're insinuating."

Detective Washington looked at Liston with an expression telling him to cool it.

"Okay, Olive, we believe you. How about the day in question? What happened after you got there?"

"Barry met us at the door. We started to walk in when the guy in the baby doll mask approached from behind us. He had me get down on my knees and I thought he might kill me. Instead, I guess he just knocked me out. I came to when the police arrived."

"And you never went upstairs?"

"No. What the hell is going on?"

They ignored my question.

"Did Barry Gant ever tell you that he had money in his safe?"

"No."

"But he did ask you to come back to his place?"

"Yes. Many times. It had become a joke, because he knew I was never going to come. He'd say things like 'So I'll see you at 4:00 at my place.' But no, I never went and never had plans to."

"So why was this time different?"

"Because I really liked Austin and thought this was going to help him out."

"You thought the guy with $3,000 in his checking account was going to open up a bar?"

"I didn't know that at the time. I was duped. He told me he was some rich guy who had worked on Wall Street."

"And you believed him?"

"Sadly, yes."

"You didn't have all that much money either, did you, Olive?" Liston asked.

Washington was noticeably quiet.

"I'm a bartender and I put half my tips toward rent, so no, I'm not rich either. Tell me what the fuck you are suggesting!"

I rarely swore, but the circumstances called for it. They were asking me some pointed questions and not even telling me why.

"We're just trying to make sure it wasn't you and Austin who planned this whole thing."

My stomach dropped. This wasn't what I had expected at all. Suddenly, I felt nervous as hell.

"Of course not!"

"You want us to believe that you thought a guy who had $3,000 dollars to his name was going to open a bar?"

"I already told you, I didn't know he was that broke."

"Why do you think you were so naive with regards to Austin?"

"Probably because I thought I was falling in love," I said.

I lowered my head and started crying. I'd fallen for the wrong guy, wound up at the scene of a triple murder, and hired a private detective who was subsequently killed. And now they were accusing me of being involved.

It was suddenly all too much.

Detective Washington handed me some tissues and I used them to pat down my eyes and my runny nose.

"I'm sorry," I said.

Washington looked on compassionately, Liston suspiciously.

I gathered myself.

"I was an idiot for falling for Austin. But I had nothing to do with Barry's death, or the others."

I looked across the table, not sure if they believed me. "You asked me if I went upstairs, so you must be trying to say I took money myself. Look at my checking account. Search my apartment. Do whatever the hell you want."

I sounded defensive, and felt I had a right to be. Neither one said anything.

"What's brought about your suspicion of me?" I asked.

They looked at each other and I noticed a small nod from Liston to Washington. Detective Washington spoke.

"We received something," he said. "It says that you were the one who orchestrated the robbery."

After all the questioning, I should have expected it, but it still hit me like a ton of bricks.

"And you believe it?"

"Sorry, Olive, but we have to follow up."

I realized that I hadn't mentioned Richard Levert. I wasn't sure if it was the right thing to do. For the first time, I really wished I'd had a lawyer present. But asking for one would have just made them more suspicious.

My mind raced and I figured I probably looked like someone guilty of a crime.

"Did the letter come from Las Vegas?" I asked.

The idea had entered my mind abruptly, and I just as abruptly blurted it out.

"When I said we received something, I meant an email. Not a letter. Why are you guessing Vegas?"

Should I tell them about Richard Levert? I had to decide quick. They were looking at me, waiting for an answer on Vegas.

Screw them! They were treating me like a suspect. I wasn't going to tell them about Richard. For one thing, they'd just think I was more fucked up. I'd allege that Becca Poe had killed him and they'd find out that it was a heart attack.

"Why are you guessing Vegas?" Officer Liston repeated.

"Never mind," I said. "Just a random guess."

They both looked at me with narrowed eyes.

Did they really think I was involved?

"You're acting a little weird today, Olive. Is there something you'd like to get off your chest?"

"I can't believe this is happening. I was set up by Austin to get him close to Barry Gant. I was almost killed and now you're accusing me of being involved."

"We're not accusing, we're just asking questions."

"Sure doesn't feel that way."

"Why don't we do this again in a few days?" Detective Washington asked.

"Fine," I said, just wanting to get out of there. "But nothing is going to change. I was set up by Austin and Becca Poe and you guys don't believe me."

"For the thousandth time, there is zero evidence that a woman named Becca Poe is involved. No fingerprints at the scene, not one email or text to or from Chet Watkins or Jared Austin Jenkins. Don't you find that weird?"

"She's brilliant, what can I say? Maybe she had ways of contacting them that she thought were better than cell phones. I don't know. I'm just telling you that I know she was involved."

"We don't think so," Detective Liston said.

"Can I go?" I asked.

"Yes."

I got up.

"One more thing," I said.

"What is it?"

"If I'm murdered in the coming days or weeks, I hope you'll investigate Becca Poe, because she's the one who is going to do it," I said and walked away.

"Olive," Detective Washington yelled.

But I was already out the door and heading toward the front exit.

49

BECCA

After much debate, I had decided it was time to go back to the scene of the crime. The best decision? No, and I knew that. But as always, I had to be in the center of things. I wanted to see Olive twisting in the wind. If my email had worked, maybe she'd already come under investigation by the Los Angeles Police Department. The thought of it made me smile.

What if she got wrongly convicted and was put on death row? My smile only got bigger.

The one thing that would make me happier would be killing Olive myself. And that's the other reason I was headed to LA.

I emailed the man who'd rented me the suite at Veer Towers in Vegas. I told him I'd be traveling abroad for a few months and wouldn't be occupying the suite. Just in case he came back and I was nowhere to be seen, I didn't want him filing a missing persons case on my behalf or anything else that would lead to police intervention. By informing him that I was eventually coming back, I ensured he would do nothing. The first three months of rent had already been paid, so I didn't have any worries.

I came up with conflicting answers to the question of why I wanted to kill Olive so badly. On the one hand, it served as a preemptive strike, since she seemed to be the only one who might suspect me in the murders of Richard Levert and the others. But there was another reason. One more primal. She had put me in harm's way when she hired Richard Levert. And for that, I wanted her dead.

As much as I wanted to stay in LA for a long time, I knew it was best to get in and out. The connections between me and dead people continued to mount and would only get worse when Olive "went missing." I needed to head out of the country, preferably to somewhere that didn't have an extradition policy with the United States. I googled that information, immediately regretting it. If the authorities ever got ahold of my laptop, that would be some pretty incriminating evidence.

But through my search, I learned that every country in Central and South America would extradite. I had to assume that's because we were the big dick on the block. It would be bad business for poorer Latin American countries to show up the mighty U.S. Cuba was the closest country that didn't extradite, but I knew flying there could be problematic, so I ruled it out.

Going down the list, I was left with mainly Middle Eastern or African countries. None of them sounded enticing. Maybe it was the racist in me, but I wanted to be surrounded by whites, not back on my high school bus, surrounded by dirty minorities. I'd become rich for a reason and it was to hang out with fellow wealthy people.

I decided I'd rather be looking over my shoulder in Europe than comfortable in Bahrain, wherever the fuck that was.

The other possibility was going over the border and into Mexico. Not my first choice, but if I couldn't find a way to launder my money, flights might become impossible. Mexico could be a shithole country, but it also had some beautiful beaches and island towns where I could slum it before I made it to Europe.

That decision could wait. Be better not to book a flight too far ahead in case they were checking my credit cards.

I looked down at my phone and saw the date: February 8th. In six days, it was going to be Valentine's Day. What a great day that would be to kill Olive.

50

OLIVE

I considered asking Sheri if she wanted to move in with me. She had four other college students as roommates and she'd often complain that it was like living in a female Animal House. But I couldn't do it. If I was really in harm's way, I couldn't bring someone else into the middle of it. For the same reason, I couldn't ask someone if I could shack up with them until this all blew over.

And when was this going to blow over? As long as Becca Poe was alive, I'd be living in fear. It was unfair to the nth degree. I had realized she orchestrated the robbery and murder at Barry Gant's, and because of my resourcefulness, I had to suffer. Life could be such bullshit sometimes.

And now I had to deal with the detectives who, at worst, suspected me of being in on the murders at Barry Gant's house, and at best, still had to investigate that possibility.

I felt I could deal with them, though.

Becca Poe, on the other hand, could be anywhere and that truly scared me. Every time I turned a corner, I thought I saw her. My mind played tricks on me. It didn't help that each time I'd actually seen her, she'd looked completely different. I started questioning whether I'd even recognize her.

While my life had become a mess, there was a silver lining. A guy, Rory, came around Rick's a couple of times a week and I enjoyed talking to him. He looked pretty dorky, with glasses and a unique taste in fashion. Which probably worked to his advantage. After Austin, I knew I couldn't date a suave, good-looking guy. It would bring back too many bad memories. Not that Rory and I were dating, but he was definitely the first guy I was interested in since Austin. And it's not that Rory wasn't handsome, just not in the overt way that Austin was.

He stood around six feet tall, with dark brown hair parted from left to right. It didn't look like a hair was ever out of place, which added to Rory's dorkiness. He always wore his wire-rimmed glasses, and if it was midweek, he was always in a suit. After the laziness of Austin, it was nice to see Rory out working each and every day.

He worked in finance, but that wasn't what interested me. He was a big reader, movie buff, music aficionado, and so much more. He'd traveled the world, and even though I once had a travel blog, I hadn't experienced anything near what he had.

I'd ask him about it, and I guess what I liked most about Rory was that he turned reticent when it came to his worldwide travels. He was the opposite of braggadocious, and I'd have to repeatedly ask him before he'd tell me about all the adventures he'd been on. But when I cajoled him enough, he wouldn't hold back.

He talked about doing the Running of the Bulls, Carnival in Brazil, and New Year's Eve in Dubai. I took it very slow, but I found myself enjoying Rory's company more and more each time I saw him.

Of course, with the whole Becca thing looming over my head, it didn't seem like the right time to get close to anyone. So I'd turned down Rory for three different dates, telling him the timing wasn't ideal. I was nice about it, but never told him why and he didn't press me on it.

I really hoped that he didn't grow tired of waiting, but I had to stick to my guns.

I called Cora out of the blue one day. She had given me her number at the memorial and I hoped I could learn some more about Richard and his connections. Maybe I could get some information on Becca. I felt like the hunted and wanted to change that. I told her a few of my suspicions, hoping that would convince her to come.

She agreed and we met at Gramercy for lunch. It had been less than four months since Austin and I had our first date at Gramercy, and I couldn't help but think about it as I walked in. Cora was already there, sitting in a booth in the corner. A good choice, I thought.

"Hi, Olive," the bartender said.

I'd come by and grab lunch about once a week and a few of the bartenders had remembered my name. Unfortunately, I hadn't remembered his, so I just gave him a wave as I headed to the corner and joined Cora. We looked at the menus and made a little small talk. A few minutes later, after we ordered, I got down to the reason I'd invited her out.

"I'm wondering if there's any information you could give me about Richard. I'm trying to find out any connections he had or people who helped him out. Hopefully I can find out more about what he was doing in Vegas."

"When we talked, you said the police wouldn't listen to you about Richard."

I had to throw Cora a bone, so I'd mentioned Becca Poe, the money, and my fear that she had killed Richard.

"I didn't get a chance to explain it fully, but yes, they are not investigating Richard's death right now," I said.

"Why not?"

"Because they're investigating me. They got an email saying I was the one who orchestrated the killing of Barry Gant."

"Do they believe it?"

"I don't know, but they at least have to follow up. I mean, I guess it makes some sense. I knew Barry and helped set up the meeting with him. To the police, it seems logical that a bartender and her poor boyfriend might set up her boss and steal his money. For all I know, they really do believe it."

"And now you want to do your own investigating? That didn't turn out too well for Richard."

That hit hard, but I deserved it.

"I just want to know who Richard may have talked to. If they knew where Becca was living, it would be a huge help."

"My guess is that no one knew. That's probably why Richard had me pretend to be you. To get her to come out of the shadows."

"You're right. That being said, I'd still like to talk to someone. If you know of anyone."

"Well, I know he had a lot of connections around LA. Snitches and things like that. But I didn't know many of them. In fact, his only acquaintance I also got acquainted with was a man named Hector Reyes. Richard used him all the time and was actually very good friends with the guy, away from their jobs. I'd probably consider him Richard's best friend. He didn't have many. When we were dating, we'd have lunch with Hector about once a month. They'd never talk business in front of me, but Richard would always tell me that Hector made his life easier."

"Sounds like they were pretty close."

"They were," Cora said. "Initially, I was surprised that he didn't come to the memorial at your old bar, but if he had helped Richard with any information pertaining to Vegas, he'd probably want to stay clear of his friends and family."

"Makes sense. Listen, Cora, do you have Hector's phone number?"

"Yeah. Like I said, we had become pretty close with him."

"Could you give me it?"

She paused for a second, but then scrolled through her phone and read the number to me.

"Thanks, Cora."

Our timing was on point, as a chicken sandwich (hers) and lobster roll (mine) arrived just as we finished the important part of our conversation. We each took a bite and I could tell she liked hers.

"It's delicious," she said.

"On my first date with Austin, I was having a chicken sandwich just like yours."

"Here, at Gramercy?"

"Yeah."

"Doesn't bring back bad memories?"

"He does. Not the restaurants or bars we ate at."

"How's your lobster roll?" she said, changing the subject.

"As good as if I was in Maine."

"I haven't been back east in years. In fact, when Richard had said he wanted to take a vacation, New York, Boston, and the whole Eastern Seaboard came to mind."

We ate for a few minutes in silence.

"I'm really sorry for your loss, Cora," I finally said.

"It's not your fault, I hope you know that. From all you've told me, it sounds like his greed is what did him in."

"Thanks. I know you're right, but I still beat myself about it."

"Have you ever thought what you would do if you caught Becca and she had a whole bunch of money?"

"I have."

"And?"

"And what?"

"And would you turn the money in?"

"Of course," I said. "That's blood money."

"Yeah, I guess you're right," Cora said, but I suspected she was still dreaming about a trip back east.

"Catching her and finding out exactly what went down would be enough for me."

"Of course. We both lost people we cared about," she said.

I didn't like the morose way the conversation was headed.

"Thanks for giving me Hector's phone number, Cora. I don't know if it's going to lead anywhere, but I greatly appreciate it."

"You're welcome. I hope you or the police catch that evil bitch."

"Me too," I said.

"Better yet, I hope Hector catches her. He's got a teddy bear exterior, but Richard told me he can be a mean SOB when he needs to be."

I took note of that.

As we finished up our meals, I motioned for the bartender.

"Can I get a bill?" I asked.

"Sure, Olive."

I really needed to find out the guy's name. I saw Cora take the final bite of her chicken sandwich.

"How was it?"

"Fantastic. Thanks for the meal."

"You're welcome. Let me close the bill and I'll walk out with you."

"Sounds good."

I called Hector Reyes early the next day. I was in my bed, under my covers, Macbook sitting on the comforter. It was a non-work day and I planned on it being a quiet one—but productive.

"Hello?"

"Hector, my name is Olive Fairbanks and I think we have a mutual friend."

"And who might that be?"

His voice sounded like sandpaper mixed with Maker's Mark whiskey. It was deep, gruff, and none too friendly. But I stood my ground.

"Richard Levert. I'm the one who hired him to investigate Becca Poe and I think he may have contacted you."

"And why might you think that?"

He sure was consistent with his responses.

"I talked to Cora and she said Richard used you every time he could. Look, I'm not trying to get you into trouble. I'm just trying to find out some information."

I heard him exhale on the other end.

"Yeah, he called me. Told me about you and about a woman named Becca Poe. Did she kill him? I heard heart attack, but you never know when you're out there following someone."

I figured giving him a little information could only help me get some in return. Plus, there was no harm in telling him.

"I'm guessing that she killed him, but I can't get the Las Vegas police department to answer any of my questions."

"I could inquire. I have some connections out there," he said.

"I'd appreciate that," I said. "And what information did you give him?"

I hoped I wasn't pushing it, but I had to ask.

"He was trying to find out if Becca Poe had used a credit card, gas card, or anything like that."

"And had she?" I asked.

"No."

"Then how did…"

"I found something better," Hector interrupted.

"What was it?"

"First, I'd like to ask you something."

"Anything," I said.

"How much money did Becca Poe escape with?"

"Richard told you that?"

"Actually, he didn't. Probably thought I'd go after it myself." Hector laughed. "But once I found out she had two safety-deposit boxes, I made that leap."

"He never told me about any safety-deposit boxes."

"I'm sure you can guess why."

I had been betrayed again. No doubt of it now. Though not at the level of Austin's betrayal, it still cut deep.

"Would be a pretty big coincidence if he really died of a heart attack," I said.

"Yeah, I'm guessing it's related to the money."

"And Becca."

"Yup."

"As for your question about how much money Becca escaped with, I don't know. But I'll ask you this. How much would there have to be for you to leave 75k at the scene?"

"I get your point."

"I'm guessing several hundred thousand," I said.

"Sounds logical. To answer your earlier question, the two safety-deposit boxes were better than any credit card receipt…"

"That would confirm to Richard that she'd escaped with money."

"Exactly," Hector said.

It started to come together. Once Richard Levert found out about the safety-deposit boxes, he gave me the cold shoulder because he was after the money himself.

"Now I know why he went after Becca Poe," I said.

"He wouldn't be the first private investigator to betray his client."

"Yeah, I'm sure you're right," I said.

"Is there anything else I can help you with?" he asked.

I realized there was.

"If I could ask for one more favor, it would really help me."

"What is it?"

"Could you find out if those safety-deposit boxes are still current?"

"You afraid that Becca Poe may have skipped town?"

"Yes," I said.

"I'll get back to you within the hour," he said.

"Thanks for your help, Hector."

"I'm doing it because I was friends with Richard."

"Do you want to help me get Becca?"

"Hmm, that's tempting," he said, but didn't answer one way or the other.

He called back twenty minutes later.

"Becca Poe no longer has any safety-deposit boxes in Las Vegas. Nor anywhere in the U.S., for that matter."

I wasn't surprised, but it still raised my level of anxiety to a new high.

"Thank you. I have one last favor to ask," I said.

"You're a pushy one."

"I can be. I'd be willing to pay for it."

"What did you have in mind?"

"Could you update me every few days on whether Becca Poe has used a credit card, or opened a new bank account or a safety-deposit box somewhere?"

"Sure, I can do that."

"Thanks for your help, Hector. And if it happens to be Los Angeles, could you let me know right away?"

"Yes. I normally wouldn't be so generous, but like I said, I was really close with Richard. I'd like to find the woman who killed him. Assuming you are right."

"So are you answering yes to my earlier question?"

"I can't just drop all of my cases to go after Becca Poe. But let's say that I'm going to start taking an interest in her."

"I can live with that."

"You'll have to," he said sternly.

"I'll keep you informed of anything I learn on my end."

"Do you think she's coming for you?"

"I think it's a possibility," I said.

"I know a lot of people in the protection business. If you would like someone to look after you, let me know."

"Not yet, but I might take you up on it at some point. Thank you for everything, Hector."

"Stay safe, Olive."

51

BECCA

Since I'd be staying in Los Angeles for less than a week, I decided to do it in style.

At The Montage Beverly Hills, a five-star hotel located a block from Rodeo Drive, I'd spend in one day what it cost to rent my old, shitty apartment in Phoenix for a month. It certainly wouldn't have suited as a long-term plan, but for a week, I could afford it. Plus, I would try to make some connections while I was there. When someone found out I was staying at The Montage, any bullshit story I made up would immediately be believed.

I booked the room from February 9th to February 14th. That would be quite the day. Valentine's Day. Checking out of The Montage. Killing Olive. Fleeing the country.

I had less than twenty-four-hours left in Las Vegas. I'd closed my two safety-deposit boxes the day before, putting the money back in my trusted suitcase and hiding it in my suite at Veer Towers.

While I wanted to do Vegas right on my last night, I decided it was smarter to stay in. I had all the money in my room and I had some planning to do with regards to Los Angeles. So I poured myself a glass of white wine and started brainstorming how I was going to kill my last remaining nemesis.

And then I'd be off to Europe or Mexico, where there would be an all-new challenge. But I knew I was up for it.

This wasn't some movie where the good guy had to win.

No one could stop me.

The bad guy, or in this case, bad girl, was going to be the one smiling at the end.

The next morning, I set off for LA in my shitty car, which I had used sparingly since arriving in Vegas.

The drive took me a little under four hours and I pulled into The Montage with my old, ratty car, provoking some curious looks.

But while a few people looked down on me, those idiots didn't know I was carrying hundreds of thousands of dollars in my suitcase. So fuck them! I was rich, even if the car may have said otherwise.

The Montage was absolutely gorgeous, with a fountain on the ground and the rooms, all equipped with a patio, rising up several stories high. Around the fountain, little batches of lawns, immaculately clean, were surrounded by beautiful trees. They had a rooftop pool that, even in February, I'd be using. It was 75 degrees, after all.

From where I stood, I could see Mastro's Steakhouse and Sugarfish Sushi, two of the best restaurants in Beverly Hills.

I checked in and told them that I would be paying cash. They said they needed a card, but that they would only process it if I didn't pay with cash. That wasn't going to be a problem.

I turned down the bellhop for obvious reasons. No one else would be handling my money.

Once I'd settled in my room, I walked out on the balcony, looking out at the expensive stores below me and the mountains in the background. I could get used to this.

But I'd need a lot more money if I ever wanted to live at The Montage full-time. I'd always heard of famous, often eccentric Hollywood types who lived at extravagant hotels, and I would definitely be up for that. I'd much rather have a room at The Montage and walk around Beverly Hills every day than have some white picket fence in the suburbs. I was never going to have kids, so owning some yard where children could play was unimportant to me. No, The Montage would suit me just fine.

But at upwards of $800 a night, I was looking at over $200,000 a year. And while I had built myself a nice little nest egg, that cost made The Montage currently unfeasible. Maybe in the future. I needed to find another Barry Gant. Maybe I'd keep this one alive and just have him spoil me. Or put me in his will and have him suffer a terrible "accident" a few months later.

Yeah, that sounded good.

As I unpacked, I threw about half of the money in the large safe that they provided. The rest I left in the suitcase and put my other two bags on top of it in the huge walk-in closet. I could never be too careful and always left the suitcase holding the cash covered by other bags in case some woman from housekeeping liked to look through other people's stuff. She wasn't going to risk knocking all my bags over by looking through the bottom one.

I lay on the bed and googled something on my phone. After I got what I wanted, I used The Montage's phone to dial out.

"Hi, you've reached The Belly Flop."

"Hello. I'm an old friend of Olive Fairbanks who's staying in LA for a few days. Was hoping to surprise her."

"She doesn't work here anymore,"

"Do you know where her new job is?" I asked.

"Hold on a second. Sheri, where does Olive work now?" I heard the young, muffled voice ask.

She came back to the line. "She is at Rick's Tavern on Main Street."

"Thanks so much. She's going to be so happy to see me," I said.

52

OLIVE

My talks with Hector and Cora had done nothing to calm my nerves. In fact, they had only made things worse. I'd worked at Rick's both days since I'd talked to Hector, constantly looking at people along Main Street to see if Becca Poe walked by.

But what was I looking for? A blonde pixie cut? Jet black long hair? I had looked directly at her outside of her parents' house without recognizing her. And she was undoubtedly going to look different. If this was a race, I lagged way behind.

I decided to take matters into my own hands. While no evidence had been found of any text messages between Becca and Austin or Chet Watkins, I had to assume she owned a cell phone. I found Becca's parents' number again and called.

"Hello?" a woman's voice answered. It had to be her mother, who had greeted me upon my visit.

"Hi, Mrs. Poe. This is Becca's friend. You met me when I came to the door when I was in Atlanta."

"We're actually in Roswell."

"Yes, I'm sorry. Roswell."

"And you wanted to talk to Becca?"

"Yeah."

I wasn't sure if she was going to give up her daughter's number. She seemed guarded.

"Well, I think that would be just swell. Becca doesn't have many friends right now."

Because she's a freaking murderer! Of course, I couldn't say that. I actually felt really bad for her mother. She must have known that she hadn't raised the nicest child. What she didn't know was that she had actually raised a deranged criminal. But I couldn't break the news to her.

"Well, I'm trying to reach out to her, but I only have an old cell phone number which is no longer hers."

"I didn't know she had changed it."

"I had one from several years ago. I forgot to ask her for her new number when I saw her in Roswell."

"Hold on just a second. I don't know it offhand and have to look at contacts on my cell."

She came back to the phone a minute later.

"I've got two. The last one I have for Becca is 602-555-8295. No, wait, I don't think that one is still active. Try this Atlanta one. 770-216-9091."

"Thanks so much, Mrs. Poe. Where was the 602 is located?"

"That one was Phoenix. Becca lived there a while back, I believe."

Something about Phoenix rang a bell. Chet Watkins! He had been from Phoenix.

All the puzzle pieces were slowly coming together.

"Thank you so much, Mrs. Poe. You've been a great help."

"If you talk to Becca, please tell her to call home. My husband and I haven't heard from her since she left. She didn't leave on good terms, but I still love my daughter."

"I will," I said.

Even though I felt bad for her, I hoped the next call she got from Becca was from jail.

I pondered all the information I had just received. I could go to the police. The confirmation that Becca Poe had lived in the same city as Chet Watkins must be important evidence to the LAPD. But I wasn't exactly feeling the love from them right now, especially after being accused of being part of Barry Gant's robbery and murder.

No, I needed to wait until I had an open and shut case against Becca Poe.

I looked at flights to Phoenix. I had the next few days off at Rick's. This was about getting some closure for Barry Gant. And to a lesser degree, Austin and Richard, though they weren't innocent in all of this. Most of all, it was about bringing the sick, deranged Becca Poe to justice.

If I could undeniably tie Becca to Chet Watkins and bring that to the LAPD, it would be game, set, and match.

A flight took off the next morning at 8:30 from Los Angeles to Phoenix Sky Harbor International Airport, arriving at 10:45 after the hour time change.

I planned to be on it.

Part of me wanted to text Becca and tell her I was closing in on her. But I knew it wasn't the best idea. This woman had killed a seasoned private eye and had arranged or carried out the deaths of three other grown men.

She was no one to screw with, and I decided to err on the side of caution.

_53_
<u>BECCA</u>

I had disregarded many texts from my mom since leaving my childhood home a few months previously, vowing never again to talk to my parents. But there was no ignoring this one.

Your friend who came to say hi in Roswell asked for your cell number. I gave it to her. I think you could use a few more friends, Becca. Love, Mom.

I typed back. *What else did you discuss with her?*

Just that you had lived in Phoenix a while back.

I wanted to kill my mother. What a stupid bitch!!

Instead, I typed…

Does your home phone register incoming calls?

Yeah, I think so

Could you go back and see if you can find her number? Thanks, Mom.

I felt no gratitude toward her, but it might make her more likely to help me. I didn't get a text back for a few minutes.

There's a 310 number. Is that it?

With LA's area code, it had to be.

Yeah.

My mom sent me the number.

When did she call?

Earlier today.

Please text me back immediately if she reaches out again.

Okay, Becca. What is going on?

I'll tell you later, Mom.

Please text me and your father from time to time.

I needed to have my mother on my side in case I required help with Olive, so I continued to play nice. Not that I'd forgotten how my father kicked me permanently out of their house and my mother hadn't stood up for me.

I will, Mom. Love you, bye.

I love you too.

I set my phone down on the bed at The Montage.

"FUCK!!!" I yelled at the top of my lungs.

I grabbed a lamp and ripped it out of the outlet and threw it across the room.

"Goddamn, Olive!"

I was about to throw the remote control at the television, but held back. I needed to calm down. I took a few deep breaths and slowly got my temper under control.

"I'm going to kill you, Olive Fairbanks, if it's the last thing I do on this earth."

54

OLIVE

The flight from Los Angeles to Phoenix was easy, only being in the air for fifty-eight minutes. I'd visited Phoenix one other time, for a bachelorette party when I was twenty-two. It was the first of my girlfriends to get married and none of us liked the groom-to-be, not to mention Stella seemed too young.

We were proved correct, and Stella got divorced less than two years later. But Phoenix had been fun, I'd remembered that. They had a great downtown with lots of high-level clubs that my twenty-two-year-old self really enjoyed. Of course, this was not going to be a partying trip. I was here to get information tying Becca Poe and Chet Watkins together.

My inner Nancy Drew had been reawakened.

I'd called Hector the night before flying and asked for another favor: checking Chet Watkins' credit card information in Phoenix before he died. About to enter a gray area, I wasn't sure if what I asked for was completely legal, but I still felt the LAPD suspected me, and I had to do this to clear my good name.

So I didn't beat myself up about it.

He said he'd have to pull a few favors, but it's info he could get. And he was proved correct.

There were the usual transactions you'd expect. Trader Joe's, gas stations, fast food. But employees wouldn't remember him at places like that. He had also used his credit card frequently at two different bars, and being a bartender, I knew these were different. You got to know your regulars at a bar. You knew them as a person, unlike some checker at Trader Joe's.

The two bars were called Chalky's and Mahoney's. They were going to be my first, and possibly only, stops.

I booked myself into a cheap Red Roof Inn in North Phoenix, only $70 a night. I wasn't going to be there much and I saw no reason to spend money unnecessarily. Much like my trip to Atlanta.

From the airport, the cab driver took Interstate 10 to Interstate 17 north and we arrived at the Red Roof Inn in under twenty-five minutes. Chalky's and Mahoney's both opened at noon, so I didn't have much time to kill. I surfed the internet for a few minutes and got ready to go. I'd put on a red sweatshirt and jeans that morning and saw no reason to change. Usually a sweatshirt would be too warm for the Phoenix desert, but the weather was surprisingly cold. It was still relatively early February, after all.

I got an Uber driven by a vulgar middle-aged white guy. Traveling solo as a young woman always carried some risk, and while most of the time I felt safe, creeps like this always made me uncomfortable, and sometimes threatened.

"What brings you to Phoenix?" he said, turning around to look at me.

"Just seeing some old friends," I said. "They'll all be at Chalky's."

That's where I had decided to go first. And I'd mentioned my non-existent friends to prevent him from getting any ideas about following me in.

"Your friends drink at noon on Wednesdays at a dive bar? I think I like your friends."

He didn't believe my story and I could understand why.

"It's a dive bar?"

"That's an understatement. Are you sure you don't need someone to look after you?"

If we weren't on a desolate highway, I would have had him pull over right there, but I had to tough it out.

"Like I said, my friends will be there to look after me."

"Whatever floats your boat," he said and stared at me once again.

I responded monosyllabically the rest of the trip until we mercifully arrived at Chalky's. It was a dump, no doubt about it. A gas station slumped to its left and some sort of leasing office to its right.

The paint job, a puke yellow, was quickly fading. I passed by a motorcycle out front and asked myself what the hell I was doing there. Had I come to a biker bar? Making my way toward the front door as a few tumbleweeds blew by right in front of me, I vowed to get in and out of Chalky's as quickly as possible.

When I walked in, I was happy to see a woman working behind the bar. We could be terrible as well (see: Poe, Becca), but after my experience with the creepy Uber driver, I would take my changes with a fellow female.

Aside from a man shooting pool by himself, no one else occupied the bar. He had a Hell's Angels jacket on and obviously owned the motorcycle. I sat at the far end of the bar, away from the pool tables, hoping he wouldn't be able to hear the questions I wanted to ask the bartender.

"What can I getchoo?" the woman said. She was probably around fifty years old and I could tell she had been through a lot in her life. *Haggard* would be the right word. *Tough* would probably fit as well.

I had barely drunk in the last few months, but figured it would build up some goodwill if I ordered a drink and left a nice tip.

"I'll take a Tito's greyhound."

I immediately regretted it. This kind of bar didn't stock grapefruit. This was a beer and whiskey type of bar. But I turned out to be wrong.

"We only have pre-made grapefruit. Is that alright?" she said.

It was a subtle jab. I might be someone used to fresh squeezed, but I wasn't getting it here.

"That's fine. I'm a bartender too, I'm not trying to make your job difficult."

I smiled, hoping to get on her good side.

"Oh yeah, where do you bartend?"

I looked down at the pool table and the man didn't seem to be listening in.

"Los Angeles."

"Long way from Los Angeles."

She was going to be a tough egg to crack.

"Did you know a man named Chet Watkins?" I asked, figuring it was as good a time as any.

When she brought over my drink, I paid and pushed three dollars in her direction as a tip.

"Yeah, I knew Chet. Was sad to hear he passed. Especially how he went. You know Chet?"

"Sort of."

"I'll be honest, young lady," she said with obvious condescension, "you don't look like the type of girl who would have known Chet."

"He almost killed me," I said.

I figured honesty was the best policy. If she had been good friends with him, she wasn't going to give me any information anyway.

She grunted. "How'd he do that?"

"He took a gun and brought in down on the back of my head."

Something registered in her eyes. "You were at the robbery?"

"I was the only one who lived," I said, not bringing up my suspicions about Becca.

Her rough exterior faded away and I saw genuine empathy.

"I'm so sorry," she said. "Chet was a scumbag."

"Can I ask you something?"

"I'll help if I can."

She seemed to be on my side and for that, I was grateful.

"The police in Los Angeles think I might have been involved and I'm trying to clear my name. I think that Chet might have been hanging out with a woman in Phoenix who helped set it all up."

"Chet was with a lot of women."

"This woman would have been young, in her late twenties."

I grabbed something from my pocket: a high school yearbook picture of Becca that I had printed.

Before I even showed her the picture, she stared at me.

"Ten to one, it's Holly!"

"Holly?" I asked.

"She was the prettiest girl in Chet's rotation but I just knew she was bad news. Always manipulating, always probing. She was extremely intelligent and knew how to use her sexiness. And guys, being the idiots they are, fell for it. But as a woman, I knew this girl was no good. So show me your picture, but I'm laying ten to one, it's Holly."

I handed the picture over to the bartender, who I realized had never given me her name.

"Well, this is an old picture, and it's hard to be certain, but I'm pretty sure it's Holly."

"Does the name Becca Poe ring a bell?"

"No. Is it supposed to?"

"It's this woman's real name."

"Well, she was known as Holly around these parts."

"And you're sure that's her?"

"99%."

"I have one more favor to ask."

"You're a little tougher than I thought," she said.

"I'll take it as a compliment," I said.

"It is. What's your favor?"

"If I have a Los Angeles police detective call here, would you tell them what you just told me?"

"If they call me, I'll do that for you. If they ask me to fly out to Los Angeles to testify, you've got the wrong woman."

She pronounced it *Los Angle-less*.

"You've been so helpful…"

"Mable. And you are?"

"I'm Olive."

"You should be drinking a martini, girl,"

I laughed. I found myself enjoying Mable's company. Chalky's was obviously a rough spot, but I figured I could stay and have one more drink.

"You know what, I'll take you up on that, Mabel. One gin martini, please."

Mabel smiled. She made me a Beefeater Gin martini, putting the biggest green olive on the rim of the glass.

Twenty minutes later, I finished my martini and thanked Mable for her help. I ordered an Uber from inside and when it was two minutes away, walked out. Luckily it didn't turn out to be the same driver as the one who brought me to Chalky's. I would have cancelled it.

I looked down at my phone to check for the car's arrival when I saw a text had just come in.

My little Olive. You look so cute in your jeans and red sweatshirt. It's not quite blood red, but I'm looking forward to changing that. Sure hope you're enjoying Phoenix.

My blood ran cold. There was only one person this could be. Becca.

I looked around. No one else stood outside of Chalky's or the leasing office. I saw people milling around the gas station, but I couldn't tell if one of them was Becca. I considered walking in that direction, but I just wanted to get the hell out of there.

I kept turning around every few seconds, expecting Becca to be coming at me with a gun. She could easily shoot me and drive away. The people from the gas station were too far away to see what was going on.

When I looked down at my phone, the Uber was still one minute away. What was taking so fucking long?

A loud noise popped behind me. I swiveled around, but it was just the door of Chalky's being opened by the biker. He had a cigarette in his hand and nodded in my direction. I just felt happy to see another person.

I saw a car pulling up with the Uber sticker. I looked in the driver's seat, half expecting to see Becca. It wasn't, of course—the driver's name had been Fernando—but I was a nervous mess. I got in the back of the Uber, looking over my shoulder as we pulled away from Chalky's.

How the hell did Becca Poe know I was in Phoenix? And how did she know what I was wearing?

My whole body went numb. I was now involved in a game I wasn't meant for. And if I kept it up, I might well end up dead.

As I made my way back to the hotel, a steely resolve came over me. I felt pretty confident about two things. First, Becca Poe wasn't in Phoenix. If she had been, no way would she have warned me. No, she was just trying to scare me. And that meant, secondly, that she was back in Los Angeles and had staked out my apartment in Santa Monica, seeing me leave in my red sweatshirt and jeans that morning.

It made sense. She knew where I lived from my time dating Austin. My guess was that her mom called and told her what she'd told me about Phoenix. It seemed the only way she could know.

The Uber arrived at the Red Roof Inn and despite my logical conclusions, I still scanned the parking lot for anyone who resembled Becca. I didn't see anything as I made my way down the hallway, turning around halfway when I heard something, but realized it was just housekeeping.

I opened my door slowly, just in case Becca sat waiting there and I needed to run. My imagination was getting the best of me. The room was vacant.

Looking down at my phone, I read her text again. The LAPD had screwed up this case from the beginning and I wasn't going to call them, even if some might say I should. No, I was doing this myself from here on in.

I picked up my phone and started typing. I sent the following two-word response to Becca:

GAME ON!!

BECCA

After hearing from my mother about Phoenix, I just knew Olive was heading there. We didn't have much in common, but shared the attribute of resiliency. The bitch had some cockroach-like qualities, I'll give her that.

I got up early the next morning and headed to Santa Monica. I parked my car a few blocks from Olive's apartment, hoping she hadn't moved, and settled in at a Starbucks whose window had a view of the front gate of her complex.

If she crossed the street and went into the Starbucks she'd probably see me, but that seemed highly unlikely. I had only been there an hour when I saw Olive walk out of her complex in a red sweatshirt and jeans, wheeling a suitcase and carrying a small bag.

An Uber picked her up, surely taking her to the airport. I waited till later that day to send her a thinly veiled threat. I was delighted when, about thirty minutes later, I got a return message.

GAME ON!!

She had no chance, but despised me so thoroughly that she wanted to settle this one on one. *Mano a mano* as they say, which actually means hand to hand. I had already started scheming the demise of Olive and it would be violent and ugly. I couldn't wait.

I called Olive's new bar.

"Hello, you've reached Rick's on Main."

"Hi, I was wondering the next time that Olive works?"

"Olive is on tomorrow afternoon. Two to eight."

"Thanks so much."

I decided to do my thinking at The Montage Lobby Lounge. Anyone who sat at that bar was undoubtedly going to be rich. My kind of people. I know people love to say that "money doesn't buy you happiness," but that always came from poor losers. Have you ever looked at the people sitting courtside at an NBA game? They are all fucking smiling! And that was going to be me. Not at NBA games per se, but opening night at the opera, wearing an expensive ensemble at the Kentucky Derby, clutching my hat in strong winds while sailing in Nantucket.

All of this would come true. $600,000 was a lot of money and if I could find a way to invest that money, it would last me a long time. So while I sipped my drink and thought about ways to kill Olive, my eyes checked to see if any rich men sat down near me.

A few couples sat close, but while I could tell they came from wealth, I couldn't exactly jump in on a couple's conversation. A B-list actor had a drink with his agent, but that didn't interest me. His movies were garbage anyway.

About forty-five minutes later, two men sat down at the bar next to me and started talking about the stock market. They were both in their late forties and dressed like they had just finished a round of golf. The way they talked led me to believe that they might not always do everything by the book.

"Yeah, but they don't have to know about that."

"Hardly insider training, it was just a talk amongst friends."

To which they both laughed extra hard.

I hoped they wouldn't leave at the same time. Two guys, even if they are both shady individually, are tougher to crack collectively. If it's just one man, I can usually get what I want.

At one point, one of the men got up to use the bathroom. I turned to the other one.

"When your friend leaves, I'd love to discuss my portfolio," I said.

I realized he might take "my portfolio" to mean something different, and I was fine with that.

"I'm busy for the next few hours. Are you staying at The Montage?"

"I am," I said and he smiled. Immediate respect. Like being rich.

"How about meeting back at this bar, 8:00 p.m. tonight?"

"I'll be here," I said.

His friend came back and I signed for my two drinks and headed back to my room.

I came back to the lobby bar a few minutes before 8:00 and was pleasantly surprised to see the man already there. He had changed, wearing a white polo shirt and khakis this time. His light brown hair was parted precisely and he had a pair of sunglasses hanging from his polo.

Next, I saw two things that seemed to be at odds. He wore a wedding ring, but the seat next to him had a drink in front of it. Having dealt with married men many times, I could tell the fact that he had already bought me a drink superseded the fact that he was married. This guy wanted to sleep with me if I was willing. I guess we'd have to see what he had to offer.

"Nice to officially meet you," he said. "My name is Brandt. B-R-A-N-D-T."

Of course it was. While I wanted to be rich more than anything in life, the names the wealthy gave their children were absurd.

"I'm Holly," I said, using my name from Phoenix. If it came to the point where I needed to invest with my real name, I'd just say I was scared to use it. And with the story I had devised, there would be a good reason for that.

"What brings you to LA?" he asked.

"Lived here last year and considering moving back. Figured a week at The Montage might push me in that direction."

He smiled, not taking his eyes off of mine.

"And you?" I asked.

"Some work buddies—the guy I was talking with earlier was one of them—and I come to LA for a golf trip every year. Four of us total. Hit a different golf course each day."

"Sounds fun. No wives on the trip," I said, not so subtly.

"No." He blushed. "No wives."

I always found it amusing that a 5'5" woman like myself could make men cower in fear or have them eating out of my hand.

"I guess you're wondering why I wanted to talk to you."

"It crossed my mind," he said.

"You work in the stock market, right? I couldn't help but hear some of your conversation earlier."

"More generally, I work in finance. But yes, I deal quite regularly in the market."

Perfect. And now for my bullshit story.

"I have this friend. She's going through a divorce and has a lot of cash. I mean, a lot. And she doesn't want her husband to know about it. How would she go about handling that? She doesn't want to put it in a checking account or something obvious that could easily be found."

I gauged his reaction. He didn't flinch, which was a good sign.

"How much money does your friend have?"

"She's told me that it's over $600,000."

"That's a lot of cash."

We were the only patrons and the bartender was, intentionally or not, working on the other side of the bar.

"Cheers to my friend," I said and we clinked glasses together. "What am I drinking, by the way?"

"That is a Kettle martini, but no olives," he said.

"No Olives. I like the sound of that," I said.

He smiled at me, having no idea what I meant.

"It's very good. Thanks," I continued.

"I should have put it on your friend's tab." He smiled.

"Yeah, she can afford it."

"So, I've got a few ideas for your friend."

"I'd love to hear them."

And we talked for the next thirty minutes about ways "my friend" could hide money. What the guy was outlining wasn't exactly on the level, but he didn't seem to mind bending the rules. My initial impression had been correct.

"Tomorrow is a full day with the guys, so let's meet up Saturday night and you can give me the money for the first deposit. It's so nice of you to be the middlewoman for your friend," he said and let out a laugh.

I joined him. We were both in on the joke.

I had some questions, like what I would do with the rest of the money in the meantime. But just getting some of it off of my hands was a great start.

Flying might be back in the picture soon. He could answer the rest on Saturday.

He reached his hand across the table and gently touched mine.

"Can I get a check?" he asked the bartender.

While I felt sure this guy was rich as hell, there was still no way I'd invite a man back to my room who I'd basically just told I had $600,000. It looked like I'd be joining him in his. Which was my plan all along. Not only would it have him indebted to me, I'd always have a little something to blackmail him with.

I reminded myself to subtly take some pictures once we got to his room.

"I'm getting a little tired. I think I'm going to head up to my room for the evening," he said.

I leaned in and whispered, already knowing his answer, "Would you like some company?"

Men were so damn easy.

56

OLIVE

The trip back to LA was full of thinking, rethinking, and rethinking my rethinking. If I hadn't already been neck-deep in this, I certainly was now. Becca had come to Los Angeles, and not only that, she had staked out my apartment. This wasn't even a fair fight. She knew where I was and I had no idea of her whereabouts.

In order to make this a fight I had a chance to win, I enlisted the help of Hector Reyes. I called him when I landed at LAX and asked whether, if I gave him a phone number, he could track it.

He said that was easy.

And just like that, I was back in the game.

While I was generally a mild-mannered twenty-six-year-old woman, that didn't mean I couldn't fight back. And if my life was genuinely at risk, I wasn't going to go down quietly. When I'd texted "GAME ON!!" to Becca, she probably just thought it was some line meant to alarm her. It wasn't. Now she had me fully immersed in this, I was all-in on getting Becca.

Hopefully, it would be with the help of the police, but I wasn't exactly in their good graces at the moment. If it had to be by other methods, I felt ready.

I arrived back at my apartment complex, grabbing my cosmetics and clothes for three or four days. No way would I stay there, where Becca could easily ambush me when I slept. I loaded up my car and headed east on Wilshire.

Friends of mine had stayed at the Wilshire Motel, a little dive motel about three blocks from the Wilshire Exit off Interstate 405, when they visited LA. They said the rooms were clean and the price was right. That was enough for me. I called and booked a room for three days, hoping that would be enough time.

I took my bags to the front desk and checked in. They had actual, old school keys that you used to get into your room. Not an electric strip card to be seen.

But I didn't mind.

I propped the lone two pillows they gave me up against the headboard and called Hector Reyes back.

"Hello?"

"Hi, Hector, it's Olive."

"I'm currently tracking the phone number you gave me. Right now, it's in Beverly Hills at Sugarfish Sushi, The Montage Hotel, or Citibank. I can't be too precise, but it's currently roaming in that area. It's been like that since you called me, so my guess would be The Montage. She wouldn't spend that much time at Citibank, and this would be a long lunch at Sugarfish."

"Remind me never to get on your bad side, Hector."

I heard him laugh on the other end.

We had never met in person, but I had come to enjoy our brief talks. He had done and seen more than I ever would and he was a good guy to have on your side.

"Where is your office located, Hector?"

"Downtown. 5th and Broadway."

"Could I come and meet you tomorrow? I'd rather discuss my plans in person, but I have to work this afternoon."

"Sure. How about 3:00 p.m. tomorrow?"

"I'll be there," I said.

"And Olive, take a cab here and get dropped off right out front of my place. This area is pretty dangerous these days and not meant for a pretty girl like yourself."

"How do you know what I…" I started to say.

"Richard told me," Hector interrupted.

That explained it.

"I'll come straight to your work. Tomorrow at 3:00."

"See you then."

I showered and got dressed for work at the Wilshire Motel. The room was neat, but tiny, and the amenities almost non-existent. The water barely came out of the shower, and the bar of soap was the size of a dinner mint, leaving me unsure I'd properly cleansed.

I threw on some jeans and a loose-fitting gray sweater. The sweater had been through the wringer over the years, but I had no problem wearing it into work.

Rick's was quiet when I got there, fortunately. I had so much on my mind, the last thing I wanted to deal with was a packed bar. One table was filled with tourists from Ireland, an older couple sat at one end of the bar, and two guys in their mid-thirties took seats in the middle. No one seemed too drunk—it was 2:00 p.m., after all—and they seemed like a low-maintenance crowd.

It gave me time to think.

57

BECCA

After my night with Brandt, I'd taken a twenty-minute shower that morning. Not that he was bad; on the contrary, he was quite good in bed. But The Montage shower had one-of-a-kind water pressure and it was next to impossible to get out. Finally, fearing I'd start looking like a prune, I exited, then threw on some leggings and a striped blue and white shirt, something that wouldn't stand out. My hair was still auburn red and I planned to keep it that way for a while. The only person who had seen me with this hair was Richard Levert, and he wouldn't be telling anyone.

I got an Uber, which crossed under Interstate 405 and headed down Wilshire toward the ocean before taking a left and following Main Street to Rick's. I had my driver park two blocks away and walked, taking it all in. It wasn't the quickest route, but I wanted to see the water and all the tourists. Shorts and fanny packs were out aplenty. Tourism certainly didn't reach its peak in February, but it looked like plenty of Europeans wanted to get away from their cold winters. And what better place than LA?

An Irish contingent passed by and I watched as they entered Rick's, joining two other small groups already sitting at the bar. But my eyes went at once to Olive. She was gorgeous, no question about it. I couldn't wait to make her look ugly. The urge had become all-consuming now. I not only wanted to kill her, I wanted to disfigure her in the process.

Someone bumped into me right out front of Rick's and it caught a few people's attention. I realized I needed to calm down. Getting fixated could land me in trouble. I walked to a coffee shop a block down and ordered a latte.

Coffee stimulated most people, but it worked the opposite way on me. I drank the coffee and started to relax. I asked the barista for a napkin and a pen, and after a dirty look, she obliged.

I uncapped the pen and wrote on the napkin,

Nice to see you changed from that hideous red sweatshirt. This gray sweater is much more your style.

I returned the pen to the employee.

"Thank you so, so, so much for letting me borrow your pen."

I'm not sure she even picked up on my sarcasm. Dumb bitch!

I walked back over to Rick's, pausing just before I could come into view of the big windows. After a few false alarms, I saw a good-looking man in his early thirties about to walk in.

I approached him with the napkin in my hand.

"Can you give this to the bartender? Thanks a lot," I said.

"You know Olive?" he asked.

It was not the answer I was expecting.

"Oh, we're old friends. I'd give it to her myself, but I'm in a huge rush. How do you know Olive?"

"I come to Rick's a lot and we've started up a friendship," he said.

But I knew the look on his face. A friendship was the last thing he was looking for.

"I'm Nancy. Nancy Drew," I said.

His expression turned quizzical.

"Like the character?"

"Exactly like the character. Been a burden my whole life."

"I'm Rory. Not sure there even are any famous Rorys. Rory McIlroy, I guess," he said.

I had no idea who he was talking about. But Rory seemed like a nice guy and probably would have treated Olive right. Especially compared to how Austin had used her. Sadly, it was fated to be a very short relationship. Olive wouldn't be around much longer.

"Thanks for giving it to her," I said.

"You sure you don't want to do it? I can see her right there."

"I'm really in a rush. Tell her I'll be seeing her soon though. Thanks, Rory," I said.

"You're welcome, Nancy."

Rory said goodbye and headed into Rick's.

As soon as he did, common sense returned. I had to get out of there! What was I thinking?

I started running down Main Street, surely looking like a bat out of hell. After putting a block between me and Rick's, I slowed down to a speedwalking pace. I had brought attention to myself—not smart. I kept moving until I saw another coffee shop, this one known as Bulletproof Coffee. I crossed the street and walked in.

I looked in the direction of Rick's Tavern and sure enough, Olive and Rory came running down Main, looking up and down each side street. I realized they hadn't seen me enter the coffee shop.

I ducked behind a few customers, but kept my eyes on Olive. And Rory.

You were close to me, Olive, but not close enough.

I vowed not to make the same mistake again. The next time I saw her, murder would be the only reason.

I watched as Olive and her friend started heading back in the direction of Rick's. A few minutes later, I ordered an Uber with plans to return to The Montage.

58

OLIVE

"This is from your friend, Nancy Drew."

Fear quickly replaced my joy at seeing Rory when he handed me the note. I read it quickly, confirming Becca had written it. Not that there was much doubt after I'd heard "Nancy Drew."

"Which way did she go?" I asked.

"I'm guessing to the left. I really don't know."

I ran outside and Rory followed behind me. We took a left on the street and started sprinting. If it had been night time, I might not have been so exuberant to chase after a murderer, but I didn't think Becca was going to do anything in broad daylight. She was just out to scare me.

And she had.

We got about two blocks down without any sign of her.

"Do you see her?" I asked Rory.

"No."

I realized I couldn't just run all over Santa Monica; I had a bar to watch. Rory and I headed back toward Rick's. We got a few perplexed looks from some of the customers when we returned, but no one asked any questions.

Rory took a stool at the far end of the bar, where no one else was sitting.

"What is going on, Olive?"

I couldn't say nothing was wrong. It wasn't believable any more. And Rory had been more than patient with me. He deserved an explanation.

But I didn't want to tell the story at the bar, with other people milling around.

"What are you doing tonight at eight?" I asked.

"Trying to kick me out already?"

"I'm serious."

"No plans," he said.

"Pick me up here at eight and I'll explain everything," I said.

"I'll come back. But for now, I'd like a beer. I got my daily exercise in, now I can imbibe."

I didn't hold his playful manner against him. He couldn't know how serious this was. After that night, he would.

Rory stayed for the one beer and we talked about everything except what had just happened. He could tell I didn't want to discuss it, and I appreciated him stepping back. The note had described my clothing and nothing else. It must be eating him up to know why I'd gone apeshit over something so seemingly trivial.

We had a great back and forth, with never an awkward pause, feeding off each other. He was funny and quick-witted. No doubt I enjoyed his company.

The rest of the shift went relatively easily. The Irish group got a little drunk and started singing songs, but they were fun to be around. A couple of semi-regulars came in. I knew most of them by that point.

I texted Hector Reyes an hour after the incident, and he told me that Becca Poe's cell phone was back in the Beverly Hills area, so I rested easier. For a while.

As the sun went down, I felt a tightening in my stomach. If Becca was really going to do something, it wouldn't be with the sun out in front of hundreds of people on Main Street. But the dark brought a strong foreboding and I looked forward to ending my shift.

I flip-flopped on how much to tell Rory, but decided it was better to just be up front with him. He'd asked me out several times, and for that reason alone, he deserved to know the truth. Plus, he had just met Becca face-to-face and he needed to be warned.

Becca wouldn't go after Rory, would she? I didn't think so.

But he'd told Becca he knew me. And I wasn't putting anything past her at this point.

So I would tell Rory everything. It was the right thing to do.

Rory arrived at 8:00 sharp. My replacement was on time, so I was able to get out of there within ten minutes of clocking out. I was able to do some of my post-work work beforehand so I wouldn't have to leave Rory waiting too long.

We hadn't talked about what exactly we were doing, besides me offering an explanation of the note, but Rory appeared to have made the decision.

"You hungry?" he asked as we walked outside.

"Starving," I said.

I usually wouldn't say that to a guy, but I hadn't eaten all day, save for a few peanuts on the plane and some bar snacks behind the bar.

It had been the longest day in memory. Phoenix this morning, a flight back, moving from my apartment to the motel, working, Becca coming so close, and now a date with Rory.

Was it a date?

"Have you been to The Galley?"

Even though I had lived in LA for seven years, including college, I hadn't yet. "No, but I've heard good things."

"You're going to love it," he said.

We arrived at his car.

Rory drove about five blocks north on Main Street. We took a side street and found parking fairly easily. That wasn't always the case in Santa Monica.

The Galley's blue facade featured a man in a rowboat just below its sign. The entrance was very much an ode to the sea with the whole awning looking like a naval vessel. Assuming they specialized in seafood, I was surprised to see a bar as well. I'd expected more of a restaurant feel, but this place had both. Safe to say I liked it right away.

We approached the maître d'.

"Can we get a table for two?" Rory asked. "Hopefully in a corner, if you can."

He had read my mind.

"It will be a few minutes," the highly freckled young woman said.

We went to the bar and waited.

"Want a glass of white wine? Looks like you could use it!"

No question about that. "Sure," I said.

I'd been pretty good since decided to slow down on alcohol. But I wasn't perfect. And with all that was going on, a glass of wine sounded nice.

The bartender poured us two glasses and several minutes later the woman came and took us to our table.

We made small talk at first, but then Rory stared at me.

"Alright, Olive. Let's hear it. Why did you go running like Usain Bolt when I gave you that napkin?"

I told him everything. Starting with Barry hitting on me over the years, my first meeting Austin, the robbery and murders, my interviews with the police, the murder of Richard, my trip to Roswell where I talked to Becca, and finally my trip to Phoenix and the text message about my red sweatshirt.

"Jesus H. Christ," Rory said.

"So now you know why I acted crazy after I read that note."

"I don't blame you."

"So, what do you think?" I asked.

"You have no choice," he said. "You have to go back to the police."

I should have known that was going to be his answer. I realized I hadn't told him quite everything.

"There's one thing I left out," I said. "Richard has this friend named Hector Reyes. And I think there could be another option."

I did, in fact, head back to The Montage, but I knew I'd be back on Main Street just a few hours later. When I'd called the day before to ask about Olive, they said she'd work from two to eight, and I planned on being back when her shift ended. I considered going to another Rite Aid and picking up some more sleeping pills and Clorox.

It had worked on Richard Levert, after all.

I decided that might be a possibility in a few days' time, but tonight was merely going to be a reconnaissance mission.

I wanted to know if Olive was still staying at her apartment. After my text to her in Phoenix, she'd probably figured out I'd seen her in LA, and it seemed unlikely she'd return to her home.

And if that was the case, I needed to know where she did lay her head. Once I knew that, I could finalize how I was going to kill her.

I arrived back at Rick's just a few minutes before eight to be greeted with a nice surprise. As I sat in my car across the street, I saw the man from earlier that day, Rory, enter the bar. Unless, by a huge coincidence, he was walking in right as she got off, he'd come there to pick up Olive.

Maybe Olive was staying at his house. Maybe this was her rebound from Austin. Maybe she had told him everything. Maybe I could get rid of both at the same time.

I realized I was getting too manic. I couldn't just kill everyone. I had prided myself on being deliberate and planning my crimes meticulously. I had to calm down and think this through.

As I sat and watched Rory walk in, I wondered if I really needed to kill Olive at all.

I had never texted or called Jared/Austin or Chet Watkins. I'd deleted our old conversations from Chet's phone. I had done the same on my end. Leaving no trace, I really had committed the perfect murder.

But if I tried to kill Olive, it could all go wrong. And if it did, I'd spend the rest of my life in prison. I hadn't risked everything just to end up rotting inside of a cell. As much as I wanted to kill Olive, and see her squirm before doing so, I reconsidered the necessity.

I decided I could reassess tomorrow, but since I was already at Rick's, I owed it to myself to at least follow Olive and Rory around.

They left around ten minutes later, walking out the front entrance. Rory had parked a block north and a block east. I slowly followed them to his car, being as discreet as possible.

He came around to the passenger side and opened the door for Olive. What a gentleman! Definitely trying to get laid. And maybe if they went back to his house, I could...

My mind raced. I once again told myself that Olive didn't have to die.

But I had never been good at letting a sleeping dog lie. I wanted Olive dead. And I decided then and there I was going to make it happen.

I followed them to a place called The Galley and parked my car.

I peeked in the windows a few times, but I couldn't risk going into the restaurant. And what would that accomplish, anyway? Nothing.

It wasn't time to leave, however. I needed to find out if she was shacking up with the new guy. I walked back to my car and parked it with a good view of the entrance. And I bided my time. Something I was getting good at.

As I waited, I ran through ways I could kill Olive.

I could go to Skid Row and ask where to buy a gun. Once I knew where she lived currently, it would be easy to make good use of it.

I could do what I'd done to Richard Levert. The risk was in getting close enough to inject the concoction when she knew what I looked like. Maybe I could do it at night.

I could pretend to be someone else in order to lure her out. I could call Rick's and say "I'm Betsy, the new girl at The Belly Flop, and we found something interesting about Barry Gant." Curiosity would get the best of her and I could ambush her in the back alley of the bar.

Options crowded my brain. I still had a few days. Ideally, I wanted to kill her on Valentine's Day. Obviously, though, if the opportunity availed itself earlier, I would take full advantage.

As I continued going over ways to kill Olive, she and Rory walked out of The Galley. I followed them. To my delight, Rory did not drop her off back at Rick's Tavern. They went to an apartment complex that had underground parking.

So that's where Olive would stay! Rory had said they were just friends. Bullshit!

I couldn't continue my reconnaissance, but I was still smiling. I had my best idea yet. If I could get ahold of a gun and hide in the underground parking complex, I could shoot Olive and Rory before walking up to my waiting car and driving away. It was risky, but if they were the only ones in the garage at the time, it was very doable.

And I'd make sure to shoot Rory first. Then I could lock eyes with Olive for a split second before I killed her. I'd want her to know I was ending her life, that she'd fucked with the wrong woman.

What a great moment that would be.

It was time to get a gun.

60

OLIVE

I had no plans to sleep with Rory that night. But as we started talking about all that had happened, he asked if I wanted to come over to his house for a cup of coffee. Though unsure if it was a line or not, I agreed.

Once we drove over, parked in the underground garage, and made our way up to his apartment, I had changed my mind and thought maybe I would. Sure, it was our first date, but we had known each other for over a month now, and had flirted many, many times at the bar. So it didn't feel like a first date. Plus, I was ready to have sex again. Not just for the enjoyment and the stress relief I sorely needed. I hated thinking that Austin was the last guy I'd made love to. And let's be honest, it wasn't love, it was sex, merely to get me closer to him, and in turn, get him closer to Barry.

I hated constantly being reminded of the last time I'd been with a man. Maybe that was about to change, I thought to myself.

Turned out, it wasn't in the cards. Rory hadn't been using a line. He had this huge espresso maker and started brewing some Americanos as soon as we walked in. No massage, no kiss, no nothing.

He truly did just want to have me over for coffee.

And I appreciated it. While I had talked myself into sex, it would have been pretty scummy of him to initiate it after I'd told him everything regarding Austin.

"So how exactly do you want to use this guy Hector Reyes?" Rory asked me instead.

His apartment was big and beautiful. I knew he did well financially and the vaulted ceilings, hardwood floors, and spacious interior proved that. He'd brought our coffees over to the couch where I sat, setting them on the glass table in front of me. He also carried over some sort of wafer cookie, setting a plateful next to the coffee.

He joined me on the couch, but didn't sit too close. I could read the intentional signal that he wasn't hitting on me. Not on this night, at least.

"I don't know exactly," I said. "I just need one last piece of incriminating evidence and I'll go to the police. I know you want me to go now, but I want it to be foolproof this time."

"You don't think her knowing Chet Watkins in Phoenix is enough?"

Obviously he had been paying attention at dinner. He'd asked the right question.

"It's close. But the bartender told me she wouldn't come out and testify. And she had I.D.'d Becca based on a high school yearbook photo. Also, it's not illegal to know someone. They'd still have to prove that Chet and Becca worked together and I think she was too smart for that."

"You said something about that at The Galley. There was nothing tying these people together?"

"Nothing. No emails, no text messages. Becca must have really thought this thing out. She's very smart. That's why I'm telling you we have to be vigilant."

I felt bad, already saying "we" had to be vigilant. I'd dragged another innocent person into my mess. In my defense, it wasn't a mess I had wanted or created, but guilt still riddled me.

"I'd like you to stay with me until this is over," he said.

"I told you, I've got a room at the Wilshire Motel."

"If you think I'm going to let you go back to a motel by yourself, you're as crazy as Becca Poe."

"Rory, I can't."

"Of course you can. This couch is comfortable as hell. I've got a blanket and some pillows. Tomorrow, I'll go with you and we'll pick up your stuff."

"I don't know how to thank you," I said.

It was nice to know a man had my best interest in mind. After Austin, and to a lesser extent, Richard, I needed a man who cared about me and not for his own selfish interests. Rory's stock rose in my book.

"There is one thing you can do," he said.

"What is it?" I said, having a sip of the Americano.

"You can promise me you'll go to the cops tomorrow."

"I want to get more evidence."

"Olive, they need to know that this crazy woman is out there after you. I can tell them that I saw her today. That, along with what you found in Phoenix, has to be enough to at least bring her in."

"The last time I saw them, they accused me of being in on the robbery and murders."

"You said that's because Becca Poe sent them an email."

"So?" I said, running out of excuses.

"So they were just doing their job, following up on a lead."

"I know, but I need something concrete. I'm tired of this going in circles. I want to end it once and for all."

"I understand, Olive. How about this? We go to the police tomorrow and if they don't believe you or put out an arrest warrant for Becca Poe, we'll never go back to them. But they are the police and deserve one last chance."

I started getting misty-eyed again. I didn't know if it was because we were recreating all that I'd gone through, or whether I was just happy to have a good man on my side.

"I have a counteroffer," I said. "Give me tomorrow and Sunday. Maybe Hector or I can figure something out. I'll go to the police first thing Monday morning."

I saw Rory thinking it over.

"I agree. On a few conditions. When you're not working or with me, you're in this apartment with the dead bolt locked at all times."

"I don't work tomorrow or Sunday, so that's not a problem."

"Neither do I. So we'll hang out or be in this apartment together. And then we can reassess on Monday after you talk to the cops."

It sounded like being held hostage, but I knew Rory was just looking after me. After all, he wanted me to go to the police the next morning. I was the one postponing this.

"Thanks for doing all this. You don't have to," I said.

"I want to. I like you, Olive, and you need someone's help right now."

"Alright, I agree. Are there any more contingencies?"

"Yes."

"What?" I asked, expecting some other restriction.

"Sunday is Valentine's Day. You have to join me for a nice dinner. As friends, of course," he said and smiled.

"That sounds great." I leaned over and kissed him on the cheek.

Our eyes met and there was a brief period of indecision on both sides.

"Let's wait till this is all over," Rory said.

"Yeah, that's probably for the best," I said, not sure I truly believed it.

Rory went to grab a few more pillows and a blanket, tucking me in as much as one could on a couch. He said goodnight and went off to his room.

61

BECCA

Saturday morning arrived and I knew everything was coming to a head. My plan was still to get out of the country on Sunday night, but I realized Europe wasn't going to happen. I trusted Brandt. The guy was probably worth millions. That being said, I didn't intend to give the guy $600,000. And I couldn't risk carrying the rest through an airport.

Mexico brought its own potential problems, so my plan was to stay in the continental United States until all my money was safely laundered with Brandt. Then I'd set off to Europe.

As for Olive, my only fear was that she and Rory would stay in on Sunday night, but on Valentine's Day I figured they'd be out on the town. And I'd be in the parking garage waiting for them.

I grabbed my car from the valet at The Montage at 8:00 a.m. and started heading toward downtown Los Angeles, Skid Row to be exact. It's not exactly a place I'd visited often, but many people told me that the homelessness and drug situation downtown had gotten way worse over the years.

I headed to 3rd and Figueroa, which was basically the epicenter for the homeless in Los Angeles. I couldn't just go out and buy a gun and have the ballistics come back to me, so I had to get imaginative. Still, driving down Figueroa, I started to reconsider my idea. Trash lay all over the ground, graffiti splattered the walls and windows of closed businesses, and people crowded the ground, covered in makeshift tents.

These were drug addicts, not gun sellers.

I saw a man standing up, a rare site, and I approached him, rolling down my window. I leaned a twenty dollar bill out and he approached the car.

He was rail thin, with pasty, thinning hair.

"I've got a husband who wants to kill me and I need a gun," I said.

The defaults "my husband wants to kill me" and "my husband wants to take my money" had worked well for me over the years. I saw no reason to change now.

The man looked me over. "Why'd he want to hurt a little muffin like you?"

Muffin? Fucking loser.

"I don't have time to talk, I need a gun. Can you get me one?" I asked.

"I could get you drugs, but no g…" he said.

I was driving off before he finished speaking.

For the next forty-five minutes, I drove around Skid Row. Sure never to get out of my car, I must have asked fifteen people for help. The answer was almost always the same. "I can get you drugs, but no weapons." Several asked if I was a cop.

I wished I'd made some fake Olive Fairbanks business cards. I'd have had her phone number on there and her address, and left them with every drug addict who had made a pass on me. Tell them to swing by my house or stop by Rick's when they had the chance.

Man, did I have an evil mind.

Unfortunately for Olive, she wasn't going to be around in two days' time, and would miss all these great guys.

They truly were a despicable lot. I wanted to tell them they were human scum and I hoped they all died grotesque deaths. But I had more important things ahead, and used some rare restraint.

Finally, almost an hour in, I got my first lead. An African-American man—that's what you have to call them, right?— was getting out of his tent when I pulled up. I almost told him if he added another Glad bag he could double his square footage, but figured he wouldn't get the joke.

Instead, I said, "My husband is trying to kill me, do you know where I could get a gun?"

"You're not a cop, are you?"

"Do I look like a cop?" I asked.

"No, you don't."

He didn't seem drugged out and for a brief moment, I worried that maybe he was the cop.

"I don't have a gun myself, but I know someone who could sell you one. How much you willing to spend?"

"Whatever it takes to get a gun," I said.

I had my foot hovering above the gas, just in case he thought I had a lot of money on me and lunged toward me.

"Can you come back in an hour?" he asked.

"Yes."

"You come back to this same spot, I'll have someone here."

"It's 9:15. One hour?"

"To be safe, let's say 10:30."

I wanted to ask him why he was living on Skid Row. He didn't have that zombie quality shared by so many others I'd talked to. I decided to just be happy I was getting what I wanted.

"I'll be here at 10:30."

"And bring cash. He don't take no credit cards."

"Understood. And please, have him bring five to ten bullets for the gun. And a silencer," I added.

"He'll bring both."

I nodded in his direction and sped away. I realized that I very easily might have been set up. Tell the mark to bring cash and then rob her when she comes back. It's something I would have thought of.

But I didn't have much choice. I had a timeline to keep.

If there was a heaven or hell, then I'm sure Austin, Barry, Chet, and Richard would look on in utter joy if I got robbed and killed on Skid Row.

Sorry fellas, but that wasn't going to happen.

I came back a little over an hour later, no longer nervous. Do you know when you have the sense nothing can go wrong? That's how I felt. I knew I was going to get the gun. I knew I was going to kill Olive and her new boy toy. I knew I was going to get out of LA. And I knew I was going to live happily ever after.

The African-American man from earlier was flanked by another black guy, who must have been the brains behind the operation. He had glasses and looked scholarly, out of place surrounded by drug addicts in tents.

The other man had seemed pretty with it too, and I wondered if possibly he wasn't homeless but planted there to sell drugs. Or handguns.

I pulled up alongside them, but didn't get out of my car. Being confident doesn't mean I wasn't cautious as well.

"Just you." I pointed to the new guy wearing the glasses. "And walk slowly."

The guy deliberately made his way toward my car and spoke.

"I'm not here to rob you, if that's what you're worried about. I'm here to make a business transaction."

"All the same, please move slowly, or I'll hit the gas and you'll never see me again."

"I understand," he said.

Obviously, I couldn't trust the guy. He was selling guns and almost certainly drugs as well. That being said, his words had a conviction, and I did believe him.

"How many options did you bring?"

"Two. One is a little pistol and one is a bigger handgun. My friend told me your husband wants to kill you. Either will prevent that from happening."

"My husband is as big as two people. I'd have to shoot him twice. At least. Will the pistol be able to handle that?"

Little did he know the two shots were going to be for two separate people.

"Yes. This isn't the 1940s. Any gun made these days will get off a bunch of shots in rapid succession. And kill quite easily."

"I'll take the smaller pistol."

He handed it to me. It was compact and sleek. I liked the way it felt in my hands.

"This is the Kahr Arms P380," the man said. "There's very little recoil on this, which might be better for a lady like yourself."

If he only knew what I had done, he might not refer to me as a lady.

"And you brought bullets?"

"I did. The chamber takes six bullets, and I brought you twelve."

"And a silencer?"

"I brought what is referred to as a suppressor. It reduces the muzzle flash when you fire and helps reduce the intensity of the sound."

"That will work."

"The suppressor works well. And twelve bullets should be plenty to kill one man."

"Don't get funny if you want this sale," I said.

He nodded as if he understood. I had yet to find a man I couldn't intimidate in some way.

"And I'm assuming there's no serial number."

"I wouldn't be in business long if things traced back to me."

He smiled and I smiled back. Two criminals respecting each other's game.

The man I had met earlier this morning stood to the side, his head on a swivel.

"He's looking for cops, right?" I asked.

"Yup."

"And he's not even a drug addict, is he? Probably just here to get you business."

"Yup."

"Pretty nice little setup you guys have."

"You sure you're just getting this gun for protection? You've got a criminal mind on you. And I say that as a compliment."

"It means a lot," I said, meaning every word of it.

He smiled, but I could tell he wanted to finalize the deal.

"The Kahr Arms P380 would cost you over $600 in the store. Out here on the street, it's yours for $350."

I whipped out four one-hundred-dollar bills and gave them to him. He handed me the box of bullets.

"Keep the change," I said.

"You've got some flair to you, I have to say. We could use the help of a woman."

"In the next life," I said. "I'm just a housewife fearful of her husband."

"You know, when I take my wedding ring off, it still leaves a noticeable mark."

He was good, I had to give it to him.

"Love to stay and talk, and I really do mean that, but I should probably go now," I said.

"This has been a pleasure. And I do actually mean that as well."

We smiled at each other once more. Honor amongst thieves.

Although in reality, I had no honor. And I was going to prove that with my new little friend, the Kahr Arms P380.

I nodded to the man and then drove away.

62

OLIVE

I woke up on Saturday, February 13th in a strange apartment on a strange couch.

Ten minutes later, Rory emerged from his room. He wore a pair of striped boxers with no shirt. I took a quick peek and liked what I saw.

"How did you sleep?" he said.

"Pretty well. This couch is really comfortable."

"Glad to hear it."

"What time is it?" I asked.

"8:45."

"Wow, it really must have been comfortable. I rarely sleep in this late. Do you?"

"No. I've been up since 7:00, but stayed in my room because I didn't want to wake you up."

Now that's the way to win a girl's heart.

"Thanks. A long night's sleep is just what I needed."

"You're welcome."

He came over and sat on the couch next to me. "I meant what I said last night," he said. "I don't want you going to that motel or your apartment without me. I acquiesced on not going to the cops today, but I'm not budging on this."

I appreciated his firmness on the issue as I checked out his strong body one more time. Obviously, more important things were going on, but with a shirtless guy right in front of me, it was hard not to.

"Thanks for everything. What's your plan today?" I asked.

"I don't want to be stuck in this apartment all day. Neither one of us works, let's go have some fun. You could use a day away from Los Angeles and worrying about Becca."

"What did you have in mind?"

"Have you ever been to Catalina?"

Santa Catalina Island, more often referred to as Catalina Island, or just Catalina, is the most famous of the Channel Islands, located just twenty-two miles off the coast of Southern California. I had never been and told Rory so, and didn't take much convincing once he extolled its virtues. The island housed a tiny little town called Avalon, its lifestyle casual and carefree with sailboats lining the shore.

Despite it being February and not exactly prime island weather, it still sounded like the perfect trip at the perfect time. Getting out of LA for twenty-four hours seemed like paradise.

Of course, the real world wouldn't stop, and I needed to talk to Hector Reyes. I asked Rory for a little bit of privacy and he said I could talk in his room.

"Hello?"

"Hi, Hector, it's Olive."

"How are you, Olive?"

"I've been better. But I'm staying with a guy now and I've agreed that I'll go to the police on Monday if we don't find anything else on Becca Poe."

"That's probably a good idea. Contacting the police isn't always my go-to move, but I think it's right in your case."

"I'm not going to be able to make it down to your office today. Is that alright?"

"That's fine. I'm sure we'll meet each other soon enough."

"Great."

"So why'd you call?"

"Can you ping Becca's phone right now?" I asked.

"You do know that I have like thirty other cases I'm currently working on."

"I'm sorry. I said I would pay you."

"For now, don't worry about it. I'm doing it for Richard. But I can't bring up Becca's location ten times a day. I just don't have the time."

"I'm sorry, I won't ask again."

"Give me a minute to load this up."

I didn't want to poke around, but I found myself looking at some of the plaques in Rory's spacious bedroom. He seemed to be a big deal, even appearing in a picture with former President Obama. He had a framed photo of his first communion, in which he wore a disheveled suit and wasn't looking at the camera. A caption said the communion took place in 1995. I knew those happened around the time you were eight years old, so I guessed he was about thirty-two. It had never come up in our discussions.

Unlike Austin, who had told me his age the first time we had met.

I stopped looking at Rory's pictures. I felt bad, even though these were obviously things he was proud of.

Finally, Hector got back on the line.

"It appears she is currently downtown, not too far from me. Looks like she might be around Skid Row."

"What the hell would she be doing there?" I asked.

"She's not a drug addict, is she?"

"I don't know, but with all she's accomplished, I doubt it."

I knew accomplished was the wrong word, but it was too late to take it back.

"She's not a prostitute on the side?"

"I doubt that as well."

"I'd say she's looking at the local businesses, but that seems unlikely this early."

"Anything else you could think of?" I asked.

"You don't want to hear it," Hector said.

"Tell me."

"If you were trying to find a gun, it's the place you might go."

In a long line of gut punches, this was just another one. I'd say I had become immune, but that wasn't true. They all hurt, and this one put me more on edge than ever.

"Great," I sarcastically said.

"Are you sure you don't want to go to the police today?"

"My friend Rory and I are going to Catalina."

"You trust him?"

"He's one of the good ones."

"With your recent history of men, I had to make sure."

Another punch to the stomach.

"That hurt, Hector."

"It was meant to."

"About this guy, I'm positive. And he's got money. That seemed to be the starting point for Austin and Richard."

"It's the root of all evil, as the saying goes."

"I'll be back tomorrow and probably go out to dinner, stay at his place, and go to the police Monday morning."

"A Valentine's Day dinner?"

I found myself laughing. "When did you turn into my dad?"

"Just looking after you, Olive. I feel a bond with you."

I felt it as well.

"It's mutual. I'll call you tomorrow when I get back. If you have any ideas how we can get a little last-minute evidence on Becca, let me know."

"Will do. Be safe, Olive."

"I will. Thanks for everything, Hector."

I hung up and walked back to the living room.

"Everything okay?" Rory asked.

"Yeah, we're fine. Just some last-minute things with Hector. He also thinks I should go to the police."

"I knew I liked Hector."

"I don't think we have anything to worry about. We're going to be gone all day and it doesn't sound like you're going to allow me to venture out on my own tomorrow."

"You got that right. You're mine for the next few days."

He said it with a smile, knowing what I'd been through in recent months.

"By the way, I made reservations. One of the last available on the island. Because of Valentine's Day on Sunday."

"Is it weird we're going there as friends?"

"I don't think so."

"Neither do I." I smiled. "I need to take a shower. But…"

He looked at me and then it hit him.

"Ah, but you need some clothes first. Let's go by the motel and your place and pick up whatever you may need for the next few days."

"Thanks."

"You're welcome. Ready to go?"

"Yeah."

We went by the motel first and I grabbed my clothes. I went to the front desk and asked if I could get Saturday and Sunday's payment taken off of my credit card since I wouldn't be staying. The man there pulled some strings and made it happen.

Next, we went to my apartment. Rory insisted coming to the door with me, having heard my suspicions that Becca had spied on me there. Nothing seemed amiss and I picked up a few extra things.

The stereotypical woman, I had grabbed six different outfits for what was supposed to be just two days with Rory.

"You moving in?" he said.

"Oh, you mean these? That's just for today."

We got a good laugh out of that.

I locked the apartment and we walked to his waiting car, then drove back to his beautiful apartment and alternated taking showers.

Please, please, please, make sure Rory is a good guy, I thought to myself. I was 99.9% sure of it, but if he turned out to be a jerk as well, I didn't know if I could ever trust a man again. I didn't know him that well, after all, and here I was joining him on an island for the night.

On the other hand, we'd built a good rapport as a regular and a bartender at Rick's. It's not like we didn't know anything about each other. And he had acted like a perfect gentleman the night before, so I didn't think I had anything to worry about.

After we finished getting ready, it was almost noon, and we drove south to Long Beach, where the ferry to Catalina Island awaited.

Surreal is an overused word, but it's how I felt riding on a big, beautiful white catamaran while knowing that a murderer was loose in LA and likely out to harm me. I tried not to concentrate on Becca, instead enjoying the time at hand. Rory and I stood on the top of the vessel with the beautiful Pacific below us.

It quickly reminded me of the trip that Austin and I took out on the Pacific, but I just as quickly pushed the memory out of my mind.

Rory would touch my shoulder occasionally, but for the most part, he let me be. I realized it had to be a tough spot for him as well, not wanting to come off as hitting on me, but also being there for me if I needed someone.

"I saw that picture of you and Obama in your room," I said.

"Pretty cool, huh?"

"Yeah, I'd say."

"I won an award for our company. They sent like twenty of us out there and we got to meet him. The owner of our company knew President Obama back in Chicago and I think that's why it was set up."

"How was he?"

"As kind and respectful as you'd imagine."

"I also saw your first communion picture."

"Now that was not my finest moment," Rory said.

"What exactly where you looking at?"

"Well, there was this cute nun to the right."

I started laughing.

"And your jacket?"

"I know, right? I was a pretty sloppy dresser back in the day."

I pulled on the brown sweater he wore.

"I like how you dress now," I said.

He smiled. Tepidly, however.

"I'm looking forward to Becca Poe being behind bars. I'll better know how to proceed. With us, I mean."

"I'm not made of porcelain," I said. "I'm a tough cookie. If I don't want something, I'll let you know."

We both looked in each other's eyes. Another day of resisting our urges was going to be difficult.

63

BECCA

I decided to make one stop on my way back from downtown LA. I wanted to see if anything was going on around Rory's apartment. If I didn't see anything, then I'd return to Beverly Hills and wait to meet up later that day with Brandt. Couldn't believe I was giving some of my money to a silver-spooned East Coaster named Brandt.

In actuality, that's the exact type of person you want to give your money to. They're often unscrupulous, just in it for the money. A bit like me in some ways.

I took Interstate 10 toward Santa Monica, taking the Bundy Drive exit before driving west on Wilshire toward the Pacific Ocean. I drove to Rory's apartment complex and parked kitty-corner to it. I told myself I'd stay there for one hour and if I didn't see anything, I'd head back to The Montage.

I wasn't sure exactly what I waited for, but any new information would be welcomed.

One piece of information came pretty quickly. I watched the gate as it opened upward, counting how long until it returned back to the ground. It took a solid fifteen seconds to hit its apex and then return to the ground. That would give me plenty of time to sneak into the parking garage after one of the cars pulled out.

I'd stealthily enter, hide until Olive and Rory entered, shoot them, run back up to my car, drive away, and disappear again.

Forever this time.

But then my plans changed once again. I'd learned you had to be adaptable when it came to crime. It's why, when I had the opportunity, I shot Austin and Chet. It's why I followed Richard Levert and killed him. You had to take your chance when it presented itself.

As I watched the parking garage, I saw Rory's car pull out. Olive was in the front seat, smiling and looking happy.

Rage went through my body. I didn't want this girl to be happy, I wanted her suffering.

I quietly started following at a safe distance. They made their way to Interstate 10, heading in the direction I had just come from. On Saturday the traffic wasn't bad, and I was able to follow at a safe distance.

They eventually got onto Interstate 405 South and I briefly thought they were going to San Diego, or better yet, Mexico. Instead, they got on Interstate 705 South, getting off in Long Beach and heading down toward the water.

I never thought they'd become aware of being followed. I had a nondescript car and in LA, with cars flying by you every second, I was positive I hadn't been seen.

They got out of the car and walked toward the water, each carrying a little overnight bag, I parked the car, getting as close as I could to the ocean. They just stood around for a good fifteen minutes before walking onto a big catamaran docked there.

As soon as the boat left the dock, I went to the ticket booth. The girl working there couldn't have been more than sixteen. Probably some high school job set up by her parents. Kind of like how my parents made me earn money to save up when I was that age.

"Where did that catamaran just go to?" I asked.

"Avalon on Catalina Island."

"When's the next boat going there?"

"In about three hours."

"Give me a ticket for that."

The girl, in her own world, didn't seem to care how rude and demanding I behaved. She gave me the ticket and I went back to my car to kill some time. I opened the latch and saw the gun sitting in the console. I grabbed it along with some gloves.

Looked like I was going to be killing a little more than time.

_64_
<u>OLIVE</u>

I didn't have many fears in life, but heights were one of them. Of course, being made to feel like a chicken didn't resonate with me either. So with a little goading from Rory, I decided to do the zip line that Catalina offered.

We had arrived at the Avalon Hotel, sitting above Avalon Bay with great views of the Pacific and the sailboats docked right off of Catalina Island. It was gorgeous.

We got a quizzical look as we checked in, but Rory just politely said we'd like two beds, so our room had them.

The hotel itself stood three stories high, and in a city where casual ruled, it was quite elegant. Every room had a patio. I looked at some of the hotels next to ours and they paled in comparison. As we sat on the patio of our room and took in the surroundings, Rory brought up zip-lining, to which I finally agreed.

An hour later we stood on a big wooden deck overlooking the valley below. It was quite a sight. There were lush mountains and beyond that, the enormity of the Pacific Ocean. We waited about ten minutes until it was our turn. Butterflies flew around my stomach, but no way could I stop now.

I listened to the advice of the guide, grabbing the top of the harness, and they sent me on my way.

It was exhilarating!

I was flying down the valley, looking at the bright green of the mountains below, when the ocean came into view. I moved fast and my stomach tied in knots, but no longer the nervous kind. They were the intoxicating type.

You moved so fast that before you knew it, the trip was over. But what transpired in that time proved unforgettable.

I landed on another makeshift deck, with the guides there to make sure I arrived softly.

I looked behind me to see Rory approaching. He had a giant smile on his face.

The guides gave him a hand as he finished and removed the harness from him. We walked toward each other and embraced.

"So, what'd you think?" he asked me.

"Beyond my wildest expectations. I loved it."

"I thought you might," he said.

And then I kissed him on the lips. Just like that, in front of the guides and everything.

He kissed me back, but it was more perfunctory. I could tell he wanted to do more, but he was in an awkward situation and I knew that.

He put his arm around my shoulder and led me off the deck.

"I'm trying to be a good guy," he said.

"You are a good guy, Rory."

We walked around the city for two hours, absorbing the tranquil atmosphere. We stopped in some shops and grabbed a small bite to eat to tide us over till dinner. We didn't mention the kiss.

By time we got back to the hotel, dinner was only an hour away. Just as we had that morning, we took turns showering and getting dressed. But not before going out on our patio for a few minutes. I sat and looked out on the gorgeous blue of the Pacific. I could have stayed there all night if we didn't have reservations.

We were eating at a place called Bluewater Grill, a restaurant that apparently sat right on the water. I wore a long red dress and had a tan jacket that would surely come in handy. Being so close to the ocean made a stiff breeze inevitable.

Rory looked sharp in khakis and a lime green dress shirt. He also had a jacket, flung it over his shoulder like some type of model.

He was handsome enough to be one. Well, maybe not handsome per se, but he definitely had the sexy look about him.

"Ready to go?" he asked.

"Yeah."

He opened the door for me as we headed out. He was doing everything right.

We walked to the restaurant, all the businesses standing so close in Avalon. The Bluewater Grill was about as centrally located as you could be, with the huge deck extending over the Pacific. I ordered crab cakes and Rory picked the catch of the day, salmon served with mashed potatoes and fresh veggies. You pretty much had to order seafood at a place like this.

After the waiter left, I leaned in toward Rory.

"Why didn't you kiss me back earlier?"

"You get right to it, don't you?" he responded.

"That's not an answer, Rory."

"You know the answer, though."

I did.

"I think you're gorgeous," he said. "I've asked you out like five times. I want to date you, I really do. But I just think we should wait until this is all over before we get physical."

"Do you really believe that, or are you just saying that because you're trying to protect me?"

His silence spoke volumes. I leaned in closer.

"You're going to get lucky tonight," I said. "And I don't want to hear you protest. I've thought you were sexy for the last month we've been hanging out at Rick's. But I was scared of getting involved after what happened with

Austin. But I'm no longer scared. I want to have sex with someone I care about. And that's you."

I leaned back to my natural position. And this time it was he who leaned in. But it wasn't to talk.

He grabbed the back of my head and moved my face toward his. He kissed me passionately, cupping my head so our faces weren't going anywhere. Not that I wanted them too.

After about ten seconds, our lips separated. I noticed some eyes on us, but I didn't care. It was a great kiss and one I'd remember forever.

"Pretty good dinner so far," Rory said.

I laughed.

"Not bad."

"And we haven't even had our appetizers yet."

"I didn't order an appetizer," I said.

"This whole dinner is an appetizer. The main course is what's coming back at the hotel."

I started to tingle in all the right places. He was right. Making love to a man who actually cared about me would far surpass whatever we ate.

I felt like I was seventeen again, when having sex was just about the most exciting thing on earth. I was no longer the worried, emotionally scarred Olive. The girl who had been used by Austin.

I was Olive: independent, attractive, and in charge.

I had gotten my mojo back.

That may have been overstating it, but it's truly how I felt going through dinner that night. The crab cakes were good, but the expectation of what was to come next dominated my thoughts.

The waiter came over and asked if we wanted dessert.

"No, I think we're alright, thanks. Neither one of us wants to get too full. We've got some other activities planned after this."

The waiter smiled devilishly. Rory hadn't been very subtle and anyone would have understood what he was alluding to.

"You're a naughty boy," I said.

"I feel like the shackles are off." He laughed. "But this hasn't been an act, I am a nice guy."

"I know you are. I told you earlier."

He leaned over and kissed me again. "You know I've been wanting to kiss you since I first walked into Rick's."

"I thought you were attractive too. But there was the whole Becca situation," I said.

"Let's not mention her again tonight," Rory said. "We can deal with her and the police and everything else on Monday. But tonight, I just want it to be Olive and Rory."

"That sounds perfect."

He paid the bill and we left the restaurant. We could have gone straight to the hotel and gotten down to business, but we walked around the island for a little bit instead.

He took my hand in his and it was all very romantic. The lights of the local businesses lit up Avalon Bay and we just enjoyed each other's company as we followed the coastline.

We didn't say much, just holding each other's hands and occasionally trading a kiss or two.

After about fifteen minutes, Rory asked me, "You ready to go back?"

"I thought you'd never ask," I playfully said.

We strode in the direction of the hotel. I was as content as I had been in a long time.

The hotel looked beautiful as we approached it. Before we entered, we turned around one last time to look out on Avalon Bay and the sailboats docked on it.

We entered the hotel and took the elevator up to the second floor. We walked, arm in arm, to the room, exchanging knowing glances.

Rory opened the door and let me in first.

Against a nice reflection from the lights of the bay, the room held the perfect mixture of dark and light for what was to come.

He lay his jacket down and started kissing me. I kissed him back and about a minute in, took off my jacket as well. We kept on kissing as we removed articles of clothing.

Rory kicked off his shoes, and I helped him pull his green dress shirt over his head. I stepped out of my heels and he helped me slide out of my dress. I grabbed his pants and slid them down his legs. He kicked them off and threw them in the corner.

We stood facing each other. I was in my bra and panties and he was shirtless, wearing only a pair of boxers. I went for the boxers and removed them, happy with what I saw below.

He took off my bra and started kissing my breasts. It was executed to perfection. I didn't have to tell him what to do next. It's like he was reading my mind. He pushed me down on the bed, gently, but with enough force to show he was boss. I slid my panties off and shimmied further back on the bed.

Rory followed and braced himself with his arms as he leaned down and kissed me. I grabbed his penis as he used a finger, and then two, to enter me. This went on for a few minutes until the foreplay became too much for me.

"I want you inside me," I said.

He smiled and kissed me.

"You're beautiful," he said.

He repositioned himself and entered me. The euphoria of the moment overtook me and I leaned back and moaned like I hadn't in a long time. He was great, no question, and my experiences of the last few months just made it all the more meaningful. He started thrusting, and I felt an ecstasy that very few men had ever given me.

My eyes had been closed as I moaned in pleasure, but I wanted to see Rory on top of me. I lifted my eyelids and he stared down at me, both of us fully immersed in the moment. He continued to thrust, every time making my body feel the joy of being a woman.

I leaned back and closed my eyes again, taking in all the elation I was feeling.

After a few more thrusts, each one seemingly deeper than the last, a loud noise came from the direction of our closet. Rory pulled out of me and something emerged the shadows.

It all happened so quick, but as I looked over, I saw a woman with a gun, pointing it at Rory.

"No," I heard him scream.

She fired twice, hitting him both times in the chest. He tumbled off of the bed and fell between the edge of the mattress and the wall.

I jumped at the woman, more out of instinct than anything else. I was able to grab ahold of the gun as she rotated it in my direction. I bent her wrist back, knowing if she repositioned the gun , she could pull the trigger and kill me.

As I continued pushing her wrists back, I looked up in her eyes. It was Becca, of course.

She had killed Rory. I was sure of it.

My heart might never recover, but I tried not to think about it in the moment. If I didn't concentrate on restricting the gun, I'd be joining Rory on the ground.

As we each tried to gain control of the weapon, I heard voices around the entrance to the room. If I could just last long enough for someone to break it down, they would tackle Becca and I would be saved.

People started banging on the door, and I felt I was gaining the upper hand. Becca noticed this, and with her free hand, she opened up the chamber and all the bullets fell to the ground. She then let go of the gun, allowing me to hold it. But it didn't do me any good at that point.

Becca ripped a lamp from the wall and wildly swung it toward my head. I saw it coming, but was only able to block some of the blow. She hit me again on the side of my head, and I fell over the bed and on top of Rory.

For a split second I had a chance to look down into his eyes, still open, wide as can be, a look of shock filling them. He was obviously dead, but it was as if his eyes were taking time to catch up to the rest of his body.

I tried to get up by pushing up off of him, but as I began to rise, Becca again swung the lamp, hitting me flush on the jaw. I fell back on Rory. I looked up and saw the devil staring down at me as she brought the lamp down on my head. It happened again and again. My hands did little to soften the blows.

On her fingers wrapped around the lamp, Becca wore gloves. She was going to get away with two more murders. I couldn't let that happen.

Using all my remaining energy, I leaned up and scratched her. My hope was that even if I died, they would find Becca's DNA underneath my fingernails.

A few seconds later, she hit me one last time and everything went black.

_65_
BECCA

I had first seen them walking around Avalon, smiling and enjoying each other's company. I guess it shouldn't have come as some great surprise. Avalon was a tiny little city without a stoplight in the whole town. At least, that's what I was told on the ferry over.

Still, the fact that I saw them within twenty minutes of the catamaran dropping me off seemed like divine intervention. Someone was looking after me.

They walked around the city for the next hour or so. I saw them stop in a little cafe for a bite to eat, but I kept my distance.

Getting a hat seemed like a good idea, so as they sat over a late lunch, I went to a nearby shop and grabbed one of those big, white ones with a low brim. Hopefully it would help hide my face if they ever looked in my direction.

There was no way they'd suspect I'd be in Avalon, but after seeing me yesterday, they were probably vigilant everywhere they went.

I'd encountered a problem that I hadn't been able to foresee. The island had no rooms available. Everything was fully booked, thanks, no doubt, to Valentine's Day the following day.

I was here and so were they. I'd never have a better chance. The lack of a room wasn't going to stop me.

If I had to spend the night in a room with two corpses, so be it.

As they started heading back to their hotel, I followed from a safe distance. I was getting good at this, whether by car or by foot. They entered the Avalon Hotel and I knew I couldn't continue on the elevator.

I looked up and saw each room had a patio with a deck that, to varying degrees, faced the Pacific. Wouldn't you want to sit out there after a long walk through the city?

Turned out that Olive did. A few minutes later, as I subtly walked the perimeter of the Avalon Hotel, I saw her appear on a second-floor balcony. There was no mistaking her, even from my distance.

She stood on the patio on the far left of the second floor. This was going to be easy.

About an hour later, after Olive and Rory left the hotel, likely on their way to dinner, I took the stairs up to the second floor, hoping I might find an easy way inside their hotel room. That wasn't the case, however.

I went back down to the ground floor and spotted some stairs on the left side, next to the patio. I realized I could lean across those stairs and grab onto the patio railing.

I put on my gloves.

I made my way up the stairs and, making sure no one was looking, extended my arms and grabbed ahold of the railing. Clutching it, I prepared to leap a few feet, over the small drop between the stairs and the patio.

It worked.

A couple approached the hotel, looking in my direction. I sat down in one of the chairs like I was staying there. They wouldn't know any better. I even gave them a wave.

I hoped the door would be unlocked—after all, it was just a patio door— but no such luck. I guess I had myself to blame. Scared people generally locked their doors.

The room had one of those typical glass doors with a lock switch that you could see from the outside. I prided myself on being a white collar criminal, but I liked to learn the tricks of the grifter's trade, and had been taught how to pick some locks over the years. Luckily, this was one of the easier types. The front door likely had a stronger lock that I wouldn't have been able to pick.

After checking that nobody looked in my direction from the other patios or the street, I grabbed a credit card and shimmied it back and forth against the lock. The black plastic knob shuffled back and forth. I knew it wasn't going to take long.

Another couple walked by below and I straightened up.

"Beautiful night, isn't it?" I said.

"Sure is," one of them replied.

After they passed, I went back to working on the lock. After a few minutes, I heard that sweet pop, and the lock came loose.

I entered and shut the glass door behind me. Taking in the room, I deliberated on the best way to "surprise" them.

I couldn't be in the open; they'd just run back out the door when they saw me. I decided to wait in the closet. That way, I could wait while they entered and gauge the best time to come out and start shooting.

As I sat in the closet, I asked myself a question: Why hadn't I just broken into Olive's place and killed her when I first got to LA? Obviously, a big part of that was because I had only just recently purchased the gun. And trying to kill someone with a knife could be much more problematic.

But more than that, I liked having Olive alive. It gave me a target. Someone to compete against. An opponent. But since I'd be on the move soon, it was time to cut all ties to the crime at Barry Gant's house. She had been a worthy adversary, I'll give her that.

I couldn't wait to see her face when I killed Rory. Shooting a strong man first was advisable anyway, but I planned to do it more for my own ego. To get to see Olive recognize that I had won, that I had killed another person she cared about. It was going to be fantastic.

I waited in the closet for what seemed like forever.

I looked down at my phone. They had been gone a little over two hours.

I didn't have to wait much longer. I heard the door open soon thereafter. Within seconds, they were taking each other's clothes off.

How could things have worked out any better for me? A couple couldn't be more defenseless than when they are lying in bed naked. Part of me advised myself to wait till they fell asleep, but it was hard not to jump at the chance of killing them mid-fuck.

I remained in the closet a few more minutes and then Olive started moaning.

I almost felt jealous. She was getting to enjoy her last few minutes on earth. But that would change once I shot Rory.

Her last few seconds on earth would be dreadful. And that's what mattered.

Usually, I wasn't an impulsive woman, but this time, I couldn't hold back. I wasn't going to wait until they fell asleep.

They'd had enough fun. I quietly pushed the closet door open, the gun in my right hand. I started closing the short distance to the bed.

Rory was on top of Olive and saw me approaching first. I raised the pistol.

He yelled "No!" as I fired two bullets into his chest. He fell off the bed into the space between it and the wall.

I had no doubt I'd killed him.

Next, I turned toward Olive, who had a look of disbelief on her face. The horror of her expression brought me great joy. I probably spent too much time enjoying it, because she leapt at me before I had time to swivel the gun.

She grabbed the weapon and we struggled for it. I had the upper hand, but she'd tilted the barrel upward so I couldn't shoot her. There was no use pulling the trigger at this point, because the bullet would just hit the ceiling.

I heard voices outside of the room and knew I had to act fast.

We wrestled for the gun for about thirty seconds.

Olive was starting to gain control, so I used my free hand to open the chamber of the gun and let the bullets fall to the floor. I then let go, allowing her to take hold of the now worthless weapon.

As she stumbled away, I ripped out the nearest lamp, and in one single motion, I swung it around and hit her. The first blow didn't do much, but the second one sent her flying. She hit the bed and then bounced off it, landing on the corpse of Rory.

At this point, the voices were getting louder and I knew I had to get out of there.

Olive tried to rise, but I was on her. She had her hands up, but I connected the lamp several times with her face. At one point, she went to scratch me.

How did she think she was going to win if she fought like a girl? She was no match for me.

It wasn't the heaviest lamp and I didn't think I could kill her with it, but I'd managed to knock her out and then hit her a few more times as she lay defenseless.

A voice outside said, "I'm going to break the door down!"

I had two choices. I could grab one of the bullets from the ground, put it back in the chamber, and finish off Olive once and for all. Probably, by the time I did that, they would have broken down the door, and I'd spend the rest of my life in jail.

I decided to go with my other option. I ran out to the patio and, seeing no one, quickly jumped to the ground floor. There, I strolled away from the hotel. It sounded like the voices remained inside. No one was following me.

I'd left the stolen gun at the scene, but had been wearing gloves. It wasn't going to be traced to me.

I walked briskly up the road. When I turned around, I saw people had started to gather out front of the hotel, surely having heard the gunshots. Maybe the door had been broken down by now.

I noticed I had a little of Olive's blood on my gloves, so I took them off. I couldn't ditch them anywhere, as they'd surely be found in a search, so I dug them deep into my jeans.

As small as the island was, I assumed Avalon had a police department who'd arrive at the hotel shortly.

For once, I hadn't thought everything out. I had been impulsive, following them to Catalina without planning a proper escape. I'd told myself that after killing them, I'd stay in their hotel room, leaving the next morning on the ferry.

That was no longer possible and I didn't have a hotel for the night. And I couldn't just walk the streets with the police sure to be looking around for suspects. I had to come up with something. And fast.

I figured if I could last the night, I'd be alright. Two days, even better. Rory was dead and I assumed Olive would be taken to a hospital on the mainland. They were the only two people who knew what I looked like.

And if someone asked for my driver's license, I always had a plan for that. In Long Beach, I had kept my real driver's license in the car and would be going by Nicole Kaffy. I'd purchased this license when in Phoenix, but the driver's license was from Colorado. I'd had a Colorado I.D. when I was living in San Francisco, so I had the answers to all the questions a Colorado ID might elicit.

While I thought I'd be fine if I made it through till morning, if they saw me roaming the streets that night, I'd be toast.

I racked my brain. The island rose into mountains as you got away from the water, but it was too risky to walk in that direction. I'd be out in the open for too long.

The other people on the streets tonight seemed to be headed in the direction of the Avalon Hotel. Word spread around quickly. I kept walking away from it and the milling crowd gathering there.

Finally, it came to me. It was risky, but nothing wasn't at this point.

I took a left off a paved street and headed closer to the water, away from the heavily lit part of the island. I continually glanced back, making sure no one followed me. It appeared I was alone.

I looked out at the ocean and the anchored boats, knowing what I had to do. I couldn't risk leaving my clothes on the shore and having them discovered.

So I waded in fully dressed.

At this point, most people would have swum to the boat furthest away. But I was smarter than your average bear. The boats docked close to the shore were more likely to be staying there awhile. The ones further out were likely there for shorter trips.

That the next day was Valentine's worked to my advantage as well. If you had brought a boat to this beautiful location with your wife or girlfriend, why would you leave on Valentine's Day? Short answer: you wouldn't. So if I could get on one of these boats, I was probably good till Monday.

Going with my gut, I swam to the very first boat. It couldn't have been more than two hundred feet from shore. I held my cell phone above water, but everything else got drenched. In jeans, it was tough to swim, yet another reason to pick a boat near shore.

I slowly glided up the back of the boat, a large green and white speedboat that could probably fit fifteen people. This far end of the bay was not well lit. No way anyone near the Avalon Hotel could have seen me.

I scanned the top of the boat, but knew I couldn't stay up there, so I headed down below.

In the lower level, I found a makeshift bed and a bathroom. While I would have loved to have slept on the mattress, I worried that they might scan the harbor with a floodlight and maybe see me down below. I decided to stay in the bathroom.

It was as tiny as you'd expect a speedboat's bathroom to be. I grabbed a few stray towels from the cabinets and took them in with me. I peeled off my wet clothes and wrapped myself in the towels. I took out my cash and my Nicole Kaffy driver's license out of my purse, patting them with the towel and hoping they'd dry out a little overnight.

I sat on the minuscule toilet.

A few hours of silence went by, but I then heard a boat patrolling the harbor. The rooms around me lit up as a huge floodlight came through the windows of my refuge, sweeping back and forth across the water.

I thought I was a goner.

"Avalon Police," they said several times, as if that would get the killer to expose himself. Or herself, as was the case.

I never heard them board a boat, and after about thirty minutes I no longer saw the floodlight. A few minutes later, I didn't hear them at all.

Soon thereafter, I was able to fall asleep.

I awoke the next morning as the first bit of sunlight hit the boat. I didn't hear anything, so I quietly opened the bathroom door and walked to the top deck, barely peeking out at the island. A few police cars littered the shore.

It was too soon to go back to land. While I'd be taking a risk by staying on the boat another night, I had no choice.

It was going to be quite the lonely Valentine's Day for me. Knowing Monday would follow buoyed my emotions, however. A great many people would need to get back to Southern California and it's not like they could quarantine the island. I would be on one of those ferries.

A tiny bikini lay on the bottom deck of the boat, along with some flip flops. I didn't have much choice. I couldn't swim back to the shore in my jeans again. Walking around the island in a wet pair of jeans might arouse suspicion.

But a girl with a great figure emerging from the ocean? That would arouse something besides suspicion.

I went back to the bathroom and prayed the owners of the boat stayed on the island one more day.

As Valentine's Day passed, I heard the Avalon police again, as well as many engines starting in the bay, but never heard a noise from upstairs on the boat I inhabited.

I managed to fall asleep around 10:00 p.m. I awakened a few times during the night, as was inevitable when sleeping on a toilet. On Monday, once again, I woke up with the first sign of sunlight.

As I had done the day before, I carefully walked to the main deck of the boat and looked out at the island. I no longer saw any police cars. Surely they were still on the lookout, but maybe they assumed I'd somehow accomplished an escape from the island. One could hope.

I turned on my phone. I had made sure I'd powered it down the first night I swam to the boat.

I used Google to find out when the first ferry left the island. 7:45 a.m.

No texts had arrived from my parents, which surprised me a bit. Maybe the police hadn't released my name yet.

I stayed on the boat, since it still seemed the safest place for me.

At 7:20, I threw on the bikini. It was a bit small, but maybe that would work to my advantage. Guys thought with their dicks and no way would they cast their suspicion on me. They'd be checking me out, but for different reasons.

I grabbed one of the towels that I'd used as a blanket and wrapped my wallet, cell phone, and purse in it. I lowered myself into the water, hoping to make as little noise as possible. Holding the towel in the dry air, I made my way to the shore. It only took a few minutes.

It was too early for anyone to be out on the beach.

Upon my arrival, I put everything in my purse and wrapped the towel around my midsection. I headed toward the ferry.

There were many questions I didn't have a good answer for: *Where is your bag? Where did you stay? Why are you in a bikini this early in the morning?*

But what I did have was a driver's license saying that I was not Becca Poe. And without Olive there to identify me, I thought this just might work.

I made my way to the ticket seller.

"One way for Long Beach at 7:45."

"That will be $36.75."

I looked behind her and spotted souvenir clothes with Avalon's name and picture on them.

"I'll also take a pair of those sweatpants and that sweatshirt. Medium."

"You got it. That's $96.75."

I gave her five twenties that were still slightly damp.

"Jumped in with my wallet on me," I said.

She smiled.

"Keep the change," I said.

I quickly slid the sweatpants over my bikini bottoms, then took off the towel and put the sweatshirt over my bikini top. Once dressed, I joined the line, trying to look innocuous in case the police made their way over to us.

They never did. I could only assume that after searching Saturday night and then all day Sunday, they assumed I was no longer on the island.

A few minutes later, we boarded the ferry. I looked back on Avalon, a smile starting to fill my face.

When we arrived back in Long Beach, no police waited there either. I went directly to my car and headed for Beverly Hills. I absolutely had to get the fuck out of LA, but needed to do a few things first.

I returned to The Montage. I had put my credit card down originally, but they said they wouldn't run it through if I paid cash.

I approached the hotel lobby and for a brief moment my heart sunk. When was I supposed to have checked out? I couldn't remember. If I was a day late, they would have processed my credit card and surely the police would have found out. And they'd be there waiting.

The days had blended together when I'd slept on the boat, but I knew it was the day after Valentine's Day. February 15th. The day I was supposed to check out.

The clock showed only 10:00 a.m. No way would they have ran the credit card yet. I breathed easier.

I went to my room, grabbed my suitcase with the money, and changed out of my Avalon sweats. There was no need to let people know I'd been to the Channel Islands recently. I checked out at the front desk, being sure to pay cash.

After making my way back to the valet, I got the car I had left only minutes before.

The car was registered under my real name. I knew I couldn't drive it around much longer, for the police surely had an APB out on it. But I couldn't leave it at The Montage either, or they could tie all of my LA movements together.

I came up with an idea.

I drove back down to Skid Row, looking for the man who'd help me buy the gun. After driving around for a bit, I saw him. Once again, he was standing, unlike all the deadbeats and drug addicts sleeping the day away.

I ordered an Uber, then got out of the car and approached the man.

"You again?"

"I'm giving you this car. Get rid of it. Take it to a chop shop and sell the parts. I don't care." I pulled my phone out and took a picture of him. "But if you go to the police, I will say that you and your friend sold me a weapon. And I'll show them this picture."

The guy looked on in amazement, not sure what to say.

"Call your friend. Tell him to come pick this car up and get it off the streets," I yelled. "If you don't, it will tie you to a crime."

"I will," he finally said.

"Don't look so mad," I said. "You probably just made a thousand bucks."

He waved me off, but I knew he'd do exactly what I asked. I grabbed a backpack with my laptop, a suitcase full of clothes, and the suitcase full of cash from my now former car.

My Uber arrived a minute later and I got in.

I would have gone to Enterprise and rented a car, but they always needed credit, and while I had an abundance of fake driver's licenses, I didn't have credit cards to go with them. So I had the Uber driver take me to the closest used car lot.

It was still in a bad part of town and I doubted the owners of the lot were on the up and up. I found an old Toyota Corolla for $2,000, gave them one of the fake I.D.s, and paid for the car in cash.

The whole deal happened in less than five minutes. No questions were asked.

I grabbed my belongings and put them in my new mode of transportation.

I left the used car lot feeling like the smartest damn criminal in the world. I had outthought the police and beaten Olive again. Literally this time. I wouldn't to be able to invest my money with Brandt, but I was in an untraceable car with $600,000 on me.

Life could be worse.

66

OLIVE

There's a time in everyone's life when they just don't give a fuck anymore.

The moment hit me as I sat in a Long Beach hospital two days after Becca Poe had killed Rory and attacked me.

My first night afterward passed at the Catalina Island Medical Center, where I was interviewed relentlessly by the police after coming to. They had to put stitches on my forehead, the back of my head, jaw, and chin. Despite all that, they still allowed the police into my room.

Before they asked their first question, I had them confirm what I suspected.

Rory was dead.

If they were ever going to catch Becca, this night seemed like their best chance, so I agreed to the interview. I was conflicted as to if she could escape. Becca had outmaneuvered the police many times. On the other hand, on an island like Catalina, where the hell could she go?

I found it almost impossible to concentrate. I couldn't believe that Rory was gone. Another person I'd dragged into Becca's world was dead.

The local cops seemed overwhelmed and I imagined they rarely had to deal with anything major on their little island. I answered all their questions, but started to lose confidence that they would catch Becca.

The next day was Valentine's. I should have been with Rory enjoying the start of a beautiful relationship. Instead, he lay in the morgue and my life would never be the same. It felt very different than Austin's death. Questions about Austin's involvement emerged from the very beginning, and it was hard to fully mourn someone who had likely used you.

No questions surrounded Rory. He had genuinely liked me and tried to protect me as well. Instead, he got in the way of a psychopath. I spent hours crying for Rory. He had always treated me with such respect, even after I turned down dates with him again and again. When we spent the previous few days together, he remained a gentleman the whole time, never overstepping his bounds or making me uncomfortable. He had really cared about me. And then, in the moment when we were most vulnerable, Becca Poe stormed out of a closet and ended his life. And had effectively ended mine.

I knew I'd never be the same.

Valentine's Day also brought my parents, who at this point were a total mess. They insisted that I was going to move back to Virginia with them. It also brought back Detectives Washington and Liston. Catalina Island was under the jurisdiction of Los Angeles County and since they had worked my previous case, they took the ferry out to Catalina to interview me.

They complimented me on scratching the suspect, saying it could be the break they needed.

I told them the evidence would only confirm what I had told them from the beginning. That Becca Poe had done it.

Their failure of good detective work, not even believing she had been part of the robbery at Barry Gant's, helped lead to the death of Rory. I no longer even pretended to be civil with them.

Sometime late on Valentine's Day they transferred me to the Long Beach Medical Center. I hoped to hear of Becca Poe's capture, but nobody had such news.

As for me, I'd be left with a few minor scars on different parts of my face, but I was going to live. I wasn't sure if I wanted to.

On Monday the 15th, I continued answering the officer's questions, as monosyllabically as I could. I wanted to shout "I told you it was Becca Poe from the beginning!" but I knew it wouldn't do any good.

They told me Becca Poe was now the target of a nationwide manhunt. I didn't have much confidence in it.

When the officers weren't interviewing me, my parents joined me in the hospital room. I knew how tough it must have been on them, but no one had suffered more than I.

I continued to think a great deal about Rory. It was way too early to say I loved him, but it had been a great start. He was kind, handsome, and knew how to take care of a woman. My mind would wander to how good he had been in those few minutes in bed, but I'd push the memories away, since they would lead to me revisiting his death.

I was due to be released from the hospital on that Tuesday when I had my "I don't give a fuck" moment. My phone had once again become part of a police investigation, so I asked my mother if I could borrow hers, along with having a few moments alone. My parents left me in the room.

I googled Hector Reyes, private investigator and dialed his number.

"Hello?"

"Hector, this is Olive."

"Olive, I'm so, so sorry. I've been following everything that happened. It's a huge story. It led the national news last night."

I didn't care.

"Can you come down and see me at the hospital?" I asked.

"Finally, I get to meet you face to face. Sorry it has to be in a hospital bed," he said.

I tried to smile for the first time since the incident.

"Can you come soon? Once I'm released, my parents aren't going to allow me out of their sight."

"I can get there in thirty minutes."

"Thanks."

My parents came back in, followed by Detectives Washington and Liston. They told me they planned to reopen the investigation of the murders at Barry Gant's house and the death of Richard Levert, which I'd finally told them about. Detective Washington looked at me and smiled.

"It won't be long now. We're going to get Becca Poe this time."

I didn't think so.

But I did think Hector Reyes might be able to find her. And I no longer gave a fuck about the rule of law.

I wanted Becca to suffer. And suffer badly.

__67__
<u>BECCA</u>

It was funny looking at the T.V. and seeing my face staring back at me. The first time happened at a gas station as I filled up the tank of the disgusting Toyota Corolla I had purchased. It was worse than the Volkswagen Golf I had when I fleeced those rich Atlanta assholes for their money. God, that felt like three lifetimes ago.

This gas station had those little monitors next to where you fill your car. And my face filled the screen. What a way to find out I'd been found out!

I knew then and there that I had to change my appearance. And fast.

I had my fake I.D.s, but this had now become a national news story and I wasn't sure they were could stand up to any reasonable amount of questioning.

So I needed a new look.

I went to a local Target and picked up some black hair dye, black lipstick, black eyeliner, dark blush, and all black clothes. I also bought a hat that I immediately put over my face.

The checkout lady was an Asian woman in her sixties who didn't seem to be all there. Which came as a relief. My purchases would have a little been suspicious to someone paying attention.

I had to find a place where I could stay for an extended period of time.

A hotel would be risky. A lot of people around. Unscrupulous cleaning ladies.

I decided to get away from Los Angeles proper. I could make some decisions once I'd settled somewhere, but getting out of LA first was all-important.

I started driving south and east from Los Angeles and ended up in Santa Ana. My eventual goal was to get down to San Diego and escape over the border, but for now I had to lie low.

My face was everywhere and even with my altered appearance, I knew it only took one person to call the police and have it all come to a crashing halt.

I pulled into a gigantic mall that had a Starbucks and logged into their Wi-Fi from my car. The less interaction with other humans, the better. I searched on Craigslist for month-long rentals. It would have to be my own place. Roommates were out of the question.

A sublease would be perfect. Someone leaving the area for a while. A landlord would bring about more problems.

I spent thirty minutes looking for the right one. Finally, I found it.

It read: *I'm backpacking in Europe for two months and looking for someone to sublet my two-bedroom home. No roommates. Stop living the apartment life and come live in your own house for a few months. Very private. Asking $3,000 for the two months. I've come down from $3,500 because I need to rent this place. Available Wednesday, February 17th.*

A day away. It was perfect.

I vowed to get rid of my cell phone once I got the place, but for now I needed it.

I called the number.

"Hello?"

"Hi, I'm calling about the house available for sublet."

"Great. It's a nice place and I need to sublet it by tomorrow."

"I'll take it."

"Do you want to come see it later today? Just to make sure?"

Time to lie. I saw no reason to deal with the girl twice in two days.

"Actually, I won't be in Santa Ana until tomorrow. But I'll take it regardless."

"You sure?"

Time for one of my go-to moves. "I'm getting out of an abusive relationship, and a place of my own for a couple of months is just what I need."

"You poor thing, I'm so sorry."

"Also, I'd prefer to just pay cash in case he's still looking for me."

"Of course. It's $3,000 for the two months."

"No problem. I'll stop at the bank on my way to Santa Ana."

"Alright. I actually fly to Europe tomorrow night, so why don't we meet in the afternoon? I'll have the keys and everything you need to move in."

"Thank you for this," I said in my most pathetic voice. "And what's the address?"

She gave it to me.

I slept in my car outside of the huge mall on Tuesday night, parking far away from anyone else, and met with the woman on Wednesday afternoon. It took me less than five minutes to get there, and I was greeted by the woman I'd talked to. A white girl in her late twenties named Tricia, she had a hippy vibe to her and her hair had all been crocheted.

The house was nothing to write home about, but it was secluded from its neighbors, a huge plus. I planned on becoming a hermit for the next few months before I made my dash for the border and this tiny, two-bedroom house would be perfect.

I laid the drama on a little thick with Tricia, who didn't bat an eye when I gave her the cash.

"How do I get ahold of you?" she asked.

"I have this cell phone, but I may get a new number."

"I'll be backpacking with two girlfriends, but we'll have our cell phones with us."

"That sounds nice," I said, trying to sound like I cared.

She grabbed a piece of paper and wrote something down. "When we're not in the mountains getting no reception, I'll be posting pictures on Instagram and Facebook. You can get ahold of me on one of those."

"Perfect. I'll keep in touch. Have a great trip," I said.

Tricia hugged me like we were long-lost friends.

"You'll get over this, Holly."

Holly had become my go-to bullshit name.

"Thanks."

After Tricia left a few minutes later, I was all alone in my own house. Likely for the next two months. Perfect.

I went to the garage to look for a hammer and found one immediately. I brought my laptop and my cell phone out there. I couldn't take a risk of the police following me through either device.

I bashed my cell phone and laptop to kingdom come. There would be no tracing me now.

I'd make a trip to a grocery store the following day and grab food for a month. Lots of boring frozen shit that wouldn't go bad.

It was time to disappear. When I re-emerged, it would be off to Mexico with all of my money. I knew how cheap property in Mexico was and I planned to get a place on the ocean, spending my days swimming in the Pacific.

In the meantime, I had the beautiful deaths of Barry Gant, Jared Austin Jenkins, Chet Watkins, Richard Levert, and Rory whatever-the-fuck-his-last-name-was to keep me company.

Olive had been the one that got away, but maybe that was for the best. I guessed she would only be a shell of herself going forward.

The phrase "a fate worse than death" came to mind.

68

OLIVE

I trusted Hector Reyes from the first time I laid eyes on him. Or more accurately, confirmed my trust, since I'd felt that way since I'd started talking on the phone with him. You just knew a seasoned, weathered guy like him could keep a secret. Probably in his late fifties, he still looked as strong as an ox. He was handsome in a rugged way, reminding me a bit of Richard Levert. Maybe all private eyes aged that way. In particular, Hector had a mustache and a full head of hair, a mixture of dark and gray. He reminded me of a Hispanic Mark Ruffalo.

He was polite, but I sensed an underlying rage. You wouldn't want to get on his bad side.

We weren't able to talk long that first meeting in the Long Beach Medical Center, but I told him I'd be getting in touch soon.

"In the meantime, why don't you try to track Becca's phone calls?"

"I tried when I found the news early on Sunday. The phone was powered off and I couldn't get a location. But I'll get back on it."

"Thanks, Hector."

He nodded and left me in the hospital room.

My parents stayed a few more days, but realized I wouldn't be joining them in Virginia. I told them I was a witness to a murder and the LAPD needed me close by. There was probably some truth to it, but they hadn't specifically advised me that I had to stay.

I told my parents I'd be staying at a friend's house, but in reality, I didn't know where I wanted to go.

"Don't worry, Mom, the last place that Becca Poe wants to be is near Los Angeles."

"She came back after fleeing the first time," my mother said.

I had no good response, so I just I told them I loved them and would be in touch daily. They didn't want to leave, but I made my opinion on the subject be known.

After they headed to the airport, I called Hector Reyes.

"Hello?"

"I'm coming to your office," I said.

"Okay."

I drove down to Hector's office. It had been only five days since Rory had been killed. My wounds had started to heal, but they were going to leave some small scarring. I tried not to think about them, knowing I had more important things to deal with.

Hector worked in a tough part of Los Angeles, but I wasn't affected. I had been through enough recently that walking past a few homeless people or drug addicts didn't bother me.

It appeared Hector was the only one there.

"Are you alone?" I asked.

He rose from his chair and pushed off the desk in front of him. Another desk and chair stood on the other side of the cramped office, vacant.

"My associate is out on a case. There's just two of us."

"I want Becca Poe to suffer," I said.

I expected warnings, cautions, and the like, but I got a completely different response.

"I know you do. She killed one of my friends. I feel the same."

"So you'll help me?"

"I'm already a step ahead. I've been on the case since I saw you at the hospital. Here, take a seat."

I sat down in a chair facing Hector's desk.

"Like I told you, I tried to track her when I first heard about what happened on Catalina. But her phone wasn't on. I'm sure that was no coincidence. I started tracking the phone again after I left the hospital. The ping came from Santa Ana. According to my Google search, she was at a place called the Main Place Mall. The phone didn't move from that destination the whole night. At least, I don't think so. I went to sleep at midnight and woke up at six a.m. and it was still there."

"You've done amazing work, Hector. I don't expect miracles," I said.

He nodded, but looked uncomfortable at the appreciation.

"Then the following morning, she moved positions, ending in the suburbs of Santa Ana. The phone pinged there for about an hour before going completely dead."

"Dead?"

"Nothing. I couldn't even ping it. And that was two days ago now."

"You're thinking she turned it off? Or destroyed it?"

"You're a quick study, Olive. Who has a phone without turning it on for two straight days?"

"I get your point."

"She's surely seen herself on T.V. She must have been worried the police were tracking her."

"So, what's our next move? Go to Santa Ana?" I asked.

"You're damn right!" Hector said feverishly. It had obviously become very personal for him as well.

He packed a gun, a Taser, some rope, masking tape, and a few sharp tools. I didn't bat an eye.

Becca Poe deserved whatever she got.

We left my car at his place and took his blue Ford F-150 down to Santa Ana.

"So how big is the radius of the ping?" I asked.

"It varies. But in the suburbs like that, my guess would be about ten blocks by ten blocks."

"That could be hundreds of houses."

"No one said this was going to be easy, Olive."

He smiled as he said it. For a big, tough guy, Hector could be very reassuring. I felt safe, but I knew not to underestimate Becca.

"Unfortunately, you can't join me if I have to go door to door," he said.

"What do you mean?"

"We'll drive through the neighborhood first, and for that you can stay in the car. We'll see if anything jumps out, or if by some miracle we actually see her. But if nothing comes of that, and I don't think anything will, then I'll have to go around asking people if they've seen her."

"And we can't take the risk that she sees me?"

"Told you you're a quick study."

"But we can't ask people if they've seen Becca Poe, can we? Surely the word would get out with all the attention the case has received."

"Right again. I'll say I'm looking for my niece, and I'll show them an older picture of Becca that I printed up. I'll say her name is Rachel or something."

"It's almost like this isn't your first rodeo," I said, getting the private eye to smile.

"I wanted to say again just how sorry I am about your friend, Rory. From all I've heard he was a great guy."

"He was," I said. "I'll never get over it."

"Then at the very least, let's get the woman responsible."

"That's why I'm here," I said.

We drove down to Santa Ana and checked into a hotel room. It was impossible to not think about the last time I'd been in one, but I tried to push it out of my mind. I had spent almost every waking moment mourning Rory, but for the time being, all my attention was on catching his killer.

We canvased the area, but saw nothing suspicious. It appeared to be a lower-middle class neighborhood with a lot of Hispanic children playing in the streets. It made me sad that the children had to grow up in less than ideal conditions, but the kids were all smiles. I guess when you're young, you don't need much. It was quite reassuring.

For our specific circumstances, I thought the demographics of the neighborhood might help. Becca was certainly not Hispanic and that might make her stand out in a neighborhood like the one we drove through.

After thirty minutes, Hector turned to me.

"This is a wild goose chase. I'm going to have to go door to door."

I didn't like it, but I knew there was no other way.

"What are you going to do with me?"

"I'll drop you off at that mall where she pinged before coming here. Maybe, by some miracle, you'll see her there."

I nodded, but didn't expect much from my end.

The Main Place Mall on Main Street had signs claiming to feature more than 200 stores on-site. It was an indoor mall, which I'm sure the heat in summer around Santa Ana made a necessity. The place looked beautiful, with two stories of a beautiful white interior. At some points, big bay windows allowed you to look up at the sky.

I walked slowly, keeping my eyes open for any sight of Becca.

I stopped in Macy's, heading to the women's section. I looked at some pretty dresses, but it made me sad. Was I ever going to be able to love again? It sure didn't seem possible after what had happened to Rory.

What guy in his right mind would ever want to date me once he found out all the baggage I came with?

That didn't even count the scarring on the side of my face, which I tried not to think about.

I left the dresses and walked out of Macy's. I found a Baskin Robbins and hoped pigging out on some ice cream might help me feel better. I sat outside the shop and watched as people passed by. No Becca.

A few hours later, I got a call from Hector.

It was go time.

I first saw the lumbering Hispanic guy when he was five houses away from mine. He had parked his car and was walking door to door. The sun had started to go down, but I could still see him clearly.

Talk about giving me enough time to prepare. I watched out my window as he went house to house, steadily approaching mine.

And I had no question he was a private eye of some sort. More likely a bounty hunter. And was he hunting me? Obviously, I couldn't be sure, but I had no choice but to assume he was.

After I'd been named the lone suspect in the murder of Rory, the robbery at Barry Gant's house had received renewed interest. The police tried to keep it under wraps, but once it came out that I had known Jared Austin Jenkins, the media ran with it. They speculated that I had indeed gotten away with money from the robbery. So it wasn't out of the realm of possibility that I was being followed by someone.

If they only knew how much, I'd have had a caravan after me.

As I saw him move a house closer, I wondered if I was just that smart, or was everyone else really that dumb? I'd never met anyone who was at my level. In fact, annoying little Olive had probably been my biggest foil. She tracked me down outside Atlanta and found out I lived in Phoenix. She'd been a tough opponent and even managed to survive two times when she should have been killed.

This waddling but sturdy Hispanic man wasn't on the same planet with me. Not the same universe.

Watching him knock on my neighbor's door, I thought he was headed to mine next. Obviously, I wouldn't be answering.

But then something funny happened. After my next-door neighbor's house, he didn't come to mine. Instead, I saw him head back to his car and drive away.

Either I was the luckiest woman in the world, or the neighbors had told him something that necessitated his leaving.

It had to be the latter.

I pulled my Toyota Corolla out of the garage, drove it onto the street, and then backed it into my driveway, so I was facing out. If I had to get the fuck out of there, every second mattered.

My life had become a series of risks, and there was another one I had to take.

I walked across the street to the last house he'd been at.

A Hispanic woman answered the door, a young child hanging on her arm.

"Hi, I'm Holly. I'm a friend of Tricia's and subletting her place. What did that guy want?" I tried to sound as playful as possible, as if no answer could matter to me.

"He was looking for his niece," she said.

Her English was better than I expected, but maybe that was just my prejudices making an appearance. I hadn't been expecting much.

"His niece?"

"Yeah, said she went missing, but he'd been told she might have moved around here."

"You didn't mention me, did you?"

"No, of course not. Are you his niece?"

"No. I'm not Hispanic," I said, thinking that was as good an excuse as any.

"Okay," she said, already looking weary of this conversation.

"Did he say his name?" I asked.

"Why?"

As usual, I needed to lie. It came so naturally for me. "He looked like an old friend of mine from when I lived in Los Angeles. But by time I got out here, he had driven away."

"He left a card. Also, he mentioned he was staying at the Motel 6 on 1st Street. Hold on, let me get that card."

The woman returned thirty seconds later.

"Hector Reyes was his name."

I grabbed the card. "Oh my God, it was him!" I exclaimed.

"How did you know him?" the woman said nervously.

"My ex-husband used to beat me and I used Hector as my private investigator."

"I'm sorry," the woman said.

"Thanks. That's why I'm trying to keep a low profile at Tricia's. Still not ready to show my face to the world."

"Understandable," she said.

"Listen, can I keep this card?"

"Of course."

"And it was the Motel 6 on 1st Street?"

"Yeah."

"Maybe I'll go pay him a visit."

"I think you should."

"It was nice meeting you. What was your name?"

"Valeria."

"Valeria, I'm Holly. Thanks for your help."

I waved goodbye, patting her little daughter, who hadn't said a word, on the head.

My timetable had been pushed ahead once again. I was going to kill this Hector Reyes and then drive down to San Diego, where I'd cross the border into Tijuana. It was time to get the fuck out of the United States. Once and for all.

I waited another hour, making sure the sun had completely set. I wanted it dark out. I grabbed two of the longest, sharpest knives that Tricia had at the house. I put on a long winter jacket and slid the knives down the longest pockets on the left and right sides.

Googling the motel, I found it was only a few miles away. I put my duffle bag and my suitcase full of cash into the Corolla and headed off toward the Motel 6.

I was many things, but gullible wasn't one of them. And when something seems too good to be true, it usually was. So I had be on the lookout at the Motel 6.

If this was all a setup, he'd have to assume I'd go to my neighbor's and they'd relay the information about the Motel 6. And then I'd decide to go to the motel itself. A stretch? Maybe, but that doesn't mean it hadn't happened.

So while I drove to the Motel 6 with the intent to kill, I remained vigilant as well. I'd scope out the place a little bit. Make sure I wasn't being set up.

I arrived and drove around the periphery, looking for anything suspicious. I drove around a second time, but saw nothing out of the ordinary. The third time I entered the motel premises, parked my car, and looked for the Hispanic man.

No sight of him.

So I waited.

After about twenty minutes, and a few false alarms, someone approached Room #104 at the far end of the first floor. It was him. I still hadn't decided how to go about killing him. Breaking into the room late at night was a possibility, but not ideal. This was likely a bounty hunter I was dealing with. He probably slept with both eyes open.

I did have two things on my side, however: some big knives and the element of surprise. Hopefully, that would be enough.

I'd escaped from three recent crime scenes and I worried my luck was running out. Of course, I had planned each one so meticulously that I had created my own luck. I planned on that continuing.

A noise came from Room #104 and I lowered my window.

"Fuck!" Hector Reyes said.

He started heading toward the lobby, but I saw he had propped his door open before he stormed down the walkway. Clothes covered the floor of his motel room.

A man several doors down approached him.

"What is it?"

"They left my room a complete mess! Didn't clean up a damn thing."

"Housekeeping isn't going to be here at this time of night," the guy said.

"Then I'm going to give the front desk a piece of my mind."

He stormed by the man. This guy was a real hothead, and I knew I'd better kill or severely disable him with my first stab wound.

I had to make a split-second decision. I got out of my car and headed toward Room #104. I turned around and as I did, I saw Hector Reyes swing open the door to the lobby. I moved quickly to his door. Another hotel room murder looked to be in the cards.

The guy who had talked to Reyes had gone back into his room. No witnesses around.

Hector Reyes hadn't lied. I'd never seen a room so messy, and I'd left dead bodies in one.

I glanced back toward the lobby and didn't see Hector Reyes emerge. If I was going to do it, it had to be now. After looking one more time and seeing no one, I entered the room.

The door stood open, so far that it was almost flat against the wall, and beyond it, to my left, I made out the bed and the closet. On the right was just openness. Reyes would see me there immediately upon entering.

Going to the left was a no-brainer.

I quickly considered whether I should hide behind the door or in the closet. In case he brought someone back from the front desk, I thought hiding in the closet was the best choice.

Just like on Catalina Island.

I turned left. I was almost fully past the door and on my way to the closet when I saw a movement in my peripheral vision.

Olive came from the space behind the door and headed toward me.

I had no time to reach for a knife.

And only a brief moment to see that Olive was moving something in my direction. I knew what it was and it didn't bode well for my future.

She pressed a button on the Taser, sending 50,000 volts into my body.

I crumpled to the floor.

OLIVE

I looked down at the quivering body in front of me. My long nightmare would soon be over. Becca Poe, murderer, wasn't going anywhere. I couldn't celebrate, not with all that I had lost, but I took some satisfaction in having caught the seemingly uncatchable woman below me.

Hector Reyes had worked as a private investigator for almost thirty years, but I was the one who came up with the plan to secure Becca. To me, it was a simple case of distraction. She'd enter the room and be so fixated on Hector coming back that she wouldn't think to look behind the door. I'd set up a situation where Becca thought she had the upper hand over her sole opponent. And that's when the second person, me, would come in handy.

I told Hector my plan before he set off for the suburbs. He was right that I shouldn't be anywhere near there. If Becca had seen me, that would have changed everything.

If she just saw some suspicious guy, she'd probably take him for a lone wolf after her money. The police had finally come around, admitting Becca Poe had probably spearheaded the Barry Gant robbery and likely escaped with some cash from the safe. The media picked this up and it became national news. The idea of a woman serial killer with possibly hundreds of thousands of dollars on her made for good television. So the possibility that someone might be after her money had to have crossed Becca's mind. I hoped that's what she saw Hector as.

I had turned to Hector as he dropped me off at the Main Place Mall.

"If someone tells you that a person matching Becca's description moved in, subtly mention you are staying at the Motel 6. If she sees someone going door to door, I can assure you she'll go ask what you wanted."

"You've met her a few times, and only briefly. How do you know that?" Hector asked.

"She'll do anything to gain the upper hand. She'd immediately be suspicious of you and would have to know what's going on. I'm beginning to learn how she thinks."

Hector believed me.

"And what will we do if she comes to the room?"

"I've got a plan for that, too," I said.

Hector left for the suburbs and I walked around the Main Place Mall until he called me a few hours later.

"A neighbor several doors down said she'd seen a girl moving into a new place a few days back. Used to belong to someone named Tricia. I didn't knock at her house, but I got closer and closer to it, taking my time and letting myself be seen. I told all the neighbors I was staying at the Motel 6."

"Great work," I said. "Now come pick me up. I'll tell you my plan for when Becca gets to the motel."

The rest had worked perfectly. It was my idea to spread clothes all over the floor just to further the idea that Hector was really pissed at housekeeping.

We had debated whether I should wait behind the door with Hector's gun or his Taser, and both decided the Taser was a better idea. If Becca saw a gun, she'd likely just run, leaving me with a tough decision of whether to shoot. A Taser would ensure she wouldn't be running anywhere.

I heard Becca enter the room, knowing I had to pounce at the precise moment she passed the door I hid behind. It's when she'd be most vulnerable.

I waited a few seconds and then pounced, immediately after she passed me. I tased Becca, then pushed the door shut as she went down. I tased her again when she went to the floor. And after she made a little whimper, I tased her a third time for good measure.

It was impossible not to feel a wave of emotion. This woman who had tormented me for months, who'd killed people close to me, was now incapacitated on the floor below me.

I took a moment to soak it in.

Hector came back a few minutes later. Him acting pissed had all been a charade to get Becca to enter the room. When Hector went to the motel lobby, he'd just asked if they had any pamphlets of things to do around Santa Ana.

But his diversion was executed flawlessly.

When he arrived back to the room, pamphlets in hand, I opened the door. Hector went to his tool box and grabbed the duct tape. He wrapped it around Becca's mouth several times, then put her wrists behind her back and duct taped them as well. And finally, he forced her ankles together and did the same with them.

She looked up at us, fear emanating from her eyes. We didn't give a shit. She deserved much worse. And she was going to get it.

We sat around till a little after midnight. Becca tried to speak, but with the duct tape over her mouth, we couldn't hear a thing. Nor did we want to. We basically just ignored her. We didn't talk to each other much either, knowing there was more to come. And it would likely be unpleasant.

When we hadn't heard a noise in almost an hour, we decided it was time. A handicapped parking spot lay in front of our room, and Hector went outside and backed his Ford truck as close as it could get.

He came back in and threw a huge Glad bag over Becca. If someone saw us, maybe they'd think we were just putting trash into the truck. If they saw a bound and gagged woman, things would be decidedly different.

Hector had me stand watch outside. The back door of the F-150 was open and waiting for Becca. It was too risky to throw her in the back of the flatbed truck.

I looked around, seeing no one.

"Coast is clear. Come now."

I watched as he carried the bag that held Becca and quickly shoved her into the back seat, shutting the door immediately behind her.

"Get in," he said.

I did, and he shut the door behind me. I heard some noises from Becca, but paid them no mind. If she thought she was going to get sympathy points, she was sorely mistaken.

Hector came back a minute later and threw his toolbox in the back. He took a penknife out and cut a little hole in the Glad bag near Becca's mouth.

"I wouldn't want her suffocating before we got where we were going. She doesn't deserve to get off that easy," he said.

I concurred.

We drove from Santa Ana back to LA, Hector keeping right around the speed limit the entire time. If we were pulled over, we'd surely be arrested for kidnapping and spend the majority of our lives in jail. People in the media had commented on all the grief I had been through, but that wouldn't be an excuse in the eyes of the law.

Not for this.

Luckily, we were never pulled over and by time we approached Los Angeles it was late at night. We headed into East LA, a particularly rough-and-tumble area.

Hector didn't say much as we drove.

We pulled into a driveway and he pressed a button above his visor. We waited for the garage door to open and drove in.

We wouldn't have to worry about dragging Becca in front of his neighbors.

Hector carried her into the house and dropped Becca on the floor. The place wasn't clean, with a kitchen full of dirty dishes to the left. On the right I saw what looked like a study, and straight ahead was the living room with a T.V. on the wall and a dirty, L-shaped couch in front of it.

Even though it was the middle of the night, Hector went over and turned down all the blinds so no one could see in.

He brought in a huge painter's cloth from a different room and laid it on the floor. He then grabbed a chair and put it in the middle of the cloth. Next, he took the Glad bag off of Becca and lifted her from the floor, setting her on the chair.

Hector grabbed the duct tape from his back pocket, and wrapped it several times around Becca's torso and the chair itself. Finally, he grabbed a couple of tethers and connected them from the chair to the base of the couch, assuring the chair wouldn't get knocked over.

Just when I thought he was done, he went to the kitchen and grabbed a few knives, a lighter, and a pair of pliers.

We remained quiet for a moment. Becca had stopped trying to yell, knowing it was a fool's errand.

Hector looked over at me.

"Give me a few minutes," I said.

Hector walked back toward the bedrooms, going into one and shutting the door hard, as if to accentuate that I was alone with Becca.

I looked down at her and gathered my thoughts.

I'd accomplished my goal, and now that I had Becca Poe in front of me, I didn't know where to start.

Hector had set a knife next to me. I grabbed it.

"I'm going to cut a little hole in the tape covering your mouth. If you say one little peep without my consent, I'm going to cover your mouth back up and let Hector go to work on you. Is that clear?"

Becca nodded with fearful eyes.

I cut a little incision in the tape.

"Say something."

"You devised a great plan. I wasn't ready for it," she said.

The incision was small and it partially muted her words, but I could understand her perfectly.

"I'm looking for one-word answers, Becca. If you deviate from that, I'll put more tape on," I said and held up the roll of duct tape.

"Sure. Olive," she said as two separate sentences.

Even in her compromised state, she couldn't behave. I wasn't going to let it stand between me and the truth, however.

"Did you have Austin come to LA to meet me?"

"Yes."

"Was that because you knew Barry Gant liked me?"

"Yes."

"And you knew that from the time you came to The Belly Flop."

"Yes."

I saw something like admiration coming from Becca's eyes.

"And I know the following question will require more than one word, so you have my permission to elaborate. How did you know Barry had all the money? And keep in mind, Becca, if I think you are lying, I'm bringing Hector back in."

"I overheard a woman in Beverly Hills saying she'd been to Gant's house and that he'd shown her several hundred thousand dollars."

Any other person would ask her at that point where she'd put the cash, but I honestly didn't care. Hector could get that information out of her. To me, it was, and always would be, blood money.

"And Austin never wanted to open a bar, did he?"

"No."

"That was how you planned to get us to Barry's house?"

"Actually, that was Austin's plan. I hadn't sorted out how we were getting in."

Some other questions would involve more than one word, so I let her speak. She wasn't going anywhere. She couldn't move her arms, torso, or legs. The woman had been a murderous thug, but she was no longer a danger to me.

"I know from the police that Barry had a gun in his safe. I'm assuming he killed Chet. Did he kill Austin or did you?"

"I killed both Chet and Austin," she said.

Her eyes told me she was proud of it.

"How?"

"Barry shot Chet, who killed him in response. I grabbed Barry's gun and, sensing my chance, finished off Chet and then shot and killed Austin."

"You're diabolical," I said.

"Thank you."

I could tell she took it as a genuine compliment.

I was growing tired of talking to the evil that was Becca, but had a few more questions.

"And you had told Chet and Austin no text messages, right? Nothing to tie you all together."

"You're good, Olive. Yes, that's right."

"And Richard Levert knew you had money?"

"That's what I assumed. Why else would he follow me from a Vegas bar? I'm guessing he was going to make me some offer to pay him off or he'd harm me. But I never gave him the chance."

At that she smiled.

It was still too fresh in my mind and I didn't want to discuss it, but I had to know.

"How'd you know Rory and I were on Catalina Island?"

"I followed you guys from The Galley one night. The next day I was scoping out his parking garage and you guys pulled out. I followed you to Long Beach and got on the next ferry. The rest was history. I loved seeing your eyes after you knew your little boy toy was dead. And during sex, to boot. What beautiful timing."

It took me a second to process all she'd said. She had been so forthcoming with her answers that I almost didn't expect her vitriol. But I should have known it was coming.

A leopard like her doesn't change her spots.

I reached for the duct tape.

"No! Don't! I'm sorry, Olive!"

Her voice was rising and I had to get the tape on her before a neighbor heard. I cut off a slab and put it over her mouth. It didn't cover it fully. She started screaming as loud as she could, but it was muffled.

I put another strip over her mouth and effectively muted her.

Hector walked out of the room.

"I've got in under control. Give me just one more minute," I said and he went back in.

I looked down at Becca, whose eyes now burned with anger. I didn't even see fear anymore. She was just disgusted that her day of reckoning had come, and it was at the hands of me.

I gathered my thoughts.

"I'm going to make this quick," I said. Her eyes rose to meet mine. "And I'm not going to give you a chance to respond this time. You've lost that right. At some point in your life, you are the actions you have taken. And you're an evil bitch. A user of people. A ruiner of lives. A murderer. And this world is going to be better off without you. You killed Austin. You killed Chet Watkins. They probably don't deserve my grief, but it's still human life. And you killed a good man in Barry Gant, merely because he was rich. And Richard Levert, even if he was after your money, didn't deserve to die. And most importantly, you murdered Rory, an honorable man who was doing nothing but looking out for me. For that, I can never forgive you. And you will deserve all that's going to happen."

I wanted to say more, but I started crying. I bowed my head and cried and cried for all that happened. And all that I had lost.

It lasted for a few minutes. All my thoughts, all the emotions I had kept to myself, all came out at once.

After gathering myself, I yelled out to Hector.

"You can come back out."

Hector emerged from the room and Becca's eyes moved from me to him.

She couldn't talk, but her eyes told the story. She knew what was to come. Her anger had turned back to fear.

Hector looked at me and I think he was half-expecting what I said next.

"I'm going to leave now," I said.

There were many reasons why I decided to leave Hector's house when I did. Despite all I'd experienced, I was not a killer.

It would take time, but I thought I might be able to overcome all I'd gone through and live a somewhat normal life. If I had stayed and helped kill Becca, I'd have become a completely different person. Similar to Becca in some small ways. And I couldn't have that.

Despite everything, I still liked myself.

So I left.

I ordered an Uber and entered an address a block away. Just in case.

As I walked out the door, I heard a piercing scream. And knowing that was coming from behind a strip of duct tape, made it all the more jarring.

I tried to not picture the horror that Hector was going to inflict on Becca, even though I knew she deserved all of it.

BECCA

I'd accomplished a lot in my criminal life, but escaping from Hector and coming back to murder Olive was my greatest feat.

At least, I told myself it would be, as Hector started taking the pliers to my toenails.

But I knew better. There was no escaping from this one. And it was going to be painful. Of that, there was no doubt.

After removing all of my nails in the most dreadful pain I'd ever experienced, Hector grabbed a small little Bic lighter. It turned out the hurt of the nails was nothing compared to what happened next.

I understood this wasn't going to be a quick death, and so, in between the unbelievable amount of pain being inflicted on me, I tried to reflect on why I'd become the murderous, immoral human being that I was.

My parents had tried their best, but I was just a bad seed. I didn't want to work for things when money could be handed to me. I would do anything to prevent being poor. And I had no empathy for anyone trying to get in my way.

All that had snowballed over the years, until I'd become a menace to society.

And that menace was now paying for her sins. In the most agonizing way possible.

After the lighter, I saw Hector reach for a small knife. I just prayed the end would come soon, but it wasn't to be.

I heard questions about the money. And wasn't able to lie about it for long. It's not like I was ever going to have the chance to spend it now.

I didn't apologize for my sins or ask for forgiveness. After all I'd done, forgiveness was out of the question. And as for my sins, I'd actively chosen to commit them. My arm wasn't twisted, I wasn't forced to do anything. I'd done them. Me alone.

What can I say? I was evil.

And as Hector grabbed a huge saw and several trash bags, I knew "was" was the right tense.

OLIVE

SIX MONTHS LATER

I hadn't talked to Hector since the night in question. I'd thought a clean break was best and he never tried to contact me, so I assume he felt the same.

In the first few months following Rory's murder, I had almost weekly interviews with the LAPD. Even though I knew they'd never find Becca, I still went in and answered their questions.

An LA neighbor of Becca's came forward, saying she thought the suspect on T.V. looked like the girl who lived next to her. They found plenty of Becca Poe's fingerprints littered throughout the apartment and the complex itself. Another neighbor came forward, saying she saw Jared Austin Jenkins come to Becca's front door a few times. Chet Watkins' fingerprints were found in the apartment as well.

Whether or not Becca was at the scene of Barry Gant's robbery remained up for debate amongst the LAPD. Detective Washington seemed to think she was, while Detective Liston still saw no evidence of that.

I couldn't tell them the truth.

The story continued to be national news for a few months, with numerous people claiming they had seen Becca Poe. In Seattle. In Detroit. In Argentina. In Paris.

But I knew better.

As for me, I am doing well.

For the first two months after Rory's death, I wouldn't give any guy the time of day. I was a robot. But slowly that started to change.

I knew I couldn't just shut myself off from the world. I'd be letting Becca win if I didn't go about enjoying life.

One day, I was writing at a coffee shop in Venice when a guy who looked like he hadn't shaved in months sat next to me.

He was attractive, in spite of the abundant facial hair. Or maybe because of it. I couldn't decide.

Turned out he was an artist and aspiring comic strip writer who also worked as a waiter.

"We're in similar fields," I told him.

"Gotta pay the bills in order to have a chance to achieve artistry. Seems stupid, doesn't it?"

"The struggle is real," I said, kicking myself for using such a lame line.

"My name is Arlo. Really."

"I'm Olive."

We went on our first date a few days later. I didn't tell him about Barry Gant's house or the death of Rory until a month in.

I'd been on the national news, but if he knew who I was, he had the discretion not to mention anything.

When I told him, he didn't respond in words, instead just bringing me in close, hugging me for a good two minutes. We never mentioned it again.

We've now been dating for almost four months and we've even talked about moving in together. When not working, I spend my days writing while he sketches on the huge drawing pad he takes everywhere. I've put the romance novel on hiatus after all that's happened, but I'm not discounting returning to it at some point.

I've never mentioned to anyone what happened to Becca Poe and never will. I find myself thinking less about her as time drags on and that's a good thing.

She will never fully be in my rearview mirror, but the distance is increasing with each passing day.

But I'm happy and that's what matters. She took a lot of things, but she couldn't take that.

I lean over and kiss Arlo. We're sitting at a restaurant a stone's throw from Venice Beach, enjoying the Los Angeles summer.

The bartender walks over. She's a few years younger than me.

"Do you guys want a drink or are you just eating?"

Arlo and I look at each other.

"Want to get drunk?" I ask.

"We've been really responsible lately. I think we can have a day for ourselves."

"Two Long Islands," I say.

I remember a time at The Belly Flop when some twenty-one-year-olds ordered Long Islands and it made me feel old.

Well, I'm tired of feeling old. I'm still a young woman and it's time to start acting like one.

"And two shots of tequila," I yell.

Arlo just looks at me.

"What, you can't hang with a girl?" I ask.

"It's on! And don't get mad at me if I'm holding your hair while you puke later."

In a weird way, that sounds oddly perfect.

When the bartender returns, we clink our glasses and each take the shot.

For the first time in I don't know how long, I don't have a worry in the world.

And it feels great.

A week later, as I walk out of my apartment, I find a flyer pinned to the door. It read:

The Los Angeles Public Library just received a donation of $600,000 from an anonymous donor. We will be breaking ground on the new wing in a ceremony on Sunday, August 29th. We hope you can join us.

I hadn't thought about the money in months, but I was delighted to see it put to good use.

"Well done, Hector," I whispered under my breath.

I exit my apartment, no longer looking over my shoulder.

Life is good. I've said it before, but this time I know it to be true.

I walk out of my complex into the beautiful, warm Los Angeles summer air and enjoy the moment.

Nothing is guaranteed in life and I'm committed to appreciating all the good times. I think I've got a long stretch of them ahead.

THE END

A note to my readers:

Thanks for reading *The Bartender*!!
I hope you enjoyed it.

If you like my writing, I'd be honored if you checked out my other novels.

The Quint Adler series:
Book 1: <u>Revenge at Sea</u>
Book 2: <u>The Bay Area Butcher</u>

Quint is a hard-headed crime reporter turned private investigator. He starts looking into a series of unsolved murders—and quickly becomes a suspect himself.

The Frankie and Evie series:
Book 1: <u>The Puppeteer</u>
Book 2: <u>The Patsy</u>

These are for the people who like political thrillers. Follow Frankie and Evie as they investigate the shadowy proprietor of a far-right website. And they better hurry! Because he's got some dirt on the President and is about to become all-powerful!

Thank you so much for your support!
It means the world.

Sincerely,
Brian O'Sullivan